Praise for *The Templar Legacy*

"Steve Berry is on a roll. . . . His most readable book yet. Berry is one of those authors who can blend history and adventure and satisfy both audiences, and he does so with precision in his latest story."
—*Newton Citizen*

"[An] extraordinary work . . . sure to pique the interest of readers who favor suspense, ancient rites, clandestine societies, and lost treasures."
—*The Oklahoman*

"Berry's latest is simultaneously a history lesson and a spellbinding mystery. Danger is ever-present, and the twists culminate in a breathtaking finale."
—*Romantic Times*

"Fascinating and impossible to put down."
—*Record-Courier*

"Berry provides *Da Vinci Code*–type suspense about a fascinating ancient order."
—*OK!* magazine

"Once again, Berry takes an unsolved historical mystery . . . and whips it into an action-packed thriller. This is the first of three books to feature Cotton Malone, and I don't plan to miss a single one."
—*Kingston Observer*

BY STEVE BERRY

NOVELS

The Amber Room
The Romanov Prophecy
The Third Secret
The Templar Legacy
The Alexandria Link
The Venetian Betrayal
The Charlemagne Pursuit
The Paris Vendetta
The Emperor's Tomb
The Jefferson Key
The Columbus Affair
The King's Deception
The Lincoln Myth

EBOOKS

"The Balkan Escape"
"The Devil's Gold"
"The Admiral's Mark"
The Tudor Plot

The
TEMPLAR
Legacy
A NOVEL

STEVE BERRY

BALLANTINE BOOKS • NEW YORK

2007 Ballantine Books Mass Market Edition

Copyright © 2006 by Steve Berry
Excerpt from *The Venetian Betrayal* copyright © 2007
by Steve Berry
Maps copyright © 2006 by David Lindroth
Interview with the author copyright © 2007 by Random House, Inc.

Published in the United States by Ballantine Books, an imprint of The Random House Publishing Group, a division of Random House, Inc., New York.

BALLANTINE and colophon are registered trademarks of Random House, Inc.

Originally published in hardcover in the United States by Ballantine Books, an imprint of The Random House Publishing Group, a division of Random House, Inc., in 2006.

ISBN 978-0-345-50441-8

Cover illustration: detail of Templar knight © AKG-Images

Printed in the United States of America

www.ballantinebooks.com

OPM 19 18 17 16 15 14 13 12 11 10

For Elizabeth,
Always

*Jesus said, "Know what is within your sight, and
what is hidden from you will become clear. For there
is nothing hidden that will not be revealed."*
—THE GOSPEL OF THOMAS

"It has served us well, this myth of Christ."
—POPE LEO X

ACKNOWLEDGMENTS

I've been lucky. The same team that produced my first novel, *The Amber Room,* in 2003 has stayed together. Few writers can claim that luxury. So, again, lots of thanks to each is in order. First, Pam Ahearn, my agent, who believed from the start. Next, to the wonderful folks at Random House: Gina Centrello, an extraordinary publisher; Mark Tavani, an editor far wiser than his years (and a great friend too); Ingrid Powell, who can always be counted on; Cindy Murray, who goes to great lengths to make me look good in the press (which is a task in and of itself); Kim Hovey who markets with the skill and precision of a surgeon; Beck Stvan, the talented artist responsible for the gorgeous cover; Laura Jorstad, an eagle-eyed copy editor who keeps me straight; Crystal Velasquez, the production editor who daily steers production on a true course; Carole Lowenstein, who once again made the pages shine; and finally to all those in Promotions and Sales—absolutely nothing could be achieved without their superior efforts.

A special thanks to one of the "girls," Daiva Woodworth, who gave Cotton Malone his name. But I can't forget my two "other girls," Nancy Pridgen and Fran Downing. The inspiration from all three remains with me everyday.

On a personal note. My daughter Elizabeth (who's growing

up so fast) brought daily joy to the incredible trials and tribulations that occurred during the production of this book. She is truly a treasure.

This book is for her.

Always.

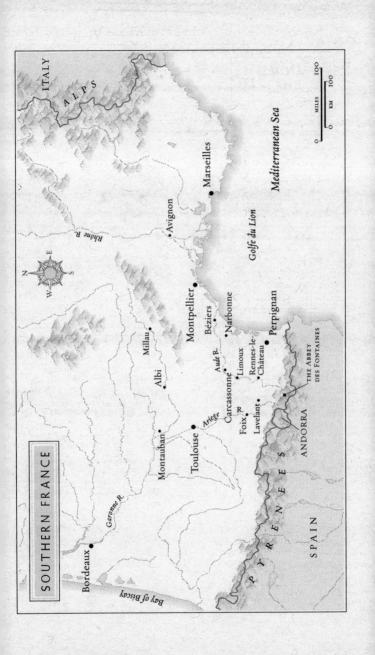

SOUTHERN FRANCE

ITALY

ALPS

Marseilles

Mediterranean Sea

Avignon

Rhône R.

Golfe du Lion

Montpellier

Béziers

Narbonne

Perpignan

Millau

Aude R.

Limoux

Albi

Carcassonne

Rennes-le-Château

THE ABBEY
DES FONTAINES

Montauban

Toulouse

Ariège

Foix

Lavelanet

R.

ANDORRA

PYRENEES

SPAIN

Garonne R.

Bordeaux

Bay of Biscay

MILES   100

KM   100

0

0   100

N
W   E
S

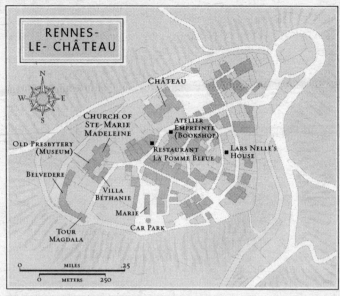

RENNES-LE-CHÂTEAU

N
W E
S

CHÂTEAU

CHURCH OF
STE-MARIE
MADELEINE

ATELIER
EMPREINTE
(BOOKSHOP)

OLD PRESBYTERY
(MUSEUM)

RESTAURANT
LA POMME BLEUE

LARS NELLE'S
HOUSE

BELVEDERE

VILLA BÉTHANIE

MARIE

CAR PARK

TOUR
MAGDALA

0   MILES   .25
0   METERS   250

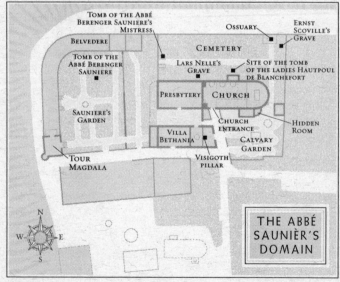

TOMB OF THE ABBÉ
BERENGER SAUNIERE'S
MISTRESS

OSSUARY

ERNST
SCOVILLE'S
GRAVE

BELVEDERE

CEMETERY

TOMB OF THE
ABBÉ BERENGER
SAUNIERE

LARS NELLE'S
GRAVE

SITE OF THE TOMB
OF THE LADIES HAUTPOUL
DE BLANCHEFORT

PRESBYTERY

CHURCH

SAUNIERE'S
GARDEN

CHURCH
ENTRANCE

HIDDEN
ROOM

VILLA
BETHANIA

CALVARY
GARDEN

TOUR
MAGDALA

VISIGOTH
PILLAR

N
W E
S

THE ABBÉ
SAUNIÈR'S
DOMAIN

The
TEMPLAR
Legacy

PROLOGUE

JACQUES DE MOLAY SOUGHT DEATH, BUT KNEW SALVATION would never be offered. He was the twenty-second master of the Poor Fellow-Soldiers of Christ and the Temple of Solomon, a religious order that had existed under God's charge for two hundred years. But for the past three months, he, like five thousand of his brothers, had been a prisoner of Philip IV, king of France.

"You will stand," Gu'llaume Imbert ordered from the doorway.

De Molay remained on the bed.

"You are insolent, even in the face of your own demise," Imbert said.

"Arrogance is about all I have left."

Imbert was an impish man with a face like that of a horse who, de Molay had noted, seemed as impassible as a statue. He was France's grand inquisitor and Philip IV's personal confessor, which meant he possessed the king's ear. Yet de Molay had many times wondered what, besides pain, brought joy to the Dominican's soul. But he knew what irritated him. "I will do nothing you desire."

"You have already done more than you realize."

That was true, and de Molay once more rued his weakness. Imbert's torture in the days after the October 13 arrests had been brutal, and many brothers had confessed to wrongdoing. De Molay cringed at the memory of his own admissions— that those who were received in the Order denied the Lord Jesus Christ and spat upon a cross in contempt of Him. De Molay had even broken down and written a letter calling on the brothers to confess as he'd done, and a sizable lot had obeyed.

But just a few days ago emissaries from His Holiness, Clement V, had finally arrived in Paris. Clement was known to be Philip's puppet, which was why de Molay had brought gold florins and twelve pack horses laden with silver with him to France last summer. If things went awry, that money would have been used to buy the king's favor. Yet he'd underestimated Philip. The king longed not for partial tributes. He wanted all that the Order possessed. So charges of heresy had been fabricated and thousands of Templar arrests made in a single day. To the pope's emissaries de Molay had reported the torture and publicly recanted his confession, which he knew would bring reprisals. So he said, "I imagine Philip is presently concerned that his pope may actually have a backbone."

"Insulting your captor is not wise," Imbert said.

"And what would be wise?"

"Doing as we wish."

"And then how would I answer to my God?"

"Your God is waiting for you, and every other Templar, to answer." Imbert spoke in his usual metallic voice, which betrayed no vestige of emotion.

De Molay no longer wanted to debate. Over the past three months he'd endured ceaseless questioning and sleep deprivation. He'd been placed in irons, his feet smeared with fat and held close to flames, his body stretched on the rack.

He'd even been forced to watch while drunken jailers tortured other Templars, the vast majority of whom were merely farmers, diplomats, accountants, craftsmen, navigators, clerks. He was ashamed of what he'd already been forced to say, and he wasn't going to volunteer anything further. He lay back on the stinking bed and hoped his jailer would go away.

Imbert motioned, and two guards squeezed through the doorway and yanked de Molay upright.

"Bring him," Imbert ordered.

De Molay had been arrested at the Paris Temple and held there since last October. The tall keep with four corner turrets was a Templar headquarters—a financial center—and did not possess any torture chamber. Imbert had improvised, converting the chapel into a place of unimaginable anguish— one that de Molay had visited often over the past three months.

De Molay was dragged inside the chapel and brought to the center of the black-and-white-checkered floor. Many a brother had been welcomed into the Order beneath this starstudded ceiling.

"I am told," Imbert said, "that this is where the most secret of your ceremonies were performed." The Frenchman, dressed in a black robe, strutted to one side of the long room, near a carved receptacle de Molay knew well. "I have studied the contents of this chest. It contains a human skull, two thighbones, and a white burial shroud. Curious, no?"

He was not about to say anything. Instead, he thought of the words every postulant had uttered when welcomed into the Order. *I will suffer all that is pleasing to God.*

"Many of your brothers have told us how these items were used." Imbert shook his head. "So disgusting has your Order become."

He'd had enough. "We answer only to our pope, as servants to the servant of God. He alone judges us."

"Your pope is subject to my liege lord. He will not save you."

It was true. The pope's emissaries had made clear they would convey de Molay's recanting of his confession, but they doubted it would make much difference as to the Templar's fate.

"Strip him," Imbert ordered.

The smock he'd worn since the day after his arrest was torn from his body. He wasn't necessarily sad to see it go, as the filthy cloth smelled of feces and urine. But Rule forbid any brother from showing his body. He knew the Inquisition preferred its victims naked—without pride—so he told himself not to shrink from Imbert's insulting act. His fifty-six-year-old frame still possessed great stature. Like all brother knights, he'd taken care of himself. He stood tall, clung to his dignity, and calmly asked, "Why must I be humiliated?"

"Whatever do you mean?" The question carried an air of incredulousness.

"This room was a place of worship, yet you strip me and stare at my nakedness, knowing that the brothers frown on such displays."

Imbert reached down, hinged open the chest, and removed a long twill cloth. "Ten charges have been leveled against your precious Order."

De Molay knew them all. They ranged from ignoring the sacraments, to worshiping idols, to profiting from immoral acts, to condoning homosexuality.

"The one that is of most concern to me," Imbert said, "is your requirement that each brother deny that Christ is our Lord and that he spit and trample on the true cross. One of your brothers has even told us of how some would piss on an image of our Lord Jesus on the cross. Is that true?"

"Ask that brother."

"Unfortunately, he was overmatched by his ordeal."

De Molay said nothing.

"My king and His Holiness were more disturbed by this one charge than all others. Surely, as a man born into the Church, you can see how they would be angered over your denial of Christ as our Savior?"

"I prefer to speak only to my pope."

Imbert motioned, and the two guards clamped shackles onto both of de Molay's wrists, then stepped back and stretched out his arms with little regard for his tattered muscles. Imbert produced a multi-tailed whip from beneath his robe. The ends clinked and de Molay saw that each was tipped with bone.

Imbert lashed the whip beneath the outstretched arms and onto de Molay's bare back. The pain surged through him then receded, leaving behind a sharpness that did not dull. Before the flesh had time to recover, another blow came, then another. De Molay did not want to give Imbert any notion of satisfaction, but the pain overcame him and he shrieked in agony.

"You will not mock the Inquisition," Imbert declared.

De Molay gathered his emotions. He was ashamed that he'd screamed. He stared into the oily eyes of his inquisitor and waited for what was next.

Imbert stared back. "You deny our Savior, say he was merely a man and not the son of God? You defile the true cross? Very well. You will see what it is like to *endure* the cross."

The whip came again—to his back, his buttocks, his legs. Blood splattered as the bone tips ripped skin.

The world drifted away.

Imbert stopped his thrashing. "Crown the master," he yelled.

De Molay lifted his head and tried to focus. He saw what looked like a round piece of black iron. Nails were bound to the edges, their tips angled down and in.

Imbert came close. "See what our Lord endured. The Lord Jesus Christ whom you and your brothers denied."

The crown was wedged onto his skull and pounded down tight. The nails bit into his scalp and blood oozed from the wounds, soaking the mane of his oily hair.

Imbert tossed the whip aside. "Bring him."

De Molay was dragged across the chapel to a tall wooden door that once had led to his private apartment. A stool was produced and he was balanced on top. One of the guards held him upright while another stood ready in case he resisted, but he was far too weak to challenge.

The shackles were removed.

Imbert handed three nails to another guard.

"His right arm to the top," Imbert ordered, "as we discussed."

The arm was stretched above his head. The guard came close and de Molay saw the hammer.

And realized what they intended to do.

Dear God.

He felt a hand clamp his wrist, the point of a nail pressed to his sweaty flesh. He saw the hammer swing back and heard metal clang metal.

The nail pierced his wrist and he screamed.

"Did you find veins?" Imbert asked the guard.

"Clear of them."

"Good. He is not to bleed to death."

De Molay, as a young brother, had fought in the Holy Land when the Order had made its last stand at Acre. He recalled the feel of a sword blade to flesh. Deep. Hard. Lasting. But a nail to the wrist was something altogether worse.

His left arm was pulled out at an angle and another nail driven through the flesh at the wrist. He bit his tongue, trying to contain himself, but the agony sent his teeth deep. Blood filled his mouth and he swallowed.

Imbert kicked the stool away and the weight of de Molay's six-foot frame was now borne entirely by the bones in his wrists, particularly his right, as the angle of his left arm stressed his right to the breaking point. Something popped in his shoulder, and pain pummeled his brain.

One of the guards grabbed his right foot and studied the flesh. Apparently, Imbert had taken care in choosing the insertion points, places where few veins coursed. The left foot was then placed behind the right and both feet were tacked to the door with a single nail.

De Molay was beyond screaming.

Imbert inspected the handiwork. "Little blood. Well done." He stepped back. "As our Lord and Savior endured, so will you. With one difference."

Now de Molay understood why they'd chosen a door. Imbert slowly swung the slab out on its hinges, opening the door, then slamming it shut.

De Molay's body was thrust one way, then another, swaying on the dislocated joints of his shoulders, pivoting off the nails. The agony was of a kind he'd never known existed.

"Like the rack," Imbert said. "Where pain can be applied in stages. This, too, has an element of control. I can allow you to hang. I can swing you to and fro. Or I can do as you just experienced, which is the worst of all."

The world was blinking in and out, and he could barely breathe. Cramps claimed every muscle. His heart beat wildly. Sweat poured from his skin and he felt as if he had the fever, his body a roaring blaze.

"Do you mock the Inquisition now?" Imbert asked.

He wanted to tell Imbert that he hated the Church for what it was doing. A weak pope controlled by a bankrupt French monarch had somehow managed to topple the greatest religious organization man had ever known. Fifteen thousand brothers scattered over Europe. Nine thousand estates. A band of brothers that had once dominated the Holy Land and spanned two hundred years. The Poor Fellow-Soldiers of Christ and the Temple of Solomon were the epitome of everything good. But success had bred jealousy and, as master, he should have fully appreciated the political storms churning around him. Been less stiff, more bending, not so outspoken. Thank heaven he'd anticipated some of what had already occurred and taken precautions. Philip IV would never see an ounce of Templar gold and silver.

And he would never see the greatest treasure of all.

So de Molay mustered his last remaining bits of energy and raised his head. Imbert clearly thought he was about to speak and drew close.

"Damn you to hell," he whispered. "Damn you and all who aid your hellish cause."

His head collapsed back to his chest. He heard Imbert scream for the door to be swung, but the pain was so intense and swept into his brain from so many directions that he felt little.

He was being taken down. How long he'd hung he did not know, but the relaxation to his limbs went unnoticed because his muscles had long ago numbed. He was carried some distance and then realized that he was back in his cell. His captors laid him onto the mattress, and as his body sunk into the soft folds a familiar stench filled his nostrils. His head was elevated by a pillow, his arms stretched out at each side.

"I have been told," Imbert quietly said, "that when a new brother was accepted into your Order, the candidate was draped about the shoulders in a linen shroud. Something about symbolizing death, then resurrecting into a new life as a Templar. You, too, will now have that honor. I have laid out beneath you the shroud from the chest in the chapel." Imbert reached down and folded the long herringbone cloth over de Molay's feet, down the length of his damp body. His gaze was now shielded by the cloth. "I am told this was used by the Order in the Holy Land, brought back here and wrapped around every Paris initiate. You are now reborn," Imbert mocked. "Lie here and think about your sins. I shall return."

De Molay was too weak to respond. He knew that Imbert had most likely been ordered not to kill him, but he also realized that no one was going to care for him. So he lay still. The numbness was receding, replaced by an intense agony. His heart still pounded and he was sweating frightening amounts of moisture. He told himself to calm down and think pleasant thoughts. One that kept coming to mind was what he knew his captors wanted to know above all else. He was the only man alive who knew. That was the way of the Order. One master passed the knowledge to the next in a way that only the next would know. Unfortunately, because of his sudden arrest and the purge of the Order, the passing this time would have to be accomplished another way. He would not allow Philip or the Church to win. They would only learn what he knew when he wanted them to know. What had the Psalm said? *Thy tongue deviseth mischiefs like a sharp razor, working deceitfully.*

But then another biblical passage occurred to him, one that brought a measure of comfort to his beleaguered soul. So as he lay wrapped in the shroud, his body pouring forth blood and sweat, he thought of Deuteronomy.

Let me alone, that I may destroy them.

PART
ONE

ONE

COTTON MALONE SPOTTED THE KNIFE AT THE SAME TIME HE saw Stephanie Nelle. He was sitting at a table outside the Café Nikolaj, comfortable in a white lattice chair. The sunny afternoon was pleasant and Højbro Plads, the popular Danish square that spanned out before him, bristled with people. The café was doing its usual brisk business—the mood feverish—and for the past half hour he'd been waiting for Stephanie.

She was a petite woman, in her sixties, though she never confirmed her age and the Justice Department personnel records that Malone once saw contained only a winking n/a in the space reserved for date of birth. Her dark hair was streaked with waves of silver, and her brown eyes offered both the compassionate look of a liberal and the fiery glint of a prosecutor. Two presidents had tried to make her attorney general, but she'd turned both offers down. One attorney general had lobbied hard to fire her—especially after she was enlisted by the FBI to investigate him—but the White House nixed the idea since, among other things, Stephanie Nelle was scrupulously honest.

In contrast, the man with the knife was short and stout, with narrow features and brush-cut hair. Something haunted loomed on his East European face—a forlornness that worried Malone more than the glistening blade—and he was dressed casually in denim pants and a bloodred jacket.

Malone rose from his seat but kept his eyes trained on Stephanie.

He thought of shouting a warning, but she was too far away and there was too much noise between them. His view of her was momentarily blocked by one of the modernistic sculptures that dotted Højbro Plads—this one of an obscenely obese woman, lying naked on her belly, her obtrusive buttocks rounded like windswept mountains. When Stephanie appeared from the other side of the cast bronze, the man with the knife had moved closer and Malone watched as he severed a strap that draped her left shoulder, jerked a leather bag free, then shoved Stephanie to the flagstones.

A woman screamed and commotion erupted at the sight of a purse snatcher brandishing a knife.

Red Jacket rushed ahead, Stephanie's bag in hand, and shouldered people out of his way. A few pushed back. The thief angled left, around another of the bronzed sculptures, and finally broke into a run. His route seemed aimed at Købmagergade, a pedestrian-only lane that twisted north, out of Højbro Plads, deeper into the city's shopping district.

Malone bounded from the table, determined to cut off the assailant before he could turn the corner, but a cluster of bicycles blocked his way. He circled the cycles and sprinted forward, partially orbiting a fountain before tackling his prey.

They slammed into hard stone, Red Jacket taking most of the impact, and Malone immediately noticed that his opponent was muscular. Red Jacket, undaunted by the attack, rolled once, then brought a knee into Malone's stomach.

The breath left him in a rush and his guts churned.

Red Jacket sprang to his feet and raced up Købmagergade.

Malone stood, but instantly crouched over and sucked a couple of shallow breaths.

Damn. He was out of practice.

He caught hold of himself and resumed pursuit, his quarry now possessing a fifty-foot head start. Malone had not seen the knife during their struggle, but as he plowed up the street between shops he saw that the man still grasped the leather bag. His chest burned, but he was closing the gap.

Red Jacket wrenched a flower cart away from a scraggly old man, one of many carts that lined both Højbro Plads and Købmagergade. Malone hated the vendors, who enjoyed blocking his bookshop, especially on Saturdays. Red Jacket flung the cart down the cobbles in Malone's direction. He could not let the cart run free—too many people on the street, including children—so he darted right, grasped hold, and twisted it to a stop.

He glanced back and saw Stephanie round the corner onto Købmagergade, along with a policeman. They were half a football field away, and he had no time to wait.

Malone dashed ahead, wondering where the man was heading. Perhaps he'd left a vehicle, or a driver was waiting where Købmagergade emptied into another of Copenhagen's busy squares, Hauser Plads. He hoped not. That place was a nightmare of congestion, beyond the web of people-only lanes that formed the shoppers' mecca known as Strøget. His thighs ached from the unexpected workout, the muscles barely recalling his days with the Navy and the Justice Department. After a year of voluntary retirement, his exercise regimen would not impress his former employer.

Ahead loomed the Round Tower, nestled firmly against the Trinity Church like a thermos bound to a lunch pail. The burly cylindrical structure rose nine stories. Denmark's Christian IV had erected it in 1642, and the symbol of his reign—a gilded

4 embraced by a C—glistened on its somber brick edifice. Five streets intersected where the Round Tower stood, and Red Jacket could choose any one of them for his escape.

Police cars appeared.

One screeched to a stop on the south side of the Round Tower. Another came from farther down Købmagergade, blocking any escape to the north. Red Jacket was now contained in the plaza that encircled the Round Tower. His quarry hesitated, seeming to appraise the situation, then scampered right and disappeared inside the Round Tower.

What was the fool doing? There was no way out besides the ground-floor portal. But maybe Red Jacket didn't know that.

Malone ran to the entrance. He knew the man in the ticket booth. The Norwegian spent many hours in Malone's bookshop, English literature his passion.

"Arne, where did that man go?" he asked in Danish, catching his wind.

"Ran right by without paying."

"Anybody up there?"

"An older couple went up a little while ago."

No elevator or stairs led to the top. Instead, a spiral causeway wound a path straight to the summit, originally installed so that bulky seventeenth-century astronomical instruments could be wheeled up. The story local tour guides liked to tell was of how Russia's Peter the Great once rode up on horseback while his empress followed in a carriage.

Malone could hear footfalls echoing from the flooring above. He shook his head at what he knew awaited him. "Tell the police we're up there."

He started to run.

Halfway up the spiraling incline he passed a door leading into the Large Hall. The glassed entrance was locked, the lights off. Ornamented double windows lined the tower's outer walls, but each was iron-barred. He listened again and could still hear running from above.

He continued ahead, his breathing growing thick and hampered. He slowed his pace when he passed a medieval planet plotter affixed high on the wall. He knew the exit onto the roof platform was just a few feet away, around the ramp's final bend.

He heard no more footsteps.

He crept forward and stepped through the archway. An octagonal observatory—not from Christian IV's time, but a more recent incarnation—rose in the center, with a wide terrace encircling.

To his left a decorative iron fence surrounded the observatory, its only entrance chained shut. On his right, intricate wrought-iron latticework lined the tower's outer edge. Beyond the low railing loomed the city's red-tiled rooftops and green spires.

He rounded the platform and found an elderly man lying prone. Behind the body, Red Jacket stood with a knife to an older woman's throat, his arm encasing her chest. She seemed to want to scream, but fear quelled her voice.

"Keep still," Malone said to her in Danish.

He studied Red Jacket. The haunted look was still there in the dark, almost mournful eyes. Beads of sweat glistened in the bright sun. Everything signaled that Malone should not step any closer. Footfalls from below signaled that the police would arrive in a few moments.

"How about you cool down?" he asked, trying English.

He could see the man understood him, but the knife stayed in place. Red Jacket's gaze kept darting away, off to the sky then back. He seemed unsure of himself and that concerned Malone even more. Desperate people always did desperate things.

"Put the knife down. The police are coming. There's no way out."

Red Jacket looked to the sky again, then refocused on Malone. Indecision stared back at him. What was this? A purse snatcher who flees to the top of a hundred-foot tower with nowhere to go?

Footfalls from below grew louder.

"The police are here."

Red Jacket backed closer to the iron railing but kept his grip tight on the elderly woman. Malone sensed the steeliness of an ultimatum forcing some choice, so he made clear again, "There's no way out."

Red Jacket tightened his grip on the woman's chest, then he staggered back, now firmly against the waist-high outer railing, nothing beyond him and his hostage but air.

The eyes lost their panic and a sudden calm swept over the man. He shoved the old woman forward and Malone caught her before she lost her balance. Red Jacket made the sign of the cross and, with Stephanie's bag in hand, pivoted out over the railing, screamed one word—*"beauseant"*—then slashed the knife across his throat as his body plunged to the street.

The woman howled as the police emerged from the portal.

Malone let her go and rushed to the rail.

Red Jacket lay sprawled on the cobbles one hundred feet below.

He turned and looked back to the sky, past the flagpole atop the observatory, the Danish Dannebrog—a white cross upon a red banner—limp in the still air.

What had the man been looking at? And why did he jump?

He gazed back down and saw Stephanie elbowing her way through the growing crowd. Her leather bag lay a few feet from the dead man and he watched as she yanked it from the cobbles, then dissolved back into the spectators. He followed her with his gaze as she plowed through the people and scuttled away, down one of the streets that led from the Round Tower, deeper into the busy Strøget, never looking back.

He shook his head at her hasty retreat and muttered, "What the hell?"

TWO

STEPHANIE WAS SHAKEN. AFTER TWENTY-SIX YEARS WORKING for the Justice Department, the past fifteen heading the Magellan Billet, she'd learned that if it stood on four legs, had a trunk, and smelled like peanuts, it was an elephant. No need to hang a sign across its torso. Which meant the man in the red jacket was no purse snatcher.

He was something else altogether.

And that meant somebody knew her business.

She'd watched as the thief leaped from the tower—the first time she'd ever actually witnessed death. For years she'd heard her agents talk about it, but a vast chasm lay between reading a report and seeing someone die. The body had slammed into the cobbles with a sickening thud. Did he jump? Or had Malone forced him over? Was there a struggle? Had he spoken before leaping?

She'd come to Denmark for a singular purpose and had decided, while there, to visit with Malone. Years ago he'd been one of her original twelve choices for the Magellan Billet. She'd known Malone's father and watched the steady rise of the son, glad to have him when he accepted her offer and moved from Navy JAG to Justice. He eventually grew to be her best agent, and she was saddened when he'd decided last year that he wanted out.

She'd not seen him since, though they'd talked on the phone a few times. When he'd given chase to the thief, she'd noticed that his tall frame remained muscular and his hair thick and wavy, carrying the same light sienna tint she remembered, similar to the olden stone in the buildings surrounding her. For the dozen years he'd worked for her, he'd always been forthright and independent, which had made him a good operative—one she could trust—yet there was compassion, too. He'd actually been more than an employee.

He was her friend.

But that didn't mean she wanted him in her business.

Pursuing the man in the red jacket was like Malone, but it was also a problem. Visiting with him now would mean there'd be questions, ones she had no intention of answering.

Time with an old friend would have to await another occasion.

MALONE EXITED THE ROUND TOWER AND STARTED AFTER Stephanie. As he'd left the roof, paramedics were tending to the older couple. The elderly man was shaken from a blow to the head, but would be all right. The woman remained hysterical and he'd heard one of the attendants urge that she be taken to a waiting ambulance.

Red Jacket's body still lay on the street, beneath a pale yellow sheet, and police were busy moving people out of the way. Edging through the crowd, Malone watched as the sheet was lifted away and the police photographer went to work. The thief had clearly slit his throat. The bloodied knife lay a few feet away from one arm contorted at an unnatural angle. Blood had poured from the neck gash, settling across the cobbles in a dark pool. The skull was caved in, the torso crushed, the legs twisted as if they contained no bone.

The police had told Malone not to leave—they would need a statement—but at the moment he needed to find Stephanie.

He emerged from the gawkers and glanced back up into the evening sky, where the late-afternoon sun shone with spendthrift glory. Not a cloud loomed in sight. Should be an excellent night to view the stars, but no one would visit the observatory atop the Round Tower. No. That was closed for the evening, as a man had just jumped to his death.

And what of that man?

Malone's thoughts were a tangle of curiosity and apprehension. He knew he should go back to his bookshop and forget all about Stephanie Nelle and whatever she was doing. Her business was no longer his. But he knew that wasn't going to happen.

Something was unfolding, and it wasn't good.

He spotted Stephanie fifty yards ahead on Vestergade, another of the long lanes that spiderwebbed Copenhagen's shopping district. Her pace was brisk, undaunted, then she abruptly veered right and disappeared into one of the buildings.

He trotted forward and saw HANSEN'S ANTIKVARIAT—a bookshop, its proprietor one of the few people in town who'd not offered Malone a warm welcome. Peter Hansen did not like foreigners, especially Americans, and had even tried to block Malone's induction into the Danish Antiquarian Booksellers Association. Thankfully, Hansen's distaste had not proven contagious.

Old instincts were taking over, feelings and senses that had lain dormant since his retirement last year. Sensations he did not like. But ones that had always driven him forward.

He stopped short of the front doorway and saw Stephanie inside, talking to Hansen. The two then retreated deeper into the store, which filled the ground floor of a three-story building. He knew the interior layout, having last year studied the Copenhagen bookstores. Nearly all of them were a testament to Nordic neatness, the stacks organized by subject, books carefully shelved. Hansen, though, was more haphazard. His was an eclectic mix of old and new—mainly new, since he was not one to pay top dollar for private acquisitions.

Malone slipped into the dim space and hoped none of the employees called out his name. He'd had dinner a couple of times with Hansen's manager, which was how he'd learned that he was not Hansen's favorite person. Luckily, she was not around and only ten or so people perused the shelves. He quickly moved toward the back where, he knew, there were myriad cubbyholes, each one brimming with shelves. He was not comfortable being here—after all, Stephanie had merely called and said she'd be in town for a few hours and wanted to say hello—but that was before Red Jacket. And he was damn curious to know what that man died wanting.

He shouldn't be surprised by Stephanie's behavior. She'd always kept everything close to her vest, too close sometimes, which had often generated clashes. One thing to be safe in an Atlanta office working a computer, quite another being out in the field. Good decisions could never be made without good information.

He spotted Stephanie and Hansen inside a windowless alcove that served as Hansen's office. Malone had visited there once when he'd first tried to make friends with the idiot. Hansen was a heavy-chested man with a long nose that overhung a grizzly mustache. Malone positioned himself behind a row of overloaded shelves and grabbed a book, pretending to read.

"Why have you come such a long way for this?" Hansen was saying in his tight, wheezy voice.

"Are you familiar with the Roskilde auction?"

Typical Stephanie, answering a question she didn't want to answer with another question.

"I attend often. Lots of books for sale."

Malone, too, was familiar with the auction. Roskilde lay thirty minutes west of Copenhagen. The town's antique-book dealers convened once a quarter for a sale that brought buyers from all over Europe. Two months after opening his shop, Malone had earned nearly two hundred thousand euros there from four books he'd managed to find at an obscure estate sale in the Czech Republic. Those funds had made his transition from salaried government employee to entrepreneur a lot less stressful. But they also bred jealousy, and Peter Hansen had not hidden his envy.

"I need the one book we spoke about. Tonight. You said there would be no problem buying it," Stephanie said, in the tone of someone accustomed to giving orders.

Hansen chuckled. "Americans. All alike. The world revolves around you."

"My husband said you were a man who could find the unfindable. The book I want is already found. I just need it purchased."

"It does go to the highest bidder."

Malone winced. Stephanie did not know the perilous territory she was navigating. The first rule of the bargain was never to reveal how badly you wanted something.

"It's an obscure book that no one cares about," she said.

"But apparently you do, which means there will be others."

"Let's make sure we're the highest bidder."

"Why is this book so important? I've never heard of it. Its author is unknown."

"Did you question my husband's motives?"

"What does that mean?"

"That it's none of your business. Secure the book and I'll pay your fee, as agreed."

"Why don't you buy it yourself?"

"I don't plan to explain myself."

"Your husband was much more agreeable."

"He's dead."

Though the declaration carried no emotion, a moment of silence passed.

"Are we to travel to Roskilde together?" Hansen asked, apparently getting the message that he was going to learn nothing from her.

"I'll meet you there."

"I can hardly wait."

Stephanie bounded from the office and Malone shrank farther into his alcove, his face turned away as she passed. He heard the door to Hansen's office slam shut and took the opportunity to stride back toward the front entrance.

Stephanie exited the darkened shop and turned left. Malone waited, then crept forward and watched his former boss weave her way through afternoon shoppers back toward the Round Tower.

He dropped back and followed.

Her head never turned. She seemed oblivious that anyone might be interested in what she was doing. Yet she should be, especially after what happened with Red Jacket. He wondered why her guard was not up. Granted, she wasn't a field agent, but she wasn't a fool either.

At the Round Tower, instead of turning right and heading toward Højbro Plads where Malone's bookshop stood, she kept straight. After another three blocks, she disappeared inside the Hotel d'Angleterre.

He watched as she entered.

He was hurt that she was intent on purchasing a book in Denmark and had not asked him to assist. Clearly, she didn't want him involved. In fact, after what happened at the Round Tower, she apparently didn't even want to speak with him.

He glanced at his watch. A little after four thirty. The auction started at six PM, and Roskilde was half an hour's drive away. He'd not planned on attending. The catalog sent out weeks ago contained nothing of interest. But that was no longer the case. Stephanie was acting strange, even for her. And a familiar voice deep inside his head, one that had kept him alive through twelve years as a government operative, said she was going to need him.

THREE

ABBEY DES FONTAINES
FRENCH PYRÉNÉES
5:00 PM

THE SENESCHAL KNELT BESIDE THE BED TO COMFORT HIS DY-ing master. For weeks he'd prayed that this moment would not come. But soon, after ruling the Order wisely for twenty-eight years, the old man lying on the bed would achieve a well-earned peace and join his predecessors in heaven. Unfortunately for the seneschal, the tumult of the physical world would continue, and he dreaded that prospect.

The room was spacious, the ancient stone-and-wood walls free of decay, only the pine-hammered ceiling beams blackened by age. A solitary window, like a somber eye, broke the exterior wall and framed the beauty of a waterfall matted by a stark gray mountain. A growing dusk thickened the room's corners.

The seneschal reached for the old man's hand. The grip

was cold and clammy. "Can you hear me, Master?" he asked in French.

The tired eyes opened. "I am not gone as yet. But soon."

He'd heard others in their final hour make similar statements and wondered if the body simply did exhaust itself, lacking the energy to compel lungs to breathe or a heart to beat, death finally conquering where life had once flourished. He gripped the hand tighter. "I'll miss you."

A smile came to the thin lips. "You have served me well, as I knew you would. That's why I chose you."

"There will be much conflict in the days ahead."

"You are ready. I have seen to it."

He was the seneschal, second only to the master. He'd risen fast through the ranks, too fast for some, and only the master's firm leadership had quelled the discontent. But death would soon claim his protector and he feared open revolt might follow.

"There is no guarantee I'll succeed you."

"You underestimate yourself."

"I respect the power of our adversaries."

A silence washed over them, allowing the larks and blackbirds beyond the window to announce their presence. He stared down at his master. The old man wore an azure smock besprinkled with golden stars. Though the facial features were sharpened by his approaching death, there remained a vigor to the old man's lean form. A gray beard hung long and unkempt, the hands and feet constricted with arthritis, but the eyes continued to glisten. He knew twenty-eight years of leadership had taught the old warrior much. Perhaps the most vital lesson was how to project, even in the face of death, a mask of civility.

The doctor had confirmed the cancer months ago. As required by Rule, the disease was allowed to run its course, the natural consequences of God's action accepted. Thousands of brothers through the centuries had endured the same end, and it was unthinkable that the master would soil their tradition.

"I wish I could smell the water's spray," the old man whispered.

The seneschal glanced toward the window. Its sixteenth-century panes were swung open, allowing the sweet aroma of wet stone and verdant greens to seep into his nostrils. The distant water roared in a bubbly tenor. "Your room offers the perfect venue."

"One of the reasons I wanted to be master."

He smiled, knowing the old man was being facetious. He'd read the Chronicles and knew that his mentor had ascended by being able to grasp each turn of fortune with the adaptiveness of a genius. His tenure had been one of peace, but all that would soon change.

"I should pray for your soul," the seneschal said.

"Time for that later. Instead, you must prepare."

"For what?"

"The conclave. Gather your votes. Be ready. Do not allow your enemies time to rally. Remember all I taught you." The hoarse voice cracked with infirmity, but there was a firmness in the tone's foundation.

"I'm not sure that I want to be master."

"You do."

His friend knew him well. Modesty required that he shun the mantle, but more than anything he wanted to be the next master.

He felt the hand within his shiver. A few shallow breaths were needed for the old man to steady himself.

"I have prepared the message. It is there, on the desk."

He knew it would be the next master's duty to study that testament.

"The duty must be done," the master said. "As it has been done since the Beginning."

The seneschal did not want to hear about duty. He was

more concerned with emotion. He looked around the room, which contained only the bed, a prie-dieu that faced a wooden crucifix, three chairs protected by an old tapestried cushion, a writing desk, and two aged marble statues standing in wall niches. There was a time when the chamber would have been filled with Spanish leather, Delft porcelain, English furniture. But audacity had long been purged from the Order's character.

As from his own.

The old man gasped for air.

He stared down at the man lying in an uneasy slumber of disease. The master gathered his wind, blinked a few times, then said, "Not yet, old friend. But soon."

FOUR

ROSKILDE
6:15 PM

MALONE WAITED UNTIL AFTER THE AUCTION STARTED BEFORE slipping into the hall. He was familiar with the setup and knew bidding would not begin before six twenty, as there were preliminary matters of buyer registration and seller agreements that had to be verified before any money began changing hands.

Roskilde was an ancient town nestled beside a slender saltwater fjord. Founded by Vikings, it had served as Denmark's capital until the fifteenth century and continued to exude a regal grace. The auction was held downtown, near the Domkirke, in a building off Skomagergade, where shoe- makers had once dominated. Bookselling was an art form in Denmark. There was a nationwide appreciation for the writ- ten word—one Malone, as a lifelong bibliophile, had come to admire. Where once books were simply a hobby, a diversion from the pressures of his risky career, now they were his life.

Spotting Peter Hansen and Stephanie near the front, he stayed toward the rear, behind one of the stone pillars sup- porting the vaulted ceiling. He had no intention of bidding, so it mattered not if the auctioneer could see him.

Books came and went, some for respectable numbers of kroner. But he noticed Peter Hansen perk up as the next item was displayed.

"*Pierres Gravées du Languedoc,* by Eugène Stüblein. Copy- right 1887," the auctioneer announced. "A local history, quite common for the time, printed in only a few hundred copies. This is part of an estate we recently acquired. This book is very fine, leather-bound, no marks, with some extraordinary prints—one is reproduced in the catalog. Not something we normally bother with, but the volume is quite lovely, so we thought there may be some interest. An opening bid, please."

Three came fast, all low, the last at four hundred kroner. Malone did the math. Sixty dollars. Hansen then weighed in at eight hundred. No more bids came from the other potential buyers until one of the representatives who worked phones for those unable to attend called out a bid of one thousand kroner.

Hansen seemed perturbed by the unexpected challenge, especially from a long-distance bidder, and upped his offer to 1,050. Phone Man retaliated with two thousand. A third bidder joined the fray. Shouts continued until the bid soared to nine thousand kroner. Others appeared to sense there might be something more to the book. Another minute of intense bidding ended with Hansen's offer of twenty-four thousand kroner.

More than four thousand dollars.

Malone knew Stephanie was a salaried civil servant, somewhere in the seventy- to eighty-thousand-dollar-a-year range. Her husband had died years ago and left her with some assets, but she was not wealthy and certainly not a book collector, so he wondered why she was willing to pay so much for an unknown travel log. People brought them into his shop by the box, many from the nineteenth and early twentieth centuries, a time when personal accounts of far-away places were popular. Most sported purple prose and were, by and large, worthless.

This one clearly seemed an exception.

"Fifty thousand kroner," the representative for Phone Man called out.

More than double Hansen's last bid.

Heads turned and Malone retreated behind the pillar as Stephanie whirled to face the phone bank. He peered around the edge and watched as Stephanie and Hansen conversed, then returned their attention to the auctioneer. A moment of silence passed while Hansen seemed to consider his next move, but he was clearly taking his cue from Stephanie.

She shook her head.

"Item is sold to the telephone bidder for fifty thousand kroner."

The auctioneer retrieved the book from the display stand and a fifteen-minute break was announced. Malone knew the house was going to take a look at *Pierres Gravées du Languedoc* to see what made it worth more than eight thousand dollars. He knew the Roskilde dealers were astute and unaccustomed to treasures slipping past them. But apparently, something had this time.

He continued to hug the pillar while Stephanie and Hansen remained near their seats. A number of familiar faces filled the hall and he hoped no one called out his name. Most were idling toward the other corner where refreshments were being offered. He noticed two men approach Stephanie and introduce themselves. Both were stocky, with short hair, dressed in chinos and crew-necked shirts beneath loose-fitting tan jackets. As one bent to shake Stephanie's hand, Malone noticed the distinctive bulge of a weapon nestled against his spine.

After some discussion, the men withdrew. The conversation had appeared friendly, and while Hansen drifted toward the free beer, Stephanie approached one of the attendants, spoke a moment, then left the hall through a side door.

Malone moved straight for the same attendant, Gregos, a thin Dane whom he knew well.

"Cotton, so good to see you."

"Always on the lookout for a bargain."

Gregos smiled. "Tough to find those here."

"Looked like that last item was a shock."

"I thought it would fetch maybe five hundred kroner. But fifty thousand? Amazing."

"Any idea why?"

Gregos shook his head. "Beyond me."

Malone motioned toward the side door. "The woman you were just talking to. Where was she headed?"

The attendant gave him a knowing look. "You interested in her?"

"Not like that. But I am interested."

Malone had been a favorite of the auction house since a few months back when he helped find a wayward seller who'd offered three volumes of *Jane Eyre,* circa 1847, that turned out to be stolen. When the police seized the books from the new buyer, the auction house had to refund every krone, but the seller had already cashed the house check. As a favor, Malone found the man in England and retrieved the money. In the process, he'd made some grateful friends in his new home.

"She was asking about the Domkirke, where it is located. Particularly the chapel of Christian IV."

"She say why?"

Gregos shook his head. "Only that she was going to walk over."

He reached out and shook the man's hand. In his grasp lay a folded thousand-krone note. He saw that Gregos appreciated the offering and casually slipped the money into his pocket. Gratuities were frowned upon by the auction house.

"One more thing," he said. "Who was the high bidder on the phone for that book?"

"As you know, Cotton, that information is strictly confidential."

"As *you* know, I hate rules. Do I know the bidder?"

"He owns the building that you rent in Copenhagen."

He nearly smiled. Henrik Thorvaldsen. He should have known.

The auction was reconvening. As buyers retook their seats, he made his way toward the entrance and noticed Peter Hansen sitting down. Outside, he stepped into a cool Danish evening, and though nearly eight PM the summer sky remained backlit with bars of dull crimson from a slowly setting sun. Several blocks away loomed the redbrick cathedral, the Domkirke, where Danish royalty had been buried since the thirteenth century.

What was Stephanie doing there?

He was just about to head that way when two men approached. One pressed something hard into his back.

"Nice and still, Mr. Malone, or I will shoot you here and now," the voice whispered in his ear.

He glanced left and right.

The two men who'd been talking to Stephanie in the hall flanked him. And in their features he saw the same anxious look he'd seen a few hours ago on Red Jacket's face.

FIVE

STEPHANIE ENTERED THE DOMKIRKE. THE MAN AT THE AUCTION had said the building was easy to find and he'd been right. The monstrous brick edifice, far too big for the town around it, dominated the evening sky.

Inside the grandiose building she found extensions, chapels, and porches, all topped by a high vaulted ceiling and towering stained-glass windows that lent the ancient walls a celestial air. She could tell the cathedral was no longer Catholic—Lutheran from the décor, if she was not mistaken—with architecture that cast a distinctively French air.

She was angry that she'd lost the book. She'd thought it would sell for no more than three hundred kroner, fifty dollars or so. Instead, some anonymous buyer paid more than eight thousand dollars for an innocuous account of southern France written over a hundred years ago.

Again, somebody knew her business.

Maybe it was the person waiting for her? The two men who'd approached her after the bidding had said all would be explained if she would simply walk to the cathedral and find Christian IV's chapel. She'd thought the trip foolish, but what choice did she have? She had a limited amount of time in which to do a great deal.

She followed the directions provided to her and circled the

vestibule. A service was being held in the nave to her right, before the main altar. About fifty people knelt in the pews. Music from a pipe organ banged through the interior with a metallic vibration. She found Christian IV's chapel and entered through an elaborate iron grille.

Waiting for her was a short man with wispy, iron-gray hair that lay flat upon his head like a cap. He had a rugged, clean-shaven face and wore light-colored cotton trousers beneath an open collar shirt. A leather jacket covered his thick chest, and as she drew closer, she noticed that his dark eyes cast a look she immediately thought cold and suspicious. Perhaps he sensed her apprehension because his expression softened and he threw her a disarming grin.

"Ms. Nelle, so good to meet you."

"How do you know who I am?"

"I was well acquainted with your husband's work. He was a great scholar on several subjects that interest me."

"Which ones? My husband dealt in many subjects."

"Rennes-le-Château is my main interest. His work on the so-called great secret of that town and the land surrounding it."

"Are you the person who just outbid me?"

He held up his hands in mock surrender. "Not I, which is why I asked to speak with you. I had a representative bidding but—like you, I'm sure—I was shocked at the final price."

Needing a moment to think, she wandered around the royal sepulcher. Monstrous wall-sized paintings, encased with elaborate trompe l'oeil, sheathed the dazzling marble walls. Five embellished coffins filled the center beneath an enormous arched ceiling.

The man motioned to the coffins. "Christian IV is regarded as Denmark's greatest monarch. As with Henry VIII in England, Francis II in France, and Peter the Great of Russia, he fundamentally changed this country. His mark remains everywhere."

She wasn't interested in a history lesson. "What do you want?"

"Let me show you something."

He stepped toward the metal grating at the chapel's entrance. She followed.

"Legend says that the devil himself designed these ironworks. The craftsmanship is extraordinary. It contains the king and queen's monograms and a multitude of fabulous creatures. But look closely at the bottom."

She saw words engraved into the decorative metal.

"It reads," he said, "*Caspar Fincke bin ich genannt, dieser Arbeit binn ich bekannt.* Caspar Fincke is my name, to this work I owe my fame."

She faced him. "Your point?"

"Atop the Round Tower in Copenhagen, around its edge, is another iron grating. Fincke designed that, too. He fashioned it low so the eye could see the city rooftops, but it also makes for an easy leap."

She got the message. "That man who jumped today worked for you?"

He nodded.

"Why did he die?"

"Soldiers of Christ securely fight the battles of the Lord, fearing no sin from the slaughter of the enemy, nor danger from their own death."

"He killed himself."

"When death is to be given, or received, it has naught of a crime in it but much glory."

"You don't know how to answer a question."

He smiled. "I was merely quoting a great theologian, who wrote those words eight hundred years ago. St. Bernard of Clairvaux."

"Who are you?"

"Why not call me Bernard."

"What do you want?"

"Two things. First, the book we both lost in the bidding. But I recognize you cannot provide that. The second, you do have. It was sent to you a month ago."

She kept her face stoic. This was indeed the man who knew her business. "And what is that?"

"Ah, a test. A way for you to judge my credibility. All right. The package sent to you contained a journal that once belonged to your husband—a personal notebook he kept until his untimely death. Did I pass?"

She said nothing.

"I want that journal."

"Why is it so important?"

"Many called your husband odd. Different. New age. The academic community scoffed at him, and the press made fun of him. But I called him brilliant. He could see things others never noticed. Look what he accomplished. He originated the entire modern-day attraction with Rennes-le-Château. His book was the first to realert the world to the locale's wonders. Sold five million copies worldwide. Quite an accomplishment."

"My husband sold many books."

"Fourteen, if I'm not mistaken, but none was of the magnitude of his first, *The Treasure at Rennes-le-Château*. Thanks to him, there are now hundreds of volumes published on that subject."

"What makes you think I have my husband's journal?"

"We both know that I would have it now but for the interference of a man named Cotton Malone. I believe he once worked for you."

"Doing what?"

He seemed to understand her continued challenge. "You are a career official with the United States Justice Department and head a unit known as the Magellan Billet. Twelve lawyers, each chosen specially by you, who work under your sole direction and handle, shall we say, *sensitive* matters.

Cotton Malone worked a number of years for you. But he retired early last year and now owns a bookshop in Copenhagen. If not for the unfortunate actions of my acolyte, you
would have enjoyed a light lunch with Mr. Malone, bid him
farewell, and headed here for the auction, which was your
true purpose for coming to Denmark."

The time for pretense was over. "Who do you work for?"

"Myself."

"I doubt that."

"Why would you?"

"Years of practice."

He smiled again, which annoyed her. "The notebook, if
you please."

"I don't have it. After today, I thought it needed safekeeping."

"Does Peter Hansen have it?"

She said nothing.

"No. I assume you would not admit to anything."

"I think this conversation is over." She turned for the open
gate and hurried through it. To her right, back toward the
main doors, she spied two more men with short hair—not
the same ones from the auction house—but she instantly
knew who gave them orders.

She glanced back at the man whose name was not
Bernard.

"Like my associate today on the Round Tower, there is no
place for you to go."

"Screw you."

And she spun left and rushed deeper into the cathedral.

SIX

MALONE ASSESSED THE SITUATION. HE WAS STANDING IN A public place, adjacent to a crowded street. People were coming and going from the auction hall, while others were waiting for their cars to be brought by attendants from a nearby lot. Clearly his surveillance of Stephanie had not gone unnoticed, and he cursed himself for not being more alert. But he decided that, contrary to the threats made, the two men on either side of him would not risk exposure. He was being detained, not eliminated. Perhaps their task was to give whatever was happening in the cathedral with Stephanie time to unfold.

Which meant he needed to act.

He watched as more patrons spilled out from the auction hall. One, a gangly Dane, owned a bookshop in the Strøget, near Peter Hansen's store. He watched as a valet delivered the man's car.

"Vagn," Malone called out, stepping away from the gun to his back.

His friend heard his name and turned.

"Cotton, how are you?" the man answered in Danish.

Malone casually walked toward the car and looked back to see the short-haired man quickly conceal the weapon beneath his jacket. He'd caught the man off his guard, which only confirmed what he already thought. These guys were amateurs. He was ready to bet that they didn't speak Danish, either.

"Might I trouble you for a ride back to Copenhagen?" he asked.

"Certainly. We have room. Climb in."

He reached for the rear passenger door. "I appreciate it. My ride is going to hang around awhile and I need to get back home."

As he slammed the car door shut, he waved through the window and saw a confused look on the two men's faces as the car eased away.

"Nothing interest you today?" Vagn asked.

He turned his attention to the driver. "Not a thing."

"Me, either. We decided to leave and take an early dinner."

Malone glanced over at the woman next to him. Another man sat in the front. He did not know either, so he introduced himself. The car slowly made its way out of Roskilde's warren of tight streets toward the Copenhagen highway.

He spied the twin spires and copper roof of the cathedral. "Vagn, could you let me out? I need to hang around a little longer."

"You sure?"

"I just remembered something I need to do."

STEPHANIE PARALLELED THE NAVE AND PLUNGED DEEPER INTO the cathedral. Past the massive pillars rising to her right, the church service was still in progress. Her low heels clicked off the flagstones, but only she could hear them, thanks to the ponderous organ. The path ahead rounded the main altar, and a series of half walls and memorials divided the ambulatory from the choir.

She glanced back to see the man calling himself Bernard sauntering forward, but the two other men were nowhere to be seen. She realized that she would soon be heading back toward the church's main entrance, only on the other side of the building. For the first time, she fully appreciated the risks her agents took. She'd never worked in the field—that was not part of her job—but this was not an official assignment. This was personal and she was officially on vacation. No one knew she'd traveled to Denmark—no one besides Cotton Malone. And considering her present predicament, that anonymity was becoming a problem.

She rounded the ambulatory.

Her pursuer stayed a discreet distance back, surely knowing that she had nowhere to go. She passed a set of stone stairs that dropped down into another side chapel and then saw, fifty feet ahead, the two other men appear in the rear vestibule, blocking her way out of the church. Behind her, Bernard continued his steady advance. To her left was another sepulcher, this one identified as the Chapel of Magi.

She darted inside.

Two marble tombs lay within the brilliantly decorated walls, both reminiscent of Roman temples. She retreated toward the farther. Then a wild unreasoning terror seized her as she realized the worst.

She was trapped.

MALONE JOGGED TO THE CATHEDRAL AND ENTERED THROUGH the main doors. To his right he spotted two men—stocky, short hair, plainly dressed—similar to the two he'd just evaded outside the auction. He decided not to take any chances and reached beneath his jacket for a Beretta automatic, standard issue to all Magellan Billet agents. He'd been allowed to keep the weapon when he retired and managed to smuggle it into Denmark—owning a handgun here was illegal.

He palmed the stock, finger on the trigger, and brought out

the gun, shielding it with his thigh. He'd not held a weapon in more than a year. It was a feeling he'd thought part of his past, one he hadn't missed. But a man leaping to his death had grabbed his attention, so he'd come prepared. That was what a good agent did, and one of the reasons he'd served as the pallbearer for a few friends instead of being hauled down the center aisle of a church himself.

The two men were standing with their backs to him, arms at their sides, hands empty. Thunderous organ music masked his approach. He stepped close and said, "Busy night, fellows."

Both turned and he flashed the gun. "Let's keep this civil."

Over the shoulder of one of the men he caught sight of another man, a hundred feet down the transept, casually striding toward them. He saw the man reach beneath his leather jacket. Malone did not wait for what was next, and dove left into an empty row of pews. A pop echoed over the organ and a bullet tore into the wood pew ahead of him.

He saw the two other men reach for weapons.

From his prone position, he fired twice. The shots exploded through the cathedral, piercing the music. One of the men went down, the other fled. Malone came to his knees and heard three new pops. He dove back down as more bullets found wood near him.

He sent two more shots in the direction of the lone gunman.

The organ stopped.

People realized what was happening. The crowd started flooding from the pews past where Malone was hiding, seeking safety outside through the rear doors. He used the confusion to peer above the pew and saw the man in the leather jacket standing near the entrance to one of the side chapels.

"Stephanie," he called out over the mayhem.

No answer.

"Stephanie. It's Cotton. Let me know if you're okay?"

Still no answer.

He belly-crawled forward, found the opposite transept, and rose to his feet. The path ahead rounded the church and led to the other side. Pillars lining the way would make any shot at him difficult, and then the choir would block him completely, so he ran forward.

STEPHANIE HEARD MALONE CALL HER NAME. THANK GOODness he never could mind his own business. She was still in the Magi Chapel, hiding behind a black marble tomb. She heard shots and realized Malone was doing what he could, but he was outnumbered at least three to one. She needed to help him, but what good could she be? She carried no weapon. At least she ought to let him know she was all right. But before she could answer, through another elaborate iron grille that opened into the church, she saw Bernard, gun in hand.

Fear seized her muscles and gripped her mind in an unfamiliar panic.

He entered the chapel.

MALONE ROUNDED THE CHOIR. PEOPLE WERE STILL RUSHING from the church, voices excited, hysterical. Surely someone had called the police. He just needed to contain his attackers until help arrived.

He looped the ambulatory and saw one of the men he'd shot helping the other out the rear doors. The one who'd started the attack was not in sight.

That worried him.

He slowed his pace and brought his gun to the ready.

STEPHANIE STIFFENED. BERNARD WAS TWENTY FEET AWAY.

"I know you're in here," he said in a deep, throaty voice.

"Your savior arrived, so I have no time to deal with you. You know what I want. We shall meet again."

The prospect was not appealing.

"Your husband was unreasonable, too. He was made a similar offer eleven years ago with regard to the journal and refused."

She was stung by the man's words. She knew that she should remain silent, but there was no way. Not now. "What do you know of my husband?"

"Enough. Let's leave it at that."

She heard him walk away.

MALONE SAW LEATHER JACKET STEP FROM ONE OF THE SIDE chapels.

"Stop," he called out.

The man whirled and leveled his gun.

Malone dove toward a set of steps that led to another room jutting from the cathedral and rolled down half a dozen stone risers.

Three bullets smacked off the walls above him.

Malone scampered back up, ready to return fire, but Leather Jacket was a hundred feet away, running toward the rear vestibule, turning for the other side of the church.

Malone came to his feet and trotted forward.

"Stephanie," he called out.

"Here, Cotton."

He saw his old boss appear at the far side of the chapel. She walked toward him, a stony expression spread over her calm face. Sirens could be heard outside.

"I suggest we get out of here," he said. "There are going to be a lot of questions and I have the feeling you're not going to want to answer any of them."

"You got that right." She brushed by him.

He was just about to suggest that they use one of the other

exits when the main doors were flung open and uniformed police swarmed inside. He still held his gun and they spotted it immediately.

Feet were planted and automatic weapons raised.

He and Stephanie froze.

"Hen til den landskab. Nu," came the command. To the ground. Now.

"What do they want us to do?" Stephanie asked.

Malone dropped his gun and started down to his knees. "Nothing good."

SEVEN

RAYMOND DE ROQUEFORT STOOD OUTSIDE THE CATHE-dral, beyond the circle of onlookers, and watched the un-folding drama. He and his two associates had dissolved into the web of shadows cast by the thick trees that rose across from the cathedral plaza. He'd managed to slip out a side door and retreat just as the police stormed the main entrance. No one seemed to notice him. The authorities would, for the moment, be focused on Stephanie Nelle and Cotton Malone. It would be awhile before witnesses described other men with guns. He was familiar with these kinds of situations and knew how calm heads always prevailed. So he told him-self to relax. His men must know that he was in control.

The front of the brick cathedral was awash with strobing red and white light. More police arrived, and he marveled how a town of Roskilde's size possessed so much law enforcement. People were flooding over from the nearby main plaza. The whole scene was quickly turning chaotic. Which was perfect. He'd always found tremendous freedom of movement within chaos, provided he controlled the chaos.

He faced the two who'd been with him inside the church. "Are you injured?" he asked the one who'd been shot.

The man peeled back his jacket and showed him how the body armor had done its job. "Just sore."

From the crowd he saw his remaining two acolytes emerge—the ones he'd sent to the auction. They'd reported through their radios that Stephanie Nelle had not prevailed in the bidding. So he'd ordered them to send her his way. He'd thought perhaps she could be intimidated, but the effort had failed. Worse, he'd drawn a great deal of attention to his activities. But that was thanks to Cotton Malone. His men had spotted Malone at the auction, so he'd instructed them to detain him while he spoke with Stephanie Nelle. Apparently, that effort had failed, too.

The two approached and one of them said, "We lost Malone."

"I found him."

"He's resourceful. With nerve."

He knew that to be true. He'd checked out Cotton Malone after learning Stephanie Nelle would be traveling to Denmark to visit with him. Since Malone could have well been a part of whatever she was planning, he'd made a point to learn all he could.

His given name was Harold Earl Malone. He was forty-six years old, born in the American state of Georgia. His mother was a native Georgian, his father a career military man, an Annapolis graduate, who rose to the rank of navy commander before his submarine sank when Malone was ten years old.

The son followed in the father's footsteps, attending the Naval Academy and graduating in the top third of his class.

He was admitted to flight school, eventually earning high enough marks to choose fighter pilot training. Then, interestingly, midway through, he abruptly sought reassignment and was admitted to Georgetown University Law School, earning his law degree while stationed at the Pentagon. After graduation he was transferred to the Judge Advocate General's corps, where he spent nine years as a staff lawyer. Thirteen years ago he was reassigned to the Justice Department and Stephanie Nelle's newly formed Magellan Billet. He remained there until last year, retiring out early as a full commander.

On the personal side, Malone was divorced and his fourteen-year-old son lived with his ex-wife in Georgia. Immediately upon retiring, Malone had left America and moved to Copenhagen. He was a confirmed bibliophile and born Catholic, but not noted as overly religious. He was reasonably fluent in several languages, possessed of no known addictions or phobias, and prone to extreme self-motivation and obsessive dedication. He also possessed an eidetic memory. All in all, just the kind of man de Roquefort would rather have *in* his employ than working against him.

And the past few minutes had proven that.

Three-to-one odds had not seemed to bother Malone, especially when he thought Stephanie Nelle was in jeopardy.

Earlier, de Roquefort's young associate had demonstrated loyalty and courage, too, though the man had acted in haste stealing Stephanie Nelle's bag. He should have waited until *after* her visit with Cotton Malone, when she was on the way back to her hotel, alone and vulnerable. Perhaps he'd been trying to please, knowing the importance of their mission. Maybe it was simply impatience. But when cornered at the Round Tower, the young man had correctly chosen death over capture. A shame, but the learning process was like that. Those with brains and ability rose. Everyone else was eliminated.

He turned to one of his associates who'd been inside the

auction hall and asked, "Did you learn who was the high bidder for the book?"

The young man nodded. "It cost a thousand kroner to bribe the attendant."

He wasn't interested in the price of weakness. "The name?"

"Henrik Thorvaldsen."

The phone in his pocket vibrated. His second in command knew he was occupied, so the call had to be important. He flipped the unit open.

"The time is close," the voice said in his ear.

"How close?"

"Within the next few hours."

An unexpected bonus.

"I have a task for you," he said into the phone. "There's a man. Henrik Thorvaldsen. A wealthy Dane, lives north of Copenhagen. I know some, but I need complete information on him within the hour. Call me back when you have it."

Then he clicked off the phone and turned to his subordinates.

"We must return home. But first there are two more tasks we have to complete before dawn."

EIGHT

MALONE AND STEPHANIE WERE TRANSPORTED TO A POLICE building on the outskirts of Roskilde. Neither of them spoke on the way, as they both knew enough to keep their mouths shut. Malone fully realized that Stephanie's presence in Denmark had nothing to do with the Magellan Billet. Stephanie never worked the field. She was at the apex of the triangle—everyone reported to her in Atlanta. And besides, when she'd called last week and said she wanted to drop by and say hello, she'd made clear she was coming to Europe on vacation. Some vacation, he thought, as they were left alone in a brightly lit, windowless room.

"Oh, by the way, the coffee was great at the Café Nikolaj," he said. "I went ahead and drank yours. Of course that was *after* I chased a man to the top of the Round Tower and watched while he jumped."

She said nothing.

"I did manage to see you snatch your bag from the street. Did you happen to notice the dead man lying next to it? Maybe not. You seemed in a hurry."

"That's enough, Cotton," she said in a tone he knew.

"I don't work for you anymore."

"So why are you here?"

"I was asking myself the same thing in the cathedral, but the bullets distracted me."

Before she could say anything further, the door opened and a tall man with reddish blond hair and pale brown eyes entered. He was the Roskilde police inspector who'd brought them from the cathedral and he held Malone's Beretta.

"I made the call you requested," the inspector said to Stephanie. "The American embassy confirms your identity and status with your Justice Department. I'm awaiting word from our Home Office as to what to do." He turned. "You, Mr. Malone, are another matter. You are in Denmark on a temporary residence visa as a shopkeeper." He displayed the gun. "Our laws do not sanction the carrying of weapons, not to mention discharging it in our national cathedral—a World Heritage Site, no less."

"I like to break only the most important laws," he said, not letting the man think he was getting to him.

"I do love humor, Mr. Malone. But this is a serious matter. Not for me, but for you."

"Did the witnesses mention that there were three other men who started the shooting?"

"We have descriptions. But it is unlikely they are around any longer. You, though, are right here."

"Inspector," Stephanie said. "The situation that developed was of my doing, not Mr. Malone's." She threw him a glare. "Mr. Malone once worked for me and thought I required his assistance."

"Are you saying the shooting would not have occurred but for Mr. Malone's interference?"

"Not at all. Only that the situation grew out of control—through no fault of Mr. Malone's."

The inspector appraised her observation with obvious apprehension. Malone wondered what Stephanie was doing.

Lying was not her forte, but he decided not to challenge her in front of the inspector.

"Were you in the cathedral on official United States government business?" the inspector asked her.

"That I cannot say. You understand."

"Your job involves activities that cannot be discussed? I thought you were a lawyer?"

"I am. But my unit is routinely involved in national security investigations. In fact, that's our main purpose for existing."

The inspector did not seem impressed. "What is your business in Denmark, Ms. Nelle?"

"I came to visit Mr. Malone. I haven't seen him in more than a year."

"That was your only purpose?"

"Why don't we wait for the Home Office."

"It is a miracle that no one was hurt in that mélange. There is damage to a few sacred monuments, but no injuries."

"I shot one of the gunmen," Malone said.

"If you did, he did not bleed."

Which meant they were armored. The team had come prepared, but for what?

"How long will you be staying in Denmark?" the inspector asked Stephanie.

"Gone tomorrow."

The door opened and a uniformed officer handed the inspector a sheet of paper. The man read, then said, "You apparently have some well-placed friends, Ms. Nelle. My superiors say to let you go and ask no questions."

Stephanie headed for the door.

Malone stood, too. "That paper mention me?"

"I'm to release you, as well."

Malone reached for the gun. The man did not offer it.

"There is no instruction that I am to return the weapon."

He decided not to argue. He could deal with that issue later. Right now, he needed to speak with Stephanie.

He rushed off and found her outside.

She whirled to face him, her features set tight. "Cotton, I appreciate what you did in the cathedral. But listen to me, and listen good. Stay out of my business."

"You have no idea what you're doing. In the cathedral you walked right into something with no preparation. Those three men wanted to kill you."

"Then why didn't they? There was every opportunity before you arrived."

"Which raises even more questions."

"Don't you have enough to do at your bookshop?"

"Plenty."

"Then do it. When you quit last year, you made clear that you were tired of getting shot at. I believe you said that your new Danish benefactor offered a life you always wanted. So go enjoy it."

"You're the one who called me and wanted to stop by for a visit."

"Which was a bad idea."

"That was no purse snatcher today."

"Stay out of this."

"You owe me. I saved your neck."

"Nobody told you to do that."

"Stephanie—"

"Dammit, Cotton. I'm not going to say it again. If you keep on, I'll have no choice but to take action."

Now his back was stiff. "And what do you plan to do?"

"Your Danish friend doesn't have all the connections. I can make things happen, too."

"Go for it," he said to her, his anger building.

But she did not reply. Instead, she stormed off.

He wanted to go after her and finish what they'd started, but decided she was right. This was none of his concern. And he'd made enough trouble for one night.

Time to go home.

NINE

DE ROQUEFORT APPROACHED THE BOOKSHOP. THE PEDESTRIANS-only street out front was deserted. Most of the district's many cafés and restaurants were blocks away—this part of the Strøget closed for the night. After tending to his two remaining chores, he planned to leave Denmark. His physical description, along with those of his two compatriots, had now most likely been obtained from witnesses in the cathedral. So it was important that they linger no longer than necessary.

He'd brought all four of his subordinates from Roskilde with him and planned to supervise every detail of their action. There'd been enough improvising for one day, some of which had cost the life of one of his men earlier at the Round Tower. He did not want to lose anyone else. Two of his men were already scouting the rear of the bookshop. The other two stood ready at his side. Lights burned on the building's top floor.

Good.

He and the owner needed to talk.

MALONE GRABBED A DIET PEPSI FROM THE REFRIGERATOR and walked down four flights of stairs to the ground floor. His shop filled the entire building, the first floor for books and customers, the next two for storage, the fourth a small apartment that he called home.

He'd grown accustomed to the cramped living space, enjoying it far better than the two-thousand-square-foot house he'd once owned in north Atlanta. Its sale last year, for a little over three hundred thousand dollars, had netted him sixty thousand dollars to invest into his new life, one offered to him by, as Stephanie had early chided, his *new Danish benefactor,* an odd little man named Henrik Thorvaldsen.

A stranger fourteen months ago, now his closest friend.

They'd connected from the beginning, the older man seeing in the younger something—what, Malone was never sure, but something—and their first meeting in Atlanta one rainy Thursday evening had sealed both of their futures. Stephanie had insisted he take a month off after the trial of three defendants in Mexico City—which involved international drug smuggling and the execution-style murder of a DEA supervisor who happened to be a personal friend of the president of the United States—had resulted in carnage. Walking back to court during a lunch break, Malone had been caught in the crossfire of an assassination, an act wholly unrelated to the trial, but something he'd tried to stop. He'd come home with a bullet wound to his left shoulder. The final tally from the shooting—seven dead, nine injured, one of the dead a young Danish diplomat named Cai Thorvaldsen.

"I came to speak with you in person," Henrik Thorvaldsen had said.

They were sitting in Malone's den. His shoulder hurt like hell. He didn't bother to ask how Thorvaldsen had located him, or how the older man knew that he understood Danish.

"My son was precious to me," Thorvaldsen said. "When he joined our diplomatic corps I was thrilled. He asked for the assignment to Mexico City. He was a student of the Aztecs. He would have made a worthy member of our Parliament one day. A statesman."

A swirl of first impressions raced through Malone's mind. Thorvaldsen was certainly high bred with an air of distinction, at once elegant and rakish. But the sophistication was in stark contrast to a deformed body, his spine humped in a grotesque exaggeration and stiff, shaped like an egret. A leathery face suggested a lifetime of impossible choices, the wrinkles more like deep clefts, the crow's-feet sprouting legs, liver spots and forked veins discoloring the arms and hands. Pewter-colored hair was piled thick and bushy and matched the eyebrows—dull silver wisps that made the older man look anxious. Only in the eyes was there passion. Gray-blue, strangely clairvoyant, one flawed from a star-shaped cataract.

"I came to meet the man who shot my son's killer."

"Why?" he asked.

"To thank you."

"You could have called."

"I prefer to face my listener."

"At the moment, I prefer to be left alone."

"I understand you were nearly killed."

He shrugged.

"And you are quitting your job. Resigning your commission. Retiring from the military."

"You know an awful lot."

"Knowledge is the greatest of luxuries."

He was not impressed. "Thanks for the pat on the back. I have a hole in my shoulder that's throbbing. So since you've said your peace, could you leave?"

Thorvaldsen never moved from the sofa. He simply stared around at the den and the surrounding rooms visible through an open archway. Every wall was sheathed in books. The house seemed nothing but a backdrop for the shelves.

"I love them, too," his guest said. "My home is likewise full of books. I've collected them all my life."

He could sense that this man, sixty-plus years old, was given to grandiose tactics. He'd noticed when answering the door that he'd arrived via a limousine. So he wanted to know, "How did you know I speak Danish?"

"You speak several languages. I was proud to learn that my native tongue was one."

Not an answer, but had he really expected one?

"Your eidetic memory must be a blessing. Mine has gone the way of age. I can hardly remember much anymore."

He doubted that. "What do you want?"

"Have you considered your future?"

He motioned around the room. "Thought I'd open an old-book shop. Got plenty to sell."

"Excellent idea. I have one for sale, if you'd like it."

He decided to play along. What the hell. But there was something about the tight points of light in the old man's eyes that told him his visitor was not joking.

Hard flinty hands searched a suit coat pocket and Thorvaldsen laid a business card on the sofa.

"My private number. If you're interested, call me."

The old man stood.

He stayed seated. "What makes you think I'm interested?"

"You are, Mr. Malone."

He resented the assumption, particularly when the old man was right. Thorvaldsen shuffled toward the front door.

"Where is this bookstore?" he asked, cursing himself for even sounding interested.

"Copenhagen. Where else?"

He remembered waiting three days before calling. The prospect of living in Europe had always appealed to him. Had Thorvaldsen known that, too? He'd never thought living overseas possible. He was a career government man. American, born and bred. But that was before Mexico City. Before seven dead and nine injured.

He could still see his estranged wife's face the day after he made the call to Copenhagen.

"I agree. We've had enough separation, Cotton, it's time for a divorce." The declaration came with the matter-of-factness of the trial lawyer that she was.

"Is there someone else?" he asked, uncaring.

"Not that it matters, but yes. Hell, Cotton, we've been apart five years. I'm sure you haven't been a monk during that time."

"You're right. It's time."

"You really going to retire from the navy?"

"Already have. Effective yesterday."

She shook her head, like she did when Gary needed motherly advice. "Will you ever be satisfied? The Navy, then flight school, law school, JAG, the Billet. Now this sudden retirement. What's next?"

He'd never liked her condescending tone. "I'm moving to Denmark."

Her face registered nothing. He might as well had said he was moving to the moon. "What is it you're after?"

"I'm tired of being shot at."

"Since when? You love the Billet."

"Time to grow up."

She smiled. "So you think moving to Denmark will accomplish that miracle?"

He had no intention of explaining himself. She didn't care. Nor did he want her to. "It's Gary I need to talk with."

"Why?"

"I want to know if he's okay with that."

"Since when have you cared what we thought?"

"He's why I got out. I wanted him to have a father around—"

"That's bullshit, Cotton. You got out for yourself. Don't use that boy as an excuse. Whatever it is you're planning, it's for you, not him."

"I don't need you telling me what I think."

"Then who does tell you? We were married a long time. You think it was easy waiting for you to come back from who-knows-where? Wondering if it was going to be in a body bag? I paid the price, Cotton. Gary did, too. But that boy loves you. No, he worships you, unconditionally. You and I both know what he'll say, since his head is screwed on better than either of ours. For all our failures together, he was a success."

She was right again.

"Look, Cotton. Why you're moving across the ocean is your business. But if it makes you happy, then do it. Just don't use Gary as an excuse. The last thing he needs is a discontented parent around trying to make up for his own sad childhood."

"You enjoy insulting me?"

"Not really. But the truth has to be said and you know it."

He stared around at the darkened bookshop. Nothing good ever came from thinking about Pam. Her animosity toward him ran deep and stemmed back fifteen years to when he was a brash ensign. He'd not been faithful and she knew it. They'd gone to counseling and resolved to make the marriage work, but a decade later he'd returned home one day from an assignment to find her gone. She'd rented a house on the other side of Atlanta for her and Gary, taking only what they needed. A note informed him of their new address and that the marriage was over. Pragmatic and cold, that was

Pam's way. Interestingly, though, she'd not sought an immediate divorce. Instead, they'd simply lived apart, remained civil, and spoke only when necessary for Gary's sake.

But eventually the time came for decisions—across the board.

So he quit his job, resigned his commission, ended his marriage, sold his house, and left America, all in the span of one long, terrible, lonely, exhausting, but satisfying week.

He checked his watch. He really should e-mail Gary. They communicated at least once a day, and it was still late afternoon in Atlanta. His son was due in Copenhagen in three weeks to spend a month with him. They'd done the same thing last summer, and he was looking forward to the time together.

His confrontation with Stephanie still bothered him. He'd seen naïveté like hers before in agents who, though aware of risks, simply ignored them. What was it she always told him? *Say it, do it, preach it, shout it, but never, absolutely never, believe your own bullshit.* Good advice she should heed. She had no idea what she was doing. But then, did he? Women were not his strong point. Though he'd spent half his life with Pam, he never really took the time to know her. So how could he possibly understand Stephanie? He should stay out of her business. After all, it was *her* life.

But something nagged at him.

When he was twelve he'd learned that he'd been born with an eidetic memory. Not *photographic,* as movies and books liked to portray, just an excellent recall of details that most people forgot. It certainly helped with studying, and languages came easy, but trying to pluck one detail from so many could, at times, aggravate him.

Like now.

TEN

DE ROQUEFORT TRIPPED THE FRONT DOOR LOCK AND ENTERED the bookshop. Two of his men followed him inside. The other two were stationed outside to watch the street.

They crept past darkened shelves to the rear of the cluttered ground floor and climbed narrow stairs. No sound betrayed their presence. On the top floor, de Roquefort stepped through an open doorway into a lit apartment. Peter Hansen was ensconced in a chair reading, a beer on the table beside him, a cigarette burning in an ashtray.

Surprise flooded the book dealer's face. "What are you doing here?" Hansen demanded in French.

"We had an arrangement."

The dealer sprang to his feet. "We were outbid. What was I to do?"

"You told me there'd be no problem." His associates moved to the far side of the room, near the windows. He stayed at the door.

"That book sold for fifty thousand kroner. An outrageous price," Hansen said.

"Who outbid you?"

"The auction will not reveal such information."

De Roquefort wondered if Hansen thought him that stupid. "I paid you to ensure that Stephanie Nelle was the purchaser."

"And I tried. But no one told me the book would go for such a price. I stayed with the bidding, but she waved me off. Were you willing to pay more than fifty thousand kroner?"

"I would have paid whatever it took."

"You weren't there, and she was not as determined." Hansen seemed to relax, the initial surprise replaced with a smugness de Roquefort fought hard to ignore. "And besides, what makes that book so valuable?"

He surveyed the tight room, which reeked of alcohol and nicotine. Hundreds of books lay scattered among stacks of newspapers and magazines. He wondered how anyone lived in such disarray. "You tell me."

Hansen shrugged. "I have no idea. She wouldn't say why she wanted it."

De Roquefort's patience was wearing thin. "I know who outbid you."

"How?"

"As you well know, the attendants at the auction are negotiable. Ms. Nelle contacted you to act as her agent. I contacted you to make sure she obtained the book so that I might have a copy before you turned it over to her. Then you arranged for a telephone bidder."

Hansen smiled. "Took you long enough to figure that one out."

"Actually it took me only a few moments, once I had information."

"Since I now have control of the book and Stephanie Nelle is out of the picture, what is it worth for just you to have it?"

De Roquefort already knew what course he would be taking. "Actually, the question is, how much is the book worth to you?"

"It means nothing to me."

He motioned and his two associates grabbed Hansen's arms. De Roquefort jammed a fist into the book dealer's abdomen. Hansen spit out a breath, then slumped forward, held upright by his limbs.

"I wanted Stephanie Nelle to have the book, after I made a copy," de Roquefort said. "That was what I paid you to do. Nothing more. You once possessed a use to me. That's no longer the case."

"I . . . have the . . . book."

He shrugged. "That's a lie. I know exactly where the book is."

Hansen shook his head. "You won't . . . get it."

"You're wrong. In fact, it will be an easy matter."

MALONE FLIPPED ON THE FLUORESCENT LIGHTS OVER THE HIS-tory section. Books of every shape, size, and color consumed the black lacquered shelves. But there was one volume in particular he recalled from a few weeks back. He'd bought it, along with several other mid-twentieth-century histories, from an Italian who'd thought his wares worth far more than Malone was willing to pay. Most sellers did not understand that value was a factor of desire, scarcity, and uniqueness. Age was not necessarily important since, just as in the twenty-first century, a lot of junk had always been printed.

He recalled selling a few of the Italian's books, but was hoping that one of them was still around. He could not remember it leaving the store, though one of his employees might have made a sale. But thankfully the book remained on the second row from the bottom, precisely where he'd first placed it.

No dust jacket protected the clothbound cover, which was once surely a deep green, now faded to light lime. Its pages were tissue-thin, gilt-edged, and littered with engravings. The title was still visible in patchy gold lettering.

The Knights of the Temple of Solomon.

The copyright read 1922 and, when he first saw it, Malone had become interested since the Templars were a subject he'd read little about. He knew they were not mere monks, more religious warriors—a sort of spiritualized special forces unit. But his rather simplistic conception was of white-clad men sporting stylish red crosses. A Hollywood stereotype, surely. And he recalled being fascinated as he'd thumbed through the volume.

He carried the book to one of several club chairs that dotted the store, settled himself into the soft folds, and started to read. Gradually, a summary began to formulate.

By AD 1118 Christians once again controlled the Holy Land. The First Crusade had been a resounding success. And though the Muslims were defeated, their lands confiscated, their cities occupied, they'd not been vanquished. Instead, they remained on the fringe of the newly established Christian kingdoms, wreaking havoc on all who ventured to the Holy Land.

Safe pilgrimage to holy sites was one of the reasons for the Crusades, and road tolls were the chief revenue source for the newly formed Christian Kingdom of Jerusalem. Pilgrims were streaming by the day into the Holy Land, arriving alone, in pairs, groups, or sometimes as entire uprooted communities. Unfortunately, the roads in and out were not secure. Muslims lay in wait, bandits roamed freely, even Christian soldiers were a threat since pillage was, to them, a normal course of forage.

So when a knight from Champagne, Hugh de Payens, founded a new movement consisting of himself and eight others, a monastic order of fighting brothers dedicated to providing safe passage to pilgrims, the concept was met with widespread approval. Baldwin II, who ruled Jerusalem, granted the new order shelter under the al Aqsa mosque, a place Christians believed to be the former

Temple of Solomon, so the new order took its name from its headquarters: the Poor Fellow-Soldiers of Christ and the Temple of Solomon at Jerusalem.

The brotherhood initially stayed small. Each knight pledged vows of poverty, chastity, and obedience. They owned nothing individually. All of their worldly goods became the Order's. They lived in common and took their meals in silence. They cropped their hair, but let their beards grow. Charity supplied their food and clothing and St. Augustine provided the model for their monasticism. The Order's seal was particularly symbolic: two knights riding a single mount—a clear reference to the days when knights could not afford their own horse.

A religious order of fighting men was not, to the medieval mind, a contradiction. Instead, the new Order appealed to both religious fervor and martial prowess. Its creation also solved another problem—that of manpower— since now there existed a constant presence of trusted fighters.

By 1128 the fellowship had expanded, finding political support in powerful places. European princes and prelates donated land, money, and materials. The pope ultimately sanctioned the Order, and soon the Knights Templar became the only standing army in the Holy Land.

A strict Rule of 686 laws governed them. Hunting was forbidden. No gaming, hawking, or gambling. Speech was practiced sparingly and without laughter. Ornamentation was banned. They slept with the lights on, dressed in shirts, vests, and pantaloons, ready for battle.

The master was absolute ruler. Next were the seneschals, who acted as deputies and advisers. Marshals commanded troops during battles. Servientes in Latin, sergents in French, were the craftsmen, laborers, and attendants who supported the brother knights and formed the backbone of the Order. By a papal decree in 1148, each knight wore the red cross patee of four equal arms, wide at the ends, atop a white mantle. They were the first disciplined, equipped, and regulated standing army since Roman times. The brother knights participated in each of the subsequent Crusades, being the first into the fray, the last to retreat, and never were they ransomed. They believed service to the Order would clean their slate with heaven and, over the course of two hundred years of constant warring, twenty thousand Templars gained their martyrdom by dying in battle.

In 1139 a papal bull placed the Order under the exclusive control of the pope, which allowed it to operate freely throughout Christendom, unaffected by monarchs. It was an unprecedented action and, as the Order gained political and economic strength, it amassed a huge reserve of wealth. Kings and patriarchs left great sums in their wills. Loans were made to barons and merchants on the promise that their houses, lands, vineyards, and gardens would pass to the Order at their death. Pilgrims were given safe transport to and from the Holy Land in return for generous donations. By the beginning of the fourteenth century the Templars rivaled the Genovese, the Lombards, and even the Jews as controllers of currency. The kings of France and England kept their treasury in the Order's vaults. Even the Muslims banked with them.

The Order's Paris Temple became the center of the world's currency market. Slowly, the organization evolved into a financial and military complex, both self-supporting and self-regulating. Eventually Templar property, some 9,000 estates, was wholly exempt from taxation, and that unique position led to conflicts with local clergy since their churches suffered while Templar lands prospered. Competition from other Orders, particularly the Knights Hospitallers, only heightened tension.

During the twelfth and thirteenth centuries control of the Holy Land seesawed back and forth between Christian and Arab. The rise of Saladin, as ruler of the Muslims, provided the Arabs with their first great military leader, and Christian Jerusalem finally fell in 1187. In the chaos that followed the Templars confined their activities to Acre, a fortified stronghold close to the Mediterranean shore. For the next hundred years they languished in the Holy Land but flourished in Europe, where they established an extensive network of churches, abbeys, and estates. When Acre fell in 1291, the Order lost both its last base in the Holy Land and its purpose for existence.

Its own rigid adherence to secrecy, which initially set it apart, eventually encouraged slander. Philip IV of France, in 1307, eyeing the vast Templar assets, arrested many of the brothers. Other monarchs followed suit. Seven years of accusations and trials followed. Clement V formally dissolved the Order in 1312. The final blow came on March 18, 1314, when the last master, Jacques de Molay, was burned at the stake.

Malone kept reading. There was still that tug at the back of his brain—something he'd read when he'd first thumbed through the book weeks ago. Paging through, he read about how, before the suppression in 1307, the Order became expert in seafaring, property development, animal husbandry, agriculture, and, most important, finance. While the Church forbade scientific experimentation, the Templars learned from their enemy, the Arabs, whose culture encouraged independent thought. The Templars also secreted away, much as modern banks scatter wealth among so many vaults, a vast amount of assets. There was even a medieval French verse quoted that aptly described the overly solvent Templars and their sudden disappearance:

The brethren, the masters of the Temple,
who were well filled and ample
with gold and silver and with wealth.
Where are they? How have they fared?
Who had such power that none dared
take aught from them, no man so bold:
forever buying, they never sold.

History had not been kind to the Order. Though they captured the imagination of poets and chroniclers—the Knights of the Grail in *Parzival* were Templars, as were the demonic antiheroes in *Ivanhoe*—as the Crusades acquired the label of European aggression and imperialism, the Templars became an integral part of their brutal fanaticism.

Malone continued to scan the book until he finally found the passage he recalled from his first perusal. He knew it was there. His memory never failed him. The words talked of how, on the battlefield, the Templars always displayed a vertical banner divided into two blocks—one black to represent the sin that brother knights had left behind, the other white to symbolize their new life within the Order. The banner was labeled in French. Translated it meant a lofty, noble, glorious state. The term also doubled as the Order's battle cry.

Beauseant. Be glorious.

Precisely the word Red Jacket had uttered as he'd leaped from the Round Tower.

What was happening?

Old motivations stirred inside him. Feelings he'd thought a year of retirement had quelled. Good agents were both inquisitive and cautious. Forget either attribute and something was inevitably overlooked—something potentially disastrous. He'd made that mistake once years ago on one of his early assignments, and his impetuousness cost the life of a hired operative. It would not be the last person he felt responsible for getting killed, but it was the first, and he never forgot his carelessness.

Stephanie was in trouble. No question. She'd ordered him to stay out of her business, so talking to her again would be useless. But maybe Peter Hansen would prove informative.

He glanced at his watch. Late, but Hansen was known as a night owl and should still be up. If not, he'd awaken him.

He tossed the book aside and headed for the door.

ELEVEN

"WHERE IS LARS NELLE'S JOURNAL?" DE ROQUEFORT ASKED.

Still in the grasp of the two men, Peter Hansen stared up at him. He knew Hansen had once been closely associated with Lars Nelle. When he'd discovered that Stephanie Nelle was coming to Denmark to attend the Roskilde auction, he'd surmised that she might contact Peter Hansen. Which was why he'd approached the book dealer first.

"Surely Stephanie Nelle mentioned her husband's journal?"

Hansen shook his head. "Nothing. Nothing at all."

"When Lars Nelle was alive, did he mention that he kept a journal?"

"Never."

"Do you understand your situation? Nothing I wanted has occurred and, worse, you deceived me."

"I know that Lars kept meticulous notes." Resignation filled Hansen's voice.

"Tell me more."

Hansen seemed to steel himself. "When I'm released."

De Roquefort allowed the fool a victory. He motioned and his men released their hold. Hansen quickly gulped a deep swallow of beer, then tabled the mug. "Lars wrote lots of books about Rennes-le-Château. All that stuff about lost parchments, hidden geometry, and puzzles made for great sales." Hansen seemed to catch hold of himself. "He alluded to every treasure he could imagine. Visigoth gold, Templar wealth, Cathar loot. *Take a thread and weave a blanket,* that's what he used to say."

De Roquefort knew all about Rennes-le-Château, a tiny hamlet in southern France that had existed since Roman times. A priest in the latter part of the nineteenth century spent enormous sums of money remodeling the local church. Decades later, rumors started that the priest financed the decorations with a great treasure he'd found. Lars Nelle learned of the intriguing place thirty years ago and wrote a book about the tale, which became an international bestseller.

"So tell me what was recorded in the notebook," he asked. "Information different from Lars Nelle's published material?"

"I told you, I don't know anything about a notebook." Hansen grabbed the mug and savored another gulp. "But knowing Lars, I doubt he told the world everything in those books."

"And what was it he concealed?"

A sly smile came to the Dane's lips. "As if you don't already know. But I assure you, I have no idea. *I* only know what I read in Lars's books."

"I wouldn't assume anything, if I were you."

Hansen seemed unfazed. "So tell me, what's so important about that book tonight? It's not even about Rennes-le-Château."

"It is the key to everything."

"How could a nothing book, more than a hundred and fifty years old, be the key to anything?"

"Many times it's the simplest of things that are most important."

Hansen reached for his cigarette. "Lars was a strange man. I never could figure him out. He was obsessed with the whole Rennes thing. He loved the place. Even bought a house there. I went once. Dreary."

"Did Lars say if he found anything?"

Hansen appraised him again with a suspicious glare. "Like what?"

"Don't be coy. I'm not in the mood."

"You must know something or you wouldn't be here." Hansen bent down to balance the cigarette back onto the ashtray. But his hand kept going, straight into an open drawer in the side table, and a gun appeared. One of de Roquefort's men kicked the pistol from the book dealer's grip.

"That was foolish," de Roquefort said.

"Screw you," Hansen spat out, rubbing his hand.

The radio clipped to de Roquefort's waist crackled in his ear, and a voice said, "A man is approaching." A pause. "It's Malone. Coming straight for the shop."

Not unexpected, but perhaps it was time to send a clear message that this was not Malone's affair. He caught the attention of his two subordinates. They advanced and again seized Peter Hansen by the arms.

"Deceit has a price," de Roquefort said.

"Who the hell are you?"

"Someone you should not have toyed with." De Roquefort made the sign of the cross. "May the Lord be with you."

MALONE SAW LIGHTS IN THE THIRD-FLOOR WINDOWS. THE street in front of Hansen's bookshop was empty. Only a few parked cars lined the dark cobbles, which he knew would all be gone by morning, when shoppers once again invaded this part of the pedestrians-only Strøget.

What had Stephanie said earlier when she'd been inside Hansen's shop? *My husband said you were a man who could find the unfindable.* So Peter Hansen was apparently connected to Lars Nelle, and that former association would explain why Stephanie had sought out Hansen, rather than coming to him. But it did not answer the multitude of other questions Malone possessed.

Malone had never met Lars Nelle. He died about a year after Malone joined the Magellan Billet, at a time when he and Stephanie were just getting to know one another. But he'd subsequently read all of Nelle's books, which were mixtures of history, fact, conjecture, and grand coincidence. Lars was an international conspiratorialist who'd thought the region of southern France known as the Languedoc harbored some sort of great treasure. Which was partly understandable. The area had long been the land of troubadours, a place of castles and crusades, where the legend of the Holy Grail was first born. Unfortunately, Lars Nelle's work had not generated any serious scholarship. Instead, his theories only stirred the interest of new age writers and independent filmmakers who expanded on his original premise, ultimately proposing theories that ranged from extraterrestrials, to Roman plunder, to the hidden essence of Christianity itself. Nothing, of course, had ever been proven or found. But Malone was certain the French tourist industry loved the speculation.

The book Stephanie had tried to buy at the Roskilde auction was titled *Pierres Gravées du Languedoc*. Inscribed Stones of the Languedoc. An odd title on an even odder subject. What relevance could it have? He knew that Stephanie had always been unimpressed with her husband's work. That dispute was the number one problem in their marriage and eventually led to a continental separation—Lars living in France, she in America. So what was she doing in Denmark eleven years after his death? And why were others intent on interfering with her—even to the point of dying?

He kept walking and tried to organize his thoughts. He knew Peter Hansen would not be glad to see him, so he told himself to choose his words carefully. He needed to placate the idiot and learn what he could. He'd even pay if he had to.

Something burst from one of the top-floor windows in Hansen's building.

He stared up as a body ejected headfirst, flipped in midair, then slammed onto the bonnet of a parked car.

He raced forward and saw Peter Hansen. He tried for a pulse. Faint.

Amazingly, Hansen opened his eyes.

"Can you hear me?" he asked Hansen.

No response.

Something whizzed by close to his head and Hansen's chest lurched upward. Another swoosh and the skull ripped apart, blood and sinew splattering his jacket.

He whirled around.

In the shattered window three floors above, a man with a gun stood. The same man in the leather jacket who'd started the shooting in the cathedral—the one intent on assaulting Stephanie. In the instant it took the shooter to re-aim, Malone leaped behind the car.

More bullets rained down.

The pop of each shot was muffled, like hands clapping. A sound-suppressed weapon. One bullet pinged off the hood next to Hansen. Another shattered the windshield.

"Mr. Malone. This affair does not concern you," the man said from above.

"Does now."

He wasn't going to stay around and debate the point. He crouched low and used the parked cars as shields while working his way down the street.

More shots, like pillows fluffing, tried to find a way through metal and glass.

Twenty yards away, he glanced back. The face disappeared from the window. He stood and ran, turning at the first corner. He rounded another, trying to use the labyrinth of streets to his advantage, stacking buildings between him and his pursuers. Blood pounded in his temples. His heart thumped. Damn. He was back in the game.

He stopped a moment and gulped in the cool air.

Running footsteps were approaching from behind. He wondered if his pursuers knew their way around the Strøget. He had to assume they did. Around another corner and more darkened shops encased him. Tension built in his stomach. He was running out of options. Ahead was one of the district's many open squares, a fountain churning in the center. All the cafés lining its perimeter were closed for the night. No one was in sight. Hiding places here would be in short supply. Across the empty expanse rose a church. A faint glow was evident through darkened stained-glass windows. In summer, Copenhagen's churches were all left open to midnight. He needed a place to hide, at least for a while. So he raced across to its marble portal.

The lock clicked open.

He shoved the leadened door inward, then closed it gently, hoping his pursuers wouldn't notice.

Scattered incandescent fixtures lit the empty interior. An impressive altar and sculpted statues cast ghostly images through the sullen air. He searched the darkness toward the altar and spotted stairs and a pallid glow from below. He headed for it and descended, a cold cloud of worry filling him.

An iron gate at the bottom opened into a three-naved wide space with a low vaulted ceiling. Two stone sarcophagi topped with immense slabs of carved granite stood in the center. The only break in the darkness came from a tiny amber light near a small altar. This seemed like a good place to park for a while. He couldn't go back to his shop. They certainly knew where he lived. He told himself to calm down, but his momentary relief was shattered by a door opening above. His gaze shot to the top of the vault not three feet from the crown of his head.

Two sets of footsteps bounded across the floor above.

He moved deeper into the shadows. His mind filled with a familiar panic, which he suppressed with a wave of self-control. He needed something to defend himself with, so he searched the darkness. In an apse twenty feet away he spotted an iron candelabrum.

He crept over.

The ornament stood about five feet tall, a solitary wax candle, about four inches thick, rising from its center. He removed the candle and tested the metal stem. Heavy. With the candelabrum in hand, he tiptoed across the crypt and took up a position behind another pillar.

Someone started down the steps.

He peered past the tombs, through the blackness, his body alive with an energy that had always, in the past, clarified his thoughts.

At the base of the stairs appeared the silhouette of a man. He carried a gun, a sound suppressor at the end of the barrel distinctive even in shadow. Malone tightened his grip on the iron stem and cocked his arm. The man was moving toward him. His muscles tensed. He silently counted to five, clenched his teeth, then swung the candelabrum and caught the man square in the chest, propelling the shadow back onto one of the tombs.

He tossed the iron aside and swung his fist into the man's jaw. The pistol flew away and rattled across the floor.

His attacker went down.

He searched for the gun as another set of footsteps bounded into the crypt. He found the pistol and locked his hand on the grip.

Two shots came in his direction.

Dust snowed down from the ceiling as bullets found stone. He dove for the nearest pillar and fired. A muffled retort sent a shot through the darkness, ricocheting off the far wall.

The second attacker stopped his advance, taking up a position behind the farther tomb.

Now he was trapped.

Between him and the only way out was an armed man. The first pursuer was starting to come to his feet, groaning from the blows. Malone was armed, but the odds weren't good.

He stared through the dimly lit chamber and readied himself.

The man rising from the floor suddenly collapsed back down.

A few seconds passed.

Silence.

One set of footsteps echoed from above. Then the church door opened and closed. He did not move. The stillness was unnerving. His gaze raked the darkness. No movement anywhere.

He decided to risk it and crept forward.

The first assailant lay sprawled on the floor. The other man was likewise prone and still. He checked both men for pulses. Beating, but weak. Then he spotted something at the back of one of the necks. He bent close and plucked out a small dart, the tip a half-inch needle.

His savior was privy to some sophisticated equipment.

The two men lying on the floor were the same two from outside the auction earlier. But who'd disabled them? He bent back down and retrieved both guns, then searched the bodies. No identification on either. One man wore a radio beneath his jacket. He removed the unit along with the earpiece and microphone.

"Anyone there?" he said into the mike.

"And who is this?"

"You the same man that was in the cathedral? The one who just killed Peter Hansen."

"Half correct."

He realized no one was going to say much over an open channel, but the message was clear. "Your men are down."

"Your doing?"

"Wish I could take credit. Who are you?"

"That's not relevant to our discussion."

"How was Peter Hansen a problem for you?"

"I detest those who deceive me."

"Obviously. But somebody just caught your two guys by surprise. I don't know who, but I like them."

No response. He waited a moment more and was about to speak when the radio crackled. "I trust you will take advantage of your good fortune and go back to selling books."

The other radio clicked off.

TWELVE

ABBEY DES FONTAINES
FRENCH PYRÉNÉES
11:30 PM

THE SENESCHAL AWOKE. HE'D DRIFTED OFF IN A CHAIR BESIDE the bed. A quick glance at the clock on the night table told him that he'd been asleep for about an hour. He glanced over at his sick master. The familiar sound of labored breath was gone. In the scattered rays of incandescent light that washed in from the abbey's exterior, he saw the film of death had gathered in the old man's eyes.

He felt for a pulse.

The master was dead.

His courage forsook him as he knelt and said a prayer for his departed friend. The cancer had won. The battle was over. But another conflict of differing proportion would soon begin. He beseeched the Lord to allow the old man's soul into heaven. No one deserved salvation more. He'd learned everything from the master—his personal failings and emotional loneliness long ago tossed him under the old man's influence. His had been a quick education, and he'd tried never to disappoint. *Mistakes are tolerated, so long as they are not made again,* he'd been told—only once, since the master never repeated himself.

Many of the brothers took that directness for arrogance. Others resented what they believed to be a condescending attitude. But none ever questioned the master's authority. A brother's duty was to obey. The time for inquiry came only with the selection of the master.

Which was what the day ahead now promised.

For the sixty-seventh time since Inception, a point dating back to the early part of the twelfth century, another man would be chosen master. For the sixty-six who'd come before, the average tenure was a mere eighteen years, the contributions varying from nonexistent to beyond compare. Each, though, had served the Order until death. Some had even died fighting, but the days of open warfare were long over. The quest today was more subtle, modern battle-grounds places the Fathers could never have imagined. The courts, the Internet, books, magazines, newspapers—all were venues that the Order regularly patrolled, making sure its secrets were safe, its existence unnoticed. And every master, no matter how inept he might have been, had succeeded in that singular goal. But the seneschal feared that the next tenure would be particularly decisive. A civil war was brewing, one the dead man lying before him had kept in check with an uncanny ability to predict his enemy's thoughts.

In the silence that engulfed him the rushing water from outside seemed closer. During summer the brothers often visited the falls and enjoyed a swim in the frigid pool, and he longed for such pleasures but knew there'd be no respites anytime soon. He decided not to alert the brotherhood of the master's death until prayers at Prime, which would not be for another five hours. In times past they'd all gathered just after midnight for Matins, but that devotional went the way of many Rules. A more realistic schedule now governed, one that recognized the importance of sleep, geared to the practicalities of the twenty-first rather than the thirteenth century.

He knew that no one would dare enter the master's chamber. Only he, as seneschal, was granted that privilege, particularly while the master lay ill. So he reached for the comforter and stretched the blanket over the old man's dead face.

Several thoughts raced through his mind and he fought the rising temptation. Rule, if nothing else, instilled a sense of discipline, and he was proud that he'd never knowingly committed any violations. But several were now screaming to him. He'd thought about them all day while he watched his friend die. If death had claimed the master while the abbey was alive with activity, it would have been impossible to do what he now contemplated. But at this hour he would have free reign, and depending on what happened over the next day this might be his only chance.

So he reached down, slid back the blanket, and parted the azure robe, exposing the old man's lifeless chest. The chain was there, precisely where it should be, and he slipped the gold links over the head.

A silver key dangled from the end.

"Forgive me," he whispered as he replaced the blanket.

He hustled across the room to a Renaissance armoire darkened by countless waxings. Inside lay a bronze box adorned with a silver crest. Only the seneschal knew of its existence, and he'd seen the master open it many times, though he'd never been allowed to study its contents. He carried the container to the desk, inserted the key, and once again begged for forgiveness.

He was searching for a leather-bound volume that the master had possessed for several years. He knew it was kept inside the strongbox—the master had placed it there in his presence—but when he hinged open the lid, he saw that there was only a rosary, a few papers, and a missal. No book.

His fear was now a reality. Where before he'd only suspected, now he knew.

He replaced the strongbox in the armoire and left the bedchamber.

The abbey was a maze of multistory wings, each added in a differing century, the architecture conspiring to create a jumbled complex that now housed four hundred brothers. There was the obligatory chapel, a stately cloister garth, workshops, offices, a gym, common rooms for hygiene, eating, and entertainment, a chapter house, a sacristy, a refectory, parlors, an infirmary, and an impressive library. The master's bedchamber was situated in a section built originally in the fifteenth century, facing sheer rock precipices that towered over a narrow glen. Lodgings for the brothers were nearby, and the seneschal passed an arched portal that led into the cavernous dormitory where lights burned, as Rule forbid the chamber to ever be totally dark. He noticed no movement and heard nothing except intermittent snores. Centuries ago a guard would have been posted at the door, and he wondered if perhaps that custom would have to be revived in the days ahead.

He glided down the wide passageway, following the crimson carpet runner that shielded the rough flagstones. On

either side paintings, statuary, and scattered memorials recalled the abbey's past. Unlike at other Pyrenean monasteries,
no looting had occurred here during the French Revolution,
so both its art and message had survived.

He found the main staircase and descended to ground
level. Through more vaulted corridors he passed areas where
visitors were schooled in the monastic way of life. There
were not many invitees, a few thousand each year, the income a modest supplement to the annual operating ex-
penses, but enough visited that care was taken to ensure the
brothers' privacy.

The entrance he sought stood at the end of another
ground-floor corridor. The door, laced with medieval iron-
work, was swung open, as always.

He entered the library.

Few collections could claim to have never been disturbed,
yet the innumerable volumes that surrounded him had remained inviolate for seven centuries. Started with only a score
of books, the collection had grown through gift, bequest, purchase, and, in the beginning, production from scribes who labored day and night. The subject matters then and now varied,
with emphases on theology, philosophy, logic, history, law,
science, and music. The Latin phrase etched into the mortar
above the main doorway was fitting. CLAUSTRUM SINE AR-
MARIO EST QUASI CASTRUM SINE ARMAMENTARIO. A monastery
without a library is like a castle without an armory.

He stopped and listened.

No one was around.

Security was of no real concern, as eight hundred years of
Rule had proven more than effective in guarding the
stacks. No brother would dare intrude without permission.
But he was no brother. He was the seneschal. At least for one
more day.

He navigated his way through the shelves, toward the
rear of the massive expanse, and stopped at a black metal

door. He raked a plastic card across the scanner affixed to the wall. Only the master, marshal, archivist, and himself possessed the cards. Access to the volumes beyond was gained only with the master's direct permission. Even the archivist had to obtain an okay before entering. Stored inside were a variety of precious books, old charters, title deeds, a register of members, and, most important, the Chronicles, which contained a narrative history of the Order's entire existence. As minutes memorialized what the British Parliament or U.S. Congress accomplished, the Chronicles detailed the Order's successes and failures. Written journals remained, many with brittle covers and brazen clasps, each one looking like a tiny trunk, but the bulk of the data had now been scanned into computers— making it a simple matter to electronically search the Order's nine-hundred-year record.

He entered, navigated the dimly lit shelving, and found the codex lying in its designated spot. The tiny volume measured eight inches square and an inch thick. He'd come across it two years ago, its pages bound in wooden boards sheathed with blind-stamped calf. Not quite a book, but an ancestor—an early effort that replaced rolled parchment and allowed text to be inscribed on two sides of a page.

He carefully opened the front cover.

There was no title page, the cursive Latin script framed by an illuminated border of dull red, green, and gold. He'd learned that it had been copied in the fifteenth century by one of the abbey's scribes. Most of the ancient codices had fallen victim, their parchment used to either bind other books, cover jars, or simply kindle a fire. Thank goodness this one survived. The information it contained was priceless. He'd never told anyone what he'd found within the codex, not even the master, and since he might need the information, and there would be no chances better than the present, he slipped the book into the fold of his cassock.

He walked an aisle over and found another thin volume, its script also hand-penned, but in the latter part of the nineteenth century. Not a book written for an audience, but instead a personal record. He might need it, as well, so he slipped it into his cassock.

He then left the library, knowing that the computer that controlled the security door had recorded the time of his visit. Magnetic strips affixed in each of the two volumes would identify that both had been removed. Since there was no other way out except through the doorway lined with sensors, and removing the tags could well damage the books, little choice existed. He could only hope that in the confusion of the days ahead, no one would take the time to examine the computer log.

Rule was clear.

Theft of Order property was punishable by banishment.

But that was a chance he would have to take.

THIRTEEN

11:50 PM

MALONE TOOK NO CHANCES AND DEPARTED THE CHURCH through a rear door, beyond the sacristy. He could not worry about the two unconscious men. Right now, he needed to get to Stephanie, her surly attitude be damned. Clearly, the man from the cathedral, the one who'd killed Peter Hansen, had his own problems. Somebody had taken out his two accomplices.

Malone had no idea who or why, but he was grateful, since escaping from that crypt could have proven tough. He cursed himself again for getting involved, but it was too late to walk away now. He was in—whether he liked it or not.

He took a roundabout path out of the Strøget and eventually made his way to Kongens Nytorv, a typically busy city square encircled by stately buildings. His senses were on maximum alert and he kept a sharp lookout for any tails, but no one was behind him. At this late hour, traffic in the square was light. Nyhavn, just beyond the square's east side, with its colorful harbor promenade of gabled houses, continued to accommodate waterfront diners at outdoor tables lively with music.

He hustled down the sidewalk toward the Hotel d'Angleterre. The brightly lit seven-story structure faced the sea and stretched an entire city block. The elegant building dated from the eighteenth century, its rooms, he knew, having hosted kings, emperors, and presidents.

He entered the lobby and passed the desk. A soft melody drifted from the main lounge. A few late-night patrons milled about. A row of house phones dotted a marble counter and he used one to call Stephanie Nelle's room. The phone rang three times before it was answered.

"Wake up," he said.

"You don't listen well, do you, Cotton?" The voice still carried the same desultory tone from Roskilde.

"Peter Hansen is dead."

A moment of silence passed.

"I'm in six ten."

HE STEPPED INTO THE ROOM. STEPHANIE WORE ONE OF THE HOtel's signature robes. He told her everything that had just happened. She listened in silence, just like in years past when he'd made reports. But he saw a sense of defeat in her tired features, one he hoped signaled a change in attitude.

"Are you going to let me help you now?" he asked.

She studied him through eyes that, he'd often noticed, changed shades as her mood shifted. In some ways she reminded him of his mother, though Stephanie was only a dozen or so years older than him. Her anger from earlier was not out of character. She didn't like making mistakes and she hated having them pointed out. Her talent was not in gathering information but in analyzing and assessing—a meticulous organizer who plotted and planned with the cunning of a leopard. He'd watched her many times make tough decisions without hesitation—both attorneys general and presidents had relied on her cool head—so he wondered about her present quandary and its strange effect on her usually sound judgment.

"I pointed them to Hansen," she muttered. "In the cathedral, I didn't correct him when he implied Hansen may have Lars's journal." She told him about the conversation.

"Describe him." When she did he said, "That's the same guy who started the shooting and the one who shot Hansen."

"The jumper from the Round Tower worked for him. He came to steal my bag, which contained Lars's journal."

"Then he goes to the same auction, knowing you'd be there. Who knew you were going?"

"Just Hansen. The office knows only that I'm on vacation. I have my world phone, but I left word not to be disturbed unless it was a catastrophic emergency."

"Where did you learn about the auction?"

"Three weeks ago a package arrived postmarked from Avignon, France. Inside was a note and Lars's journal." She paused. "I hadn't seen that notebook in years."

He knew this would ordinarily be a forbidden subject. Lars Nelle had taken his own life eleven years ago, found hanging from a bridge in southern France, a note in his pocket that merely said GOODBYE STEPHANIE. For an academician who'd penned a multitude of books, such a simple salutation seemed almost an insult. Though she and her husband were separated at the time, Stephanie took the loss hard, and Malone recalled how difficult the months after had been. Never had they spoken about his death, and for her to even mention it now was extraordinary.

"Journal of what?" he asked.

"Lars was fascinated with the secrets of Rennes-le-Château—"

"I know. I read his books."

"You never mentioned that before."

"You never asked."

She seemed to sense his irritation. A lot was happening and neither one of them had time for chitchat.

"Lars made a living expounding theories on what may or may not be hidden in and around Rennes-le-Château," she said. "But he kept many of his private thoughts in the journal, which stayed with him always. After he died, I thought Mark had it."

Another bad subject. Mark Nelle had been an Oxford-educated medieval historian who taught at the University of Toulouse, in southern France. Five years ago he was lost in the Pyrénées. An avalanche. His body never found. Malone knew that tragedy had been accentuated by the fact that Stephanie and her son had not been close. A lot of bad blood flowed in the Nelle family, none of which was any of his business.

"That damn journal was like a ghost come back to haunt me," she said. "There it was. Lars's handwriting. The note told me about the auction and the availability of the book. I remembered Lars speaking of it, and there were references in the journal, so I came to buy it."

"And danger bells weren't clanging in your head?"

"Why? My husband was not involved in my line of work. His was a harmless quest for things that don't exist. How was I to know there were people involved who would kill?"

"That man leaping from the Round Tower was clear enough. You should have come to me then."

"I need to do this alone."

"Do what?"

"I don't know, Cotton."

"Why is that book so important? I learned at the auction that it's a nondescript account of no importance. They were shocked it sold for so much."

"I have no idea." Exasperation returned to her tone. "Truly, I don't. Two weeks ago I sat down, read Lars's notebook, and I have to say I became fascinated. I'm ashamed to say I never read one of his books until last week. When I did, I began to feel awful about my attitude toward him. Eleven years can add a lot of perspective."

"So what did you plan to do?"

She shook her head. "I don't know. Just buy the book. Read it and see what happened from there. While I was over here, I planned to go to France and spend a few days at Lars's house. I haven't been there in a while."

She apparently was trying to make peace with demons, but there was reality to consider. "You need help, Stephanie. There's more happening here, and this is something I do have experience handling."

"Don't you have a bookshop to run?"

"My employees can handle things for a few days."

She hesitated, seemingly considering his offer. "You were the best I ever had. I'm still mad you quit."

"Had to do what I had to do."

She shook her head. "To have Henrik Thorvaldsen steal you away. Insult to injury."

Last year, when he'd retired and told her he planned to move to Copenhagen, she'd been happy for him, until learning about Thorvaldsen's involvement. Characteristically, she'd never explained herself and he knew better than to ask.

"I have some more bad news for you," he said. "The person who outbid you for the book? On the phone? It was Henrik."

She cast him a look of disdain.

"He was working with Peter Hansen," he said.

"What led you to that conclusion?"

He told her what he learned at the auction and what the man had said to him over the radio. *I detest those who deceive me.* "Apparently Hansen was playing both ends against the middle and the middle won."

"Wait outside," she said.

"That's why I came. You and Henrik need to talk. But we need to leave here with caution. Those men may still be out there."

"I'll get dressed."

He moved toward the door. "Where's Lars's journal?"

She pointed to the safe.

"Bring it."

"Is that wise?"

"The police are going to find Hansen's body. It won't take them long to connect the dots. We need to be ready to move."

"I can handle the police."

He faced her. "Washington bailed you out of Roskilde because they don't know what you're doing. Right now, I'm sure someone in Justice is trying to find out. You hate questions, and you can't tell the attorney general to go to hell when he calls. I'm still not sure what you're doing, but I know one thing, you don't want to talk about it. So pack up."

"I don't miss that arrogance."

"And your ray-of-sunshine personality has left my life incomplete, too. Could you just for once do what I ask? It's tough enough in the field without acting stupid."

"I don't need to be reminded of that."

"Sure you do."

And he left.

FOURTEEN

Malone and Stephanie rode out of Copenhagen on Highway 152. Though he'd driven from Rio de Janeiro to the Petropolis and along the sea from Naples to the Amalfi, Malone believed the path north to Helsingør, along Denmark's rocky east shore, was by far the most charming of the seaside routes. Fishing villages, beech forest, summer villas, and the gray expanse of the tideless Øresund all combined to offer an ageless splendor.

The weather was typical. Rain peppered the windshield, whipped by a torrential wind. Past one of the smaller seaside resorts, closed for the night, the highway wound inland into a forested expanse. Through an open gate, beyond two white cottages, Malone followed a grassy drive and parked in a pebbled courtyard. The house beyond was a genuine specimen of Danish baroque—three stories, built of brick encased in sandstone, and topped with a gracefully curving copper roof. One wing turned inland. The other faced the sea.

He knew its history. Named Christiangate, the house was built three hundred years ago by a clever Thorvaldsen who'd converted tons of worthless peat into fuel to produce porcelain. In the 1800s the Danish queen proclaimed the glassworks the official royal provider, and Adelgate Glasvaerker, with its distinctive symbol of two circles with a line beneath, still reigned premier throughout Denmark and Europe. The conglomerate's current head was the family patriarch, Henrik Thorvaldsen.

The manor's door was answered by a steward who was not surprised to see them. Interesting, considering it was after midnight and Thorvaldsen lived as solitary as an owl. They were shown into a room where oak beams, armor, and oil portraits conveyed the appurtenances of a noble seat. A long table dominated the great hall—four hundred years old, Malone remembered Thorvaldsen once saying, its dark maple reflecting a finish that came only from centuries of dedicated use. Thorvaldsen sat at one end, an orange cake and a steaming samovar on the table before him.

"Please, come in. Take a seat."

Thorvaldsen rose from the chair with what appeared to be great effort and flashed a smile. His stooped arthritic frame stood no more than five and a half feet, the hump in his spine barely concealed by the folds of an oversized Norwegian sweater. Malone noticed a glint in the bright gray eyes. His friend was up to something. No question about it.

Malone pointed to the cake. "So sure we'd come you baked us a cake?"

"I wasn't sure both of you would make the journey, but I knew you would."

"Why's that?"

"Once I learned you were at the auction, I knew it was only a matter of time before you discovered my involvement."

Stephanie stepped forward. "I want my book."

Thorvaldsen appraised her with a tight gaze. "No hello? Nice to meet you? Just, 'I want my book.'"

"I don't like you."

Thorvaldsen retook his seat at the head of the table. Malone decided that the cake looked good, so he sat and cut a slice.

"You don't like me?" Thorvaldsen repeated. "Odd, considering we've never met."

"I know of you."

"Does that mean the Magellan Billet has a file on me?"

"Your name turns up in the strangest places. We call you an *international person of interest*."

Thorvaldsen's face grimaced, as if he were undergoing some agonizing penance. "You'd think me a terrorist or a criminal."

"Which one are you?"

The Dane stared back at her with a sudden curiosity. "I was told you possess the genius to conceive great deeds and the industry to see them through. Strange, with all that ability, you failed so utterly as a wife and mother."

Stephanie's eyes instantly filled with indignation. "You know nothing of me."

"I know you and Lars had not lived together for years before he died. I know you and he differed on a great many things. I know you and your son were estranged."

A flush of rage colored Stephanie's cheeks. "Go to hell."

Thorvaldsen seemed unfazed by her rebuke. "You're wrong, Stephanie."

"About what?"

"A great many things. And it's time you know the truth."

DE ROQUEFORT FOUND THE MANOR HOUSE PRECISELY WHERE the information he'd requested had directed. Once he'd learned who was working with Peter Hansen to buy the book, it had taken his lieutenant only half an hour to compile a dossier. Now he was staring at the stately home of the book's high bidder—Henrik Thorvaldsen—and it all made sense.

Thorvaldsen was one of the wealthiest citizens in Denmark, with family roots reaching back to the Vikings. His corporate holdings were impressive. In addition to Adelgate Glasvaerker, he possessed interests in British banks, Polish mines, German manufacturing, and European transportation. On a continent where old money meant billions, Thorvaldsen was at the top of most fortune lists. He was an odd sort, an introvert who ventured from his estate only sparingly. His charitable contributions were legendary, especially to Holocaust survivors, anti-communist organizations, and international medical relief.

He was sixty-two years old and close with the Danish royal family, especially the queen. His wife and son were dead, the wife from cancer, the son shot more than a year before while working for the Danish mission in Mexico City. The man who'd taken down one of the killers was an American lawyer-agent named Cotton Malone. Even a link to Lars Nelle existed, though not a favorable one, as Thorvaldsen was credited with some unflattering public comments about Nelle's research. A nasty incident fifteen years ago at the Bibliothèque Sainte-Genevieve in Paris, where the two had engaged in a shouting match, had been widely reported in the French press. All of which might explain why Henrik Thorvaldsen had been interested in Peter Hansen's offer, but not entirely.

He needed to know it all.

Bracing ocean air whipped in off the black Øresund and the rain had slackened into a mist. Two of his acolytes stood beside him. The other two waited in the car, parked beyond the property, their heads woozy from whatever drug had been shot into them. He was still puzzled by who'd interfered. He'd sensed no one watching him all day, yet somebody had covertly traced his movements. Somebody with the sophistication to utilize tranquilizing darts.

But first things first. He led the way across the spongy yard to a row of hedges that fronted the elegant house. Lights burned in a ground-floor room that would, in daylight, offer a spectacular seaside view. He'd observed no guards, dogs, or alarm system. Curious, but not surprising.

He approached the lighted window. He'd noticed a car parked in the drive and wondered if his luck was about to change. He carefully peered inside and saw Stephanie Nelle and Cotton Malone talking with an older man.

He smiled. His luck was indeed changing.

He motioned and one of his men produced a nylon case. He unzipped the pouch and removed a microphone. He carefully affixed its rubber suction cup to the corner of the damp window pane. The state-of-the-art receiver inside the nylon bag could now hear every word.

He wedged a tiny speaker into his ear.

Before he killed them, he needed to listen.

"WHY DON'T YOU SIT?" THORVALDSEN SAID.

"So kind of you, *Herr* Thorvaldsen, but I prefer to stand," Stephanie made clear, contempt in her voice.

Thorvaldsen reached for the coffee and filled his cup. "I would suggest calling me anything but *herr*." He set the samovar down. "I detest all things even remotely German."

Malone watched as Stephanie took in the command. Surely, if he was a "person of interest" within Billet files, she knew that Thorvaldsen's grandfather, uncles, aunts, and cousins had all fallen victim to the Nazi occupation of Denmark. Even so, he expected her to retaliate, but instead her face softened. "Henrik it is, then."

Thorvaldsen dropped one lump of sugar into his cup. "Your facetiousness is noted." He stirred his coffee. "I learned long ago that all things can be settled over a cup of coffee. A person will tell you more of their private life after one good cup of coffee than after a magnum of champagne or a quart of port."

Malone knew Thorvaldsen liked to ease his listener with nonsense while he appraised the situation. The old man sipped from the steaming cup.

"As I said, Stephanie, it is time you learn the truth."

She approached the table and sat across from Malone. "Then by all means, destroy all my preconceived notions about you."

"And what would those be?"

"I could go on for a while. Here are the highlights. Three years ago you were linked to an art theft syndicate with radical Israeli connections. You interfered last year in the German national elections, funneling money illegally to certain candidates. For some reason, though, both the Germans and Israelis chose not to prosecute you."

Thorvaldsen made an impatient gesture of assent. "Guilty on both counts. Those *radical Israeli connections,* as you call them, are settlers who do not feel their homes should be bargained away by a corrupt Israeli government. To help their cause, we provided funds from wealthy Arabs who trafficked in stolen art. The items were simply stolen back from the thieves. Perhaps your files noted the art was returned to its owners."

"For a fee."

"Which any private art investigator would charge. We merely channeled the money raised to more worthy causes. I saw a certain justice in the act. And the German elections? I financed several candidates who faced stiff opposition from the radical right. With my help, they all won. I saw no reason to allow fascism to gain any foothold. Do you?"

"What you did was illegal and caused a multitude of problems."

"What I did was solve a problem. Which is far more than the Americans have done."

Stephanie seemed unimpressed. "Why are you in my business?"

"How is this your business?"

"It concerns my husband's work."

Thorvaldsen's face stiffened. "I don't recall you having any interest in Lars's work when he was alive."

Malone caught the critical words *I don't recall*. Which meant a high level of past knowledge concerning Lars Nelle. Uncharacteristically, Stephanie seemed not to be listening.

"I don't intend to discuss my private life. Just tell me why you bought that book tonight."

"Peter Hansen informed me of your interest. He also told me that another man wanted you to have the book, too. But not before the man made a copy. He paid Hansen a fee to make sure that happened."

"He say who?" she asked.

Thorvaldsen shook his head.

"Hansen's dead," Malone said.

"Not surprising." No emotion claimed Thorvaldsen's voice.

Malone told him what had happened.

"Hansen was greedy," the Dane said. "He believed the book had great value, so he wanted me to purchase it secretly so he could offer it to the other man—at a price."

"Which you agreed to do, being the humanitarian sort you are." Stephanie was apparently not going to cut him any slack.

"Hansen and I did much business together. He told me what was happening and I offered to assist. I was concerned he would simply go somewhere else for an anonymous buyer. I, too, wanted you to have the book, so I agreed to his terms, but I had no intention of turning the book over to Hansen."

"You don't honestly believe—"

"How is the cake?" Thorvaldsen asked.

Malone realized that his friend was trying to take control of the conversation. "Excellent," he said through a mouthful.

"Get to the point," Stephanie demanded. "That truth I need to know."

"Your husband and I were close friends."

Stephanie's face darkened into a look of disgust. "Lars never mentioned a word of that to me."

"Considering your strained relationship, that's understandable. But, even so, just as in your profession, there were secrets in his."

Malone finished his cake and watched as Stephanie contemplated what she clearly did not believe.

"You're a liar," she finally declared.

"I can show you correspondence that will prove what I am saying. Lars and I communicated often. Ours was a collaborative effort. I financed his initial research and helped him out when times were tough. I paid for his house in Rennes-le-Château. I shared his passion, and was glad to accommodate him."

"What passion?" she asked.

Thorvaldsen appraised her with an even glare. "You know so little about him. How your regrets must torment you."

"I don't need analyzing."

"Really? You come to Denmark to buy a book you know nothing about that concerns the work of a man dead for more than a decade. And you have no regrets?"

"You sanctimonious ass, I want that book."

"You must first listen to what I have to say."

"Hurry up."

"Lars's first book was a resounding success. Several million copies worldwide, though it sold only modestly in America. His next were not as well received, but they sold—enough to finance his ventures. Lars thought an opposing point of view might help popularize the Rennes legend. So I financed several authors who wrote books critical of Lars, books that analyzed his conclusions on Rennes and pointed out fallacies. One book led to another and another. Some good, some bad. I myself even made some rather unflattering public remarks once about Lars. And soon, as he wanted, a genre was born."

Her eyes were aflame. "Are you nuts?"

"Controversy generates publicity. And Lars was not writing to a mass audience, so he had to generate his own publicity. After a while, though, it took on a life of its own. Rennes-le-Château is quite popular. Television specials have been made, magazines devoted to it, the Internet is loaded with sites dedicated solely to its mysteries. Tourism is the region's number one draw. Thanks to Lars, the town itself has now become an industry."

Malone knew that hundreds of books existed on Rennes. Several shelves in his shop were filled with recycled volumes. But he needed to know, "Henrik, two people died today. One leaped from the Round Tower and slit his throat on the way down. The other was tossed through a window. This isn't some public relations ploy."

"I would say that today at the Round Tower you came face-to-face with a brother of the Knights Templar."

"Ordinarily I'd say *you're* nuts, but the man screamed something before he jumped. *Beauseant.*"

Thorvaldsen nodded. "The battle cry of the Templars. The screaming of that word by a mass of charging knights was enough to instill absolute fear in an enemy."

He recalled what he read in the book earlier. "The Templars were eradicated in 1307. There are no knights."

"Not true, Cotton. An attempt was made to eradicate, but the pope reversed himself. The Chinon Parchment absolves the Templars of all heresy. Clement V issued that bull himself, in secret, in 1308. Many thought the document lost when Napoléon looted the Vatican, but recently it was found. No. Lars believed the Order still exists, and so do I."

"There were a lot of references in Lars's books to Templars," Malone said, "but I never recall him writing that they still actually exist."

Thorvaldsen nodded. "Intentional on his part. Such a great contradiction they were, and are. Poor by vow, yet rich in assets and knowledge. Introspective, but skilled in the ways of the world. Monks and warriors. The Hollywood stereo-type and the real Templar are two different beings. Don't be swept into the romance. They were a brutal lot."

Malone was not impressed. "How have they survived for seven hundred years without anyone knowing?"

"How does an insect or animal live in the wild without anyone knowing it exists? Yet new species are cataloged every day."

Good point, Malone thought, but he still was not convinced. "So what's this all about?"

Thorvaldsen leaned back in the chair. "Lars was looking for the treasure of the Knights Templar."

"What treasure?"

"Early in his reign, Philip IV devalued the French currency as a way to stimulate the economy. The act was so unpopular a mob came to kill him. He fled his palace for the Paris Temple and sought protection with the Templars. That was when he first spied the Order's wealth. Years later, when he was desperate for funds, he concocted a plan to convict the Order of heresy. Remember, anything a heretic owned became the property of the state. Yet, after the 1307 arrests, Philip found that not only the Paris vault, but also every other vault in Temples across France was empty. Not an ounce of Templar wealth was ever found."

"And Lars thought that treasure was in Rennes-le-Château?" he asked.

"Not necessarily there, but somewhere in the Languedoc," Henrik said. "There are enough clues to warrant that conclusion. But the Templars made finding its location difficult."

"So what does the book you bought tonight have to do with this?" Malone asked.

"Eugène Stüblein was the mayor of Fa, a village close to Rennes. He was highly educated, a musician, and an amateur astronomer. He first penned a travel book about the region, then wrote *Pierres Gravées du Languedoc*. Inscribed Stones of the Languedoc. An unusual volume that depicts gravestones in and around Rennes. A strange interest, granted, but not uncommon—the south of France is noted for unique tombs. In the book is a sketch of a headstone that caught Stüblein's eye. That drawing is important because the tombstone no longer exists."

"Could I see what you're talking about?" Malone asked.

Thorvaldsen pushed himself up from the chair and lumbered over to a server table. He came back with the book from the auction. "Delivered an hour ago."

Malone parted the binding to a marked page and studied the drawing.

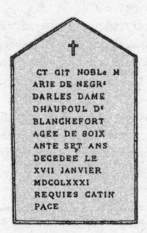
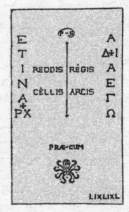

"Assuming Stüblein's sketch is accurate, Lars believed the gravestone was a clue that pointed the way to the treasure. Lars searched for that book for many years. One should be in Paris, as the Bibliothèque Nationale maintains a copy of every printing in France. But, though one is cataloged, no copy is there."

"Was Lars the only one who knew about this book?" Malone asked.

"I have no idea. Most believe the book does not exist."

"Where was this one found?"

"I spoke with the auction. A railway engineer who built the line from Carcassonne south to the Pyrénées owned it. The engineer retired in 1927 and died in 1946. The book was among his daughter's possessions when she recently died. The grandson placed it for auction. The engineer had been interested in the Languedoc, especially Rennes, and kept an inventory of tombstone rubbings himself."

Malone wasn't satisfied with his explanation. "So who alerted Stephanie to the auction?"

"Now, that is the question of the night," Thorvaldsen said.

Malone faced Stephanie. "Back at the hotel, you said a note came with the journal. You have it?"

She reached into her bag and retrieved a tattered leather notebook. Tucked within its pages was a folded sheet of taupe-colored paper. She handed the paper to Malone and he read the French.

On the 22nd of June in Roskilde a copy of Pierres Gravées du Languedoc *will be offered at auction. Your husband searched for this volume. Here is an opportunity for you to succeed where he failed. Le bon Dieu soit loué.*

Malone silently translated the last line. God be praised. He gazed across the table at Stephanie. "Where did you think this note came from?"

"One of Lars's associates. I just thought one of his cronies wanted me to have the journal and thought I'd be interested in the book."

"After eleven years?"

"I agree, it seems odd. But three weeks ago I thought little about it. Like I said before, I always believed Lars's quests were harmless."

"So why did you come?" Thorvaldsen asked.

"As you say, Henrik, I have regrets."

"And I do not want to aggravate those. I don't know you, but I did know Lars. He was a good man and his quest was, as you say, harmless. But it was nonetheless important. His death saddened me. I always questioned whether it was suicide."

"So did I," she said in a whisper. "I tried to place blame everywhere to rationalize it, but in my gut I never accepted that Lars killed himself."

"Which explains, more than anything, why you're here," Henrik said.

Malone could tell she was uncomfortable, so he offered her emotions a way out. "Let me see the journal?"

She handed him the book and he thumbed through the hundred or so pages, seeing lots of numbers, sketches, symbols, and pages of handwritten text. He then examined the binding with a bibliophile's trained eye and something caught his attention. "Pages are missing."

"What do you mean?"

He showed her the top edge. "Look here. See those tiny spaces." He parted the binding to one. Only a sliver of the original paper remained where it had once adhered to the binding. "Slit with a razor. I watch for this all the time. Nothing destroys the value of a book like missing pages." He restudied the top and bottom and determined that eight pages were gone.

"I never noticed," she said.

"A lot slipped by you."

A hectic flush came to her face. "I'm willing to concede that I screwed up."

"Cotton," Thorvaldsen said, "this whole endeavor could mean much more. The Templar archives could well be part of any find. The Order's original archives were kept in Jerusalem, then moved to Acre, and finally to Cyprus. History says that after 1312 the archives passed to the Knights Hospitallers, but there's no proof that ever occurred. From

1307 to 1314 Philip IV searched for the archives, but he found nothing. Many say that reserve was one of the medieval world's greatest collections. Imagine what locating those writings would mean."

"Could be the greatest book find ever made."

"Manuscripts no one has seen since the fourteenth century, many surely unknown to us. The prospect of finding such a cache, however remote, is worth exploring."

Malone agreed.

Thorvaldsen turned to Stephanie. "How about a truce? For Lars. I'm sure your agency works with many 'persons of interest' to achieve a mutually beneficial goal. How about we do that here?"

"I want to see those letters between you and Lars."

He nodded. "You may have them."

Stephanie's gaze caught his. "You're right, Cotton, I do need some help. I'm sorry about my tone earlier. I thought I could do this on my own. But since we're all asshole buddies now, let's you and I go to France and see what's in Lars's house. I haven't been there in some time. There's also a few people in Rennes-le-Château we can talk with. People who worked with Lars. Then we'll go from there."

"Your shadows might come, too," he said.

She smiled. "Lucky for me I have you."

"I'd like to come," Thorvaldsen said.

Malone was surprised. Henrik rarely traveled from Denmark. "And the purpose of you gracing us with your company?"

"I know a bit about what Lars sought. That knowledge might prove useful."

He shrugged. "Fine by me."

"Okay, Henrik," Stephanie said. "It'll give us time to come to know one another. Apparently, as you say, I have some things to learn."

"As do we all, Stephanie. As do we all."

DE ROQUEFORT FOUGHT TO RESTRAIN HIMSELF. HIS SUSPI-
cions were now confirmed. Stephanie Nelle was on the trail
that her husband had blazed. She also was the custodian of
her husband's notebook, along with a copy of *Pierres
Gravées du Languedoc,* perhaps the only copy still in existence. That was the thing about Lars Nelle. He'd been good.
Too good. And now his widow owned his clues. He'd made
a mistake trusting Peter Hansen. But at the time, the approach seemed the right one. He would not make that mistake again. Too much was riding on the outcome to trust any
aspect to another stranger.

He continued to listen as they finalized what to do once in
Rennes-le-Château. Malone and Stephanie would travel
there tomorrow. Thorvaldsen would come in a few days.
When he'd heard enough, de Roquefort freed the microphone from the window and withdrew with his two associates to the safety of a thick stand of trees.

There'd be no more killing tonight.

Pages are missing.

He would need that missing information from Lars Nelle's
journal. The sender of the notebook had been smart. Divid-
ing the spoils prevented rash acts. Clearly, there was more to
this intricate puzzle than he knew—and he was playing
catch-up.

But no matter. Once all of the players were in France, he
could easily deal with them.

PART
TWO

FIFTEEN

THE SENESCHAL STOOD BEFORE THE ALTAR AND STARED AT the oak coffin. The brothers were entering the chapel, marching in solemn order, their sonorous voices chanting in unison. The melody was ancient, sung at every master's funeral since the Beginning. The Latin lyrics spoke of loss, sorrow, and pain. Renewal would not be discussed until later in the day, when the conclave would convene to choose a successor. Rule was clear. Two suns could not set without a master and, as seneschal, he must ensure that Rule was maintained.

He watched as the brothers completed their entrance and positioned themselves before polished oak pews. Each man was cloaked in a plain russet frock, a cowl concealing his head, only his hands visible, folded in prayer.

The church was formed as a Latin cross with a single nave and two aisles. Little decoration existed, nothing to distract the mind from considering heaven's mysteries, but it was nonetheless majestic, the capitals and columns projecting an impressive energy. The brothers had first gathered here after the Purge in 1307—those who'd managed to escape Philip

IV's grasp, retreating to the countryside and stealthily migrating south. Eventually they'd convened here, safe within a mountain fortress, and dissolved into the fabric of religious society, making plans, pledging commitments, always remembering.

He closed his eyes and allowed the music to fill him. No tinkling accompaniment, no organ, nothing. Just the human voice, swelling and breaking. He sapped strength from the melody and steeled himself for the hours ahead.

The chanting stopped. He allowed a minute of silence to pass, then stepped close to the coffin.

"Our most exalted and reverent master has left this life. He hath ruled this Order with wisdom and justice, pursuant to Rule, for twenty-eight years. A place for him is now set within the Chronicles."

One man shoved back his cowl. "On that I challenge."

A shudder swept over the seneschal. Rule granted any brother the right to challenge. He'd expected a battle later, in conclave, but not during the funeral. The seneschal turned to the first row of pews and faced the speaker.

Raymond de Roquefort.

A stump of a man with an expressionless face and a personality of which the seneschal had always been wary, he'd been a brother for thirty years and had risen to the rank of marshal, which placed him third in the chain of command. In the Beginning, centuries ago, the marshal was the Order's military commander, the leader of the knights in battle. Now he was the minister of security, charged with making sure the Order stayed inviolate. De Roquefort had held that post for nearly two decades. He and the brothers who worked under him were allowed the privilege to come and go from the abbey at will, reporting to no one other than the master, and the marshal had made no secret of the contempt he felt for his now dead superior.

"Speak your challenge," the seneschal said.

"Our departed master weakened this Order. His policies lacked courage. The time has come to move in a different direction."

De Roquefort's words carried not a hint of emotion, and the seneschal knew how the marshal could clothe wrongs in eloquent language. De Roquefort was a fanatic. Men like him had kept the Order strong for centuries, but the master had many times counseled that their usefulness was waning. Others disagreed, and two factions had emerged—de Roquefort heading one, the master the other. Most brothers had kept their choice private, as was the Order's way. But the interregnum was a time of debate. Free discussion was how the collective decided which course it would follow.

"Is that the extent of your challenge?" the seneschal asked.

"For too long the brothers have been excluded from the decision process. We have not been consulted, nor has the counsel we offered been heeded."

"This is not a democracy," the seneschal said.

"Nor would I want it to be. But it is a brotherhood. One based on common needs and community goals. Each of us has pledged his life and possessions. We do not deserve to be ignored."

De Roquefort's voice had a calculating and deflationary effect. The seneschal noted that none of the others stirred the solemnity of the challenge and, for an instant, the sanctity that had for so long loomed within the chapel seemed tainted. He felt as if he was surrounded by men of a different mind and purpose. One word kept ringing through his mind.

Revolt.

"What would you have us do?" the seneschal asked.

"Our master does not deserve the usual respect."

He stayed rigid and made the required inquiry, "Do you call for a vote?"

"I do."

Rule required a vote, when demanded, on all issues during the interregnum. With no master, they governed as a whole. To the remaining brothers, whose faces he could not see, he said, "A show of hands as to who would deny our master his rightful place in the Chronicles."

Some arms went up immediately. Others hesitated. He gave them the full two minutes that Rule required to make their decision. Then he counted.

Two hundred ninety-one arms pointed to heaven.

"Greater than the required seventy percent are in favor of the challenge." He repressed his anger. "Our master shall be denied in the Chronicles." He could not believe he'd said the words. May his old friend forgive him. He stepped away from the coffin, back toward the altar. "Since you have no respect for our departed leader, you are dismissed. For those who wish to participate, I will proceed to the Hall of Fathers in one hour."

The brothers filed out in silence until only de Roquefort remained. The Frenchman approached the coffin. Confidence showed on his rugged face. "It is the price he pays for cowardice."

No need for appearances existed any longer. "You will regret what you just did."

"The student thinks himself master? I look forward to the conclave."

"You will destroy us."

"I will resurrect us. The world needs to know the truth. What happened all those centuries ago was wrong, and it is time to right that wrong."

The seneschal didn't disagree with that conclusion, but there was another point. "There was no need to desecrate a good man."

"Good to who? You? I was treated with contempt."

"Which is far more than you deserved."

A grim smile spread across de Roquefort's pale face. "Your protector is no more. It's now just you and me."

"I look forward to the battle."

"As do I." De Roquefort paused. "Thirty percent of the brotherhood did not support me, so I will leave it to you and them to say goodbye to our master."

His enemy turned and paraded from the chapel. The seneschal waited until the doors had closed, then laid a trembling hand on the coffin. A network of hate, treachery, and fanaticism was closing around him. He heard again his words to the master from yesterday.

I respect the power of our adversaries.

He'd just sparred with his adversary and lost.

Which did not bode well for the hours ahead.

SIXTEEN

RENNES-LE-CHÂTEAU, FRANCE
11:30 AM

MALONE TURNED THE RENTAL CAR EAST OFF THE MAIN HIGHway, just outside Couiza, and started up a twisting incline. The rising road offered stunning vistas of nearby tawny hillsides thick with summer rock roses, lavender, and thyme. The lofty ruins of a fortress, its charred walls standing like gaunt fingers, rose in the distance. The land, as far as the eye could see, oozed the romance of history when marauding knights swooped like eagles from the fortified heights to prey on their foe.

He and Stephanie had left Copenhagen around four AM and flown to Paris, where they caught the first Air France shuttle of the day south for Toulouse. An hour later they were on the ground and motoring southwest into the region known as the Languedoc.

On the way Stephanie told him about the village that stood fifteen hundred feet atop the bleak mound they were now climbing. Gauls were the first to inhabit the hilltop, drawn by the prospect of being able to see for miles across the expansive Aude River valley. But it was the Visigoths in the fifth century who built a citadel and adopted the ancient Celtic name for the location—Rhedae, which meant "chariot"—eventually developing the place into a trading center. Two hundred years later, when the Visigoths were driven south into Spain, the Franks converted Rhedae into a royal city. By the thirteenth century, though, the town's status had declined, and toward the end of the Albigensian Crusade it was razed. Ownership passed through several wealthy houses of both France and Spain, eventually resting with one of Simon de Montfort's lieutenants, who founded a barony. The family built themselves a château, around which a tiny hamlet sprouted, and the name eventually changed from Rhedae to Rennes-le-Château. Their issue ruled the land and the town until 1781, when the last heir, Marie d'Hautpoul de Blanchefort, died.

"Before her death, it was said that she passed on a great secret," Stephanie had said, "one that her family kept for centuries. She was childless and her husband died before her, so with no one left, she told the secret to her confessor, the abbé Antoine Bigou, who was the parish priest for Rennes."

Now, as Malone stared ahead at the last bend in the narrow road, he imagined what it must have been like to live then in such a remote place. The isolated valleys formed a perfect repository for both fleeing fugitives and restless pilgrims. Easy to see why the region had become a theme park for the imagination, a mecca for mystery buffs and new agers, a place where writers with a unique vision could forge a reputation.

Like Lars Nelle.

The town came into view. He slowed the car and eased through a gate framed by limestone pillars. A sign warned FOUILLES INTERDITES. Excavating prohibited.

"They had to post a notice about digging?" he asked.

Stephanie nodded. "Years ago, people were shoveling dirt in every corner looking for treasure. Even dynamiting. It had to be regulated."

Daylight dimmed beyond the town gate. The limestone buildings were packed tight, like books on a shelf, many with pitched roofs, thick doors, and rusted iron verandas. A narrow and flinty *grand rue* wound up a short incline. People with backpacks and Michelin Green Guides hugged the walls on either side, parading single-file back and forth. Malone saw a couple of stores, a bookshop, and a restaurant. Alleys led off the main *rue* to nests of buildings, but not many. The entire town was less than five hundred yards across.

"Only about a hundred people live here full time," Stephanie said. "Though fifty thousand visit each year."

"Lars had quite an effect."

"More than I ever realized."

She pointed ahead and directed him to turn left. They eased past kiosks peddling rosaries, medals, pictures, and souvenirs to more camera-toting visitors.

"They come by the busload," she said. "Wanting to believe in the impossible."

Up another incline and he parked the Peugeot in a sandy lot. Two buses were already there, their drivers milling about smoking. A water tower rose to one side, its tattered stone adorned with a zodiac sign.

"The crowds come early," Stephanie said as they climbed out. "Here to see the *domaine d'Abbé Saunière*. The priest's domain—what he built with all that mysterious treasure he supposedly found."

Malone stepped close to a waist-high rock wall. The panorama below, a patchwork of field, forest, valley, and rock, stretched for miles. The silver-green hills were dotted with chestnut and oak. He checked his bearings. The great bulk of the snowcapped Pyrénées blocked the southern horizon. A stiff wind howled from the west, thankfully warmed by the summer sun.

He glanced to the right. A hundred feet away the neo-Gothic tower, with its crenellated roof and single round turret, had graced the cover of many a book and tourist brochure. It stood on the edge of a cliff, grim and defiant, seemingly clinging to rock. A long belvedere stretched from its far side and rounded back toward an iron glasshouse, then to another cluster of olden stone buildings, each topped with orange-tiled roofs. People milled back and forth on the ramparts, cameras in hand, admiring the valleys below.

"The tower is the Tour Magdala. Quite a sight, isn't it?" Stephanie asked.

"Seems out of place."

"That's what I always thought, too."

To the right of the Magdala rose an ornamental garden that led to a compact Renaissance-style building that also seemed from another locale.

"The Villa Béthanie," she said. "Saunière built it, too."

He noted the name. Bethany. "That's biblical. In the Holy Land. It meant 'house with an answer.'"

She nodded. "Saunière was clever with names." She pointed to more buildings behind them. "Lars's house is down that alley. Before we head there, I have to do something. As we walk, let me tell you about what happened here in 1891. What I read about last week. What brought this place back from obscurity."

The abbé Bérenger Saunière pondered the daunting task before him. The Church of Mary Magdalene had been built upon Visigoth ruins and consecrated in 1059. Now, eight centuries later, the inside was in ruin, thanks to a roof that leaked as if it weren't there. The walls themselves were crumbling, the foundations slipping away. It would take both patience and stamina to repair the damage, but he thought himself up to the task.

He was a husky man, muscular, broad-shouldered, with a head of close-cropped black hair. His one endearing feature, which he used to his advantage, was the cleft in his chin. It added a whimsical air to the stiff countenance of his black eyes and thick eyebrows. Born and raised a few miles away, in the village of Montazels, he knew the geography of the Corbières well. From childhood he'd been familiar with Rennes-le-Château. Its church, dedicated to St. Mary Magdalene, had been in limited use for decades, and he'd never imagined that one day its many problems would be his.

"A mess," the man known as Rousset said to him.

He glanced at the mason. "I agree."

Another mason, Babou, was busy shoring up one of the walls. The region's state architect had recently recommended that the building be razed, but Saunière would never allow that to happen. Something about the old church demanded that it be saved.

"It will take much money to complete the repairs," Rousset said.

"Enormous amounts of money." He added a smile to let the older man know that he understood the challenge. "But we shall make this house worthy of the Lord."

What he did not say was that he'd already secured a fair amount of funds. A bequest from one of his predecessors had left six hundred francs especially for repairs. He'd also managed to convince the town council to loan him another fourteen hundred francs. But the bulk of his money had come in secret five years ago. Three thousand francs had been donated by the countess of Chambord, the widow of Henri, the last Bourbon claimant to the defunct French throne. At the time Saunière had managed to bring a great deal of attention to himself with anti-republican sermons, ones that stirred monarchist feelings in his parishioners. The government reeled from the comments, withdrawing his yearly stipend and demanding that he be fired. Instead the bishop suspended him for nine months, but his actions caught the attention of the countess, who'd made contact through an intermediary.

"Where do we start?" Rousset asked.

He'd given that matter a great deal of thought. The stained-glass windows had already been replaced and a new porch, outside the main entrance, would be completed shortly. Certainly the north wall, where Babou was working, must be mended, a new pulpit installed, and the roof replaced. But he knew where they must start.

"We will begin with the altar."

A curious look came to Rousset's face.

"The people's focus is there," Saunière said.

"As you say, Abbé."

He liked the respect his older parishioners showed him, though he was only thirty-eight. Over the past five years he'd come to like Rennes. He was near home, with plenty of opportunities to study Scriptures and perfect his Latin, Greek, and Hebrew. He also enjoyed trekking in the mountains, fishing, and hunting. But the time had come to do something constructive.

He approached the altar.

The top was white marble pitted by water that had rained down for centuries from the porous ceiling. The slab was supported by two ornate columns, their exteriors adorned with Visigoth crosses and Greek letters.

"We shall replace the top and the pillars," he declared.

"How, Abbé?" Rousset asked. "There is no way we can lift that."

He pointed to where Babou stood. "Use the sledgehammer. There is no need for delicacy."

Babou brought the heavy tool over and surveyed his task. Then, with a great heave, Babou hoisted the hammer and crashed it down onto the center of the altar. The thick top cracked, but the stone did not give way.

"It's solid," Babou said.

"Again," Saunière said with a flourish.

Another blow and the limestone shattered, the two halves collapsing into each other between the still-standing pillars.

"Finish," he said.

The two pieces were quickly busted into many.

He bent down. "Let's haul all this away."

"We'll get it, Abbé," Babou said, setting the sledgehammer aside. "You pile it for us."

The two men lifted large chunks and headed for the door.

"Take it around to the cemetery and stack it. We should have use for it there," he called out to them.

As they left, he noticed that both pillars had survived the demolition. With a swipe he cleared dust and debris away from the crown of one. On the other a piece of limestone still lay, and, when he tossed the chunk into the pile, he noticed beneath, in the crown of the pillar, a shallow mortise hole. The space was no bigger than the palm of his hand, surely designed to hold the top's locking pin, but inside the cavity he caught sight of a glimmer.

He bent close and carefully blew away the dust.

Yes, something was there.

A glass vial.

Not much longer than his index finger and only slightly wider, the top sealed with crimson wax. He looked close and saw that the vessel contained a rolled piece of paper. He wondered how long it had been there. He was not aware of any recent work done to the altar, so it must have been secreted there a long time ago.

He freed the object from its hiding place.

"That vial started everything," Stephanie said.

Malone nodded. "I read Lars's books, too. But I thought Saunière was supposed to have found three parchments in that pillar with some sort of coded messages."

She shook her head. "That's all part of the myth others added to the story. This, Lars and I did talk about. Most of the fallacies were started in the fifties by a Rennes innkeeper who wanted to generate business. One lie built on another. Lars never accepted that those parchments were real. Their supposed text was printed in countless books, but no one has ever seen them."

"Then why did he write about them?"

"To sell books. I know it bothered him, but he did it anyway. He always said that whatever wealth Saunière found could be traced to 1891 and whatever was inside that glass vial. But he was the only one who believed that." She pointed off to another of the stone buildings. "That's the presbytery where Saunière lived. It's a museum about him now. The pillar with the small niche is in there for all to see."

They passed the crowded kiosks and kept to the rough-paved street.

"The Church of Mary Magdalene," she said, pointing at a Romanesque building. "Once the chapel for the local counts. Now, for a few euros, you can see the great creation of Abbé Saunière."

"You don't approve?"

She shrugged. "I never did. That was the problem."

Off to their right he saw a tumbled-down château, its mud-colored outer walls baked by the sun. "That's the Hautpouls estate," she said. "It was lost during the Revolution to the government and has been a mess ever since."

They rounded the far end of the church and passed beneath a stone gateway that bore what looked like a skull and crossbones. He recalled from the book he'd read last night that the symbol appeared on many Templar gravestones.

The earth beyond the entrance was littered with pebbles. He knew what the French called the space. *Enclos paroissiaux.* Parish close. And the enclosure seemed typical—one side bounded by a low wall, the other nestled close to a church, its entrance a triumphal arch. The cemetery hosted a profusion of table tombs, headstones, and memorials. Floral tributes topped some of the graves, and many were adorned, in the French tradition, with photographs of the deceased.

Stephanie walked to one of the monuments that displayed neither flowers nor images, and Malone let her go alone. He knew that Lars Nelle had been so liked by the locals that they'd granted him the privilege of being buried in their cherished churchyard.

The headstone was simple and noted only the name, dates, and an epitaph of HUSBAND, FATHER, SCHOLAR.

He eased up beside her.

"They never once wavered in burying him here," she muttered.

He knew what she meant. In sacred ground.

"The mayor at the time said there was no conclusive evidence he killed himself. He and Lars were close, and he wanted his friend buried here."

"It's the perfect place," he said.

She was hurting, he knew, but to recognize her pain would be viewed as an invasion of her privacy.

"I made a lot of mistakes with Lars," she said. "And most of them eventually cost me with Mark."

"Marriage is tough." His own failed through selfishness, too. "So is parenthood."

"I always thought Lars's passion silly. I was a government lawyer doing important things. He was searching for the impossible."

"So why are you here?"

Her gaze stayed on the grave. "I've come to realize that I owe him."

"Or do you owe yourself?"

She turned away from the grave. "Perhaps I do owe us both," she said.

He let it drop.

Stephanie pointed to a far corner. "Saunière's mistress is buried there."

Malone knew about the mistress from Lars's books. She was sixteen years Saunière's junior, a mere eighteen when she quit her job as a hatmaker and became the abbé's housekeeper. She stayed by his side for thirty-one years, until his death in 1917. Everything Saunière acquired was eventually placed in her name, including all of his land and bank accounts, which subsequently made it impossible for anyone, including the Church, to claim them. She continued to live in Rennes, dressing in somber clothes and behaving as strangely as when her lover was alive, until her death in 1953.

"She was an odd one," Stephanie said. "She made a statement, long after Saunière died, about how with what he left behind you could feed all of Rennes for a hundred years, but she lived in poverty till the day she died."

"Any one ever learn why?"

"Her only statement was, *I cannot touch it.*"

"Thought you didn't know much about all this."

"I didn't, until last week. The books and journal were informative. Lars spent a lot of time interviewing locals."

"Sounds like that would have been double or triple hearsay."

"For Saunière, that's true. He's been dead a long time. But his mistress lived till the fifties, so there were many still around in the seventies and eighties who knew her. She sold the Villa Béthanie in 1946 to a man named Noël Corbu. He was the one who converted it into a hotel—the innkeeper I mentioned who made up much of the false information about Rennes. The mistress promised to tell Saunière's great secret to Corbu, but at the end of her life she suffered a stroke and was unable to communicate."

They trudged across the hard ground, grit crunching with every step.

"Saunière was once buried here, too, beside her, but the mayor said the grave was in danger from treasure hunters." She shook her head. "So a few years ago they dug the priest up and moved him into a mausoleum in the garden. Now it costs three euros to see his grave . . . the price of a corpse's safety, I assume."

He caught her sarcasm.

She pointed at the grave. "I remember coming here once years ago. When Lars first arrived in the late sixties, nothing but two tattered crosses marked the graves, overgrown with vines. No one tended to them. No one cared. Saunière and his lover were totally forgotten."

An iron chain encircled the plot and fresh flowers sprouted from concrete vases. Malone noticed the epitaph on one of the stones, barely legible.

HERE LIES BÉRENGER SAUNIÈRE
PARISH PRIEST OF RENNES-LE-CHÂTEAU
1853–1917
DIED 22 JANUARY 1917 AGED 64

"I read somewhere that the marker was too fragile to move," she said, "so they left it. More for the tourists to see."

He noticed the mistress's gravestone. "She wasn't a target of opportunists, too?"

"Apparently not, since they left her here."

"Wasn't it a scandal, their relationship?"

She shrugged. "Whatever wealth Saunière acquired, he spread around. The water tower back at the car park? He built it for the town. He also paved roads, repaired houses, made loans to people in trouble. So he was forgiven whatever weakness he may have possessed. And it was not uncommon for priests of that time to have female housekeepers. Or at least that's what Lars wrote in one of his books."

A group of noisy visitors rounded the corner behind them and headed for the grave.

"Here they come to gawk," Stephanie said, a touch of contempt in her voice. "I wonder if they would act that way back home, in the cemetery where their loved ones are buried?"

The boisterous crowd drew close, and a tour guide started talking about the mistress. Stephanie retreated and Malone followed.

"This is nothing but an attraction to them," Stephanie said in a low voice. "Where the abbé Saunière found his treasure and supposedly decorated his church with messages that somehow led the way to it. Hard to imagine that anyone buys that crap."

"Isn't that what Lars wrote about?"

"To an extent. But think about it, Cotton. Even if the priest found a treasure, why would he leave a map for someone else to find it? He built all of this during his lifetime. The last thing he'd want was for someone to jump his claim." She shook her head. "It all makes for great books, but it's not real."

He was about to inquire further when he noticed her gaze drift to another corner of the cemetery, past a set of stone stairs that led down to the shade of an oak towering above more markers. In the shadows, he spied a fresh grave decorated with colorful bouquets, the silvery lettering on the headstone bright against a crisp gray matte.

Stephanie marched toward it and he followed.

"Oh, dear," she said, concern in her face.

He read the marker. ERNST SCOVILLE. Then he did the math from the dates noted. The man was seventy-three years old when he died.

Last week.

"You knew him?" he asked.

"I talked with him three weeks ago. Just after receiving Lars's journal." Her attention stayed riveted on the grave. "He was one of those people I mentioned who worked with Lars that we needed to speak with."

"Did you tell him what you planned to do?"

She slowly nodded. "I told him about the auction, the book, and that I was coming to Europe."

He couldn't believe what he was hearing. "I thought you said last night no one knew anything."

"I lied."

SEVENTEEN

ABBEY DES FONTAINES
1:00 PM

DE ROQUEFORT WAS PLEASED. HIS FIRST CONFRONTATION with the seneschal had been a resounding victory. Only six masters had ever been successfully challenged, those men's sins ranging from thievery, to cowardice, to lust for a woman, all from centuries ago, in the decades after the Purge, when the brotherhood was weak and chaotic. Unfortunately, the penalty of a challenge was more symbolic than punitive. The master's tenure would still be noted within the Chronicles, his failures and accomplishments duly recorded, but a notation would proclaim that his brothers had deemed him *unworthy of memory*.

In recent weeks his lieutenants had made sure the requisite two-thirds percent would vote and send a message to the seneschal. That undeserving fool needed to know how difficult the fight ahead was going to be. True, the insult of being challenged mattered not to the master. He would be entombed with his predecessors no matter what. No, the denial was more a way to deflate the supposed successor—and to motivate allies. It was an ancient tool, created by Rule, from a time when honor and memory meant something. But one he'd successfully resurrected as the opening salvo in a war that should be over by sunset.

He was going to be the next master.

The Poor Fellow-Soldiers of Christ and the Temple of Solomon had existed, unbroken, since 1118. Philip IV of France, who'd borne the despicable misnomer of Philip the Fair, had tried in 1307 to exterminate them. But like the seneschal, he'd also underestimated his opponent, and managed only to send the Order underground.

Once, tens of thousands of brothers manned commanderies, farms, temples, and castles on nine thousand estates scattered across Europe and the Holy Land. Just the sight of a brother knight clad in white and wearing the red cross patee brought fear to enemies. Brothers were granted immunity from excommunication and were not required to pay feudal duties. The Order was allowed to keep all its spoils from war. Subject only to the pope, the Knights Templar was a nation unto itself.

But no battles had been fought for seven hundred years. Instead, the Order had retreated to a Pyrenean abbey and cloaked itself as a simple monastic community. Connections to the bishops in Toulouse and Perpignan were maintained, and all of the required duties were performed for the Roman Church. Nothing occurred that would draw attention, set the abbey apart, or cause people to question what may be happening within its walls. All brothers took two vows. One to the Church, which was done for necessity. The other to the brotherhood, which meant everything. The ancient rites were still conducted, though now under cover of darkness, behind thick ramparts, with the abbey gates bolted.

And all for the Great Devise.

The paradoxical futility of that duty disgusted him. The Order existed to guard the Devise, but the Devise would not exist but for the Order.

A quandary, for sure.

But still a duty.

His entire life had been only the preamble to the next few hours. Born to unknown parents, he was raised by the Jesuits at a church school near Bordeaux. In the Beginning, brothers were mainly repentant criminals, disappointed lovers, outcasts. Today they came from all walks. The secular world spawned the most recruits, but religious society produced its true leaders. The past ten masters all claimed a cloistered education. His had begun at the university in Paris, then been completed at the seminary in Avignon. He'd stayed on there and taught for three years before the Order approached him. Then he'd embraced Rule with an unfettered enthusiasm.

During his fifty-six years he'd never known the flesh of a woman, nor had he been tempted by a man. Being elevated to marshal, he knew, had been a way for the former master to placate his ambition, perhaps even a trap whereby he might generate enough enemies that further advancement would be impossible. But he'd used his position wisely, making friends, building loyalties, accumulating favors. Monastic life suited him. For the past decade he'd pored through the

Chronicles and was now versed in every aspect—good and bad—of the Order's history. He would not repeat the mistakes of the past. He fervently believed that, in the Beginning, the brotherhood's self-imposed isolation was what hastened its downfall. Secrecy bred both an aura and suspicion—a simple step from there to recrimination. So it must end. Seven hundred years of silence needed to be broken.

His time had come.

Rule was clear.

It is to be holden that when anything shall be enjoined by the master, there be no hesitation, but the thing must be done without delay, as though it had been enjoined from heaven.

The phone on his desk gave a low trill and he lifted the receiver.

"Our two brothers in Rennes-le-Château," he was told by his under-marshal, "have reported that Stephanie Nelle and Malone are now there. As you predicted, she went straight to the cemetery and found Ernst Scoville's grave."

Good to know one's enemy. "Have our brothers merely observe, but be ready to act."

"On the other matter you asked us to investigate. We still have no idea who assaulted the brothers in Copenhagen."

He hated to hear about failure. "Is everything prepared for this evening?"

"We will be ready."

"How many accompanied the seneschal to the Hall of Fathers?"

"Thirty-four."

"All identified?"

"Every one."

"They shall each be given an opportunity to join us. If not, deal with them. Let's make sure, though, that most join us. Which should not pose a problem. Few like to be part of a losing cause."

"The consistory starts at six PM."

At least the seneschal was discharging his duty, calling the brothers into session before nightfall. The consistory was the one variable in the equation—a procedure specially designed to prevent manipulation—but one he'd long studied and anticipated.

"Be ready," he said. "The seneschal will use speed to generate confusion. That's how his master managed election."

"He will not take defeat lightly."

"Nor would I expect him to. Which is why I have a surprise waiting for him."

EIGHTEEN

RENNES-LE-CHÂTEAU
1:30 PM

MALONE AND STEPHANIE MADE THEIR WAY ACROSS THE crowded hamlet. Another bus churned up the central *rue,* easing its way toward the car park. Halfway down the street Stephanie entered a restaurant and spoke with the proprietor. Malone eyed some delicious-looking fish the diners were enjoying, but realized food would have to wait.

He was angry that Stephanie had lied to him. Either she didn't appreciate or didn't understand the gravity of the situation. Determined men, willing to die and kill, were after something. He'd seen their likes many times, and the more information he possessed the better the chances of success.

Hard enough dealing with the enemy, but worrying about an ally simply compounded the situation.

Leaving the restaurant, Stephanie said, "Ernst Scoville was hit by a car last week while he took his daily walk outside the walls. He was well liked. He'd lived here a long time."

"Any leads on the car?"

"No witnesses. Nothing to go on."

"Did you actually know Scoville?"

She nodded. "But he didn't care for me. He and I spoke rarely. He took Lars's side in our debate."

"Then why did you call him?"

"He was the only one I could think of to ask about Lars's journal. He was civil, considering we hadn't spoken in years. He wanted to see the journal. So I planned on making amends while I was here."

He wondered about her. Bad blood with her husband, her son, and friends of her husband. The source of her guilt was clear, but what she planned to do about it remained cloudy.

She motioned for them to walk. "I want to check Ernst's house. He owned quite a library. I'd like to see if his books are still there."

"He have a wife?"

She shook her head. "A loner. Would have made a great hermit."

They headed down one of the side alleys between more rows of buildings that all seemed built for patrons long dead.

"Do you really believe there's a treasure hidden around here somewhere?" he asked.

"Hard to say, Cotton. Lars used to say that ninety percent of Saunière's story is fiction. I'd chastise him for wasting his time on something so foolish. But he always countered with the ten percent of truth. That's what captivated him and, to a large degree, Mark. Strange things apparently happened here a hundred years ago."

"You referring to Saunière again?"

She nodded.

"Help me understand."

"I actually need help with that, too. But I can tell you more of what I know about Bérenger Saunière."

"I cannot leave a parish where my interests keep me," Saunière told the bishop as he stood before the older man in the episcopal palace at Carcassonne, twenty miles north of Rennes-le-Château.

He'd avoided the meeting for months with statements from his doctor that he was unable to travel because of illness. But the bishop was persistent, and the last request for an audience had been delivered by a constable who'd been instructed to personally accompany him back.

"Your existence is far grander than mine," the bishop said. "I wish to have a statement as to the origin of your monetary resources, which seem so sudden and important."

"Alas, Monseigneur, you ask of me the only thing I am not able to reveal. Deep sinners to whom, with the aid of God, I have shown the way of penitence have given these considerable amounts to me. I do not wish to betray the secrets of the confessional by giving you their names."

The bishop seemed to consider his argument. It was a good one, and just might work.

"Then let us talk of your lifestyle. That is not protected by the secrets of the confessional."

He feigned innocence. "My lifestyle is quite modest."

"That is not what I am told."

"Your information must be faulty."

"Let us see." The bishop parted the cover of a thick book that lay before him. "I had an inventory performed, which was quite interesting."

Saunière did not like the sound of that. His relationship with the former bishop had been loose and cordial, and he'd enjoyed great freedom. This new bishop was another matter.

"In 1891 you started renovations on the parish church. At that time you replaced the windows, built a porch, installed a new altar and pulpit, and repaired the roof. Cost, approximately twenty-two hundred francs. The following year the exterior walls were tended to and the interior floor replaced. Then came a new confessional, seven hundred francs, statuary and stations of the cross, all hewn in Toulouse by Giscard, thirty-two hundred francs. In 1898 a collecting trunk was added, four hundred francs. Then in 1900 a bas-relief of St. Mary Magdalen, quite elaborate I'm told, was placed before the altar."

Saunière simply listened. Clearly, the bishop was privy to parish records. The former treasurer had resigned a few years ago, stating that he'd found his duties contrary to his beliefs. Someone had obviously tracked him down.

"I came here in 1902," the bishop said. "For the past eight years I have tried—in vain, I might add—to have you appear before me to answer my concerns. But during that time, you managed to build the Villa Béthanie adjacent to the church. It is, I am told, of bourgeois construction, a pastiche of styles, all from cut stone. There are stained-glass windows, a dining salon, sitting room, and bedrooms for guests. Quite a few guests, I hear. It is where you entertain."

The comment was surely designed to elicit a response, but he said nothing.

"Then there is the Tour Magdala, your folly of a library that overlooks the valley. Some of the finest woodwork around, it is reported. This is in addition to your stamp and postcard collections, which are enormous, and even some exotic animals. All costing many thousands of francs." The bishop closed the book.

"Your parish income is no more than two hundred fifty francs per year. How was it possible to amass all this?"

"As I have said, Monseigneur, I have been the recipient of many private donations from souls who want to see my parish prosper."

"You have been trafficking in masses," the bishop declared. *"Selling the sacraments. Your crime is simony."*

He'd been warned this was the charge to be leveled. *"Why do you reproach me? My parish, when I first arrived, was in a lamentable state. It is, after all, the duty of my superiors to ensure for Rennes-le-Château a church worthy of the faithful and a decent dwelling for the pastor. But for a quarter century I have worked and rebuilt and beautified the church without asking a centime from the diocese. It seems to me that I deserve your congratulations rather than accusations."*

"What do you say was spent on all those improvements?"

He decided to answer. *"One hundred ninety-three thousand francs."*

The bishop laughed. *"Abbé, that would not have bought the furniture, statues, and stained glass. To my calculation you have spent more than seven hundred thousand francs."*

"I am not familiar with accounting practices, so I cannot say what the costs were. All I know is that the people of Rennes love their church."

"Officials state that you receive one hundred to one hundred fifty postal orders a day. They come from Belgium, Italy, the Rhineland, Switzerland, and all over France. They range from five to forty francs each. You frequent the bank in Couiza, where they are converted to cash. How do you explain that?"

"All my correspondence is handled by my housekeeper.

*She both opens and answers any inquiries. That question
should be directed to her."*

"You are the one who appears at the bank."

He kept to his story. "You should ask her."

"Unfortunately, she is not subject to my authority."

He shrugged.

*"Abbé, you are trafficking in masses. It is clear, at
least to me, that those envelopes coming to your parish
are not notes from well-wishers. But there is something
else even more disturbing."*

He stood silent.

*"I performed a calculation. Unless you are being paid
exorbitant sums per mass—and last I knew, the standard
rate among offenders was fifty centimes—you would have
to say mass twenty-four hours a day for some three
hundred years to accumulate the wealth you have spent.
No, Abbé, the trafficking in masses is a front, one you
concocted, to mask the true source of your good
fortune."*

This man was far smarter than he appeared to be.

"Any response?"

"No, Monseigneur."

*"Then you are hereby relieved of your duties at Rennes
and you will report immediately to the parish in
Coustouge. In addition, you are suspended, with no right
to say the mass or administer the sacraments in church,
until further notice."*

*"And how long is this suspension to last?" he calmly
asked.*

*"Until the Ecclesiastical Court can hear your appeal,
which I am sure you will forthwith file."*

"Saunière did appeal," Stephanie said, "all the way to the
Vatican, but he died in 1917 before being vindicated. What
he did, though, was resign from the Church and never left

Rennes. He just started saying mass in the Villa Béthanie. The locals loved him, so they boycotted the new abbé. Remember, all the land around the church, including the villa, belonged to Saunière's mistress—he was clever there—so the Church couldn't do a thing about it."

Malone wanted to know, "So how did he pay for all those improvements?"

She smiled. "That's a question many have tried to answer, including my husband."

They navigated another of the winding alleyways, bordered by more melancholy houses, the stones the color of dead wood stripped of bark.

"Ernst lived up ahead," she said.

They approached an olden building warmed by pastel roses climbing a wrought-iron pergola. Up three stone stairs stood a recessed door. Malone climbed, peered in through glass in the door, and saw no evidence of neglect. "The place looks good."

"Ernst was obsessive."

He tested the knob. Locked.

"I'd like to get in there," she said from the street.

He glanced around. Twenty feet to their left, the lane ended at the outer wall. Beyond loomed a blue sky dotted with billowy clouds. No one was in sight. He turned back and, with his elbow, popped the glass pane. He then reached inside and released the lock.

Stephanie stepped up behind him.

"After you," he said.

NINETEEN

THE SENESCHAL SWUNG THE IRON GRILLE INWARD AND LED the cortège of mourners through the ancient archway. The entrance into the subterranean Hall of Fathers was located within the abbey walls, at the end of a long passageway where one of the oldest buildings butted rock. Fifteen hundred years ago monks first occupied the caverns beyond, living in the sullen recesses. As more and more penitents arrived, buildings were erected. Abbeys tended to either dramatically grow or dwindle, and this one had erupted with a burst of construction that had lasted centuries, continued by the Knights Templar, who quietly took ownership in the late thirteenth century. The Order's mother house—*maison chèvetaine,* as Rule labeled it—had first been located in Jerusalem, then Acre, then Cyprus, finally ending here after the Purge. Eventually, the complex was surrounded with battlement walls and towers and the abbey grew to become one of Europe's largest, set high among the Pyrénées, secluded by both geography and Rule. Its name came from the nearby river, the falls, and an abundance of groundwater. Abbey des Fontaines: abbey of the fountains.

He made his way down narrow steps chipped from rock. The soles of his canvas sandals were slippery on the moist stone. Where oil torches once provided light, electric sconces now lit the way. Behind him came the thirty-four brothers who'd decided to join him. At the bottom of the stairs, he padded forward until the tunnel opened into a vaulted room. A stone pillar rose from the center, like the trunk of an aging tree.

The brothers slowly gathered around the oak coffin, which had already been brought inside and laid on a stone plinth. Through clouds of incense came melancholy chants.

The seneschal stepped forward and the chanting stopped. "We have come to honor him. Let us pray," he said in French.

They did, then a hymn was sung.

"Our master led us well. You, who are loyal to his memory, take heart. He would have been proud."

A few moments of silence passed.

"What lies ahead?" one of the brothers quietly asked.

Caucusing was not proper in the Hall of Fathers, but with apprehension looming he allowed a bending of Rule.

"Uncertainty," he declared. "Brother de Roquefort is ready to take charge. Those of you who are selected for the conclave will have to work hard to stop him."

"He will be our downfall," another brother muttered.

"I agree," the seneschal said. "He believes that we can somehow avenge seven-hundred-year-old sins. Even if we could, why? We survived."

"His followers have been pressing hard. Those who oppose him will be punished."

The seneschal knew that this was why so few had come to the hall. "Our ancestors faced many enemies. In the Holy Land they stood before the Saracens and died with honor. Here, they endured torture from the Inquisition. Our master, de Molay, was burned at the stake. Our job is to stay faithful." Weak words, he knew, but they had to be said.

"De Roquefort wants to war with our enemies. One of his followers told me that he even intends to take back the shroud."

He winced. Other radical thinkers had proposed that show of defiance before, but every master had quelled the act. "We must stop him in conclave. Luckily, he cannot control the selection process."

"He frightens me," a brother said, and the quiet that followed signaled that the others agreed.

After an hour of prayer the seneschal gave the signal. Four bearers, each dressed in a crimson robe, hoisted the master's coffin.

He turned and approached two columns of red porphyry between which stood the Door of Gold. The name came not from its composition, but from what was once stored behind it.

Forty-three masters lay in their own *locoli,* beneath a rock ceiling, polished smooth and painted a deep blue, upon which gold stars spangled in the light. The bodies had long ago turned to dust. Only bones remained, encased within ossuaries each bearing a master's name and dates of service. To his right were empty niches, one of which would cradle his master's body for the next year. Only then would a brother return and transfer the bones to an ossuary. The burial practice, which the Order had long employed, belonged to the Jews in the Holy Land at the time of Christ.

The bearers deposited the coffin into the assigned cavity. A deep tranquility filled the semi-darkness.

Thoughts of his friend flashed through the seneschal's mind. The master was the youngest son of a wealthy Belgian merchant. He'd gravitated to the Church for no clear reason—simply something he felt compelled to do. He'd been recruited by one of the Order's many journeymen, brothers stationed around the globe, blessed with an eye for recruits. Monastic life had agreed with the master. And though not of high office, in the conclave after his predecessor died the brothers had all cried, "Let him be master." And so he took the oath. *I offer myself to the omnipotent God and to the Virgin Mary for the salvation of my soul and so shall I remain in this holy life all my days until my final breath.* The seneschal had made the same pledge.

He allowed his thoughts to drift back to the Order's beginning—the battle cries of war, groans of brothers wounded and dying, the anguished moans born of burying those who'd not survived the conflict. That had been the way of the Templars. First in, last to leave. Raymond de Roquefort longed for that time. But why? That futility had been proven when Church and State turned on the Templars at the time of the Purge, showing no regard for two hundred years of loyal service. Brothers were burned at the stake, others tortured and maimed for life, and all for simple greed. To the modern world, the Knights Templar were legends. A long-ago memory. No one cared if they existed, so righting any injustice seemed hopeless.

The dead must stay dead.

He again glanced around at the stone chests, then dismissed the brothers—save one. His assistant. He needed to speak with him alone. The younger man approached.

"Tell me, Geoffrey," the seneschal said. "Were you and the master plotting?"

The man's dark eyes flashed surprise. "What do you mean?"

"Did the master ask you to do something for him recently? Come now, don't lie to me. He's gone, and I'm here." He thought pulling rank would make it easier for him to learn the truth.

"Yes, Seneschal. I mailed two parcels for the master."

"Tell me of the first."

"Thick and heavy, like a book. I posted it while I was in Avignon, more than a month ago."

"The second?"

"Sent Monday, from Perpignan. A letter."

"Who was the letter sent to?"

"Ernst Scoville in Rennes-le-Château."

The younger man quickly crossed himself, and the seneschal spied puzzlement and suspicion. "What's wrong?"

"The master said you would ask those questions."

The information grabbed his attention.

"He said that when you did, I should tell you the truth. But he also said for you to be warned. Those who have gone down the path you are about to take have been many, but never has anyone succeeded. He said to wish you well and Godspeed."

His mentor was a brilliant man who clearly knew far more than he'd ever said.

"He also said that you must finish the quest. It's your destiny. Whether you realize that or not."

He'd heard enough. The empty wooden box from the armoire in the master's chamber was now explained. The book he'd sought inside was gone. The master had sent it away. With a gentle wave of his hand he dismissed the aide. Geoffrey bowed, then hustled toward the Door of Gold.

Something occurred to him. "Wait. You never said where the first package, the book, was sent."

Geoffrey stopped and turned but said nothing.

"Why don't you answer?"

"It is not right that we speak of this. Not here. With him so near." The young man's gaze darted to the coffin.

"You said he wanted me to know."

Anxiety swirled in the eyes staring back at him.

"Tell me where the book was sent." Though he already knew, he needed to hear the words.

"To America. A woman named Stephanie Nelle."

TWENTY

MALONE SURVEYED THE INSIDE OF ERNST SCOVILLE'S MODEST house. The décor was an eclectic collection of British antiques, twelfth-century Spanish art, and unremarkable French paintings. He estimated that a thousand books surrounded him, most yellowed paperbacks and aged hardcovers, each shelf fronting an exterior wall and meticulously arranged by subject and size. Old newspapers were stacked by year, in chronological order. The same was true for periodicals. Everything dealt with Rennes, Saunière, French history, the Church, Templars, and Jesus Christ.

"Seems Scoville was a Bible connoisseur," he said, pointing to rows of analysis.

"He spent his life studying the New Testament. He was Lars's biblical source."

"Doesn't seem anyone has searched this house."

"It could have been done carefully."

"True. But what were they looking for? What are we looking for?"

"I don't know. All I know is I talked to Scoville, then two weeks later he's dead."

"What would he have known that was worth killing for?"

She shrugged. "Our conversation was pleasant. I honestly thought he was the one who'd sent the journal. He and Lars worked closely. But he knew nothing of the journal being sent to me, though he wanted to read it." She stopped her perusal. "Look at all this stuff. He was obsessed." She shook her head. "Lars and I argued about this very thing for years. I always thought he was wasting his academic abilities. He was a good historian. He should have been making a decent salary at a university, publishing credible research. Instead, he traipsed around the world, chasing shadows."

"He was a bestselling author."

"Only his first book. Money was another of our constant debates."

"You sound like a woman with a lot of regrets."

"Don't you have some? I recall you taking the divorce from Pam hard."

"Nobody likes to fail."

"At least your spouse didn't kill herself."

She had a point.

"You said on the way over here that Lars believed Saunière discovered a message inside that glass vial found in the column. Who was the message from?"

"In his notebook, Lars wrote that it was probably from one of Saunière's predecessors, Antoine Bigou, who served as the parish priest for Rennes in the latter part of the eighteenth century, during the time of the French Revolution. I mentioned him in the car. He was the priest to whom Marie d'Hautpoul de Blanchefort told her family secret before dying."

"So Lars thought the family secret was recorded in the vial?"

"It's not that simple. There's more to the story. Marie d'Hautpoul married the last marquis de Blanchefort in 1732. The de Blanchefort line has a French history all the way back to the time of the Templars. The family took part in both the Crusades and the Albigensian wars. One ancestor was even master of the Templars in the middle of the twelfth century, and the family controlled the Rennes township and surrounding land for centuries. When the Templars were arrested in 1307, the de Blancheforts sheltered many fugitives from Philip IV's men. It's said, though no one knows for sure, that members of the de Blanchefort family were always part of the Templars after that."

"You sound like Henrik. Do you actually think the Templars are still out there?"

"I have no idea. But something the man in the cathedral said keeps coming back. He quoted St. Bernard of Clairvaux, the twelfth-century monk who was instrumental in the Templars' rise to power. I acted like I didn't know what he was talking about. But Lars wrote a lot about him."

Malone also recalled the name from the book he'd read in Copenhagen. Bernard de Fontaines was a Cistercian monk who founded a monastery at Clairvaux in the twelfth century. He was a leading thinker and exerted great influence within the Church, becoming a close adviser to Pope Innocent II. His uncle was one of the nine original Templars, and it was Bernard who convinced Innocent II to grant the Templars their unprecedented Rule.

"The man in the cathedral knew Lars," Stephanie said. "Even intimated that he'd spoken to him about the journal, and that Lars challenged him. The man from the Round Tower also worked for him—he wanted me to know that—and that man screamed the Templar battle cry before jumping."

"Could all be a bluff to rattle you."

"I'm starting to doubt it."

He agreed, especially with what he'd noticed on the way over from the cemetery. But for the moment he kept that to himself.

"Lars wrote in his journal about the de Blancheforts' secret, one supposedly dating from 1307, the time of the Templars' arrest. He found plenty of references to this supposed family duty in documents from the period, but never any details. Apparently he spent a lot of time in the local monasteries poring through writings. It's Marie's grave, though, the one drawn in the book Thorvaldsen bought, that seems to be the key. Marie died in 1781, but it wasn't until 1791 that Abbè Bigou erected a headstone and marker over her remains. Remember the time. The French Revolution was brewing, and Catholic churches were being destroyed. Bigou was anti-republic, so he fled into Spain in 1793 and died there two years later, never returning to Rennes-le-Château."

"And what did Lars think Bigou hid inside that glass vial?"

"Probably not the actual de Blanchefort secret, but rather a method for learning it. In the notebook, Lars wrote that he firmly believed Marie's grave held the key to the secret."

He was beginning to understand. "Which is why the book was so important."

She nodded. "Saunière stripped many of the graves in the churchyard, digging up the bones and placing them in a communal ossuary that still stands behind the church. That explains, as Lars wrote, why there are no graves there now dated prior to 1885. The locals raised a loud ruckus about what he was doing, so he was ordered by the town councilors to stop. Marie de Blanchefort's grave was not exhumed, but all of the letters and symbols were chipped away by Saunière. Unbeknownst to him, there was a sketch of the marker that survived, drawn by a local mayor, Eugène Stüblein. Lars learned of that drawing but could never find a copy of the book."

"How did Lars know Saunière defaced the grave?"

"There's a record of Maria's grave being vandalized during that time. No one attached any special significance to the act, yet who else but Saunière could have done it?"

"And Lars thought all this leads to a treasure?"

"He wrote in his journal that he believed Saunière deciphered the message Abbé Bigou left behind and that he found the Templar hiding place, telling only his mistress, and she died without telling anyone."

"So what were you going to do? Use the notebook and the book to look for it again?"

"I don't know what I would have done. I can only say that something told me to come, buy the book, and look around." She paused. "It also gave me an excuse to come, stay in his house for a while, and remember."

That he understood. "Why involve Peter Hansen? Why not just buy the book yourself?"

"I still work for the U.S. government. I thought Hansen would be insulation. That way my name appears nowhere. Of course, I had no idea all of this was involved."

He considered what she'd said. "So Lars was following Saunière's tracks, just as Saunière followed Bigou."

She nodded. "And it seems someone else is also following those same tracks."

He surveyed the room again. "We'll need to go through all this carefully to even have a hope of learning anything."

Something at the front door caught his attention. When they'd entered a stack of mail scattered on the floor had been swept close to the wall, apparently dropped in through the door slot. He walked over and lifted half a dozen envelopes.

Stephanie came close.

"Let me see that one," she said.

He handed her a taupe-colored envelope with black script.

"The note included with Lars's journal was on that color paper and the writing looks similar." She found the page in her shoulder bag and they compared the script.

"It's identical," she said.

"I'm sure Scoville won't mind." He tore open the envelope.

Nine sheets of paper came out. On one was a penned message, the ink and writing the same as Stephanie had received.

She will come. Be forgiving. You have long searched and deserve to see. Together, it may be possible. In Avignon find Claridon. He can point the way. But prend garde l'Ingénieur.

He read the last line again—*prend garde l'Ingénieur.* "Beware the engineer. What does that mean?"

"Good question."

"No mention in the journal of any engineer?"

"Not a word."

"*Be forgiving.* Apparently the sender knew you and Scoville didn't care for one another."

"That's unnerving. I wasn't aware anyone knew that."

He examined the eight other pieces of paper. "These are from Lars's journal. The missing pages." He checked the postmark on the envelope. From Perpignan, on the French coast. Five days ago. "Scoville never received this. It came too late."

"Ernst was murdered, Cotton. There's no doubt now."

He concurred, but something else bothered him. He crept to one of the windows and carefully peered past the sheers.

"We need to go to Avignon," she said.

He agreed, but as he focused out at the empty street and caught a glimpse of what he knew would be there, he said, "After we tend to one other matter."

TWENTY-ONE

DE ROQUEFORT FACED THE GATHERING. RARELY DID THE brothers don vestments. Rule required that, for the most part, they dress *without any superfluity and ostentation*. But a conclave demanded formality and each member was expected to wear his garment of rank.

The sight was impressive. Brother knights sported white woolen mantles atop short white cassocks trimmed with crimson orphrey. Silver stockings sheathed their legs. A white hood covered each head. The red cross patee of four equal arms, wide at the ends, adorned every chest. A crimson belt wrapped the waist, and where once a sword hung now only a sash distinguished knights from artisans, farmers, craftsmen, clerks, priests, and aides, who wore a similar ensemble but in varying shades of green, brown, and black, the clerics distinguished by their white gloves.

Once a consistory convened Rule required that the marshal chair the proceeding. It was a way to balance the influence of any seneschal who, as second in command, could easily dominate the assembly.

"My brothers," de Roquefort called out.

The room drained of noise.

"This is our time of renewal. We must choose a master. Before we begin, let us ask the Lord for His guidance in the hours ahead."

In the glow from the bronze chandeliers, de Roquefort watched as 488 brothers bowed their heads. The call had gone out just after dawn, and most of those who served outside the abbey had made the journey home. They'd assembled in the upper hall of the *palais,* an enormous round citadel that dated from the sixteenth century, built a hundred feet high, seventy feet in diameter, with walls a dozen feet thick. It once had served as the abbey's last line of defense in case of attack, but it had evolved into an elaborate ceremonial center. Arrow slits were now filled with stained glass, the yellow stucco coated with images of St. Martin, Charlemagne, and the Virgin Mary. The circular room, with two railed galleries above, easily accommodated the nearly five hundred men and was blessed with nearly perfect acoustics.

De Roquefort raised his head and made eye contact with the other four officers. The commander, who was both the quartermaster and treasurer, was a friend. De Roquefort had spent years cultivating a relationship with that distant man and hoped those efforts would soon reap rewards. The draper, who oversaw the Order's clothes and dress, was clearly ready to champion the marshal's cause. The chaplain, though, who supervised all spiritual aspects, was a problem. De Roquefort had never been able to secure anything tangible from the Venetian besides vague generalizations of the obvious. Then there was the seneschal, who stood holding the *beauseant,* the Order's revered black-and-white banner. He looked comfortable in his white tunic and cape, the embroidered patch on his left shoulder indicating his high office. The sight turned de Roquefort's stomach. The man had no right to be wearing those precious garments.

"Brothers, the consistory is convened. It is time to nominate the conclave."

The procedure was deceptively simply. One name was chosen from a cauldron that contained all of the brothers' names. Then that man looked out among the assembled and freely chose another. Back to the cauldron for the next name, then another open selection, with the random pattern continuing until ten were designated. The system melded an element of chance coupled with personal involvement, diminishing greatly any opportunity for organized bias. De Roquefort, as marshal, and the seneschal were automatically included, making twelve. A two-thirds vote was needed to achieve election.

De Roquefort watched as the selections were made. When finished, four knights, one priest, a clerk, a farmer, two artisans, and a laborer had been chosen. Many were his followers. Yet the cursed randomness had allowed several to be included whose allegiance was, at best, questionable.

The ten men stepped forward and fanned out in a semicircle.

"We have a conclave," de Roquefort declared. "The consistory is over. Let us begin."

Every brother shoved back his hood, signaling that the debate could now start. The conclave was not a secret affair. Instead, the nomination, the discussion, and the vote would take place before the entire brotherhood. But Rule mandated that not a sound was to be uttered by the spectators.

De Roquefort and the seneschal took their place with the others. De Roquefort was no longer the chair—in the conclave each brother was equal. One of the twelve, an older knight with a thick gray beard, said, "Our marshal, a man who has guarded this Order for many years, should be our next master. I place him in contention."

Two more gave their consent. With the required three, the nominee was accepted.

Another of the twelve, one of the artisans, a gunsmith, stepped forward. "I disagreed with what was done to the master. He was a good man who loved this Order. He should not have been challenged. I place the seneschal in contention."

Two more nodded their assent.

De Roquefort stood rigid. The battle lines were drawn.

Let the war begin.

The debate was entering its second hour. Rule set no time limit on the conclave, but required that all in attendance must stand, the idea being that the length of the proceeding could well be a factor of the participants' endurance. No vote had yet been called. Any of the twelve possessed the right, but no one wanted to lose a tally—that was a sign of weakness—so votes were called only when two-thirds seemed assured.

"I'm not impressed with what you plan," one of the conclave members, the priest, said to the seneschal.

"I was not aware that I possessed a plan."

"You will continue the ways of the master. The ways of the past. True or not true?"

"I will remain faithful to my oath, as you should, brother."

"My oath said nothing about weakness," the priest said. "It does not require that I be complacent to a world that languishes in ignorance."

"We have guarded our knowledge for centuries. Why would you have us change?"

Another conclave member stepped forward. "I'm tired of the hypocrisy. It sickens me. We were nearly extinguished by greed and ignorance. It's time we return the favor."

"To what end?" the seneschal asked. "What would be gained?"

"Justice," cried another knight, and several other conclave members agreed.

De Roquefort decided it was time to join in. "The Gospels say, *Let one who seeks not stop seeking until one finds. When*

*one finds, one will be disturbed. When one is disturbed, one
will be amazed and will reign over all.*"

The seneschal faced him. "Thomas also said, *If your leaders say to you, behold, the kingdom is in the sky, then the
birds in the sky will get there before you. If they say to you,
it is in the sea, then the fish will get there before you.*"

"We will never go anywhere if we stay the present course,"
de Roquefort said. Heads bobbed in agreement, but not
enough to call for a vote.

The seneschal hesitated a moment, then said, "I ask you,
Marshal. What are *your* plans if you achieve election? Can
you tell us? Or do you do as Jesus, disclosing your mysteries
only to those worthy of the mysteries, never letting the left
hand know what the right is doing?"

He welcomed the opportunity to tell the brotherhood what
he envisioned. "Jesus also said, *There is nothing hidden that
will not be revealed.*"

"Then what would you have us do?"

He surveyed the room, his eyes traveling from floor to
gallery. This was his moment. "Think back. To the Beginning. When thousands of brothers took the oath. These were
brave men, who conquered the Holy Land. In the Chronicles, a tale is told of one garrison who lost out to the Saracens. After the battle, two hundred of those knights were
offered their lives if they would simply abandon Christ and
join Islam. Each one chose to kneel before the Muslims and
lose his head. That is our heritage. The Crusades were *our*
crusade."

He hesitated a moment for effect.

"Which is what makes Friday, October 13, 1307—a day so
infamous, so despicable, that Western civilization continues
to label it with bad luck—so difficult to accept. Thousands
of our brothers were wrongfully arrested. One day they were
the Poor Fellow-Soldiers of Christ and the Temple of
Solomon, the epitome of everything good, willing to die for

their Church, their pope, their God. The next day they were accused heretics. And to what charge? That they spat upon the Cross, exchanged obscene kisses, held secret meetings, adored a cat, practiced sodomy, venerated some bearded male head." He paused. "Not a word of truth to any of it, yet our brothers were tortured and many succumbed, confessing to falsehoods. One hundred and twenty burned at the stake."

He paused again.

"Our legacy is one of shame, and we are recorded in history with nothing but suspicion."

"And what would you tell the world?" the seneschal asked in a calm tone.

"The truth."

"And why would they believe you?"

"They will have no choice," he said.

"And why is that?"

"I will have proof."

"Have you located our Great Devise?"

The seneschal was pressing his one weak point, but he could not show any weakness. "It's within my grasp."

Gasps came from the gallery.

The seneschal's face remained rigid. "You're saying that you have found our lost archives after seven centuries. Have you also found our treasury that eluded Philip the Fair?"

"That, too, is within my grasp."

"Bold words, Marshal."

He stared out at the brothers. "I've been searching for a decade. The clues are difficult, but I'll soon possess proof the world cannot deny. Whether any minds change is irrelevant. Rather, the victory is gained by proving that our brothers were not heretics. Instead, each and every one of them was a saint."

Applause erupted from the crowd. De Roquefort seized the moment. "The Roman Church disbanded us, claimed we were idol worshipers, but the Church itself venerates its own idols with great pageantry." He paused, then in a loud voice he said, "I will take back the shroud."

More applause. Louder. Sustained. A violation of Rule, but no one seemed to care.

"The Church has no right to *our* shroud," de Roquefort yelled over the clapping. "Our master, Jacques de Molay, was tortured, brutalized, then burned at the stake. And his crime? Being a loyal servant to his God and his pope. His legacy is not *their* legacy. It's *our* legacy. We have the means to accomplish that goal. So shall it be, under my tenure."

The seneschal handed the *beauseant* to the man beside him, stepped close to de Roquefort, and waited for the applause to subside. "What of those who do not believe as you do?"

"Whoever seeks will find, whoever knocks will be let in."

"And for those who choose not to?"

"The Gospel is clear on that, too. *Woe to you on whom the evil demons act.*"

"You are a dangerous man."

"No, Seneschal, you are the danger. You came to us late and with a weak heart. You have no conception of our needs, only what you and your master thought to be our needs. I have given my life to this Order. No one save you has ever challenged my ability. I have always adhered to the ideal that I would rather break than bend." He turned from his opponent and motioned out to the conclave. "Enough. I call for a vote."

Rule dictated that debate was over.

"I shall vote first," de Roquefort said. "For myself. All those who agree, so say."

He watched as the ten remaining men considered their decision. They'd stayed silent during his confrontation with the seneschal, but each member had listened with an intensity that signaled comprehension. Dr. Roquefort's eyes

strafed the group and zeroed tight on the few he thought absolutely loyal.

Hands started to rise.

One. Three. Four. Six.

Seven.

He had his two-thirds, but he wanted more, so he waited
before declaring victory.

All ten voted for him.

The room erupted in cheer.

In ancient times he would have been swept off his feet
and carried to the chapel, where a mass would be said in his
honor. A celebration would later occur, one of the rare
times the Order engaged in merriment. But that happened
no longer. Instead, men began to chant his name and brothers, who otherwise existed in a world devoid of emotion,
showed their approval by clapping. The applause turned
into *beauseant*—and the word reverberated throughout
the hall.

Be glorious.

As the chant continued he stared at the seneschal, who
still stood beside him. Their eyes met and, through his
gaze, he made it known that not only had the master's chosen successor lost the fight, but the loser was now in mortal danger.

TWENTY-TWO

STEPHANIE WANDERED AROUND HER DEAD HUSBAND'S HOUSE.

The look was typical for the region. Sturdy timber floors, beam ceilings, stone fireplace, simple pine furniture. Not much space, but enough with two bedrooms, a den, a bath, kitchen, and a workshop. Lars had loved wood turning and earlier she'd noticed that his lathes, skews, chisels, and gouges were all still there, each tool hanging from a Peg-Board and frosted with a thin layer of dust. He'd been talented with the lathe. She still possessed bowls, boxes, and candlesticks he'd crafted from the local trees.

During their marriage she'd visited only a few times. She and Mark lived in Washington, then Atlanta. Lars stayed mainly in Europe, the last decade here in Rennes. Neither of them ever violated the other's space without permission. Though they may not have agreed on most things, they were always civil. Maybe too much so, she'd many times thought.

She'd always believed Lars had bought the house with royalties earned from his first book, but now she knew that Henrik Thorvaldsen had aided in the purchase. Which was so like Lars. He'd possessed little regard for money, spending all of what he earned on travel and his obsessions, the task of making sure the family bills were paid left to her. She'd only recently satisfied a loan used to finance Mark's college and graduate school. Her son had several times offered to assume the debt, especially once they were estranged, but she'd always refused. A parent's job was to educate their child, and she took her job seriously. Perhaps too much, she'd come to believe.

She and Lars had not spoken at all in the months before his death. Their last encounter was a bad one, another argument about money, responsibility, family. Her attempt at defending him yesterday with Henrik Thorvaldsen had sounded hollow, but she never realized that anyone knew the truth about her marital estrangement. Apparently, though, Thorvaldsen did. Perhaps he and Lars had been close. Unfortunately, she'd never know. That was the thing about suicide—ending one person's suffering only prolonged the agony of those left behind. She so wished to be rid of the sick feeling rooted in the pit of her stomach. The pain of failure, a writer once called it. And she agreed.

She finished her tour and entered the den, taking a seat across from Malone, who had been reading Lars's journal since dinner.

"Your husband was a meticulous researcher," he said.

"A lot of it is cryptic—much like the man."

He seemed to catch her frustration. "You want to tell me why you feel responsible for his suicide?"

She decided to allow his intrusion. She needed to talk about it. "I don't feel responsible, I just feel part of it. Both of us were proud. Stubborn, too. I was with Justice, Mark was grown, and there was talk of giving me my own division, so I focused on what I thought was important. Lars did the same. Unfortunately, neither one of us appreciated the other."

"Easy to see that now, years later. Impossible to know then."

"But that's the problem, Cotton. I'm here. He's not." She was ill at ease talking about herself, but things needed to be said. "Lars was a gifted writer and a good researcher. All that stuff I told you earlier about Saunière and this town? How interesting it is? If I had paid it any mind while he was alive, maybe he'd still be here." She hesitated. "He was such a calm man. Never raised his voice. Never a bad word. Silence was his weapon. He could go weeks and never say a word. It infuriated me."

"Now, that I understand." And he added a smile.

"I know. My quick temper. Lars could never deal with it, either. Finally he and I decided that the best thing was for him to live his life and me mine. Neither of us wanted to divorce."

"Which says a lot about what he thought of you. Deep down."

"I never saw that. All I saw was Mark in the middle. He was drawn to Lars. I have a hard time with emotion. Lars wasn't like that. And Mark possessed his father's religious curiosity. They were so much alike. My son chose his father over me, but I forced that choice. Thorvaldsen was right. For someone so careful with work, I was inept at handling my own life. Before Mark was killed, I hadn't spoken to him in three years." The pain from that reality rocked her soul. "Can you imagine, Cotton? My son and I went three years without saying a word."

"What caused the split?"

"He took his father's side, so I went my way and they went theirs. Mark lived here in France. I stayed in America. After a while it became easy to ignore him. Don't ever let that happen to you and Gary. Do whatever you have to, but never let that happen."

"I just moved four thousand miles away."

"But your son adores you. Those miles mean little."

"I've wondered plenty if I did the right thing."

"You have to live your life, Cotton. Your way. Your son seems to respect that, even though he's young. Mine was much older and far tougher on me."

He glanced at his watch. "Sun's been down twenty minutes. Almost time."

"When did you first notice we were being tailed?"

"Right after we arrived. Two men. Both similar to those from the cathedral. They followed us to the cemetery, then around town. They're outside, right now."

"No danger they'll come in?"

He shook his head. "They're here to watch."

"I understand now why you got out of the Billet. The anxiety. It's tough. You can never let your guard down. You were right back in Copenhagen. I'm no field agent."

"The trouble for me came when I started to like the rush. That's what'll get you killed."

"We all live a relatively safe existence. But to have people tracing your every move, intent on killing you? I can see how that would wear on you. Eventually, you have to escape from it."

"Training helps with the apprehension. You learn how to deal with uncertainty. But you were never trained." He smiled. "You're just in charge."

"I hope you know that I never intended involving you."

"You made that point quite clear."

"But I'm glad you're here."

"Wouldn't have missed it for the world."

She smiled. "You were the best agent I ever had."

"I was just the luckiest. And I had enough sense to say when."

"Peter Hansen and Ernst Scoville were both murdered." She paused and finally voiced what she'd come to believe. "Maybe Lars, too. The man in the cathedral wanted me to know that. His way of sending a message."

"That's a big leap in logic."

"I know. No proof. But I have a feeling, and though I may not be a field agent, I've come to trust my feelings. Still, like I used to tell you, no conclusions based on assumptions. Get the facts. This whole thing is bizarre."

"Tell me about it. Knights Templars. Secrets on gravestones. Priests finding lost treasure."

She glanced over at a photo of Mark on the side table, taken a few months before he died. Lars was everywhere in the young man's vibrant face. The same cleft chin, bright eyes, and swarthy skin. Why had she let things become so bad?

"Strange that's here," Malone said, seeing her interest.

"I set it there the last time I came. Five years ago. Just after the avalanche." Hard to believe her only child had been dead five years. Children shouldn't die thinking their parents had not loved them. Unlike with her estranged husband who possessed a grave, Mark lay buried under tons of Pyrenean snow thirty miles to the south. "I have to finish this," she muttered to the picture, her voice faltering.

"I'm still not sure what *this* is."

Neither was she.

Malone gestured with the journal. "At least we know where to find Claridon in Avignon, as the letter to Ernst Scoville instructed. He's Royce Claridon. There's a notation and address in the journal. Lars and he were friends."

"I was wondering when you'd find that."

"Anything else I missed?"

"Hard to say what's important. There's a lot in there."

"You have to stop lying to me."

She'd been waiting for the scolding. "I know."

"I can't help if you hold back."

She understood. "What about the missing pages sent to Scoville? Anything there?"

"You tell me." And he handed her the eight sheets.

She decided a little thinking would take her mind off Lars and Mark, so she scanned the handwritten paragraphs. Most of it was meaningless, but there were parts that ripped at her heart.

. . . Saunière obviously cared for his mistress. She came to him when her family moved to Rennes. Her father and brother were skilled artisans and her mother maintained the parish presbytery. This was in 1892, a year after much was found by Saunière. When her family moved from Rennes to take jobs in a nearby factory, she stayed with Saunière and remained with him until he died, two decades later. At some point he titled every single thing he acquired in her name, which shows the unquestioning trust he placed in her. She was totally devoted to him, keeping his secrets for 36 years after he died. I envy Saunière. He was a man who knew the unconditional love of a woman and returned that love with unconditional trust and respect. He was by all accounts a difficult man to please, a man driven to accomplish something for which people would remember him. His garish creation in the Church of Mary Magdalene seems his legacy. There is no record of his lover ever once voicing any opposition to what he was doing. All accounts say she was a devoted woman who supported her benefactor in all that he did. Surely there were some disagreements but, in the end, she stood by Saunière until the day he died and then after, for nearly four decades. There is much to be said for devotion. A man can accomplish much when the woman he loves supports him, even if she believes that what he does is foolishness. Surely, Saunière's mistress must have shook her head more than once at the absurdity of his creations. Both the Villa Béthanie and the Tour Magdala are ridiculous for their time. But she never let a drop of water fall on his fire. She cared for him enough to let him be what he

needed to be, and that result is being seen today by the thousands who come to Rennes each year. Such is Saunière's legacy. Hers is that his still exists.

"Why did you give me this to read?" she said to Malone when she finished.

"You needed to."

Where had all these ghosts come from? Rennes-le-Château might hold no treasure, but this place harbored demons intent on tormenting her.

"When I received that journal in the mail and read it, I realized that I had not been fair to Lars or Mark. They believed in what they sought, just as I believed in my job. Mark would say I was nothing but negative." She paused, hoping the spirits were listening. "I knew when I saw that notebook again I'd been wrong. Whatever Lars was after was important to him, so it should have been important to me. That's really why I came, Cotton. I owe it to them." She looked over at him with tired eyes. "God knows I owed it to them. I just never realized the stakes were so high."

He glanced at his watch again, then stared toward the blackened windows. "Time to find out just how high. You going to be all right here?"

She grabbed hold of herself and nodded. "I'll keep mine occupied. You handle the other."

TWENTY-THREE

MALONE LEFT THE HOUSE THROUGH THE FRONT DOOR, MAKING no attempt to hide his departure. The two men he'd noticed earlier were stationed at the far end of the street, around a corner near the town wall where they could see Lars Nelle's residence. Their problem was, in order to follow him, they would have to traverse the same deserted street. Amateurs. Professionals would have split up. One at each end, ready to move in any direction. Just like in Roskilde, this conclusion lessened his apprehension. But he remained on edge, his senses alert, wondering who was so interested in what Stephanie was doing.

Could it really be the modern-day Knights Templar?

Back inside, Stephanie's lamenting had made him think of Gary. The death of a child seemed unspeakable. He could not imagine her grief. Maybe after he retired he should have stayed in Georgia, but Gary would not hear of that. *Don't worry about me,* his son had said. *I'll come see you.* Fourteen years old and the boy possessed such a level head. Still, the decision haunted him, especially now that he was once again risking his neck for somebody else's cause. His own father, though, had been the same way—dying when the submarine he commanded sank in the North Atlantic during a training exercise. Malone was ten and he remembered his mother taking the death hard. At the memorial service, she'd even refused the folded flag offered her by the honor guard. But he'd accepted it and, ever since, the red, white, and blue bundle had stayed with him. With no grave to visit, that flag was his only physical reminder of the man he barely knew.

He came to the end of the street. He didn't have to glance back to know that one of the men was following him, the other staying with Stephanie at the house.

He turned left and headed toward Saunière's domain.

Rennes was clearly not a night place. Bolted doors and shuttered windows lined the way. The restaurant, bookstore, and kiosks were all closed. Darkness sheathed the lane in deep shadow. The wind murmured beyond the walls like a soul in pain. The scene was like something from Dumas, as if life here spoke only in whispers.

He paraded up the incline toward the church. The Villa Béthanie and presbytery were shut tight, the tree garden beyond illuminated by a half-moon broken by clouds racing past overhead.

The gate to the churchyard remained open, as Stephanie said it would be. He headed straight for it, knowing that his tail would come, too. Just inside, he used the thickening darkness to slip behind a huge elm. He peered back and saw his pursuer enter the cemetery, the pace quickening. As the man passed the tree, Malone pounced and jammed a fist into the other man's abdomen. He was relieved to feel no body armor. He pounded another blow across the jaw, sending his pursuer to the ground, then yanked him up.

The younger man was short, muscular, and clean-shaven with close-cropped light hair. He was dazed as Malone patted him down, quickly finding the bulge of a weapon. He reached beneath the man's jacket and withdrew a pistol. A Beretta Bobcat. Italian made. A tiny semi-automatic, designed as a last-resort backup. He'd once carried one himself. He brought the barrel to the man's neck and pressed his opponent firm against the tree.

"The name of your employer, please."

No response.

"You understand English?"

The man shook his head, as he continued to suck air and orient himself.

"Since you understood my question, do you comprehend this?" He cocked the hammer on the gun.

A stiffening signaled that the younger man registered the message.

"Your employer."

A shot rang out and a bullet thudded into the tree trunk just above their heads. Malone whirled to see a silhouetted figure standing a hundred feet away, perched where the belvedere met the cemetery wall, rifle in hand.

Another shot and a bullet skipped off the ground within inches of his feet. He released his hold and his original pursuer bolted out of the parish close.

But he was more concerned now with the shooter.

He saw the figure abandon the terrace, disappearing back onto the belvedere. A new energy swept through him. Gun in hand, he fled the cemetery and ran toward a narrow passageway between the Villa Béthanie and the church. He recalled the geography from earlier. The tree garden lay beyond, enclosed by an elevated belvedere that wrapped U-shaped toward the Tour Magdala.

He rushed into the garden and saw the figure running across the belvedere. The only way up was a stone staircase. He raced for it and skipped up three steps at a time. On top the thin air slashed his lungs and the stiff wind attacked him without interference, molesting his body and slowing his progress.

He saw his assailant head straight for the Tour Magdala. He thought about trying a shot, but a sudden gust snatched at him, as if warning against it. He wondered where the attacker was headed. No other staircase led down, and the

Magdala was surely locked for the night. To his left stretched a wrought-iron railing, beyond which were trees and a ten-foot drop to the garden. To his right, beyond a low stone wall, was a fifteen-hundred-foot drop. At some point, he was going to come face-to-face with whomever.

He rounded the terrace, passed through an iron glasshouse, and saw the form enter the Tour Magdala.

He stopped.

He'd not expected that.

He recalled what Stephanie had said about the building's geometry. About eighteen feet square, with a round turret that housed a winding staircase leading up to a crenellated rooftop. Saunière had once housed his private library inside.

He decided he had no choice. He trotted to the door, saw it was cocked open, and positioned himself to one side. He kicked the heavy wooden slab inward and waited for a shot.

Nothing came.

He risked a glance and saw that the room was empty. Windows filled two walls. No furniture. No books. Only bare wooden cases and two upholstered benches. A brick fireplace sat dark. Then he realized.

The roof.

He approached the stone staircase. The steps were short and narrow. He climbed the clockwise spiral to a steel door and tested it. No movement. He pushed harder. The portal was locked from the outside.

The door below slammed shut.

He descended the staircase and discovered that the only other exit was now locked from the outside, too. He stepped to a pair of fixed-pane windows that overlooked the tree garden and saw the black form leap from the terrace, grab hold of a thick limb, then drop to the ground with a surprising agility. The figure ran through the trees and headed for the car park about thirty yards away, the same one where he'd left the Peugeot earlier.

He stepped back and fired three bullets into the left side of the double windows. The leaded glass shattered, then broke away. He rushed forward and used the gun to clear away the shards. He hopped onto the bench below the sill and squeezed himself through the opening. The drop down was only about six feet. He jumped, then ran toward the car park.

Exiting the garden, he heard the rev of an engine and saw the black form atop a motorcycle. The driver whipped the cycle around and avoided the only street leading out of the car park, roaring down one of the side passages toward the houses.

He quickly decided to use the village's compactness to his advantage and bolted left, rushing down a short lane and turning at the main *rue*. A downward incline helped, and he heard the motorcycle approaching from his right. There would be but one opportunity, so he raised the gun and slowed his pace.

As the cyclist popped out of the alley, he fired twice.

One shot missed, but the other caught the frame in a burst of spark, then ricocheted off.

The motorcycle roared out the town's gate.

Lights began to spring on. Gunshots were surely a strange sound here. He stuffed the gun under his jacket, retreated down another alley, and made his way back toward Lars Nelle's house. He could hear voices behind him. People were coming out to investigate. In a few moments he would be back inside and safe. He doubted that the other two men were still around—or if they were, that they'd be a problem.

But one thing nagged at him.

He'd caught a suggestion of it as he'd watched the form leap from the terrace, then race away. Something in the movement.

Hard to tell for sure, but enough.

His assailant had been a woman.

TWENTY-FOUR

THE SENESCHAL FOUND GEOFFREY. HE'D BEEN LOOKING for his assistant since the conclave dissolved and finally learned that the younger man had retired to one of the minor chapels in the north wing, beyond the library, one of many places of repose the abbey offered.

He entered the room lit only by candles and saw Geoffrey lying on the floor. Brothers many times laid themselves before the altar of God. During induction the act showed humility, a demonstration of insignificance in the face of heaven, and its continued use served as a reminder.

"We need to talk," he quietly said.

His young associate remained still for a few moments, then slowly came to his knees, crossed himself, and stood.

"Tell me precisely what you and the master were doing." He was not in the mood for coyness, and thankfully Geoffrey seemed calmer than earlier in the Hall of Fathers.

"He wanted to make sure those two parcels were posted in the mail."

"He say why?"

"Why would he? He was the master. I'm but a minor brother."

"He apparently trusted you enough to enlist your aid."

"He said you would resent that."

"I'm not that petty." He could sense that the man knew more. "Tell me."

"I cannot say."

"Why not?"

"The master instructed me to answer the question about the mailings. But I am not to say anything further . . . until more happens."

"Geoffrey, what more needs to happen? De Roquefort is in charge. You and I are practically alone. Brothers are aligning themselves with de Roquefort. What else needs to occur?"

"That's not for me to decide."

"De Roquefort cannot succeed without the Great Devise. You heard the reaction in the conclave. The brothers will desert him if he fails to deliver. Is that what you and the master were plotting about? Did the master know more than he said to me?"

Geoffrey went silent, and the seneschal suddenly detected a maturity in his aide that he'd never noticed before. "I'm ashamed to say that the master told me the marshal would defeat you in the conclave."

"What else did he say?"

"Nothing I can reveal at the moment."

The evasiveness was irritating. "Our master was brilliant. As you say, he foresaw what happened. He apparently thought ahead enough to make you his oracle. Tell me, what am I to do?" The plea in his voice could not be disguised.

"He said for me to answer that inquiry with what Jesus said. *Whoever does not hate their father and mother as I do cannot be my disciple.*"

The words were from the Gospel of Thomas. But what did

they mean in this context? He thought of what else Thomas wrote. *Whoever does not love their father and mother as I do cannot be my disciple.*

"He also wanted me to remind you that Jesus said, *Let one who seeks not stop seeking until one finds—*"

"When one finds, one will be disturbed. When one is disturbed, one will be amazed, and will reign over all," he quickly finished. "Was everything he said a riddle?"

Geoffrey did not answer. The younger man was of a much lesser degree than the seneschal, his path to knowledge only just beginning. Order membership was a steady progression toward full Gnosticism—a journey that would normally require three years. Geoffrey had only come to the abbey eighteen months ago from the Jesuit home in Normandy, abandoned as a child and raised by the monks. The master had immediately noticed him and requested that he be included on the executive staff. The seneschal had wondered about that hasty decision, but the old man had merely smiled and said, "No different than I did with you."

He placed a hand on his aide's shoulder. "For the master to enlist your help, he surely thought highly of your abilities."

A resolute look came to the pale face. "And I will not fail him."

Brothers took differing paths. Some veered toward administration. Others became artisans. Many were associated with the abbey's self-sufficiency as craftsmen or farmers. A few devoted themselves solely to religion. Only about a third were selected as knights. Geoffrey was in line to become a knight sometime within the next five years, depending on his progress. He'd already served his apprenticeship and completed the required elementary training. A year of Scriptures lay ahead before the first fidelity oath could be administered. Such a shame, the seneschal thought, that he could well lose all he'd worked to achieve.

"Seneschal, what of the Great Devise? Can it be found, as the marshal said?"

"That's our one salvation. De Roquefort does not have it, but probably thinks we know. Do we?"

"The master spoke of it." The words came quickly, as if they were not to be said.

He waited for more.

"He told me that a man named Lars Nelle came the closest. He said Nelle's path was the right one." Geoffrey's pallid face worked with a nervous excitement.

He and the master had many times discussed the Great Devise. Its origins were from a time before 1307, but its hiding place after the Purge was a way to deprive Philip IV of the Templars' wealth and knowledge. In the months prior to October 13, Jacques de Molay hid all that the Order cherished. Unfortunately, no mention of its location was recorded, and the Black Death eventually wiped out every soul who knew anything of its whereabouts. The only clue came from a passage noted in the Chronicles for June 4, 1307. *Where is it best to hide a pebble?* Subsequent masters tried to answer that inquiry and searched until the effort was deemed pointless. But only in the nineteenth century had new clues come to light—not from the Order, but from two parish priests in Rennes-le-Château. Abbés Antoine Bigou and Bérenger Saunière. The seneschal knew that Lars Nelle had resurrected their astonishing tale, writing a book in the 1970s that told the world about the tiny French village and its supposed ancient mystic. Now to learn that *he came the closest,* that *his was the right path,* seemed almost surreal.

The seneschal was about to inquire further when footfalls sounded. He turned as four brother knights, men he knew, marched into the chapel. De Roquefort followed them inside, now dressed in the master's white cassock.

"Plotting, Seneschal?" de Roquefort asked, the eyes beaming.

"Not anymore." He wondered about the show of force. "Need an audience?"

"They're here for your benefit. Though I am hoping this can be done in a civilized manner. You are under arrest."

"And the charge?" he asked, showing not a hint of concern.

"Violation of your oath."

"You intend to explain yourself?"

"In the proper forum. These brothers shall accompany you to your chambers, where you will stay the night. Tomorrow, I will find more appropriate accommodations. Your replacement will, by then, need your chamber."

"That's kind of you."

"I thought so. But be happy. A penitent cell would have been your home long ago."

He knew about them. Nothing more than boxes of iron, too small for standing or lying. Instead, the prisoner had to crouch, and no food or water only added to the agony. "You plan to resurrect the cell's use?"

He saw de Roquefort did not appreciate the challenge, but the Frenchman only smiled. Seldom had this demon ever relaxed into a grin. "My followers, unlike yours, are loyal to their oaths. There's no need for such measures."

"I almost think you believe that."

"You see, that insolence is the very reason I opposed you. Those of us trained in the discipline of our devotion would never speak to one another in such a disrespectful manner. But men, like you, who come from the secular world think arrogance appropriate."

"And denying our master his due accord was showing respect?"

"That was the price paid for *his* arrogance."

"He was raised like you."

"Which shows we, too, are capable of error."

He was tiring of de Roquefort, so he collected himself and said, "I demand my right to a tribunal."

"Which you shall have. In the meantime you will be confined."

De Roquefort motioned. The four brothers stepped forward, and though he was frightened he decided to go with dignity.

He left the chapel, surrounded by his guards, but at the doorway he hesitated a moment and glanced back, catching a final glimpse of Geoffrey. The younger man had stood silent as he and de Roquefort sparred. The new master was characteristically unconcerned with someone so junior. It would be many years before Geoffrey could pose any threat. Yet the seneschal wondered.

Not a hint of fear, shame, or apprehension clouded Geoffrey's face.

Instead, the look was one of intense resolve.

TWENTY-FIVE

RENNES-LE-CHÂTEAU
SATURDAY, JUNE 24
9:30 AM

MALONE SQUEEZED HIS TALL FRAME INTO THE PEUGEOT. Stephanie was already inside the car.

"See anybody?" she asked.

"Our two friends from last night are back. Resilient suckers."

"No sign of motorcycle girl?"

He'd told Stephanie about his suspicions. "I wouldn't expect that."

"Where are the two amigos?"

"In a crimson Renault at the far end, beyond the water tower. Don't turn your head. Let's not spook 'em."

He adjusted the outside mirror so he could see the Renault. Already tour buses and about a dozen cars filled the sandy car park. The clear weather from yesterday was gone, the sky now smeared with pewter storm clouds. Rain was on the way, and soon. They were headed to Avignon, about ninety miles away, to find Royce Claridon. Malone had already checked the map and decided on the best route to lose any tail.

He cranked the car, and they cruised out of the village. Once beyond the city gate and on the winding path down to ground level, he noticed the Renault staying a discreet distance back.

"How do you plan to lose them?"

He smiled. "The old-fashioned way."

"Always plan ahead, right?"

"Somebody I once worked for taught me that."

They found highway D118 and headed north. The map indicated a distance of twenty miles to A61, the tolled superhighway just south of Carcassonne that led northeast to Avignon. About six miles ahead, at Limoux, the highway forked, one route crossing the Aude River into Limoux, the other continuing north. He decided that would be his opportunity.

Rain started to fall. Light at first, then heavy.

He flipped on the front and rear wipers. The road ahead on both sides was clear of cars. Saturday morning had apparently kept traffic at home.

The Renault, its fog lamps piercing the rain, matched his speed and then some. He watched in his rearview mirror as the Renault passed the car directly behind him, then sped ahead, paralleling the Peugeot in the opposite lane.

The passenger window descended and a gun appeared.

"Hold on," he told Stephanie.

He floored the accelerator and whipped the car tight around a curve. The Renault lost speed and fell in behind.

"Seems there's been a change in plan. Our shadows have turned aggressive. Why don't you stay down on the floorboard."

"I'm a big girl. Just drive."

He slid around another curve and the Renault closed distance. Holding the tires to the highway was tough. The pavement was coated in a thick veil of condensation and becoming wetter by the second. No yellow lines defined anything and the asphalt's edge was partially obscured by puddles that could easily hydroplane the car.

A bullet shattered the rear windshield.

The tempered glass did not explode, but he doubted if it could take another hit. He started zigzagging, guessing where the pavement ended on each side. He spotted a car approaching in the opposite lane and returned to his own.

"Can you fire a gun?" he asked, not taking his eyes off the road.

"Where is it?"

"Under the seat. I took it off the guy last night. There's a full clip. Make 'em count. I need a little space from those guys behind us."

She found the pistol and lowered her window. He saw her reach out, aim toward the rear, and fire five rounds.

The shots had the desired effect. The Renault backed off, but did not abort its pursuit. He fishtailed around another curve, working the brake and accelerator as years ago he'd been trained to do.

Enough of being the fox.

He swerved into the southbound lane and slammed on brakes. Tires grabbed the wet pavement with a screech. The Renault shot past in the northbound lane. He released the brake, downshifted to second, then plunged the accelerator to the mat.

The tires spun, then shot the car forward.

He wound the gearshift through to fifth.

The Renault was now ahead of him. He sent more gas to the engine. Sixty. Sixty-five. Seventy miles an hour. The whole thing was curiously invigorating. He hadn't seen this kind of action in a while.

He swerved into the southbound lane and came parallel to the Renault.

Both cars were now doing seventy-five miles an hour on a relatively straight part of highway. Suddenly they crested a knoll and arched off the pavement, tires slamming hard as rubber re-found the soaked asphalt. His body jerked forward then back, rattling his brain, his shoulder harness holding him in place.

"That was fun," Stephanie said.

To their left and right stretched green fields, the countryside a sea of lavender, asparagus, and grapes. The Renault roared up beside him. He stole another glance to his right. One of the short-hairs was climbing out of the passenger-side window, curling himself up and over the roof for a clear shot.

"Shoot the tires," he told Stephanie.

She was preparing to fire when he saw a transport truck ahead, filling the Renault's northbound lane. He'd driven enough of Europe's two-laned highways to know that, unlike in America where trucks drove with reckless abandon, here they moved at a snail's pace. He'd been hoping to find one closer to Limoux, but opportunities had to be taken when offered. The truck was no more than a couple of hundred yards ahead. They would be on it in a moment, and luckily his lane ahead was clear.

"Wait," he said to her.

He kept his car parallel and did not allow the Renault a

way out. The other driver would have to either brake, crash into the truck, or veer right into the open field. He hoped the truck stayed put in the northbound lane, otherwise he'd have no choice but to find a field himself.

The other driver apparently realized his three options and veered off the pavement.

He sped past the truck down the open road. A glance in his mirror confirmed that the Renault was mired in the tawny mud.

He swerved back into the northbound lane, relaxed a bit, but kept his speed, eventually leaving the main highway, as planned, at Limoux.

They arrived in Avignon a little after eleven am. The rain had stopped fifty miles back and bright sunshine flooded the wooded terrain, the rolling hills green and gold, like a page from an old manuscript. A turreted medieval wall enclosed the city, which had once served as the capital of Christendom for nearly a hundred years. Malone maneuvered the Peugeot through a maze of narrow streets into an underground parking lot.

They climbed stairs to ground level and he immediately noticed Romanesque churches, framed by sunbaked dwellings, the roofs and walls all the tint of dirty sand, the feel clearly Italian. Being the weekend tourists were out by the thousands, the colorful awnings and plane trees in the Place de l'Horloge shading a boisterous lunch crowd.

The address from Lars Nelle's notebook led them down one of the many *rues*. As they walked Malone thought of the fourteenth century, when popes exchanged Rome's Tiber River for the French Rhône and occupied the huge palace on the hill. Avignon became an asylum for heretics. Jews bought tolerance with a modest tax, criminals lived unscathed, gaming houses and brothels flourished. Policing was lax and roaming after dark could be life threatening. What had Petrarch written? *An abode of sorrows, everything breathes lies.* He hoped things had changed in six hundred years.

Royce Claridon's address was an antiques shop—books and furniture—the front window filled with Jules Verne volumes from the early part of the twentieth century. Malone was familiar with the colorful editions. The front door was locked, but a note taped to the glass stated that business was being conducted today on the Cours Jean Jaurès, part of a monthly book fair.

They learned directions to the market, which sat adjacent to a main boulevard. Rickety metal tables dotted the treed square. Plastic crates held French books as well as a smattering of English titles, mostly movie and television picture volumes. The fair seemed to draw a different type of patron. Lots of trimmed hair, glasses, skirts, ties, and beards—not a Nikon or camcorder in sight.

Buses lumbered past with tourists on the way to the papal palace, the groaning diesels drowning out the beat of a steel band playing across the street. A Coke can clattered across the pavement and startled Malone. He was on edge.

"Something wrong?"

"Too many distractions."

They strolled though the market, his bibliophilic eye studying the wares. The good stuff was all wrapped in plastic. A card on top identified a book's provenance and price, which he noticed was high for the low quality. He learned from one of the vendors the location for Royce Claridon's booth, and they found it on the far side, away from the street. The woman tending the tables was short and stout, with bottle-blond hair tied in a bun. She wore sunglasses and any attractiveness was tempered by a cigarette stuck between her lips. Smoking was not something Malone had ever found appealing.

They examined her books, everything displayed on a tattered home entertainment center, most of the clothbound volumes in ratty condition. He was amazed anyone would buy them.

He introduced himself and Stephanie. The woman didn't offer her name, she just kept smoking.

"We went by your shop," he said in French.

"Closed for the day." The clipped tone made clear that she did not want to be bothered.

"We're not interested in anything there," he made clear.

"Then, by all means, enjoy these wonderful books."

"Business that bad?"

She sucked another drag. "It stinks."

"Why are you here then? Why not out in the country for the day?"

She appraised him with a suspicious eye. "I don't like questions. Especially from Americans who speak bad French."

"I thought mine was fair."

"It's not."

He decided to get to the point. "We're looking for Royce Claridon."

She laughed. "Who isn't?"

"Care to enlighten us on who else is?" This bitch was getting on his nerves.

She did not immediately answer. Instead, her gaze shifted to a couple of people examining her stock. The steel band from across the street struck up another tune. Her potential patrons wandered off.

"Have to watch them all," she muttered. "They will steal anything."

"Tell you what," he said. "I'll buy a whole crate if you'll answer one question."

The proposal seemed to interest her. "What do you want to know?"

"Where is Royce Claridon?"

"I haven't seen him in five years."

"That's not an answer."

"He's gone."

"Where did he go?'

"That's all the answers one crate of books will buy."

They clearly were not going to learn anything from her, and he had no intention of giving her any more money. So he tossed a fifty-euro note onto the table and grabbed his crate of books. "Your answer sucked, but I'll keep my end of the bargain."

He walked over to an open trash bin, turned the container upside down, and dumped the contents inside. Then he tossed the crate back on the table.

"Let's go," he said to Stephanie. They walked off.

"Hey, American."

He stopped and turned back.

The woman rose from her chair. "I liked that."

He waited.

"Lots of creditors are looking for Royce, but he's easy to find. Check out the sanatorium in Villeneuve-les-Avignon." She twirled an extended index finger at her temple. "Loony, that's Royce."

TWENTY-SIX

THE SENESCHAL SAT IN HIS CHAMBERS. HE'D SLEPT LITTLE LAST night as he pondered his dilemma. Two brothers guarded his door and no one was allowed inside except to bring him food. He didn't like being caged—albeit, at least for now, in a comfortable prison. His quarters were not the size of the master's or the marshal's, but they were private, with a bath and a window. Little danger existed that he'd climb through the window, the drop beyond the sill was several hundred feet down a sheer mass of gray rock.

But his fortunes were sure to change today, as de Roquefort was not going to allow him to roam the abbey at will. He'd probably be held in one of the underground rooms, places long used for cool storage, the perfect spot to keep an enemy isolated. His ultimate fate was anybody's guess.

He'd come a long way since his induction.

Rule was clear. *If any man wished to leave the mass of perdition and abandon that secular life and choose communal life, do not consent to receive him immediately, for thus said Saint Paul:* Test the soul to see if it comes from God. *If the company of the brotherhood is granted, let the Rule be read to him, and if he wishes to obey the commandments of the Rule, let the brothers receive him, let him reveal his wish and desire before all of the brothers and let him make his request with a pure heart.*

All of that had happened and he'd been received. He'd willingly taken the oath and gladly served. Now he was a prisoner. Accused of false charges leveled by an ambitious politico. Not unlike his ancient brethren, who'd fallen victim to the despicable Philip the Fair. He'd always thought the label odd. In truth, *the Fair* had nothing to do with the monarch's temperament, since the French king was a cold, secretive man who wanted to rule the Catholic Church. Instead, it referred to his light hair and blue eyes. One thing on the outside, something altogether different on the inside—a lot like himself, he thought.

He stood from his desk and paced, a habit acquired in college. Moving helped him think. On the desk lay the two books he'd taken from the library two nights ago. He realized that the next few hours might be his last opportunity to scan their pages. Surely, once they turned up missing, theft of Order property would be added to the list of charges. Its punishment—banishment—would actually be welcome, but he knew his nemesis was never going to allow him off that easily.

He reached for the codex from the fifteenth century, a treasure any museum would pay dearly to display. The pages were scripted in the curvy lettering he knew as rotunda, common for the time, used in learned manuscripts. Little punctuation existed, just long lines of text filling every page from top to bottom, edge to edge. A scribe had labored weeks producing it, holed up in the abbey's scriptorium before a writing desk, quill in hand, slowly inking each letter onto parchment. Burn marks marred the binding and droplets of wax dotted many of the pages, but the codex was in remarkably good shape. One of the Order's great missions had been to preserve knowledge, and he'd been lucky to stumble across this reservoir amid the thousands of volumes the library contained.

You must finish the quest. It is your destiny. Whether you realize that or not. That's what the master had told Geoffrey. But he'd also said, *Those who have followed the path you are about to take have been many, and never has anyone succeeded.*

But did they know what he knew? Surely not.

He reached for the other volume. Its text was also handwritten. But not by scribes. Instead, the words had been penned in November 1897 by the Order's then marshal, a man who'd been in direct contact with Abbé Jean-Antoine-Maurice Gélis, the parish priest for the village of Coustausa, which also lay in the Aude River Valley, not far from Rennes-le-Château. Theirs had been a fortuitous encounter, for the marshal had learned vital information.

He sat and again thumbed through the report.

A few passages caught his attention, words he'd first read with interest three years ago. He stood and stepped to the window with the book.

I was distressed to learn that the abbé Gélis was murdered on All Saints' Day. He was found fully dressed, wearing his clerical hat, lying in his own blood upon his kitchen floor. His watch had stopped at 12:15 AM, but the time of death was determined to be between 3 and 4 AM. Posing as the bishop's representative, I spoke with villagers and the local constable. Gélis was a nervous sort, known to keep windows closed and shutters drawn, even in summer. He never opened the presbytery's door to strangers, and since there was no sign of forced intrusion, officials concluded that the abbé had known his attacker.

Gélis died at age seventy-one. He was beaten over the head with fire tongs then hacked with an ax. Blood was copious, splatters on the floor and ceiling were found, but not one footprint lay among the various pools. This baffled the constable. The body was intentionally laid out on its back, arms crossed on the chest, in the common pose for the dead. Six hundred and three francs in gold and notes, along with another one hundred and six francs, were found in the house. Robbery was clearly not the motive. The only item that could be considered evidence was a pack of cigarette papers. Penned on one was "Viva Angelina." This was significant since Gélis was not a smoker and detested even the smell of cigarettes.

In my opinion, the true motive for the crime was found in the priest's bedroom. There, the assailant had pried open a briefcase. Papers remained inside but it was impossible to know if anything had been removed. Drops of blood were found in and around the briefcase. The constable concluded that the murderer was searching for something and I may know what that could be.

Two weeks prior to his murder, I met with Abbé Gélis. A month before that, Gélis had communicated with the bishop in Carcassonne. I appeared at Gélis's home, posing as the bishop's representative, and we discussed at length what troubled him. He eventually requested that I hear his confession. Since in truth I am not a priest, and therefore not bound by any oath of the confessional, I can report what was told me.

Sometime in the summer of 1896, Gélis discovered a glass vial in his church. The railing for the choir had required replacing and, when the wood was removed, a hiding place was found that contained a wax-sealed vial holding a single sliver of paper, upon which was the following:

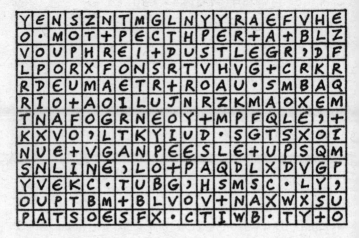

This cryptogram was a common coding device popular during the last century. He told me that six years earlier the abbé Saunière, from Rennes-le-Château, found a cryptogram in his church, too. When compared, they were identical. Saunière believed that both vials had been left by the abbé Bigou, who served at Rennes-le-Château during the French Revolution. In Bigou's time, the church in Coustausa was also served by the priest from Rennes. So Bigou would have been a frequent visitor to Gélis's present parish. Saunière also thought there was a connection between the cryptograms and the tomb of Marie d'Hautpoul de Blanchefort, who died in 1781. Abbé Bigou had been her confessor and commissioned her headstone and marker, having an assortment of unique words and symbols inscribed thereon. Unfortunately, Saunière had not been able to decipher anything, but after a year of work Gélis solved the cryptogram. He told me that he was not entirely truthful with Saunière, thinking his fellow abbé's motives unpure. So he withheld from his colleague the solution he had determined.

Abbé Gélis wanted the bishop to know the complete solution and believed he was accomplishing that act by telling me.

Unfortunately, the marshal did not record what Gélis said. Perhaps he thought the information too important to write down, or maybe he was another schemer, like de Roquefort. Strangely, the Chronicles reported that the marshal himself disappeared a year later, in 1898. He left one day on abbey business and never returned. A search yielded nothing. But thank the Lord he recorded the cryptogram.

The bells for Sext began to ring, signaling the brothers' noontime gathering. All, except the kitchen staff, would gather in the chapel for Psalm readings, hymns, and prayers until one PM. He decided to have his own time of meditation, but was interrupted by a soft rap at the door. He turned as Geoffrey stepped inside, carrying a tray of food and drink.

"I volunteered to deliver this," the younger man said. "I was told you skipped breakfast. You must be hungry." Geoffrey's tone was strangely buoyant.

The door remained open and he could see the two guards standing outside.

"I brought them some drink, too," Geoffrey said, motioning outside.

"You're in a generous mood today."

"Jesus said the first aspect of the Word is faith, the second is love, the third is good works, and from these come life."

He smiled. "That's right, my friend." He kept his tone lively for the two pairs of ears just a few feet away.

"Are you well?" Geoffrey asked.

"As well as can be expected." He accepted the tray and laid it on the desk.

"I have prayed for you, Seneschal."

"I daresay that I no longer possess that title. Surely, a new one was appointed by de Roquefort."

Geoffrey nodded. "His chief lieutenant."

"Woe be unto us—"

He saw one of the men outside the door collapse. A second later, the other man's body went limp and joined his partner's on the floor. Two goblets clattered across the flagstones.

"Took long enough," Geoffrey said.

"What did you do?"

"A sedative. The physician provided it to me. Tasteless, odorless, but fast. The healer is our friend. He wishes you Godspeed. Now we must go. The master made provisions, and it's my duty to see they're accomplished."

Geoffrey reached beneath his frock and produced two pistols. "The armory attendant is our friend, too. We may need these."

The seneschal was trained in firearms, all part of the basic education every brother received. He grabbed the weapon. "We're leaving the abbey?"

Geoffrey nodded. "It is required to accomplish our task."

"*Our* task."

"Yes, Seneschal. I've been training for this a long time."

He heard the eagerness and, though he was almost ten years older than Geoffrey, he suddenly felt inadequate. This supposed junior brother was far more than he appeared. "As I said yesterday, the master chose well in you."

Geoffrey smiled. "I think he did in both of us."

He found a knapsack and quickly stuffed a few toiletries, some personal items, and the two books he'd taken from the library inside. "I have no other clothes but for a cassock."

"We can buy some once we're gone."

"You have money?"

"The master was a thorough man."

Geoffrey crept to the doorway and checked both ways. "The brothers will all be in Sext. The way out should be clear."

Before following Geoffrey into the hall, the seneschal took one last look around his quarters. Some of the best times of his life had been spent here, and he was sad to leave those memories behind. But another part of his psyche urged him forward, to the unknown, outside, toward whatever truth the master so obviously knew.

TWENTY-SEVEN

MALONE STUDIED ROYCE CLARIDON. THE MAN WAS DRESSED in loose-fitting corduroy trousers smeared with what looked like turquoise paint. A colorful sports jersey covered the man's thin chest. He was probably in his late fifties, gangly as a praying mantis, with a comely face full of tight features. Dark eyes were sunk deep into his head, no longer bright with the power of intellect, but nonetheless piercing. His feet were bare and dirty, his fingernails unkempt, his graying hair and beard tangled. The attendant had warned them that Claridon was delusional but generally harmless, and almost everyone at the institution avoided him.

"Who be you?" Claridon asked in French, appraising them with a distant, perplexed gaze.

The sanatorium filled an enormous château that a placard out front announced had been owned by the French government since the Revolution. Wings jutted from the main building at odd angles. Many of the former salons were now converted into patient rooms. They stood in a solarium, surrounded by a broad embrasure of floor-to-ceiling windows that framed out the countryside. Gathering clouds veiled the midday sun. One of the attendants had said Claridon spent most of his days here.

"Are you from the commandery?" Claridon asked. "Did the master send you? I have much information to pass to him."

Malone decided to play along. "We are from the master. He sent us to speak with you."

"Ah, finally. I have been waiting so long." The words carried excitement.

Malone motioned and Stephanie backed off. This man obviously thought himself a Templar and women were not part of that brotherhood. "Tell me, brother, what have you to say. Tell me all."

Claridon fidgeted in his chair, then sprang to his feet, shifting his spare frame back and forth on bare feet. "Awful," he said. "So awful. We were surrounded on all quarters. Enemies as far as the eye could see. We were down to our last few arrows, the food spoiled from heat, the water gone. Many had succumbed to disease. None of us was going to live long."

"Sounds a challenge. What did you do?"

"The strangest thing we saw. A white banner was raised from beyond the walls. We all stared at one another—saying with our puzzled expressions the words each of us was thinking. *They want to talk.*"

Malone knew his medieval history. Parlays were common during the Crusades. Armies in a stalemate would many times work out terms whereby each could retreat and both claim victory.

"Did you gather?" Malone asked.

The older man nodded and held up four soiled fingers. "Each time we rode from the wall, out among their horde, they received us warmly and the discussions were not without progress. In the end, we came to terms."

"So tell me. What is your message the master needs to know?"

Claridon offered a look of annoyance. "You're an insolent one."

"What do you mean? I have much respect for you, brother. That's why I'm here. Brother Lars Nelle told me you were a man to be trusted."

The inquiry seemed to tax the older man's brain. Then recognition came to Claridon's face. "I recall him. A courageous warrior. Fought with much honor. Yes. Yes. I do recall him. Brother Lars Nelle. God rest his soul."

"Why do you say that?"

"You haven't heard?" There was incredulousness in the tone. "He died in battle."

"Where?"

Claridon shook his head. "That I don't know, only that he now dwells with the Lord. We said a mass for him and offered many prayers."

"Did you break bread with brother Nelle?"

"Many times."

"He ever speak of his quest?"

Claridon moved to his right, but kept his gaze on Malone. "Why do you ask that of me?"

The fidgety little man started to circle him, like a cat. He decided to up the ante in whatever game the man's loose mind envisioned. He grabbed Claridon by the jersey, lifting the wiry little man off the floor. Stephanie took a step forward, but he urged her back with a quick glance.

"The master is displeased," he said. "Most displeased."

"In what way?" Claridon's face was suffused with a deep blush of shame.

"With you."

"I've done nothing."

"You will not answer my question."

"What is it you wish?" More astonishment.

"Tell me of brother Nelle's quest."

Claridon shook his head. "I know nothing. The brother did not confide in me."

Fear crept into the eyes staring back at him, accented by utter confusion. He released his grip. Claridon shrank away toward the glass wall and snatched up a roll of paper towels and a spray bottle. He doused the panes and began cleaning glass that displayed not a speck of anything.

He turned to Stephanie. "We're wasting our time here."

"What tipped you off?"

"I had to try." He recalled the note sent to Ernst Scoville and decided to make one last attempt. He fished the paper from his pocket and approached Claridon. Beyond the glass, a few miles west, rose the pale gray walls of Villeneuve-les-Avignon.

"The cardinals live there," Claridon said, never stopping his cleaning. "Insolent princes, all of them."

Malone knew that cardinals once flocked to the hills outside Avignon's town walls and erected country retreats as a way to escape the town's congestion and the pope's constant eye. Those *livrées* were all gone, but the ancient city remained, still quiet, countrified and crumbling.

"We are the cardinals' protectors," Malone said, keeping up the pretense.

Claridon spat on the floor. "The pox to them all."

"Read this."

The little man took the paper and raked his gaze over the words. A look of astonishment filled the man's wide eyes. "I've stolen nothing from the Order. That I swear." The voice was rising. "This accusation is false. I would gladly pledge an oath to my God. I've stolen nothing."

The man was seeing on the page only what he wanted. Malone took back the paper.

"This is a waste of time, Cotton," Stephanie said.

Claridon drew close to him. "Who is this vixen? Why is she here?"

He nearly smiled. "She is brother Nelle's widow."

"I was not aware that the brother had been married."

He recalled some of what he'd read from the Templar book two nights before. "As you know, many brothers were once married. But she was an unfaithful one, so the bond was dissolved and she was banished to a convent."

Claridon shook his head. "She looks difficult. What is she doing *here*?"

"She seeks the truth about her husband."

Claridon faced Stephanie and pointed with one of his stubby fingers. "You are evil," the man shouted. "Brother Nelle sought penance with the brotherhood because of your sins. Shame on you."

Stephanie had the good sense to simply bow her head. "I seek nothing but forgiveness."

Claridon's face softened at her humility. "And you shall have mine, sister. Go in peace."

Malone motioned and they headed for the door. Claridon retreated to his chair.

"So sad," she said. "And frightening. Losing one's mind is terrifying. Lars often spoke of the malady and feared it."

"Don't we all." He was still holding the note found at Ernst Scoville's house. He looked at the writing again and read the last three lines:

In Avignon find Claridon. He can point the way. But prend garde l'Ingénieur

"I wonder why the sender thought Claridon could point the way to anywhere?" he asked. "We have zero to go on. This trail may be at a dead end."

"Not true."

The words were spoken in English and came from across the solarium.

Malone turned as Royce Claridon stood from the chair.

All confusion was gone from the man's bearded face. "I can provide that direction. And the advice given in that note should be heeded. You must beware the engineer. She, and others, are the reason I'm hiding here."

TWENTY-EIGHT

ABBEY DES FONTAINES

THE SENESCHAL FOLLOWED GEOFFREY THROUGH THE WARREN of vaulted corridors. He hoped Geoffrey's assessment was correct and that all of the brothers were in the chapel for noontime prayers.

So far they'd seen no one.

They made their way to the *palais* that housed the upper hall, administrative offices, and public rooms. When, in times past, the abbey had been sealed from outside contact, no one not of the Order was allowed beyond its ground-floor entrance hall. But when tourism blossomed in the twentieth century, as other abbeys opened their doors, so as not to arouse suspicions the Abbey des Fontaines followed suit, offering visits and informational sessions, many of which occurred in the *palais*.

They entered the expansive foyer. Windows filled with coarse greenish glass cast dull shafts of sunlight onto a checkered tile floor. A mammoth wooden crucifix dominated one wall, a tapestry another.

At the entrance to another passageway, a hundred feet

across the lofty expanse, stood Raymond de Roquefort, five brothers behind him, all armed with handguns.

"Leaving?" de Roquefort asked.

The seneschal froze, but Geoffrey raised his weapon and fired twice. The men on the other side dove for the floor as bullets pinged off the wall.

"That way," Geoffrey said, motioning left to another passageway.

Two shots screamed past them.

Geoffrey sent another bullet across the foyer and they assumed a defensive position just inside the corridor, near a parlor where merchants once brought their wares for display.

"All right," de Roquefort called out. "You have my attention. Is bloodshed necessary?"

"That's entirely up to you," the seneschal said.

"I thought your oath was precious. Is it not your duty to obey your master? I commanded you to stay in your quarters."

"Did you? I forgot that part."

"Interesting how one set of rules applies to you, and another governs the rest of us. Even so, can we not be reasonable?"

He wondered about the show of civility. "What do you propose?"

"I assumed you would attempt an escape. Sext seemed the best time, so I was waiting. You see, I know you well. Your ally, though, surprises me. There is courage and loyalty there. I would like you both to join my cause."

"And do what?"

"Help us reclaim our destiny, instead of hindering the effort."

Something was wrong. De Roquefort was posturing. Then it hit him. To buy time.

He whirled around.

An armed man rounded the corner, fifty feet away. Geoffrey saw him, too. The seneschal fired one shot into the lower part of the man's cassock. He heard the smack of metal tearing flesh and a shriek as the man dropped to the flagstones. May God forgive him. Rule forbid the harming of another Christian. But there was no choice. He had to escape this prison.

"Come on," he said.

Geoffrey took the lead and they bolted forward, leaping over the brother who writhed in pain.

They turned the corner and kept moving.

Footsteps could be heard behind them.

"I hope you know what you're doing," he said to Geoffrey.

They rounded another neck in the passageway. Geoffrey stopped at a partially open door and they slipped inside, closing it gently behind them. A second later men ran past, their footfalls fading.

"The route ends at the gymnasium. It won't take them long to see we're not there," he said.

They slipped back out, breathless with excitement, and headed toward the gym, but instead of heading right at an intersection they went left, toward the dining hall.

He was wondering why the gunshots had not aroused more brothers. But the music in the chapel was always loud, making it hard to hear anything beyond the walls. Still, if de Roquefort expected him to flee, it would be reasonable to assume that more brothers were waiting around the abbey.

The long tables and benches in the dining hall were empty. Smells of stewed tomatoes and okra wafted from the kitchen. In the speaker's niche carved three feet up one wall, a robed brother stood, rifle in hand.

The seneschal dove under a table, using his knapsack for cushion, and Geoffrey sought refuge beneath another table.

A bullet burrowed into the thick oak top.

Geoffrey scampered out and ticked off two shots, one of which found the attacker. The man in the alcove teetered, then dropped to the floor.

"You kill him?" the seneschal asked.

"I hope not. I think I got his shoulder."

"This is getting out of hand."

"Too late now."

They came to their feet. Men bolted from the kitchen, all dressed in food-stained aprons. The cooking staff. Not a threat.

"Back inside, now," the seneschal screamed, and none disobeyed.

"Seneschal," Geoffrey said, anticipation in his tone.

"Lead on."

They left the dining hall through another passageway. Voices were heard behind them, accompanied by the rapid sound of leather soles slapping stone. The shooting of two brothers would motivate even the meekest among their pursuers. The seneschal was angry that he'd fallen into the snare de Roquefort had laid for him. Any credibility he once possessed had vanished. No one would follow him any longer, and he cursed his foolishness.

They entered the dormitory wing. A door at the far end of the corridor was closed. Geoffrey ran ahead and tested the latch. Locked.

"Seems our options are limited," the seneschal said.

"Come," Geoffrey said.

They sprinted into the dormitory, a large oblong chamber with bunk beds standing perpendicular, in military style, beneath a row of lancet windows.

A shout came from the hallway. More voices. Excited. People were headed their way.

"There's no other way out of here," he said.

They stood halfway down the row of empty beds. Behind them was the entrance, about to be filled with adversaries. Ahead, lavatories.

"Into the bathrooms," he said. "Let's hope they move on."

Geoffrey ran to the far end where two doors led into separate facilities. "In here."

"No. Let's split up. You go into one. Hide in a stall and stand on a toilet. I'll take the other. If we're quiet, we might get lucky. Besides—" He hesitated, not liking the reality. "—it's our only play."

DE ROQUEFORT EXAMINED THE BULLET WOUND. THE MAN'S shoulder was bleeding, the brother in agony, but he was showing remarkable control, fighting hard not to go into shock. He'd stationed the shooter in the dining hall thinking the seneschal might eventually make his way there. And he'd been right. What he'd underestimated was his opponents' resolve. Brothers took an oath never to harm another brother. He'd thought the seneschal enough of an idealist that he'd stay true to that oath. Yet two men were now headed to the infirmary. He hoped neither would have to be taken to the hospital in Perpignan or Mont Louis. That might lead to questions. The abbey's healer was a qualified surgeon and possessed a well-equipped operating room, one that had been used many times in years past, but there were limits to its effectiveness.

"Take him to the physician and tell him to mend them here," he ordered a lieutenant. He checked his watch. Forty minutes before prayers at Sext ended.

Another brother approached. "The door at the far end, beyond the dorm entrance, is still locked, as you ordered."

He knew they'd not come back through the dining hall. The wounded brother had made no such report. Which left only one alternative. He reached for the man's revolver.

"Stay here. Allow no one to pass. I'll handle this myself."

THE SENESCHAL ENTERED THE BRIGHTLY LIT BATHROOM. ROWS of toilet stalls, urinals, and stainless-steel sinks encased by marble counters filled the space. He heard Geoffrey in the adjacent room, positioning himself in a stall. He stood rigid and tried to calm his nerves. He'd never been in a situation like this before. He snatched a few deep breaths then turned back and grasped the door handle, easing it open half an inch and peering through the crack.

The dormitory was still empty.

Perhaps the search had moved on. The abbey was lined like an ant mound with corridors. All they would need was a few precious minutes to make an escape. He cursed himself again for weakness. His years of careful thought and deliberate intent had all been wasted. He was now a fugitive with more than four hundred brothers about to be his enemy. *I simply respect the power of our adversaries.* That's what he'd told his master just a day ago. He shook his head. Some respect he'd shown. So far, he'd done nothing smart.

The door leading from the dormitory swung open and Raymond de Roquefort stepped inside.

His adversary locked the ponderous bolt on the door.

Any hope the seneschal may have possessed vanished.

The showdown was to be here and now.

De Roquefort held a revolver and studied the room, surely wondering where his prey might be. They'd not fooled him. But the seneschal had no intention of risking Geoffrey's life. He needed to draw his pursuer's attention. So he released his grip on the handle and allowed the door to close with a soft thud.

DE ROQUEFORT CAUGHT A FRACTION OF MOVEMENT AND HEARD the sound of a door, hydraulically hinged, gently nudge a metal frame. His gaze shot to the back of the dormitory and one of the lavatory doors.

He'd been right.

They were here.

Time to end this problem.

THE SENESCHAL SURVEYED THE BATHROOM. FLUORESCENT light illuminated everything in a daylight glow. A long wall mirror above the sink counter made the room appear even larger. The floor was tile, the toilets separated by marble partitions. Everything had been built with care and designed to last.

He ducked into the second stall and closed the swinging door. He hopped onto the toilet and folded himself over the partition until he could close and lock the doors to the first and third stalls. He then shrunk back, still standing on the toilet, and hoped de Roquefort took the bait.

He needed something to draw attention. So he freed the toilet paper from its holder.

Air rushed out as the bathroom's door swung open.

Soles swept across the floor.

He stood on the toilet, gun in hand, and told himself to breathe slow.

DE ROQUEFORT POINTED THE SHORT-BARRELED AUTOMATIC TOward the stalls. The seneschal was here. He knew it. But where? Did he dare take a moment to bend down and examine the gap at the bottom? Three doors were closed, three cocked open.

No.

He decided to fire.

THE SENESCHAL REASONED IT WOULD TAKE ONLY A MOment before de Roquefort started shooting, so he flipped the toilet paper holder beneath the partition, into the first stall.

Metal found tile with a clank.

DE ROQUEFORT FIRED A BURST INTO THE FIRST STALL AND kicked the door inward with his sandal. Marble dust clouded the air. He unleashed another round that obliterated the toilet and the plaster on the wall.

Water flooded out.

But the cubicle was empty.

IN THE INSTANT BEFORE DE ROQUEFORT REALIZED HIS MISTAKE, the seneschal fired over the stalls, sending two slugs into his enemy's chest. The gunshots reverberated off the walls, the sound waves racking his brain.

He watched as de Roquefort fell back across the marble counter and bucked as though punched in the chest. But he noticed no blood flowed from the wounds. The man seemed more dazed than anything. Then he spotted a blue-gray surface beneath tears in the white cassock.

A bulletproof vest.

He readjusted his aim and fired for the head.

DE ROQUEFORT SAW A SHOT COMING AND MUSTERED THE strength to roll off the counter just as the bullet left the barrel. His body skidded across the wet floor, through the puddled water, toward the outer door.

Bits of porcelain and stone crunched beneath him. The mirror exploded, shattering in a clangor then pulverizing onto the counter. The confines of the washroom were tight and his opponent was unexpectedly brave. So he retreated toward the door and slipped out just as a second shot careened off the wall behind him.

THE SENESCHAL JUMPED FROM THE TOILET AND BURST FROM the stall. He crept toward the door and prepared himself for an exit. De Roquefort would surely be waiting. But he wasn't going to shy away. Not now. He owed this fight to his master. The Gospels were clear. Jesus came not to bring peace, but a sword. And so did he.

He steeled himself, readied the gun, and yanked open the door.

The first thing he saw was Raymond de Roquefort. The next was Geoffrey, his gun firmly nestled to the master's neck, de Roquefort's weapon lying on the floor.

TWENTY-NINE

VILLENEUVE-LES-AVIGNON

MALONE STARED AT ROYCE CLARIDON AND SAID, "YOU'RE good."

"I've had lots of practice." Claridon looked at Stephanie. "You are Lars's wife?"

She nodded.

"He was a friend and a great man. So smart. Yet also naïve. He underestimated those who opposed him."

They were still alone in the solarium and Claridon seemed to notice Malone's interest in the door leading out.

"No one will disturb us. Not a soul wants to listen to my ramblings. I made a point to become quite a nuisance. They all look forward to my retreat here each day."

"How long have you been here?"

"Five years."

Malone was astonished. "Why?"

Claridon paced slowly among the bushy potted plants. Beyond the outer glass, black clouds girted the western horizon, the sun blazing through crevices like fire from the mouth of a furnace. "There are those who seek what Lars sought. Not openly, or with attention drawn to their quest, but they deal severely with those who stand in their way. So I came here and feigned illness. They feed you well, care for your needs, and, most important, ask no questions. I've not spoken rationally, other than to myself, in five years. And I can assure you, talking to yourself is not satisfying."

"Why are you talking to us?" Stephanie asked.

"You're Lars's widow. For him, I would do anything." Claridon pointed. "And that note. Sent by someone with knowledge. Perhaps even by those people I mentioned who don't allow anyone to stand in their way."

"Did Lars stand in their way?" Stephanie asked.

Claridon nodded. "Many wanted to know what he learned."

"What was your connection to him?" Stephanie asked.

"I had access to the book trade. He required many obscure materials."

Malone knew that secondhand-book stores were the haunts of both collectors and researchers.

"We eventually became friends and I started to share his passion. This region is my home. My family has been here since medieval times. Some of my ancestors were Cathars, burned to death by the Catholics. But then, Lars died. So sad. Others after him also perished. So I came here."

"What others?"

"A book dealer in Seville. A librarian in Marseille. A student in Rome. Not to mention Mark."

"Ernst Scoville is also dead," Stephanie said. "Run down by a car last week, just after I spoke to him."

Claridon quickly crossed himself. "Those who seek are indeed made to pay. Tell me, dear lady, do you know anything?"

"I have Lars's journal."

A look of concern swept across the man's face. "Then you are in mortal danger."

"How so?" Malone asked.

"This is terrible," Claridon said, the words coming fast. "So terrible. It's not right that you be involved. You lost your husband and your son—"

"What do you know of Mark?"

"It was just after his death that I came here."

"My son died in an avalanche."

"Not true. He was killed. Just like the others I mentioned."

Malone and Stephanie stood in silence, waiting for the odd little man to explain.

"Mark was following leads his father had discovered years before. He was not as passionate as Lars, and it took him years to decipher Lars's notes, but he finally made some sense of them. He traveled south into the mountains to look but never returned. Just like his father."

"My husband hung himself from a bridge."

"I know, dear woman. But I always wondered what truly happened."

Stephanie said nothing, but her silence signaled that at least part of her wondered, too.

"You said you came here to escape *them*. Who's *them*?" Malone asked. "The Knights Templar?"

Claridon nodded. "I came face-to-face with them on two occasions. Not pleasant."

Malone decided to let that notion simmer a moment. He was still holding the note that had been sent to Ernst Scoville in Rennes-le-Château. He motioned with the paper. "How can you lead the way? Where are we to go? And who is this engineer we're supposed to be watching out for?"

"She, too, seeks what Lars coveted. Her name is Cassiopeia Vitt."

"She good with a rifle?"

"She has many talents. Shooting, I'm sure, is one. She lives at Givors, an ancient citadel site. She's a woman of color, a Muslim, who possesses great wealth. She labors in the forest to rebuild a castle using only thirteenth-century techniques. Her château stands nearby and she personally oversees the rebuilding project, calling herself *l'Ingénieur*. The engineer. Have you met her?"

"I think she saved my hide in Copenhagen. Which makes me wonder why someone would warn us to beware of her."

"Her motives are suspect. She seeks what Lars sought, but for different reasons."

"And what is it she seeks?" Malone asked, tired of riddles.

"What the brothers of the Temple of Solomon left behind long ago. Their Great Devise. What the priest Saunière discovered. What the brothers have been searching for all these centuries."

Malone didn't believe a word of it, but motioned again with the paper. "So point us in the right direction."

"It's not that the simple. The trail has been made difficult."

"Do you even know where to start?"

"If you have Lars's notebook, you have more knowledge than I possess. He often spoke of the journal, but I was never allowed to see it."

"We also have a copy of *Pierres Gravées du Languedoc*," Stephanie said.

Claridon gasped. "I never believed that book existed."

She reached into her bag and showed him the volume. "It's real."

"Might I see the gravestone?"

She opened to the page and showed him the drawing. Claridon studied it with interest. The older man smiled. "Lars would have been pleased. The drawing is a good one."

"Care to explain?" Malone asked.

"The abbé Bigou learned a secret from Marie d'Hautpoul de Blanchefort, just before she died. When he fled France in 1793, Bigou realized that he would never return, so he hid what he knew in the church at Rennes-le-Château. That information was later found by Saunière, in 1891, within a glass vial."

"We know all that," Malone said. "What we don't know is Bigou's secret."

"Ah, but you do," Claridon said. "Let me see Lars's notebook."

Stephanie handed him the journal. He anxiously shuffled through it and showed them a page.

```
Y E N S Z N I M G L C Y • R A T E H O X
O • E O T + T E C T N G A + D E Z B O F
V O U P H R P A + D Y S T L R D A • X T
L P O C X F E I S R A V H G C K L N H N
R D M R M A A N R J , S • M B D Q A D P
R I E U Z O O T U O J I F S O E A L B N
T N A T , G R E Y I O E , T R U X , W H
K X V E V L A L P E N + L O Z J K J D G
N U E + N G E K O • I X A Z V R + S I Z
S N S I C E T B + X G A C S E D X V U A
Y V L K B • , N B W V K T P I B • J T Y
O U P E O M S U L Z R V , J R S B + C E
P A T S X E • F X , H N M Z H • Y T B C
```

"This cryptogram was supposedly inside the glass vial."

"How do you know?" Malone asked.

"To know that, you must understand Saunière."

"We're all ears."

"When Saunière was alive, not a word was ever written about the money he spent on the church or the other buildings. No one outside of Rennes even knew any of that existed. When he died in 1917, he was totally forgotten. His papers and belongings were either stolen or destroyed. In

1947 his mistress sold the entire estate to a man named Noël Corbu. The mistress died six years later. The so-called tale of Saunière, about his great treasure find, first appeared in print in 1956. A local newspaper, *La Dépêche du Midi,* published three installments that supposedly told the true story. But the source for that material was Corbu."

"I know this," Stephanie said. "He embellished everything, adding to the story, changing it all around. Afterward, more press accounts came and the story gradually became even more fantastic."

Claridon nodded. "Fiction completely took over fact."

"You talking about the parchments?" Malone asked.

"An excellent example. Saunière never found parchments in the altar pillar. Never. Corbu, and the others, added that detail. Not one person has ever seen those parchments, yet their texts have been printed in countless books, each one supposedly hiding some sort of coded message. It's nonsense, all of it, and Lars knew that."

"But Lars published the texts of the parchments in his books," Malone said.

"He and I spoke of that. All he would say is, *People love a mystery.* But I know it bothered him to do it."

Malone was confused. "So is Saunière's story a lie?"

Claridon nodded. "The modern rendition is mainly false. Most of the books written also link Saunière to the paintings of Nicolas Poussin, particularly *The Shepherds of Arcadia.* Supposedly, Saunière took the two parchments he found to Paris in 1893 for deciphering and, while there, purchased a copy of that painting, and two more, at the Louvre. They are reported to contain hidden messages. The problem with that is the Louvre did not sell copies of paintings at that time, and there is no record that *The Shepherds of Arcadia* was even stored at the Louvre in 1893. But the men who promulgated that fiction worried little about errors. They just assumed no one would check the facts, and for a while they were right."

Malone motioned to the cryptogram. "Where did Lars find this?"

"Corbu penned a manuscript all about Saunière."

Some of the words from the eight pages sent to Ernst Scoville swept through his mind. What Lars had written about the mistress. *At one point she did reveal to Nöel Corbu one of Saunière's hiding places. Corbu wrote of this in his manuscript I managed to find.*

"While Corbu spent a great deal of time telling reporters the fiction of Rennes, in his manuscript he did a credible job of detailing the true story, as he learned it from the mistress."

More of what Lars had written ran through Malone's mind. *What Corbu found, if anything, is never revealed by him. But the wealth of information contained within his manuscript makes one wonder where he could have learned all that he wrote about.*

"Corbu, of course, let no one see the manuscript, since the truth was not nearly as captivating as the fiction. He died in the late sixties from a car crash and his manuscript disappeared. But Lars found it."

Malone studied the rows of letters and symbols on the cryptogram. "So what is this? Some type of code?"

"One quite common for the eighteenth and nineteenth centuries. Random letters and symbols, arranged in a grid. Somewhere in all that chaos is a message. Basic, simple, and, for its time, quite difficult to decipher. Still so even today, without the key."

"What do you mean?"

"Some numeric sequence is needed to find the right letters to assemble the message. Sometimes, to confuse the matter further, the starting point on the grid was random, too."

"Did Lars ever decipher it?" Stephanie asked.

Claridon shook his head. "He was unable. And it frustrated him. Then, in the weeks before he died, he thought he came across a new clue."

Malone's patience was wearing thin. "I assume he didn't tell you what that was."

"No, monsieur. That was his way."

"So where do we go from here? Point the way, like you're supposed to."

"Return here at five PM, on the road just beyond the main building and wait. I'll come to you."

"How can you leave?"

"No one here will be sad to see me go."

Malone and Stephanie shared a glance. She was surely debating, as he was, if following Claridon's directions would be smart. So far this whole endeavor had been littered with either dangerous or paranoid personalities, not to mention wild speculation. But something was going on, and if he wanted to learn more he was going to have to play by the rules the odd man standing across from him was setting.

Still, he wanted to know, "Where are we going?"

Claridon turned to the window and pointed eastward. In the far distance, miles away, on a hilltop overlooking Avignon, stood a palace stronghold with an Oriental appearance, like something from Arabia. Its golden luminosity stood out against the eastern sky with a fugitive brightness and cast the appearance of several buildings piled onto one another, each rising from the bedrock, standing in clear defiance. Just as its occupants had done for nearly a hundred years, when seven French popes ruled Christendom from within the fortress walls.

"To the *palais des popes*," Claridon said.

The palace of the popes.

THIRTY

ABBEY DES FONTAINES

THE SENESCHAL STARED INTO GEOFFREY'S EYES AND SAW HA-
tred. He'd never seen that emotion there before.

"I've told our new master," Geoffrey said, nudging the
gun deeper into de Roquefort's throat, "to stand still or I will
shoot him."

The seneschal stepped close and poked a finger beneath
the white mantle, into the protective vest. "If we'd not
started the gunfire, you would have, right? The idea was for
us to be killed while escaping. That way, your problem is
solved. I'm eliminated and you're the Order's savior."

De Roquefort said nothing.

"That's why you came here alone. To finish the job yourself. I saw you lock the dormitory door. You wanted no witnesses."

"We must go," Geoffrey said.

He realized the danger that endeavor would entail, but
doubted if any of the brothers would risk the master's life.
"Where are we going?"

"I'll show you."

Keeping the gun cocked at de Roquefort's neck, Geoffrey
led his hostage across the dormitory. The seneschal kept his

own gun ready and, at the door, released the latch. In the hall stood five armed men. At the sight of their leader in peril, they raised their guns, ready to fire.

"Lower your aim," de Roquefort ordered.

The guns stayed pointed.

"I command you to lower your weapons. I want no more bloodshed."

The gallant gesture stimulated the desired effect.

"Stand away," Geoffrey said.

The brothers took a few steps backward.

Geoffrey motioned with the gun and he and de Roquefort stepped out into the hall. The seneschal followed. Bells rang in the distance, signaling one PM. Sext prayers would be ending shortly, and the corridors would once again be filled with robed men.

"We need to move quickly," the seneschal made clear.

With his hostage, Geoffrey led the way down the passageway. The seneschal followed, creeping backward, keeping his attention trained on the five brothers.

"Stay there," the seneschal made clear to them.

"Do as he says," de Roquefort called out, as they turned the corner.

DE ROQUEFORT WAS CURIOUS. HOW DID THEY EXPECT TO FLEE the abbey? What had Geoffrey said? *I'll show you.* He decided the only way to discover anything was to go with them, which was why he'd ordered his men to stand down.

The seneschal had twice shot him. If he'd not been quick, a third bullet would have found his skull. The stakes had clearly been raised. His captors were on a mission, something he believed involved his predecessor and a subject that he desperately needed to know more about. The Denmark excursion had been less than productive. So far nothing had been learned in Rennes-le-Château. And though he'd managed to discredit the former master in death, the old man might have reserved the last laugh.

He also did not like the fact that two men had been wounded. Not the best way to start off his tenure. Brothers strived for order. Chaos was seen as weakness. The last time violence had invaded the abbey's walls was when angry mobs tried to gain entrance during the French Revolution—but after several died in the attempt, they'd retreated. The abbey was a place of tranquility and refuge. Violence was taught—and sometimes used—but tempered with discipline. The seneschal had demonstrated a total lack of discipline. Stragglers who may have harbored some fleeting loyalty to him would now be won over by his grievous violations to Rule.

But still, where were these two headed?

They continued down the hallways, passing workshops, the library, more empty corridors. He could hear footfalls behind them, the five brothers following, ready to act when the opportunity arose. But there'd be hell to pay if any of them interfered until he said so.

They stopped before a doorway with carved capitals and a simple iron handle.

The master's quarters.

His chambers.

"In there," Geoffrey said.

"Why?" the seneschal asked. "We'll be trapped."

"Please, go inside."

The seneschal pushed open the door, then engaged the latch after they entered.

De Roquefort was amazed.

And curious.

THE SENESCHAL WAS CONCERNED. THEY WERE NOW IMPRIS-oned within the master's chamber, the only exit a solitary bull's-eye window that opened to nothing but air. Drops of sweat pebbled his forehead and he swiped the salty moisture from his eyes.

"Sit," Geoffrey ordered de Roquefort, and the man took a seat at the desk.

The seneschal surveyed the room. "I see you've already changed things."

A few more upholstered chairs hugged the walls. A table now stood where there had been nothing before. The bed coverings were different, as were items on the tables and desk.

"This is my home now," de Roquefort said.

He noticed the single sheet of paper on the desk, penned in his mentor's hand. The successor's message, left as required by Rule. He lifted the typewritten page and read.

Do you think that what you judge to be imperishable will not perish? You base your hope upon the world, and your god is this life. You do not realize that you will be destroyed. You live in darkness and death, drunk with fire, and full of bitterness. Your mind is deranged because of the smoldering fire within you and you are delighted by the poisoning and beating of your enemies. Darkness has risen over you like the light, for you have exchanged your freedom for slavery. You will fail, that is clear.

"Your master thought passages from the Gospel of Thomas relevant," de Roquefort said. "And he apparently believed that I, not you, would wear the white mantle once he was gone. Surely those words were not meant for his chosen one."

No, they weren't. He wondered why his mentor had so little faith in him, especially when, in the hours before he died, he'd encouraged him to seek high office.

"You should listen to him," he made clear.

"His is the advice of a weak soul."

Pounding came from the door. "Master? Are you there?" Unless the brothers were prepared to blast their way inside, there existed little danger of the heavy slabs being forced.

De Roquefort stared up at him.

"Answer," the seneschal said.

"I'm fine. Stand down."

Geoffrey moved toward the window and stared out at the waterfall across the gorge.

De Roquefort placed one knee over the other and leaned back in the chair. "What do you hope to accomplish? This is foolishness."

"Shut up." But the seneschal was wondering the same thing.

"The master left more words," Geoffrey said from across the room.

He and de Roquefort turned as Geoffrey reached into his cassock and produced an envelope. "This is his true final message."

"Give that to me," de Roquefort demanded, rising from the chair.

Geoffrey leveled his gun. "Sit."

De Roquefort stayed on his feet. Geoffrey cocked the weapon and aimed for the legs. "The vest will do you no good."

"You would kill me?"

"I'll cripple you."

De Roquefort sat. "You have a brave compatriot," he said to the seneschal.

"He's a brother of the Temple."

"A shame he will never achieve the oath."

If the words were designed to evoke a response in Geoffrey, they failed.

"You're going nowhere," de Roquefort told them.

The seneschal watched his ally. Geoffrey was again staring out the window, as if waiting for something.

"I'll enjoy seeing you both punished," de Roquefort said.

"I told you to shut up," the seneschal said.

"Your master thought himself clever. I know he wasn't."

He could tell de Roquefort had something more to say. "Okay, I'll bite. What is it?"

"The Great Devise. It's what consumed him and all of the masters. Each wanted to find it, but none succeeded. Your master spent a lot of time researching the subject, and your young friend over there helped him."

The seneschal shot a glance at Geoffrey, but his partner did not turn from the window. He said to de Roquefort, "I thought you were close to finding it. That's what you told the conclave."

"I am."

The seneschal did not believe him.

"Your young friend over there and the late master were quite a team. I've learned that recently they scoured our records with a newfound relish—one that piqued my interest."

Geoffrey turned and stomped across the bedchamber, stuffing the envelope back into his cassock. "You'll learn nothing." The voice approached a shout. "What there is to find is not for you."

"Really?" de Roquefort asked. "And what is there to find?"

"There will be no triumph for the likes of you. The master was right. You are drunk with fire and full of bitterness."

De Roquefort appraised Geoffrey with a stiff countenance. "You and the master learned something, didn't you? I know you sent two parcels in the mail, and I even know to whom. I've tended to one of the receivers and will shortly tend to the other. Soon I'll know all that you and he knew."

Geoffrey's right arm swung out and the gun he held slammed into de Roquefort's temple. The master teetered, stunned, then his eyes rolled skyward and he collapsed to the floor.

"Was that necessary?" the seneschal asked.

"He should be glad that I didn't shoot him. But the master made me promise I wouldn't harm the fool."

"You and I need to have a serious talk."

"First, we have to leave."

"I don't think the brothers out in the hall are going to allow that."

"They're not our problem."

He could sense something. "You know the way out of here?"

Geoffrey smiled. "The master was quite clear."

PART
THREE

THIRTY-ONE

DE ROQUEFORT OPENED HIS EYES. THE SIDE OF HIS HEAD pounded and he swore that brother Geoffrey would pay for his assault. He pushed himself up from the floor and tried to clear the fog. He heard frantic cries from outside the door. He dabbed the side of his head with his sleeve and the cassock came away stained with blood. He stepped into the bathroom and doused a rag with water, cleaning the wound.

He steeled himself. He must appear in charge. He slowly walked across the bedchamber and opened the door.

"Master, are you all right?" his new marshal asked.

"Come inside," he said.

The four other brothers waited in the hall. They knew better than to step into the master's chamber without permission.

"Close the door."

His lieutenant complied.

"I was struck unconscious. How long have they been gone?"

"It's been quiet in here for twenty minutes. That's what raised our fears."

"What do you mean?"

A puzzled look came to the marshal's face. "Silence. Nothing."

"Where did the seneschal and brother Geoffrey go?"

"Master, they were in here, with you. We were outside."

"Look around. They're gone. When did they leave?"

More bewilderment. "They didn't come our way."

"You're telling me those two did not walk out that door?"

"We would have shot them if they had, as you ordered."

His head started to hurt again. He lifted the wet rag to his scalp and massaged the throbbing knot. He'd wondered why Geoffrey had come straight here.

"There's news from Rennes-le-Château," the marshal said.

That revelation piqued his interest.

"Our two brothers made their presence known and Malone, as you predicted, eluded them on the highway."

He'd correctly deduced that the best way to pursue Stephanie Nelle and Cotton Malone was to let them think they were free of pursuit.

"And the shooter in the churchyard last night?"

"The person fled on a motorcycle. Our men watched as Malone gave chase. That incident, and the attack on our brothers in Copenhagen, are clearly related."

He agreed. "Any idea who?"

"Not yet."

He didn't want to hear that. "What of today? Where did Malone and Nelle go?"

"The electronic surveillance we affixed to Malone's car worked perfectly. They drove straight to Avignon. They've just left the sanatorium where Royce Claridon is a patient."

He was well acquainted with Claridon and did not for one moment believe Claridon was mentally ill, which was why he'd cultivated a source within the sanatorium. A month ago, when the master dispatched Geoffrey to Avignon to mail the package to Stephanie Nelle, he'd thought contact might have then been made. But Geoffrey paid no visit to the asylum. He suspected that the second parcel, the one sent to Ernst Scoville in Rennes, the one he knew little about, was what led Stephanie Nelle and Malone to Claridon. One thing was certain. Claridon and Lars Nelle had worked side by side, and when the son dabbled in the quest after Lars Nelle's death, Claridon had assisted him, too. The master had clearly known all that. And now Lars Nelle's widow had gone straight to Claridon.

Time to deal with that problem.

"I'll travel to Avignon within the half hour. Prepare a contingent of four brothers. Maintain the electronic surveillance and tell our people not to be tagged. That equipment has a long range, use it to our advantage." But there was still another matter and he stared around the room. "Leave me, now."

The marshal bowed, then retreated from the chamber.

He stood, his head still woozy, and surveyed the elongated chamber. Two of the walls were stone, the remaining two maple paneling framed out in symmetrical panels. A decorative armoire dominated one wall, a dresser, another chest, and a table and chairs the others. But his gaze stopped on the fireplace. It seemed the most logical location. He knew that in ancient times no room possessed only one way in and out. This particular chamber had housed masters since the sixteenth century, and if he recalled correctly, the fireplace was a seventeenth-century addition, replacing an older stone hearth. Rarely was it used now that central heating was employed throughout the abbey.

He approached the mantel and studied the woodwork, then carefully examined the hearth, noticing faint white lines stretching perpendicular toward the wall.

He bent down and gazed into the darkened hearth. With his curled hand, he probed up inside the flue.

And found it.

A glass knob.

He tried to turn it, but nothing moved. He pushed up, then down. Still nothing. So he pulled, and the knob came free. Not far, maybe half an inch, and he heard a mechanical snap. He released his grip and felt a slipperiness on his fingers. Oil. Somebody had been prepared.

He stared into the fireplace.

A crack ran the height of the rear wall. He pushed, and the stone panel swung inward. The opening was large enough to enter, so he crawled forward. Beyond the portal was a passageway the height of a man.

He stood.

The narrow corridor stretched only a few feet to a stone staircase that wound down in a tight spiral. No telling where that led. No doubt there were other entrances and exits scattered throughout the abbey. He'd been marshal for twenty-two years and never had he known of any secret routes.

The master knew, though, which was how Geoffrey knew.

He pounded his fist onto the stone and allowed his anger to work itself out. He must find the Great Devise. His entire ability to govern rested on its discovery. The master had possessed Lars Nelle's journal, as de Roquefort had known for many years, but there'd been no way to obtain it. He'd thought that with the old man gone his chance would come, but the master had anticipated his move and sent the manuscript away. Now Lars Nelle's widow and a former employee—a trained government agent—were connecting themselves with Royce Claridon. Nothing good would come of that collaboration.

He calmed his nerves.

For years he'd labored in the master's shadow. Now he was master. And he was not going to allow a ghost to dictate his path.

He sucked a few deep breaths of the dank air and thought

back to the Beginning. AD 1118. The Holy Land had finally been wrestled from the Saracens and Christian kingdoms had been established, but a great danger still existed. So nine knights banded together and promised to the new Christian king of Jerusalem that the route to and from the Holy Land would be safe for pilgrims. But how could nine middle-aged men, pledged to poverty, protect the long route from Jaffa to Jerusalem, especially when hundreds of bandits lined the way? Even more puzzling, for the first ten years of its existence no new knights were added, and the Order's Chronicles recorded nothing of the brothers helping any pilgrims. Instead, those original nine occupied themselves with a greater task. Their headquarters was beneath the old temple, in an area that had once served as King Solomon's stables, a chamber of endless arches and vaults, so large that it once housed two thousand animals. There they'd discovered subterranean passages hewn from rock centuries before, many of which contained scriptural scrolls, treatises, writings on art and science, and much about Judaic/Egyptian heritage.

And the most important find of all.

The excavations consumed those nine knights' entire attention. Then, in 1127, they loaded boats with their precious cache and sailed for France. What they found brought them fame, wealth, and powerful allegiances. Many wanted to be a part of their movement and, in 1128, a mere ten years after being founded, the Templars were granted by the pope a legal autonomy unmatched in the Western world.

And all because of what they knew.

Yet they were careful with that knowledge. Only those who rose to the highest level were privileged to know. Centuries ago, the master's duty was to pass that knowledge along before he died. But that was before the Purge. After, masters searched, all to no avail.

He pounded his fist again into the stone.

Templars had first forged their destiny in forgotten caverns with the determination of zealots. He would do the same. The Great Devise was out there. He was close. He knew it.

And the answers were in Avignon.

THIRTY-TWO

AVIGNON
5:00 PM

MALONE STOPPED THE PEUGEOT. ROYCE CLARIDON WAS WAIT-ing on the roadside, south of the sanatorium, exactly where he'd said. The man's scruffy beard was gone, as were the stained clothes and jersey. The face was clean-shaven, the nails trimmed, and Claridon was wearing a pair of jeans and a crew-necked shirt. His long hair was slicked back and tied in a ponytail, and there was vigor to his step.

"Feels good to get that beard off," he said, climbing into the rear seat. "To pretend to be a Templar, I needed to look like one. You know they never bathed. Rule forbade it. No naked-ness among the brothers and all that stuff. What a smelly lot they must have been."

Malone shifted the car into first and motored down the highway. Storm clouds filled the sky. Apparently, the weather from Rennes-le-Chateâu was finally making its way eastward. In the distance lightning forked across the rising plumes, fol-lowed by growls of thunder. No rain was falling yet, but soon.

He exchanged glances with Stephanie and she understood that the man in the rear seat needed interrogating.

She turned back. "Mr. Claridon—"

"You must call me Royce, madame."

"All right. Royce, could you tell us more of what Lars was thinking? It's important we understand."

"You don't know?"

"Lars and I were not close in the years before he died. He didn't confide much in me. But I've recently read his books and the journal."

"Might I ask, then, why are you here? He's been gone a long time."

"Let's just say I'd like to think Lars would have wanted his work finished."

"On that you are right, madame. Your husband was a brilliant scholar. His theories were well founded and I believe he would have been successful. If he'd lived."

"Tell me of those theories."

"He was following the abbé Saunière's path. That priest was clever. On the one hand, he wanted no one to know what he knew. On the other, he left many clues." Claridon shook his head. "It's said he told his mistress everything, but she died without ever saying a word. Before his death, Lars thought he'd finally made progress. Do you know the full tale, madame? The real truth?"

"I'm afraid my knowledge is limited to what Lars wrote in his books. But there were some interesting references in his journal that he never published."

"Might I see those pages?"

She thumbed through the notebook, then handed the book back to Claridon. Malone watched in the rearview mirror as the man read with interest.

"Such wonders," Claridon said.

"Could you enlighten us?" Stephanie asked.

"Of course, madame. As I said this afternoon, the fiction

Noël Corbu and others manufactured about Saunière was mysterious and exciting. But to me, and to Lars, the truth was even better."

Saunière surveyed the church's new altar, pleased with the renovations. The marble monstrosity was gone, the old top now rubble in the churchyard, the Visigoth pillars enlisted for other uses. The new altar was a thing of simple beauty. Three months ago, in June, he'd orga- nized an elaborate first communion service. Men from the village had carried a statue of the Virgin in a solemn procession throughout Rennes, ending back at the church where the sculpture was placed atop one of the discarded pillars in the churchyard. To commemorate the event, he'd carved PENITENCE, PENITENCE on the pillar's face to remind the parishioners of humility, and MISSION 1891 to memorialize the year of their collective accomplishment.

The church roof had finally been sealed, the exterior walls shored. The old pulpit was gone and another one was under construction. Soon a checkerboard tile floor would be installed, then new pews. But prior to that, the floor's substructure required mending. Water seeping from the roof had eroded many of the base stones. Patching had worked in places, but several required replacement.

Outside loomed a wet, windy September morning, so he'd managed to secure the help of half a dozen townspeople. Their job was to bust away several of the damaged slabs and install new ones before the tilers arrived in two weeks. Men were now working in three separate locations throughout the nave. Saunière himself was tending to a warped stone before the altar steps, which had always wobbled.

He remained puzzled by the glass vial found earlier in the year. When he'd melted the wax seal and removed the

*rolled paper, he found not a message but thirteen rows of
letters and symbols. When he showed them to Abbé Gélis,
a priest in a neighboring village, he was told that the
arrangement was a cryptogram, and somewhere among
the seemingly meaningless letters lay a message. All one
needed was the mathematical key to its deciphering, but
after many months of trying he was no closer to solving
it. He wanted to know both its meaning and why it had
been secreted away. Obviously, its message was of great
importance. But patience would be needed. That was
what he told himself each night after he again failed to
find the answer, and, if nothing else, he was indeed
patient.*

*He gripped a hammer with a short handle and decided
to see if the thick floor stone could be cracked. The
smaller the pieces, the easier their removal. He dropped
to his knees and slammed three blows into one end of the
yard-long slab. Cracks immediately spread down its
length. More blows lengthened them into crevices.*

*He tossed the hammer aside and used an iron bar to
pry the smaller pieces loose. He then wedged the bar
underneath a long, narrow fragment and angled the thick
chunk out of its cavity. With his foot, he slid it aside.*

Then he noticed something.

*He laid down the iron bar and brought the oil lamp
close to the exposed subfloor. He reached down and
gently swiped away debris and saw that he was staring at
a hinge. He bent close and swiped away more dust and
debris, exposing more corroded iron, his fingertips
stained with rust.*

The shape became clear.

A door.

Leading down.

But to where?

He glanced around. The other men were hard at work,

talking among themselves. He set the lamp aside and calmly replaced the pieces he'd just removed back into the cavity.

"The good priest did not want anyone to know what he'd discovered," Claridon said. "First the glass vial, now a doorway. This church of his was full of wonder."

"A doorway to what?" Stephanie wanted to know.

"That's the interesting part. Lars never told me everything. But after reading his notebook, I now understand."

Saunière cleared the last of the stone from the iron door in the floor. The church doors were locked, the sun having set hours ago. All day he'd thought about what lay beneath the door, but he'd not said a word to any of the workers, merely thanking them for their labors and explaining that he intended to take a few days' rest, so they wouldn't be needed back until next week. He'd not even told his precious mistress what he'd found, only mentioning after dinner that he wanted to inspect the church before going to bed. Rain now pelted the roof.

In the light from the oil lamp he calculated that the iron door was just over a yard long and half a yard wide. It lay flush to the floor with no lock. Thankfully its frame was stone, but he worried about the hinges, which was why he'd brought a container of lamp oil. Not the best lubricant, but it was all he could find on short notice.

He doused the hinges with oil and hoped time's grip would loosen. He then wedged the tip of an iron bar beneath one edge of the door and pried upward.

No movement.

He pried harder.

The hinges started to give.

He wiggled the bar, working the rusted metal, then

*applied more oil. After several efforts the hinges
screamed and the door pivoted open and froze in place,
pointing toward the ceiling.*

He shone the lantern into the dank opening.

*Narrow steps led down five yards to a rough stone
floor.*

*A surge of excitement swept through him. He'd heard
tales from other priests about things they'd found. Most of
it stemmed from the Revolution when churchmen hid
relics, icons, and decorations from republican looters.
Many of the Languedoc's churches fell victim. But the one
in Rennes-le-Chateâu had been in such a state of decay,
there was simply nothing to loot.*

Perhaps they'd all been wrong.

*He tested the top step and determined that they'd been
hewn from the church's rock foundation. Lamp in hand,
he crept down, staring ahead into a rectangular space, it,
too, chipped from rock. An archway divided the room in
half. Then he saw the bones. The outer walls were pocked
with ovenlike cavities, each one containing a skeletal
occupant, along with the remnants of clothing, shoes,
swords, and burial shrouds.*

*He shone the light near a few of the tombs and saw that
each was identified with a chiseled name. All were
d'Hautpouls. Dates ranged from the sixteenth to the eighteenth centuries. He counted. Twenty-three filled the
crypt. He knew who they were. The lords of Rennes.*

*Beyond the center arch, a trunk lying beside an iron
pot caught his eye.*

*He stepped over, lamp in hand, and was startled when
something glistened back. He thought at first his eyes
were deceiving him, but quickly realized the vision was
real.*

He bent down.

The iron kettle was filled with coins. He lifted one out and saw that they were French gold pieces, many bearing a date: 1768. He knew little of their value but reasoned that it was considerable. Hard to tell how many filled the cauldron, but when he tested its weight he was unable to move the container one millimeter.

He reached for the trunk and saw that its hasp was not locked. He pushed open the lid and saw that the inside was filled, on one side, with leather-bound journals and, on the other, with something wrapped in an oilskin cloth. Carefully, he poked with his finger and determined that whatever lay inside was many, small, and hard. He laid down the lamp and peeled back the top fold.

The light again caught a sparkle.

Diamond.

He laid back the rest of the oilskin and the breath left him. Lying within the trunk was a cache of jewelry.

Without question, republican looters of a hundred years ago made a mistake when they bypassed the ramshackle church at Rennes-le-Chateâu. Or maybe the person or persons who selected this as their hiding spot simply chose wisely.

"The crypt existed," Claridon said. "In the notebook you have there, I just read that Lars found a parish register for the years 1694 to 1726 that speaks of the crypt, but the register does not mention its entrance. Saunière noted in his personal diary that he discovered a tomb. He then wrote in another entry, *The year 1891 carries to the highest the fruit of that of which one speaks.* Lars always thought that entry important."

Malone eased the car to the side of the road and turned back to face Claridon. "So that gold and those jewels were Saunière's source of income. That's what he used to finance the church remodeling?"

Claridon laughed. "At first. But, monsieur, there is even more to the story."

Saunière stood.

Never had he seen so much wealth in one place. What fortune had come his way. But he needed to salvage it without arousing suspicions. To do that, he would need time. And no one could be allowed to discover the crypt.

He bent down, retrieved the lamp, and decided that he might as well start tonight. He could remove the gold and jewels, hiding both in the presbytery. How to convert them to useful currency could be decided later. He retreated toward the staircase, taking another look around as he walked.

One of the tombs caught his attention.

He approached and saw that the niche contained a woman. Her burial dress lay flat, only bones and a skull remained. He held the lamp close and read the inscription beneath:

MARIE D'HAUTPOUL DE BLANCHEFORT

He was familiar with the countess. She was the last of the d'Hautpoul heirs. When she died in 1781, control of both the village and surrounding lands slipped away from her family. The Revolution, which came only a dozen years later, forever eliminated all aristocratic ownership.

But there was a problem.

He quickly climbed back to ground level. Outside, he locked the church doors and, through a blinding rain, hustled around the building to the parish close and worked his way through the graves where the tombstones seemed to swim in the living blackness.

He stopped at the one he sought and bent down.

Shining the lamp, he read the inscription.

"Marie d'Hautpoul de Blanchefort was buried outside, too," Claridon said.

"Two graves for the same woman?" Stephanie asked.

"Apparently. But the body was in the crypt."

Malone remembered what Stephanie had said yesterday about Saunière and his mistress molesting the graves in the churchyard, then chiseling away the inscription on the countess's headstone. "So Saunière dug up the grave in the churchyard."

"That's what Lars believed."

"And it was empty?"

"Again, we'll never know, but Lars felt that to be the case. And history would seem to support his conclusion. A woman of the countess's stature would never have been buried. She would have been laid in a crypt, which is indeed where the body was found. The grave outside was something altogether different."

"The tombstone was a message," Stephanie said. "We know that. That's why Eugène Stüblein's book is so critical."

"But unless you know the story of the crypt, the grave in the cemetery would generate no interest. Just another memorial, along with all the others. The abbé Bigou was smart. He hid his message in plain sight."

"And Saunière discovered it?" Malone asked.

"Lars believed so."

Malone turned back to the wheel and motored the car onto the road. They headed down the last stretch of highway, then turned west and crossed the swift-moving Rhône. Ahead rose Avignon's fortified walls, the papal palace looming high above. Malone turned off the busy boulevard into the old city, passing the market square containing the book fair they'd visited earlier. He wound a path back toward the palace and parked in the same underground garage.

"I have a stupid question," Malone said. "Why doesn't

somebody just dig beneath the church at Rennes, or use ground radar to verify the crypt?"

"The local authorities will not allow it. Think about that, monsieur. If nothing were there, what would happen to the mystique? Rennes lives off Saunière's legend. The whole Languedoc benefits. The last thing anyone wants is proof of anything. They profit far too well from myth."

Malone reached under the seat and retrieved the gun he'd taken from his pursuer last night. He checked the magazine. Three rounds left.

"Is that needed?" Claridon asked.

"I feel a whole lot better with it." He opened his door and stepped out, stuffing the gun beneath his jacket.

"Why do we have to go inside the palace of the popes?" Stephanie asked.

"That's where the information is stored."

"Care to explain?"

Claridon opened his door. "Come and I'll show you."

THIRTY-THREE

LAVELANET, FRANCE
7:00 PM

THE SENESCHAL STOPPED THE CAR IN THE VILLAGE CENTER. HE and Geoffrey had been traveling northward in a meandering route for the past five hours. Intentionally, they'd bypassed the larger communities of Foix, Quillan, and Limoux, opting instead to stop in a tiny hamlet, nestled within a sheltered hollow, where few tourists seemed to venture.

After leaving the master's chamber, they'd exited through the secret passages near the main kitchen, the portal cleverly concealed within a brick wall. Geoffrey had explained how the master had taught him the routes, used in centuries past for escape. For the last hundred years they'd been known only to masters and rarely utilized.

Once out, they'd quickly found the garage and appropriated one of the abbey's cars, leaving through the main gate before the brothers assigned to the motor pool returned from noontime prayers. With de Roquefort unconscious in his chambers and his entourage waiting for someone to open the locked door, they'd bought themselves a solid head start.

"It's time we talk," he said, his tone conveying that there would be no more procrastinating.

"I'm prepared."

They left the car and walked to a café where an older clientele filled outside tables roofed by stately elms. Their robes were gone, replaced with clothes bought an hour ago in a quick stop. A waiter appeared and they placed an order. The evening was warm and pleasant.

"Do you realize what we did back there?" he asked. "We shot two brothers."

"The master told me violence would be inevitable."

"I know what we're running from, but what are we running to?"

Geoffrey reached into his pocket and produced the envelope he'd displayed to de Roquefort. "The master told me to give you this, once we were free."

He accepted the envelope and tore it open with a mixture of eagerness and trepidation.

My son, and in many ways I thought of you as that, I knew that de Roquefort would prevail in the conclave, but it was important that you challenge him. The brothers will recall that when your time truly arrives. For now, your destiny is elsewhere. Brother Geoffrey will be your companion.

I have faith that prior to leaving the abbey you secured the two volumes that have held your attention the past few years. Yes, I was aware of your interest. I, too, read both long ago. Theft of Order property is a serious breach of Rule, but let us not consider it a theft, merely a borrowing, as I'm sure you will return both books. The information they contain, along with what you already know, is supremely potent. Unfortunately, the puzzle is not solved solely by it. There is more to the riddle, and that is what you must now discover. Contrary to what you might think, I do not know the answer. But de Roquefort cannot be allowed to obtain the Great Devise. He knows much, including all of what you have managed to extract from our records, so do not underestimate his resolve.

It was critical that you leave the confines of our cloistered life. Much awaits you. Though I write these words in the final weeks of my life, I can only assume that your departure was not without violence. Do what is necessary to complete your quest. Masters for centuries have left words for their successors, my predecessor included. Of all who came before me, you alone possess enough of the pieces to reassemble the entire puzzle. I would have liked to have accomplished that goal with you in my lifetime, but it was not to be. De Roquefort would have never allowed our success. With brother Geoffrey's help you can now succeed. I wish you well. Take care of yourself and Geoffrey. Be patient with the lad, for he does only what I have bound him to do by oath.

The seneschal looked up at Geoffrey and wanted to know, "How old are you?"

"Twenty-nine."

"You bear a lot of responsibility for one so young."

"I was frightened when the master told me what he expected of me. I didn't want the duty."

"Why didn't he tell me directly?"

Geoffrey did not immediately answer. "The master said you withdraw in the face of controversy and shy away from confrontation. You do not, as yet, know yourself fully."

He was stung by the rebuke, but Geoffrey's look of truth and innocence stamped great emphasis onto his words. And they were true. He'd never been one to search for a fight and had avoided every one that he could.

But not this time.

He'd confronted de Roquefort head-on and would have shot him dead if the Frenchmen had not reacted quickly. This time he planned to fight. He cleared his throat of emotion and asked, "What am I to do?"

The waiter returned with two salads, crusty bread, and cheese.

Geoffrey smiled. "First, we eat. I'm starved."

He grinned. "Then what?"

"Only you can tell us that."

He shook his head at Geoffrey's fervor of hope. Actually, he'd already given their next move thought on the drive north from the abbey. And a comforting resolve formed as he realized there was only one place to go.

THIRTY-FOUR

MALONE STARED UP AT THE PALACE OF THE POPES, WHICH stretched skyward a hundred yards away. He, Stephanie, and Claridon were sitting at an outdoor café in a lively square directly adjacent to the main entrance. A north wind swept in from across the nearby Rhône—the mistral, as the locals called it—and banged through the city unchecked. Malone recalled a medieval proverb that spoke to the foul smells that once filled these streets. *Windy Avignon, with the wind loathsome, without the wind poisonous.* And what had Petrarch called the place? *The most odiferous on earth.*

From a tour book he'd learned that the mass of architecture rising before him, at once a palace, fortress, and shrine, was in reality two buildings—the old palace built by Pope Benedict XII, begun in 1334, and the new palace erected under Clement VI, finished in 1352. Both reflected the personality of their creators. The old palace was a measure of Romanesque conservatism with little flair, while the new palace exuded a Gothic embellishment. Unfortunately, both buildings had been ravaged by fire and, during the French Revolution, looted, their sculpture destroyed, all of the frescoes whitewashed. In 1810 the palace was turned into a barracks. The city of Avignon assumed control in 1906, but restoration was delayed until the 1960s. Two wings were now a convention center and the rest a grand tourist attraction that offered only fleeting glances of its former glory.

"Time we enter," Claridon said. "The last tour starts in ten minutes. We must be a part."

Malone stood. "What are we going to do?"

Thunder eased past overhead.

"The abbé Bigou, to whom Marie d'Hautpoul de Blanchefort told her great family secret, would, from time to time, visit the palace and admire the paintings. That was before the Revolution, so many were still on display. Lars discovered there was one in particular he loved. When Lars rediscovered the cryptogram, he also found a reference to a painting."

"What kind of reference?" Malone asked.

"In the parish register for the church at Rennes-le-Chateâu, on the day he left France for Spain in 1793, Abbé Bigou made a final entry that read, *Lisez les Règles du Caridad.*"

Malone silently translated. Read the Rules of the Caridad.

"Saunière found that particular entry and secreted it away. Luckily, the register was never destroyed, and Lars ultimately found it. Apparently, Saunière learned that Bigou had visited Avignon often. By Saunière's time, the late nineteenth century, the palace was nothing but a gutted shell. But Saunière could have easily discovered that there'd been a painting here in Bigou's time, *Reading the Rules of the Caridad,* by Juan de Valdés Leal."

"I assume the painting is still inside?" Malone asked, staring across the expansive courtyard toward the Chapeaux Galo, the palace's central gate.

Claridon shook his head. "Long gone. Destroyed by fire fifty years ago."

More thunder rumbled.

"Then why are we here?" Stephanie asked.

Malone tossed a few euros on the table and let his glance dart to another outdoor café two doors away. While others were heading off in anticipation of the coming storm, one woman sat under an awning and sipped from a cup. His gaze lingered only for an instant, enough for him to note well-cut features and prominent eyes. Her skin was the color of creamed coffee, her manner gracious when a waiter delivered her meal. He'd noticed her ten minutes ago, after they first sat, and he'd wondered.

Now for the test.

He grabbed a paper napkin from the table and balled it into his closed fist.

"In that unpublished manuscript," Claridon was saying, "the one I told you Nöel Corbu wrote about Saunière and Rennes, which Lars found, Corbu talked about the painting and knew Bigou referred to it in the parish register. Corbu also noted that a lithograph of the painting was still in the palace archives. He'd seen it. In the week before he died, Lars finally learned where in the archives. We were to go inside for a look, but Lars never returned to Avignon."

"And he didn't tell you where?" Malone asked.

"No, monsieur."

"There's no mention in the notebook about a painting," Malone said. "I read the whole thing. Not a word on Avignon."

"If Lars didn't tell you where the lithograph is, why are we going inside?" Stephanie asked. "You don't know where to look."

"But your son did, the day before he died. He and I were

to go inside the palace for a look when he returned from the mountains. But, madame, as you know—"

"He never came back, either."

Malone watched as Stephanie suppressed her emotions. She was good, but not that good. "Why didn't *you* go?"

"I thought staying alive more important. So I retreated to the asylum."

"The man died in an avalanche," Malone made clear. "He wasn't murdered."

"You don't know that. In fact," Claridon said, "you don't know anything." He glanced around the plaza. "We need to hurry. They are particular about the last tour. Most of the employees are older residents from the city. Many are volunteers. They lock the doors promptly at seven. There's no security system or alarms within the palace. Nothing of any real value is displayed there any longer, and besides, the walls themselves are its greatest security. We will drift off from the tour and wait till all is quiet."

They started walking.

Droplets of rain pricked Malone's scalp. With his back to the woman, who should still be seated a hundred feet away eating, he opened his hand and allowed the mistral to sweep the balled napkin away. He whirled and pretended to go after the stray paper as it danced across the cobblestones. As he retrieved the supposed errant piece of trash, he stole a glance toward the café.

The woman was no longer at her table.

She was strolling their way, toward the palace.

DE ROQUEFORT LOWERED THE BINOCULARS. HE STOOD AT THE Rocher des Doms, the rock of the doms, the most picturesque spot in Avignon. Men had occupied the summit since the neolithic age. In the days of the papal occupation the great rocky outcrop served as a natural buffer for the ever-present mistral. Today the hilltop, which sat directly adjacent to the papal palace, supported a splendid park with lakes, fountains, statuary, and grottoes. The view was breathtaking. He'd come here many times when he worked at the nearby seminary, in his time before the Order.

Hills and valleys stretched to the west and south. The swift Rhône cleaved a path below, sweeping beneath the famous Pont St. Bénézet that once bisected the river and led from the pope's city to the king's on the other side. When, in 1226, Avignon sided with the count of Toulouse against Louis VIII during the Albigensian Crusade, the French king razed the bridge. Rebuilding eventually occurred, and de Roquefort imagined the fourteenth century when cardinals rode their mules across to their country palaces in Villeneuve-les-Avignon. By the sixteenth century rains and floods had cut the restored bridge back to four spans, which were never extended to the far side, so the structure still stood uncompleted. Another failure of will for Avignon, he'd always thought. A place that seemed destined to only half succeed.

"They're headed into the palace," he said to the brother standing next to him. He checked his watch. Nearly six PM. "Which closes for the day at seven."

He brought the binoculars back to his eyes and stared down five hundred yards at the plaza. He'd traveled north from the abbey and arrived forty minutes ago. The electronic surveillance on Malone's car was still functioning and had revealed a trip out to Villeneuve-les-Avignon, then back to Avignon. Apparently, they'd gone to retrieve Claridon.

De Roquefort had climbed the tree-lined walkway from the papal palace and decided to wait here, on the summit, which offered a perfect vantage of the old city. Fortune had smiled upon him when Stephanie Nelle and her two companions emerged from the underground parking garage directly below, then took a seat in a clearly visible outdoor café.

He lowered the binoculars.

The mistral whipped past him. The north wind was howling today, sweeping the quays, swelling the river, pushing storm clouds that scudded the sky ever closer.

"They apparently intend to stay in the palace after closing. Lars Nelle and Claridon once did that, too. Do we still have a key to the door?"

"Our brother here in town keeps it for us."

"Retrieve it."

He'd long ago secured a way to enter the palace through the cathedral after hours. The archives inside had held Lars Nelle's interest, so they'd likewise drawn de Roquefort's. Twice he'd sent brothers to scurry around during the night, trying to ascertain what had attracted Lars Nelle. But the volume of material was intimidating and nothing was ever learned. Perhaps tonight he'd discover more.

He returned his eyes to the lens. Paper slipped from Malone's grip, and he watched the lawyer chase after it.

Then his three targets vanished beyond view.

THIRTY-FIVE

9:00 PM

AN EERIE FEELING SWEPT OVER MALONE AS HE STROLLED through the unadorned rooms. Halfway into the palace tour, they'd slipped away and Claridon had led them to an upper floor. There they'd waited in a tower, behind a closed door, until eight thirty, when most of the interior lights had been doused and no movement could be heard. Claridon seemed to know the procedure, and had been pleased that the staff's routine remained the same after five years.

The labyrinth of sparse halls, long passages, and barren chambers was now illuminated only by isolated pools of weak light. Malone could only imagine how they were once furnished, the walls sumptuous with colorful frescoes and tapestries, each full of personages gathered to either serve or petition the supreme pontiff. Envoys from the Khan, the emperor of Constantinople, even Petrarch himself and St. Catherine of Siena, the woman who eventually convinced the last Avignon pope to return to Rome, had all come. History was deeply rooted here, yet only remnants remained.

Outside, the storm had finally arrived and rain soaked the roof with violence, while thunder rattled window glass.

"This palace was once as grand as the Vatican," Claridon whispered. "All gone. Destroyed by ignorance and greed."

Malone did not agree. "Some would say ignorance and greed were what caused it to be built in the first place."

"Ah, Mr. Malone, you're a student of history?"

"I've read."

"Then let me show you something."

Claridon led them through open portals into more trodden rooms, each identified by placards. They stopped in one cavernous rectangle labeled the Grand Tinel, the chamber topped by a wood-paneled, barrel-vaulted ceiling.

"This was the pope's banquet hall and could hold hundreds," Claridon said, his voice echoing. "Clement VI hung blue fabric, studded with gold stars, over the ceiling to create a celestial arch. Frescoes once adorned the walls. All of it was destroyed by fire in 1413."

"And never replaced?" Stephanie asked.

"The Avignon popes were gone by then, so this palace carried no further significance." Claridon motioned to the far side. "The pope would eat alone, over there, on a dais seated on a throne, under a canopy decked with crimson velvet and ermine. Guests sat on wooden benches that lined the walls— cardinals to the east, others to the west. Trestle tables formed a U and food was served from the center. All quite stiff and formal."

"A lot like this palace," Malone said. "It's like walking through a destroyed city, the building's soul bombed away. A world unto itself."

"Which was the whole idea. The French kings wanted their popes away from everyone. They alone controlled what the pope thought and did, so it wasn't necessary that their residence be an airy place. Not one of those popes ever visited Rome, since the Italians would have killed them on sight. So the seven men who served here as pope built their own fortress and did not question the French throne. They owed their existence to the king, and delighted in this repose—their Avignon Captivity, as the papacy's time here came to be called."

Into the next room the space became more confined. The Parement Chamber was identified as where the pope and cardinals would meet in secret consistories.

"This is also where the Golden Rose was presented," Claridon said. "A particularly arrogant gesture for the Avignon popes. On the fourth Sunday of Lent, the pope would honor one special person, usually a sovereign, with the presentation of a golden rose."

"You don't approve?" Stephanie asked.

"Christ had no need for golden roses. Why should popes? Just more of the sacrilege this entire place reflected. Clement VI bought the whole town from Queen Joanna of Naples. Part of a deal she made to obtain absolution for her complicity in her husband's murder. For a hundred years criminals, adventurers, counterfeiters, and smugglers all escaped justice here, provided they paid proper homage to the pope."

Through another chamber they entered what was labeled the Stag Room. Claridon switched on a series of soft incandescent lights. Malone lingered at the doorway long enough to glance back through the previous chamber into the Grand Tinel. A shadow flickered across the wall, enough for him to know they were not alone. He knew who was there. A tall, attractive, athletic woman—*of color,* as Claridon had said earlier in the car. The woman who'd followed them into the palace.

"—this is where the old and new palaces join," Claridon was saying. "Old behind us, new through that other portal. This was Clement VI's study."

Malone had read in the souvenir book about Clement, a man who enjoyed paintings and poems, pleasing sounds, rare animals, and courtly love. He was quoted as saying, *My predecessors didn't know how to be popes,* so he transformed

Benedict's old fortress into a lavish palace. A perfect example of Clement's material wants now surrounded him as painted images on the windowless walls. Fields, thickets, and streams, all under a blue sky. Men with nets by a green fishpond littered with swimming pike. Brittany spaniels. A young noble and his falcon. A child in a tree. Grasses, birds, bathers. Greens and brown predominated, but an orange dress, a blue fish, and fruit in the trees added dashes of sharp color.

"Clement had these frescoes painted in 1344. They were found beneath the whitewash the soldiers applied when the palace became a barracks in the nineteenth century. This room explains the Avignon popes, especially Clement VI. Some actually called him Clement the Magnificent. He possessed no calling for religious life. Satisfaction of penances, reversal of excommunications, remission of sins, even curtailment of years in purgatory for both the dead and living— all was for sale. You notice anything missing?"

Malone stared again at the frescoes. The hunting scenes were clearly escapism—people doing fun things—with a view that soared and dipped, but nothing particular called out to him.

Then it hit him.

"Where's God?"

"Good eye, monsieur." Claridon's arms swept out. "Not anywhere in this home of Clement VI is there a religious symbol. The omission speaks loudly. This was the bedroom of a king, not a pope, and that was how the Avignon prelates thought of themselves. These were the men who destroyed the Templars. Starting in 1307 with Clement V, who was Philip the Fair's co-conspirator, and ending with Gregory XI in 1378, these corrupt individuals crushed that Order. Lars always believed, and I agree, that this room proves what those men really valued."

"Do you think the Templars survived?" Stephanie asked.

"*Oui*. They're out there. I've seen them. What exactly they are, I do not know. But they're out there."

Malone could not decide if the declaration was fact or just the supposition of a man who saw conspiracies where none existed. All he knew was that a woman was stalking them who was expert enough to plant a slug above his head into a tree trunk, from fifty yards, at night, in a forty-mile-per-hour wind. She might even have been the one who saved his hide in Copenhagen. And she was real.

"Let's get on with it," Malone said.

Claridon switched off the light. "Follow me."

They walked across the old palace to the north wing and the convention center. A placard noted that the facility was recently created by the city as a way to raise revenue for further restoration. The former Conclave Hall, Treasurer's Chamber, and Great Cellar had been equipped with bleacher seats, a stage, and audiovisual equipment. Down more passageways they passed stone effigies of more Avignon popes.

Claridon eventually stopped at a stout wooden door and tested the latch, which opened. "Good. They still do not lock it at night."

"Why not?" Malone asked.

"There's nothing of any value here besides information, and few thieves are interested in that."

They stepped into a pitch-dark space.

"This was once the chapel of Benedict XII, the pope who conceived and built most of the old palace. In the late nineteenth century, this and the room above were converted into the district's archives. The palace keeps its records here, too."

The light spilling in from the hall revealed a towering room filled with shelving, row after row. More lined the outer walls, one section stacked on top of the other, a railed walkway encircling. Behind the shelves rose arched windows, the black panes peppered by a steady rain.

"Four kilometers of shelving," Claridon said. "A gracious plenty of information."

"But you know where to look?" Malone asked.

"I hope so."

Claridon plunged ahead down the center aisle. Malone and Stephanie waited until a lamp came on fifty feet inside.

"Over here," Claridon called out.

Malone closed the hall door and wondered how the woman was going to gain her entrance unnoticed. He led the way toward the light and they found Claridon standing next to a reading table.

"Lucky for history," Claridon said, "all the palace's artifacts were inventoried early in the eighteenth century. Then, in the late nineteenth century, photographs and drawings were made of what survived the Revolution. Lars and I both became familiar with how the information was organized."

"And you didn't come look after Mark died because you thought the Knights Templar would kill you?" Malone asked.

"I realize, monsieur, you don't believe much of this. But I assure you I did the right thing. These records have rested here for centuries, so I thought they could rest quietly awhile longer. Staying alive seemed more important."

"So why are you here now?" Stephanie asked.

"A long time has passed." Claridon stepped from the table. "Around us are the palace inventories. It will take me a few minutes to look. Why don't you sit and let me see if I can find what we want." He produced a flashlight from his pocket. "From the asylum. I thought we may need it."

Malone slid out a chair, as did Stephanie. Claridon disappeared into the darkness. They sat and he could hear rummaging, the flashlight beam dancing across the vault overhead.

"This is what my husband did," she said in a whisper. "Hiding out in a forgotten palace, looking for nonsense."

He caught the edge in her voice.

"While our marriage slipped away. While I worked twenty hours a day. This was what he did."

A peal of thunder sent tremors through both him and the room.

"It was important to him," Malone said, keeping his voice low, too. "And there might even be something to it."

"Like what, Cotton. Treasure? If Saunière discovered those jewels in the crypt, okay. Luck like that visits people every once in a while. But there's nothing more. Bigou, Saunière, Lars, Mark, Claridon. They're all dreamers."

"Dreamers have many times changed the world."

"This is a wild goose chase for a goose that doesn't exist."

Claridon returned from the darkness and dropped a musty folder on the table. Water stains smeared its outside. Inside was a three-inch stack of black-and-white photographs and pencil drawings. "Within a few feet of where Mark said. Thank heaven the old men who run this place change little about it over time."

"How did Mark find it?" Stephanie asked.

"He would hunt for clues on the weekends. He wasn't as dedicated as his father, but he came to the house in Rennes often and he and I dabbled in the search. At the university in Toulouse he came across some information on the Avignon archives. He linked the clues together and here we have the answer."

Malone spread the contents out across the table. "What are we looking for?"

"I've never seen the painting. We can only hope it's iden-tified."

They started sifting through the images.

"There," Claridon said, excitement in his voice.

Malone focused on one of the lithographs, a black-and-white drawing time-tinged, edges frayed. A handwritten

notation across the top read DON MIGUEL DE MAÑARA READ-
ING THE RULES OF THE CARIDAD.

The image was of an older man, with the dusting of a
beard and a thin mustache, seated at a table, wearing a religious habit. An elaborate emblem was stitched to one
sleeve from elbow to shoulder. His left hand touched a
book propped upright and his right hand was extended,
palm-up, motioning across an elaborately clothed desk to a
little man in a monk's robe perched on a low stool with fingers to his lips, signaling quiet. An open book lay in the little man's lap. The floor, which extended from one side to
the other, was a checkerboard arrangement, like a chessboard, and writing appeared on the stool where the little
man sat.

ACABOCE A°
DE 1687

"Most curious," Claridon muttered. "Look here."

Malone followed Claridon's finger and studied the top left
portion of the picture where, in the shadows behind the little
man, a table and shelf stood. On top lay a human skull.

"What does all this mean?" Malone asked Claridon.

"*Caridad* translates to 'charity,' which can also be love. The
black habit the man at the table wears is from the Order of the
Knights of Calatrava, a Spanish religious society devoted to
Jesus Christ. I can tell from the design on the sleeve. *Acaboce*
is 'completion.' The *A°* could be a reference to alpha and
omega, the first and last letters in the Greek alphabet—the beginning and end. The skull? I have no idea."

Malone recalled what Bigou supposedly wrote in the
Rennes parish register just before he fled France for Spain.
Read the Rules of the Caridad. "What rules are we to read?"

Claridon studied the drawing in the weak light. "Notice
something about the little man on the stool. See his shoes.

His feet are planted on black squares in the flooring, diagonal to one another."

"The floor resembles a chessboard," Stephanie said.

"And the bishop moves diagonally, as the feet indicate."

"So the little man is a bishop?" Stephanie asked.

"No," Malone said, understanding. "In French chess, the bishop is the Fool."

"You are a student of the game?" Claridon asked.

"I've played some."

Claridon rested his finger atop the little man on the stool. "Here is the Wise Fool who apparently has a secret that deals with alpha and omega."

Malone understood. "Christ has been called that."

"*Oui*. And when you add *acaboce* you have 'completion of alpha and omega.' Completion of Christ."

"But what does that mean?" Stephanie asked.

"Madame, might I see Stüblein's book?"

She found the volume and handed it to Claridon. "Let's look at the gravestone again. This and the painting are related. Remember, it was the abbé Bigou who left both clues." He laid the book flat on the table.

"You have to know the history to understand this gravestone. The d'Hautpoul family dates back to twelfth-century France. Marie married François d'Hautpoul, the last lord, in 1732. One of the d'Hautpoul ancestors penned a will in 1644, which he duly registered and placed with a notary in Espéraza. When that ancestor died, though, that will was not to be found. Then, more than a hundred years after his death, the lost will suddenly reappeared. When François d'Hautpoul went to get it, he was told by the notary that *it would not be wise for me to part with a document of such great importance.* François died in 1753, and in 1780 the will was finally given to his widow, Marie. Why? No one knows. Perhaps because she was, by then, the only d'Hautpoul left. But she died a year later and it's said she passed the will, and whatever information it contained, to the abbé Bigou as part of the great family secret."

"And that was what Saunière found in the crypt? Along with the gold coins and the jewels?"

Claridon nodded. "But the crypt was concealed. So Lars always believed the false grave of Marie in the cemetery held the actual clue. Bigou must have felt that the secret he knew was too great not to pass on. He was fleeing the country, never to return, so he left a puzzle that pointed the way. In the car, when you first showed me this gravestone drawing, many things occurred to me." He reached for a blank pad and pen that lay on the table. "Now I know this carving is full of information."

Malone studied the letters and symbols on the gravestones.

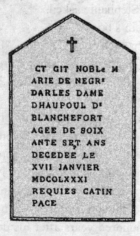

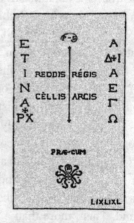

"The stone on the right lay flat on Marie's grave and does not contain the sort of inscription normally found on graves. Its left side is written in Latin." Claridon wrote ET IN PAX on the pad. "This translates to 'and in peace,' but it has problems. *Pax* is the nominative case of *peace* and is grammatically incorrect after the preposition *in*. The right-hand column is written in Greek and is gibberish. But I've been thinking about that, and the solution finally came to me. The inscription is actually all Latin, written in the Greek alphabet. When you translate into Roman, the *E, T, I, N,* and *A* are fine. But the *P* is an *R,* the *X* becomes a *K,* and—"

Claridon scribbled on the pad, then wrote his completed translation across the bottom.

ET IN ARCADIA EGO

"And in Arcadia I," Malone said, translating the Latin. "That makes no sense."

"Precisely," Claridon noted. "Which would lead one to conclude that the words are concealing something else."

Malone understood. "An anagram?"

"Quite common in Bigou's time. After all, it's doubtful Bigou would have left a message that easy to decipher."

"What about the words in the center?"

Claridon jotted them onto the pad.

REDDIS RÉGIS CÉLLIS ARCIS

"*Reddis* means 'to give back, to restore something previously taken.' But it's also Latin for 'Rennes.' *Regis* derives from *rex,* which is 'king.' *Cella* refers to a storeroom. *Arcis* stems from *arx*—a stronghold, fortress, citadel. A lot can be made of each, but together they make no sense. Then there's the arrow that connects *p-s* at the top with *præ-cum.* I have no idea what the *p-s* means. The *præ-cum* translates as 'pray to come.'"

"What is that symbol at the bottom?" Stephanie asked. "Looks like an octopus."

Claridon shook his head. "A spider, madame. But its significance escapes me."

"What about the other stone?" Malone asked.

"The left one stood upright over the grave and was the most

visible. Remember, Bigou served Marie d'Hautpoul for many years. He was extraordinarily loyal to her and took two years to produce this headstone, yet almost every line in it contains an error. Masons of that day were prone to mistakes, but this many? No way the abbé would have allowed them to remain."

"So the errors are part of the message?" Malone asked.

"It would seem. Look here. Her name is wrong. She was not Marie de Negre d'Arles dame d'Haupoul. She was Marie de Negri d'Ables d'Hautpoul. Many of the other words are also truncated. Letters are raised and dropped for no reason. But look at the date."

Malone studied the Roman numerals.

MDCOLXXXI

"Supposedly her date of death. 1681. And that's discounting the *O,* since there is no zero in the Roman numeral system, and no number was denoted by the letter *O.* Yet here it is. And Marie died in 1781, not 1681. Is the *O* there to make clear that Bigou knew the date was wrong? And her age is wrong, too. She was sixty-eight, not sixty-seven, as noted, when she died."

Malone pointed to the sketch of the right stone and the Roman numerals in the bottom corner. LIXLIXL. "Fifty. Nine. Fifty. Nine. Fifty."

"Most peculiar," Claridon said.

Malone glanced back at the lithograph. "I don't see where this painting figures in?"

"It's a puzzle, monsieur. One that has no easy solution."

"But the answer is something I'd like to know," a deep male voice said, out of the darkness.

THIRTY-SIX

MALONE HAD BEEN EXPECTING CONTACT FROM THE WOMAN, but this voice was not hers. He reached for his gun.

"Stand still, Mr. Malone. Weapons are trained on you."

"It's the man from the cathedral," Stephanie said.

"I told you we'd meet again. And you, monsieur Claridon. You weren't that convincing in the asylum. Insane? Hardly."

Malone searched the darkness. The sheer size of the chamber produced a confusion of noise. But he spotted human forms standing above them, before the upper row of shelving at the wooden railing.

He counted four.

"I am, though, impressed by your knowledge, monsieur Claridon. Your deductions about the headstone seem logical. I always believed there was much to be learned from that marker. I, too, have been here before, rummaging through these shelves. Such a difficult endeavor. So much to explore. I do appreciate you narrowing the search. *Reading the Rules of Caridad*. Who would have thought?"

Claridon made the sign of the cross and Malone spotted fear in the man's eyes. "May God protect us."

"Come now, monsieur Claridon," the disembodied voice said. "Do we need to involve heaven?"

"You are His warriors." Claridon's voice trembled.

"And what brings you to that conclusion?"

"Who else could you be?"

"Perhaps we are the police? No. You wouldn't believe that. Maybe we're adventurers—searchers—like you. But no. So, let's say for the sake of simplicity that we are His warriors. How can you three aid *our* cause?"

No one answered him.

"Ms. Nelle possesses her husband's journal and the book from the auction. She'll contribute those."

"Screw you," she spat out.

A pop, like a balloon bursting, sounded over the rain and a bullet careened off the table a few inches from Stephanie.

"Bad answer," the voice said.

"Give them to him," Malone said.

Stephanie glared at him.

"He'll shoot you next."

"How did you know?" the voice asked.

"That's what I'd do."

A chuckle. "I like you, Mr. Malone. You're a professional."

Stephanie reached into her shoulder bag and removed the book and journal.

"Toss them toward the door, between the shelves," the voice said.

She did as instructed.

A form appeared and retrieved them.

Malone silently added one more man to the list. At least five were now in the archive. He felt the gun wedged at his waist beneath his jacket. Unfortunately, there was no way to retrieve it before at least one of them was shot. And only three bullets remained in the magazine.

"Your husband, Ms. Nelle, managed to piece together many of the facts, and his deductions as to missing elements were generally correct. He was a remarkable intellect."

"What is it you're after?" Malone asked. "I only joined this party a couple of days ago."

"We seek justice, Mr. Malone."

"And it's necessary to run down an old man in Rennes-le-Château to achieve justice?" He thought he'd jostle the barrel and see what spilled out.

"And who would that be?"

"Ernst Scoville. He worked with Lars Nelle. Surely you knew of him?"

"Mr. Malone, perhaps a year of retirement has dulled your skills. I'd hope that you were better at interrogating when you were working full time."

"Since you have the journal and the notebook, don't you have to be going?"

"I need that lithograph. Monsieur Claridon, please be so kind as to take it to my associate, there, beyond the table."

Claridon clearly did not want to do it.

Another slap from a sound-suppressed weapon and a bullet thudded into the tabletop. "I hate repeating myself."

Malone lifted the drawing and handed it to Claridon. "Do it."

The sheet was accepted in a hand that trembled. Claridon took a few steps beyond the spill of the weak lamp. Thunder pounded the air and rattled the walls. Rain continued to burst forth with fury.

Then a new noise erupted.

Gunfire.

And the lamp exploded in a burst of sparks.

DE ROQUEFORT HEARD THE GUNSHOT AND SAW THE MUZZLE flash from near the archive's exit. Damn. Somebody else was here.

The room was plunged into darkness.

"Move," he screamed to his men on the second-floor cat-walk, and he hoped they knew what to do.

MALONE REALIZED SOMEBODY HAD SHOT OUT THE LIGHT. THE woman. She'd found another way in.

As darkness overtook them, he grabbed Stephanie and they dropped to the floor. He was hoping the men above him had been likewise caught off guard.

He brought out the gun from beneath his jacket.

Two more shots exploded from below, and the bullets sent the men above scurrying. Footsteps pounded on the wooden platform. He was more concerned about the man on the ground floor, but he'd heard nothing from the direction where he'd last seen him, nor had he heard anything from Claridon.

The running stopped.

"Whoever you are," the man's voice said, "must you inter-fere?"

"I could ask you the same question," the woman said in a languid tone.

"This is not your business."

"I disagree."

"You assaulted two of my brothers in Copenhagen."

"Let's say I ended your attack."

"There will be retribution."

"Come and get me."

"Stop her," the man yelled.

Black shapes rushed across overhead. Malone's eyes had adjusted and he made out a staircase at the far end of the cat-walk.

He handed Stephanie the gun. "Stay here."

"Where are you going?"

"To repay a favor."

He crouched down and hustled forward, weaving through

the shelves. He waited, then tackled one of the men as he leaped from the last tread. The size and shape of the man was reminiscent of Red Jacket, but this time Malone was ready. He brought a knee into the man's stomach, then pounded a fist to the back of the neck.

The man went still.

Malone surveyed the darkness and heard running a few aisles over.

"No. Please leave me be."

Claridon.

DE ROQUEFORT HEADED STRAIGHT FOR THE DOOR THAT LED out of the archives. He'd descended from the ramparts and knew the woman would want to make a hasty retreat, but her choices were limited. There was only the exit to the hall and one other, through the curator's office. But his man stationed there had just reported through the radio that all was quiet.

He now knew she was the same person who'd interfered in Copenhagen and probably the same one from last night in Rennes-le-Château. And that realization spurred him on. He must learn her identity.

The door leading out of the archives opened, then closed. In the wedge of light that splashed in from the hall he spied two legs lying prone on the floor between the shelves. He darted over and discovered one of his subordinates unconscious, a small dart planted in the neck. This brother had been stationed on the ground floor and had retrieved the notebook, journal, and lithograph.

Which were nowhere to be seen.

Damn her.

"Do as I instructed," he called out to his remaining men.

He raced for the door.

MALONE HEARD THE MAN'S COMMAND AND DECIDED TO HEAD
back to Stephanie. He had no idea what the men had been
commanded to do, but he assumed it included them and
wasn't good.

He crouched down and eased his way through the shelves,
toward the table.

"Stephanie," he breathed out.

"Here, Cotton."

He slipped close to her. All he could hear now was the
rain. "There must be another way out of here," she mouthed
through the darkness.

He relieved her of the gun. "Somebody left through the
door. Probably the woman. I saw only one shadow. The others must have gone after Claridon and left through another
exit."

The door leading out opened again.

"That's him leaving," he said.

They stood and rushed back across the archives. At the
exit Malone hesitated, heard and saw nothing, then led the
way out.

DE ROQUEFORT SPOTTED THE WOMAN RUNNING DOWN THE
long gallery. She whirled and, not losing a step, fired a shot
his way.

He dove to the floor, and she disappeared around a corner.

He came to his feet and bolted after her. Before she'd fired,
he'd caught sight of the journal and the book in her grasp.

She had to be stopped.

MALONE SAW A MAN, DRESSED IN BLACK TROUSERS AND A DARK
turtleneck, gun in hand, turn a corner fifty feet away.

"This is going to get interesting," he said.

They both ran.

DE ROQUEFORT KEPT UP HIS PURSUIT. THE WOMAN WAS certainly attempting to leave the palace, and she seemed to know the geography. Every turn she took was the right one. She'd deftly obtained what she came for, so he had to assume that her escape would not be left to chance.

Through another portal, he entered a rib-vaulted hall. The woman was already at the far end, turning a corner. He trotted over and saw a wide stone staircase leading down. The Great Staircase of Honor. Once, lined with frescoes, broken by iron gates, and sheathed with Persian runners, the stairway had lent itself to the solemn majesty of pontifical ceremonies. Now the risers and walls were bare. The darkness at the bottom, some thirty yards away, was absolute. He knew below were exit doors into a courtyard. He heard the woman's footsteps as she descended but could not make out her form.

So he just fired.

Ten shots.

MALONE HEARD WHAT SOUNDED LIKE A HAMMER REPEATEDLY striking a nail. One sound-suppressed shot after another.

He slowed his approach to a doorway ten feet ahead.

HINGES SQUEALED AT THE BASE OF THE INK-BLACK STAIRWAY. De Roquefort recognized the sound of a door groaning open. The storm outside grew louder. Apparently his indiscriminate shots had missed. The woman was leaving the palace. He heard footsteps behind him, then spoke into the mike clipped to his shirt.

"Do you have what I wanted?"

"We do," was the reply through his earphone.

"I'm in the Conclave Gallery. Mr. Malone and Ms. Nelle are behind me. Handle them."

He rushed down the staircase.

MALONE SAW THE MAN IN THE TURTLENECK LEAVE THE CAVernous hall that stretched out before them. Gun in hand, he ran ahead with Stephanie following.

Three armed men materialized from other portals into the room and blocked their way.

Malone and Stephanie stopped.

"Please toss the gun aside," one of the men said.

No way he could take them all before either he, Stephanie, or both of them went down. So he allowed the gun to clatter on the floor.

The three men approached.

"What do we do now?" Stephanie asked.

"I'm open to suggestions."

"There's nothing for you to do," another of the short-hairs said.

They stood still.

"Turn around," came the command.

He stared at Stephanie. He'd been in tight spots before, a few just like the one they were facing. Even if he managed to subdue one or two, there was still the third man, and all were armed.

A thud was followed by a cry from Stephanie and her body collapsed to the floor. Before he could move toward her, the back of Malone's head was pounded with something hard and everything before him vanished.

DE ROQUEFORT FOLLOWED HIS QUARRY, WHO RUSHED THROUGH the Place du Palais, quickly fleeing the empty plaza and winding a path through Avignon's deserted streets. The warm rain fell in steady sheets. The heavens suddenly opened, cleft by an immense flash of lightning that momentarily lifted the vault of darkness. Thunder shook the air.

They left buildings behind and came close to the river.

He knew, just ahead, the Pont St. Bénézet stretched out across the Rhône. Through the storm he saw the woman navigate a path straight for the bridge's entrance. What was she doing? Why go there? No matter, he had to follow. She possessed the rest of what he'd come to retrieve, and he did not plan to leave Avignon without the book and journal. Yet he wondered what the rain was doing to the pages. His hair was matted to his scalp, his clothes pasted to his body.

He saw a flash ten meters ahead of him as the woman fired a shot into the door that led to the bridge's entrance.

She disappeared inside the building.

He rushed to the door and carefully gazed inside. A ticket counter stood to his right. Souvenirs were displayed in more counters to the left. Three turnstiles led out onto the bridge. The incomplete span had long ago ceased being anything but a tourist attraction.

The woman was twenty meters away, running down the bridge, out onto the river.

Then she disappeared.

He rushed forward and leaped over the turnstiles, racing after her.

A Gothic chapel stood at the end of the second pylon. He knew that it was the Chapelle Saint-Nicholas. The remains of St. Bénézet, who was originally responsible for the bridge being built, were once preserved there. But the relics were lost during the Revolution and only the chapel remained— Gothic on top, Romanesque below. Which was where the woman had gone. Down the stone staircase.

Another greenish bolt of lightning flashed overhead.

He shook the rain from his eyes and stopped at the top riser.

Then he saw her.

Not below, but back on top, racing toward the end of the fourth span, which would take her halfway out into the Rhône with nowhere to go, since the spans to the other side of the river had washed away three hundred years ago. She'd obviously used the stairs to dip beneath the chapel as a way to block any shot he may have wanted to take.

He dashed after her, rounding the chapel.

He didn't want to shoot. He needed her alive. Even more important, he needed what she carried. So he sent a bullet to her left, at her feet.

She stopped and turned to face him.

He rushed forward, gun leveled.

She stood at the end of the fourth span, nothing but darkness and water behind her. A clap of thunder violated the air. Wind came in wild gusts. Rain poured across his face.

"Who are you?" he asked.

She wore a black bodysuit that matched her dark skin. She was lean and muscular, her head sheathed in a tight hood, only her face visible. She carried a gun in the left hand, a plastic shopping bag in the other. She extended the shopping back out over the edge.

"Let's not get hasty," she said.

"I could simply shoot you."

"Two reasons why you won't do that."

"I'm listening."

"One, the bag will drop into the river and what you really want will be lost. And two, I'm a Christian. You don't kill Christians."

"How do you know what I do?"

"You are a knight of the Templars, as are the others. You took an oath not to harm Christians."

"I have no idea whether you're a Christian."

"So let's stick with reason one. Shoot me, the books swim in the Rhône. The swift current will take them away."

"Apparently we seek the same thing."

"You're a quick one."

Her arm stayed extended out over the edge and he contemplated where best to shoot her, but she was right—the bag would be gone long before he could traverse the ten feet that separated them.

"Looks like we have a standoff," he said.

"I wouldn't say that."

She released her grip and the bag disappeared into the blackness. She then used his moment of surprise to raise her gun and fire, but de Roquefort pivoted left and dropped to the wet stones. When he shook the rain from his eyes, he saw the woman leap over the edge. He stood and rushed over, expecting to see the churning Rhône sweeping by, but instead below him was a stone platform, about eight feet down, part of a pylon that supported the outer arch. He saw the woman yank up the bag and disappear beneath the bridge.

He hesitated only an instant, then jumped, landing on his feet. His middle-aged ankles rattled from the impact.

An engine roared and he saw a motorboat shoot out from under the far side of the bridge and speed away, toward the north. He raised his gun to fire, but a muzzle flash signaled she was firing, too.

He lunged flat to more wet stone.

The boat dissolved out of range.

Who was that vixen? Clearly, she knew what he was, though not who he was since she'd not identified him. She also apparently understood the significance of the book and the journal. Most important, she knew his every move.

He came to his feet and stepped beneath the bridge, out of the rain, where the boat had been moored. She'd also planned a clever escape. He was about to climb back up, using an iron ladder affixed to the bridge's exterior, when something in the darkness caught his attention.

He bent down.

A book lay on the soaked stone beneath the overpass.

He brought it close to his eyes, straining to see what the damp pages contained, and read a few of the words.

Lars Nelle's notebook.

She'd lost it during her hasty retreat.

He smiled.

He now possessed part of the puzzle—not all, but maybe enough—and he knew precisely how to learn the rest.

THIRTY-SEVEN

MALONE OPENED HIS EYES, TESTED HIS SORE NECK, AND DETERmined nothing seemed broken. He massaged the swollen muscles with his open palm and shook off the effects of being unconscious. He glanced at his watch. Eleven twenty PM. He'd been out about an hour.

Stephanie lay a few feet away. He crawled toward her, lifted her head, and gently shook her. She blinked her eyes and tried to focus on him.

"That hurt," she muttered.

"Tell me about it." He stared around the expansive hall. Outside, the rain had slackened. "We need to get out of here."

"What about our friends?"

"If they wanted us dead, we would be. I think they're through with us. They have the notebook, the journal, and Claridon. We're unnecessary." He noticed the gun lying nearby and motioned. "That's what kind of threat they think we are."

Stephanie rubbed her head. "This was a bad idea, Cotton. I should have never reacted after that notebook was sent to me. If I hadn't called Ernst Scoville, he'd probably still be alive. And I should have never involved you."

"I believe I insisted." He slowly came to his feet. "We need to leave. At some point cleaning personnel have to come through here. And I don't feel like answering any police questions."

He helped Stephanie up.

"Thanks, Cotton. For everything. I appreciate all that you did."

"You make it sound like this is over."

"It is for me. Whatever Lars and Mark were looking for will just have to be found by somebody else. I'm going home."

"What about Claridon?"

"What can we do? We have no idea who took him or where he might be. And what would we tell the police? The Knights Templar have kidnapped an inmate from a local asylum? Get real. I'm afraid he's on his own."

"We know the woman's name," he said. "Claridon mentioned it was Cassiopeia Vitt. He told us where she is. Givors. We could find her."

"And do what? Thank her for saving our hides? I think she's on her own, too, and more than capable of handling herself. Like you say, we're not deemed important any longer."

She was right.

"We need to go home, Cotton. There's nothing here for *either* of us."

Right again.

They found their way out of the palace and returned to the rental car. After losing the first tail outside Rennes, Malone knew they'd not been followed to Avignon, so he assumed either men were already waiting in the city, which was unlikely, or some sort of electronic surveillance had been employed. Which meant the chase and shots before he managed to send the Renault into the mud was a dog-and-pony show designed to rock him to sleep.

Which worked.

But they were no longer deemed players in whatever game was unfolding, so he decided they would head back to Rennes-le-Château and spend the night there.

The drive took nearly two hours and they passed through the village's main gate just before two AM. A fresh wind raked the summit and the Milky Way streaked overhead as they walked from the car park. Not a light burned within the walls. The streets were still damp from yesterday's weather.

Malone was tired. "Let's get a little rest and we'll leave out around noontime. I'm sure there's a flight you can catch from Paris to Atlanta."

At the door, Stephanie opened the lock. Inside, Malone flipped on a lamp in the den and immediately noticed a rucksack tossed into a chair that neither he nor Stephanie had brought.

He reached for the gun at his belt.

Movement from the bedroom caught his eye. A man appeared in the doorway and leveled a Glock at him.

Malone brought his weapon up. "Who the hell are you?"

The man was young, maybe early thirties, with the same short hair and stocky build that he'd seen in abundance over the past few days. The face, though handsome, was set for combat—the eyes like black marbles—and he handled the weapon with assurance. But Malone sensed a hesitancy, as if the other man was unsure of friend or foe.

"I asked who you are."

"Lower the gun, Geoffrey," came a voice from inside the bedroom.

"Are you sure?"

"Please."

The weapon came down. Malone lowered his, too.

Another man stepped from the shadows.

He was long-limbed and squarely built with close-cropped auburn hair. He, too, held a pistol and it took Malone only an instant to register the familiar cleft, swarthy skin, and gentle eyes from the photo that still angled on the table to his left.

He heard the breath leave Stephanie.

"My God in heaven," she whispered.

He was shocked, too.

Standing before him was Mark Nelle.

STEPHANIE'S BODY SHOOK. HER HEART POUNDED. FOR A MO-ment she had to tell herself to breathe.

Her only child was standing across the room.

She wanted to rush to him, to tell him how sorry she was for all their differences, how glad she was to see him. But her muscles would not respond.

"Mother," Mark said. "Your son is back from the grave."

She caught the coolness in his tone and instantly sensed that his heart was still hard. "Where have you been?"

"It's a long story."

No shade of compassion tempered his stare. She waited for him to explain, but he said nothing.

Malone came toward her, placed a hand on her shoulder, and broke the awkward pause. "Why don't you sit."

She felt disconnected from her life, a jumble of confusion violating her thoughts, and she was having a hard time set-tling her anxiety. But dammit, she was the head of one of the most highly specialized units within the U.S. government. She dealt with crises on a daily basis. True, none was as per-sonal as the one now facing her from across the room, but if

Mark wanted their first reception to be a chilly one, then so be it, she'd not give any of them the satisfaction of thinking emotion ruled her.

So she sat and said, "Okay, Mark. Tell us your long story."

Mark Nelle opened his eyes. He was no longer eight thousand feet high in the French Pyrénées, wearing spike shoes and carrying a pick, hiking a rough trail in search of Bérenger Saunière's cache. He was inside a room of stone and wood with a blackened beamed ceiling. The man standing over him was tall and gaunt with gray fuzz for hair and a silver beard as thick as fleece. The man's eyes were a peculiar shade of violet that he could not recall ever having seen before.

"Careful," the man said in English. "You're still weak."

"Where am I?"

"A place that has been for centuries one of safety."

"Does it have a name?"

"Abbey des Fontaines."

"That's miles from where I was."

"Two of my subordinates were following and made rescue when the snow began to engulf you. I'm told the avalanche was quite intense."

He could still feel the mountain as it shook, its summit disintegrating like a great cathedral falling apart. An entire ridge had shattered above him and snow had poured down as blood would from an open wound. The chill still gripped his bones. Then he recalled tumbling downward. But had he heard the man standing over him right?

"Men were following me?"

"I ordered it. As with your father before you sometimes."

"You knew my father?"

"His theories always interested me. So I made a point to know both him and what he knew."

He tried to sit up from the bed, but his right side jarred with electric pain. He winced and clutched at his stomach.

"You have broken ribs. I, too, in youth, broke mine once. It hurts."

He lay back down. "I was brought here?"

The old man nodded. "My brothers are trained to be resourceful."

He'd noticed the white cassock and rope sandals. "This a monastery?"

"It's the place you've been seeking."

He was unsure how to respond.

"I am master of the Poor Fellow-Soldiers of Christ and the Temple of Solomon. We are the Templars. Your father sought us for decades. You, too, have sought us. So I decided the time was finally right."

"For what?"

"That's for you to decide. But I am hoping you choose to join us."

"Why would I do that?"

"Your life is, I'm sorry to say, in utter chaos. You miss your father more than you could ever voice and he's been dead a long six years now. You're estranged from your mother, which is difficult in more ways than can be imagined. Professionally you're a teacher, but you're not satisfied. You've made some attempts to vindicate your father's beliefs, but have been unable to make much progress. That's why you were in the Pyrénées— searching for the reason Abbé Saunière spent so much time there when he was alive. Saunière once scoured the region looking for something. Surely you found the coach and horse rental receipts among Saunière's papers that evidence the fees he paid to the local vendors. Amazing, isn't it, how a humble priest could afford such luxuries as a private coach and horse."

"What do you know of my father and mother?"

"I know much."

"You expect me to believe that you're the master of the Templars?"

"I can see how that premise might be hard to accept. I, too, had trouble with it when the brothers first approached me decades ago. Why don't we, for now, concentrate on mending your wounds and take this slow."

"I stayed in that bed for three weeks," Mark said. "After, my movements were restricted to certain parts of the abbey, but the master and I spoke often. Finally, I agreed to stay on and took the oath."

"Why would you do such a thing?" Stephanie asked.

"Let's be realistic, Mother. You and I had not spoken in years. Dad was gone. The master was right. I was at a dead end. Dad searched for the Templar treasure, their archives, and for the Templars themselves. One-third of what he'd been looking for had just found me. I wanted to stay."

To calm her growing agitation, Stephanie allowed her attention to stray to the younger man standing behind Mark. An aureole of freshness hovered about him, but she also registered interest, as if he were hearing things for the first time. "Your name is Geoffrey?" she asked, recalling what Mark had called him earlier.

He nodded.

"You didn't know I was Mark's mother?"

"I know little of other brothers. It is Rule. No brother speaks of himself to another. We're of the brotherhood. From where we came is immaterial to who we are now."

"Sounds impersonal."

"I consider it illuminating."

"Geoffrey sent you a package," Mark said. "Dad's journal. Did you receive it?"

"That's why I'm here."

"I had it with me the day of the avalanche. The master kept it once I became a brother. I discovered it gone after he died."

"Your master is dead?" Malone asked.

"We have a new leader," Mark said. "But he's a demon."

Malone described the man who'd confronted him and Stephanie in the Roskilde cathedral.

"That's Raymond de Roquefort," Mark said. "How do you know him?"

"We're old friends," Malone said, telling them some of what had just happened in Avignon.

"Claridon is surely de Roquefort's prisoner," Mark said. "God help Royce."

"He was terrified of the Templars," Malone said.

"With that one, he has good reason."

"You still haven't said why you stayed at the abbey for the past five years," Stephanie said.

"What I sought was there. The master became a father to me. He was a kind, gentle man, full of compassion."

She caught the message. "Unlike me?"

"Now is not the time for this discussion."

"And when would be a good time? I thought you were dead, Mark. But you were secluded in an abbey, commingling with Templars—"

"Your son was our seneschal," Geoffrey said. "He and the master ruled us well. He was a blessing to our Order."

"He was second in charge?" Malone asked. "How'd you rise so fast?"

"The seneschal is chosen by the master. He alone determines who is qualified," Geoffrey said. "And he chose well."

Malone smiled. "You have a devoted associate."

"Geoffrey is a wealth of information, though none of us is going to learn a thing from him until he's ready to tell us."

"Care to explain that one?" Malone asked.

Mark spoke, telling them what had happened over the past forty-eight hours. Stephanie listened with a mixture of fascination and anger. Her son talked of the brotherhood with reverence.

"The Templars," Mark said, "rose from an obscure band of nine knights, supposedly protecting pilgrims on the way to the Holy Land, to a multicontinent conglomerate composed of tens of thousands of brothers spread over nine thousand estates. Kings, queens, and popes cowed to them. No one, until Philip IV in 1307, successfully challenged them. You know why?"

"Military prowess, I'd assume," Malone said.

Mark shook his head. "It wasn't force that gave them strength, it was knowledge. They possessed information no one else was privy to."

Malone sighed. "Mark, we don't know each other, but it's the middle of the night, I'm sleepy, and my neck is killing me. Could we skip the riddles and get to the point?"

"Among the Templar treasure was some proof that related to Christ on the cross."

The room went silent as the words took hold.

"What kind of proof?" Malone asked.

"I don't know. But it's called the Great Devise. The proof was found in the Holy Land beneath the Jerusalem Temple, hidden away sometime between the first century and AD 70, when the Temple was destroyed. It was transported by the Templars back to France and hidden away, known only to the highest officers. When Jacques de Molay, the Templar master at the time of the Purge, was burned at the stake in 1314, the location of that proof died with him. Philip IV tried to obtain the information and failed. Dad believed that the abbés Bigou and Saunière at Rennes-le-Château succeeded. He was convinced that Saunière actually located the Templar cache."

"So was the master," Geoffrey said.

"See what I mean?" Mark glanced back at his friend. "Say the magic words and we get information."

"The master made clear that Bigou and Saunière were right," Geoffrey said.

"About what?" Mark asked.

"He didn't say. Only that they were right."

Mark looked toward them. "Like you, Mr. Malone, I've had my fill of riddles."

"Call me Cotton."

"Interesting name. How'd you get it?"

"Long story. I'll tell you sometime."

"Mark," Stephanie said, "you can't really believe that there exists any definitive proof relating to Christ on the cross? Your father never even went that far."

"How would you know?" The question carried bitterness.

"I know how he—"

"You don't know anything, Mother. That's your problem. You never knew anything about what Dad thought. You believed everything he sought was a fantasy, that he was wasting his talents. You never loved him enough to let him be himself. You thought he sought fame and treasure. No. He sought the truth. Christ has died. Christ has risen. Christ will come again. That's what interested him."

Stephanie collected her scattered senses and told herself not to react to the rebuke.

"Dad was a serious academician. His work had merit, he just never talked openly about what he really sought. When he discovered Rennes-le-Château in the seventies and told the world about Saunière's story, that was simply a way to raise money. What may or may not have happened there is a good tale. Millions of people enjoyed reading about it regardless of the embellishments. You were one of the few who didn't."

"Your father and I tried to work through our differences."

"How? By you telling him he was wasting his life, hurting his family? By telling him he was a failure?"

"All right, dammit, I was wrong." Her voice was a shout. "You want me to say it again? I was wrong." She sat up from the chair, a desperate resolution vesting her with power. "I screwed up. That what you want to hear? In my mind, you've been dead five years. Now here you are, and all you want is for me to admit I was wrong. Fine. If I could tell your father that, I would. If I could beg his forgiveness, I would. But I can't." The words were coming fast, emotion charging her, and she intended to say it all while she possessed the courage. "I came here to see what I could do. To try to follow through on whatever it was Lars *and you* thought important. That's the only reason I came. I thought I was finally doing the right thing. But don't shoot that sanctimonious crap at me anymore. You screwed up, too. The difference between us is that I learned something over the past five years."

She slumped back in the chair, feeling better, if even in a small way. But she realized the gulf between them had just widened and a shudder passed through her.

"It's the middle of the night," Malone finally said. "Why don't we sleep a little and deal with all this in a few hours."

THIRTY-EIGHT

DE ROQUEFORT SLAMMED THE DOOR SHUT BEHIND HIM. THE iron clanged against the metal frame with the retort of a rifle, and the lock engaged.

"Is all ready?" he asked one of the assistants.

"As specified."

Good. Time to make his point. He strolled ahead through the subterranean corridor. He was three floors below ground level, in a part of the abbey first occupied a thousand years ago. Endless construction had transformed the rooms surrounding him into a labyrinth of forgotten chambers, now used mainly for cool storage.

He'd returned to the abbey three hours ago with Lars Nelle's notebook and Royce Claridon. The loss of *Pierres Gravées du Languedoc,* the book from the auction, weighed heavy on his mind. He could only hope the notebook and Claridon would supply him with enough of the missing pieces.

And the dark woman—she was a problem.

His world was distinctly male. His experience with women

minimal. They were a different breed, of that he was sure, but the female he'd confronted on the Pont St.-Bénézet seemed almost alien. She'd never shown even a hint of fear, and handled herself with the cunning of a lioness. She'd lured him straight to the bridge, knowing precisely how she planned to make her escape. Her only mistake was in losing the journal. He had to know her identity.

But first things first.

He entered a chamber topped by pine rafters that had remained unaltered since the time of Napoléon. A long table spanned the room's center, upon which lay Royce Claridon, prone on his back, his arms and legs strapped to steel spikes.

"Monsieur Claridon, I have little time and I need much from you. Your cooperation will make everything so much simpler."

"What do you expect me to say?" Desperation laced the words.

"Only the truth."

"I know little."

"Come now, let us not start with a lie."

"I know nothing."

He shrugged. "I heard you in the archives. You are a reservoir of information."

"All that I said in Avignon came to me then."

De Roquefort motioned to a brother who stood across the room. The man stepped forward and laid an open tin container on the table. With three extended fingers, the brother scooped out a sticky white glob.

De Roquefort pulled off Claridon's shoes and socks.

Claridon raised his head to see. "What are you doing? What is that?"

"Cooking grease."

The brother rubbed the grease onto Claridon's bare feet.

"What are you doing?"

"Surely you know your history. When the Templars were arrested in 1307, many means were used to extract confessions. Teeth were pulled out, the empty sockets probed with metal. Wedges were driven under nails. Heat was used in a variety of imaginative ways. One technique involved greasing the feet, then exposing the oiled skin to flame. Slowly the feet would cook, the skin falling away like meat from a tenderloin. Many brothers succumbed to that agony. Those who managed to survive all confessed. Even Jacques de Molay fell victim."

The brother finished with the grease and withdrew from the room.

"In our Chronicles, there's a report of one Templar who, after being subjected to foot burning and confessing, was carried before his inquisitors clutching a bag with his blackened foot bones. He was allowed to keep them as a remembrance of his ordeal. Wasn't that kind of his inquisitors?"

He stepped over to a charcoal brazier that burned in one corner. He'd ordered it prepared an hour ago and its coals were now white hot.

"I would assume you thought this fire was to warm the chamber. Below ground is chilly here in the mountains. But I had this flame forged just for you."

He rolled the cart with the brazier within three feet of Claridon's bare feet.

"The idea, I'm told, is for the heat to be low and steady. Not intense—that tends to vaporize the grease too quickly. Just as with a steak, a slow flame works best."

Claridon's eyes went wide.

"When my brethren were tortured in the fourteenth century, it was thought God would fortify the innocent to handle the pain, so only the guilty would actually confess. Also— and quite convenient, I might add—any confession extracted from torture was nonretractable. So once a person confessed, that was the end of the matter."

He pushed the brazier to within twelve inches of the bare skin.

Claridon screamed.

"So soon, monsieur? Nothing has even happened yet. Have you no endurance?"

"What do you want?"

"A great many things. But we can start with the significance of *Don Miguel de Mañara Reading the Rules of the Caridad*."

"There's a clue there that relates to the abbé Bigou and the tombstone of Marie d'Hautpoul de Blanchefort. Lars Nelle found a cryptogram. He believed the key to solving it lay in the painting." Claridon was talking fast.

"I heard all that in the archives. I want to know what you failed to say."

"I know nothing more. Please, my feet are frying."

"That's the idea." He reached into his cassock and removed Lars Nelle's journal.

"You have it?" Claridon said in amazement.

"Why so shocked?"

"His widow. She possessed it."

"Not anymore." He'd read most of the entries on the trip back from Avignon. He thumbed through until he found the cryptogram and held the open pages up for Claridon to see. "Is that what Lars Nelle found?"

"*Oui. Oui.*"

"What's the message?"

"I don't know. Truly, I don't. Can you not remove the heat? Please, I beg you. My feet are in agony."

He decided a show of compassion might loosen the tongue quicker. He slid the cart a foot back.

"Thank you. Thank you." Claridon was breathing fast.

"Keep talking."

"Lars Nelle found the cryptogram in a manuscript that Noël Corbu wrote in the sixties."

"No one has ever found that manuscript."

"Lars did. It was with a priest, whom Corbu entrusted the pages to before he died in 1968."

He knew about Corbu from the reports one of his predecessors had recorded. That marshal, too, had searched for the Great Devise. "What about the cryptogram?"

"The painting was referenced by Abbé Bigou himself, in the parish register, shortly before he fled France for Spain, so Lars believed it held the key to the puzzle. But he died before deciphering it."

De Roquefort did not possess the lithograph of the painting. The woman had taken it, along with the book from the auction. Yet that could hardly be the only recorded image of *Reading the Rules of the Caridad*. Now that he knew what to look for, he'd find another.

"And what did the son know? Mark Nelle. What was his knowledge?"

"Not much. He was a teacher in Toulouse. He searched as a hobby on weekends. Not all that serious. But he was looking for Saunière's hiding place in the mountains when he was killed in an avalanche."

"He did not die there."

"Of course he did. Five years ago."

De Roquefort stepped close. "Mark Nelle has lived here, in this abbey for the past five years. He was pulled from the snows and brought here. Our master took him in and made him our seneschal. He also wanted him to be our next master. But thanks to me, he failed. Mark Nelle fled these walls this afternoon. For the past five years he's scoured through our records, looking for clues, while you hid like a cockroach afraid of the light in a mental asylum."

"You speak nonsense."

"I speak truth. Here is where he stayed, while you cowered in fear."

"You and your brothers were who I feared. Lars feared you, too."

"He had reason to be scared. He lied to me, several times, and I detest deceit. He was given an opportunity to repent, but he chose to offer more lies."

"You hung him from that bridge, didn't you? I always knew that."

"He was a nonbeliever, an atheist. I believe you understand that I'll do what is necessary to achieve my goal. I wear the white cassock. I'm master of this abbey. Nearly five hundred brothers await my orders. Our Rule is clear. The order of the master is as if Christ commanded it, for it was Christ who said through the mouth of David, *Ob auditu auris obedivit mihi.* He obeyed me as soon as he heard me. That, too, should place fear in your heart." He motioned with the journal. "Now tell me what this puzzle says."

"Lars thought it revealed the location of whatever it was Saunière found."

He reached for the cart. "I swear to you, your feet will become nothing but stubs if you don't answer my question."

Claridon's eyes went wide. "What must I do to prove my sincerity? I only know parts of the story. Lars was like that. He shared little. You have his journal."

An element of desperation clothed the words with believability. "I'm still listening."

"I know Saunière found the cryptogram in the Rennes church when he was replacing the altar. He also found a crypt where he discovered that Marie d'Hautpoul de Blanchefort was not buried outside in the parish close, but beneath the church."

He'd read all that in the journal, but what he wanted to know was, "How did Lars Nelle learn that?"

"He found the information about the crypt in old books discovered at Monfort-Lamaury, the fief of Simon de Montfort, which described the Rennes church in great detail. Then he found more references in Corbu's manuscript."

He despised hearing the name Simon de Montfort—another thirteenth-century opportunist who commanded the Albigensian Crusade that ravaged the Languedoc in the name of the Church. If not for him, the Templars would have achieved their own separate state, which would have surely prevented their later downfall. The one flaw in the Order's early existence had been its dependency on secular rule. Why the first few masters felt compelled to link themselves so closely with kingship had always perplexed him.

"Saunière learned that his predecessor, the abbé Bigou, erected Marie d'Hautpoul's tombstone. He thought the writing on it, and the reference Bigou left in the parish records about the painting, were clues."

"They are ridiculously conspicuous."

"Not to an eighteenth-century mind," Claridon said. "Most were illiterate then. So the simplest of codes, even words themselves, would have been quite effective. And actually they have been—staying hidden all this time."

Something from the Chronicles flashed through de Roquefort's mind, from a time after the Purge. The only clue recorded to the Great Devise's location. *Where is it best to hide a pebble?* The answer suddenly became obvious. "On the ground," he muttered.

"What did you say?"

His mind snapped back to reality. "Can you recall what you saw in the painting?"

Claridon's head bobbed up and down. "*Oui,* monsieur. Every detail."

Which gave the fool some value.

"And I also have the drawing," Claridon said.

Had he heard right? "The drawing of the gravestone?"

"The notes I made in the archive. When the lights went out, I snatched the paper from the table."

He liked what he was hearing. "Where is it?"

"In my pocket."

He decided to make a deal. "How about a collaboration? We both have certain knowledge. Why don't we pool our efforts."

"And how would that benefit me?"

"Having your feet intact would be an immediate reward."

"Quite right, monsieur. I like that a great deal."

He decided to appeal to what he knew the man wanted. "We seek the Great Devise for reasons different from you. Once it's found, I'm sure a certain monetary remuneration can compensate you for your trouble." Then he made his point crystal clear. "And besides, I'll not let you go. And if you manage to escape, I will find you."

"I seem to have little choice."

"You know they left you to us."

Claridon said nothing.

"Malone and Stephanie Nelle. They made no effort to save you. Instead, they saved themselves. I heard you pleading for help in the archives. So did they. They did nothing." He allowed his words to take root, hoping he'd correctly judged the man's weak character. "Together, Monsieur Claridon, we could be successful. I possess Lars Nelle's journal and have access to an archive you can only imagine. You have the gravestone information and know things I don't. We both want the same thing, so let's both discover it."

De Roquefort gripped a knife lying on the table between Claridon's outstretched legs and severed the bindings.

"Come, we have work to do."

THIRTY-NINE

MALONE FOLLOWED MARK AS THEY APPROACHED THE CHURCH of Saint Mary Magdalene. Services were not held there during summer. Sunday was apparently too popular a day for tourists, as a crowd was already milling about outside the church, snapping pictures and recording video.

"We'll need a ticket," Mark said. "Can't enter this church without paying a fee."

Malone stepped into the Villa Béthanie and waited in a short line. Back outside, he found Mark standing before a railed garden where the Visigoth pillar and statue of the Virgin that Royce Claridon had told him about stood. He read the words PENITENCE, PENITENCE and MISSION 1891 carved on the pillar's face.

"The Notre Dame de Lourdes," Mark said, pointing at the statue. "Saunière was enthralled by Lourdes, which was the premier Marian vision of his time. Before Fatima. He wanted Rennes to become a pilgrimage center, so he built this garden and designed the statue and pillar."

Malone gestured at the people. "He got his wish."

"True. But not for the reason he imagined. I'm sure none

of the people here today even knows that the pillar is not the original. It's a copy, put there years ago. The original is difficult to read. Weather took a toll. It's in the presbytery museum. Which is true for a lot of this place. Little is as it was in Saunière's time."

They approached the church's main door. Beneath the gilded tympanum Malone read the words, TERRIBILIS EST LOCU ISTE. From Genesis. Terrible is this place. He knew the tale of Jacob who dreamed of a ladder on which angels traveled and, after waking from his sleep, uttered the words—*Terrible is this place*—then named what he'd dreamed about Bethel, which meant "house of God." Another thought occurred to him. "But in the Old Testament, Bethel becomes a rival to Jerusalem as a religious center."

"Precisely. One more subtle clue Saunière left behind. There are even more inside."

They'd all slept late, having risen about thirty minutes ago. Stephanie had taken her husband's bedroom and was still inside with the door closed when Malone suggested that he and Mark head for the church. He wanted to talk to the younger man without Stephanie around, and he wanted to give her time to cool down. He knew she was looking for a fight, and sooner or later her son was going to have to face her. But he thought delaying that inevitability might be a good idea. Geoffrey had offered to come, but Mark had told him no. Malone had sensed that Mark Nelle wanted to speak to him alone, too.

They entered the nave.

The church was single-aisled with a high ceiling. A hideous carved devil, crouching low, clothed in a green robe, and grimacing under the weight of a holy water stoup, greeted them.

"It's actually the demon Asmodeus, not the devil," Mark said.

"Another message?"

"You apparently know him."

"A custodian of secrets, if I recall."

"You do. Look at the rest of the fount."

Above the holy water stoup stood four angels, each one enacting a separate part of the sign of the cross. Beneath them was written, PAR CE SIGNE TU LE VAINCRAS. Malone translated the French. By this sign ye shall conquer him.

He knew the significance of those words. "That's what Constantine said when he first fought his rival, Maxentius. According to the story, he supposedly saw a cross on the sun with those words emblazoned beneath."

"But there's one difference." Mark pointed to the carved letters. "No *him* in the original phrase. Only *By this sign ye shall conquer.*"

"Is that significant?"

"My father discovered an ancient Jewish legend that told of how the king managed to prevent demons from interfering with the building of the Temple of Solomon. One of those demons, Asmodeus, was controlled by being forced to tote water—the one element he despised. So this fount's symbolism is not out of character. But the *him* in the quotation was clearly added by Saunière. Some say the *him* is simply a reference to the fact that by dipping a finger in the holy water and making the sign of the cross, which Catholics do, the devil—*him*—would be conquered. But others have noticed the positioning of the word in the French phrase. *Par ce signe tu le vaincras.* The word *le,* 'him,' represents the thirteenth and fourteenth letters. 1314."

He recalled his reading from the Templar book. "The year Jacques de Molay was executed."

"Coincidence?" Mark shrugged.

About twenty people milled about snapping photographs and admiring the gaudy imagery, which all oozed a cryptic allusion. Stained-glass windows lined the outer walls, lively from the bright sun, and he noticed the scenes. Mary and Martha at Bethany. Mary Magdalene meeting the risen Christ. The resurrection of Lazarus.

"It's like a theological fun house," he whispered.

"That's one way of putting it."

Mark motioned to the checkerboard floor before the altar. "The crypt entrance is there, just before that wrought-iron grille, hidden beneath the tiles. A few years ago some French geographers conducted a covert ground-penetrating radar survey of the building and managed to make a few soundings before the local authorities stopped them. The results showed a subsurface anomaly beneath the altar that could be a crypt."

"No digging was done?"

"No way the locals would allow that. Too many risks to the tourist industry."

He smiled. "That's the same thing Claridon said yesterday."

They settled into one of the pews.

"One thing is certain," Mark said in a hushed tone. "There's no path to any treasure here. But Saunière did use this church to telegraph what he believed. And from everything I've read about the man, that act fits with his brazen personality."

Malone noticed that nothing around him was subtle. The excessive coloration and overgilding tainted any beauty. Then another point became clear. Nothing was consistent. Each artistic expression, from the statues, to the reliefs, to the windows, was individual—without regard to theme, as if similarity would somehow be offensive.

An odd collection of esoteric saints stared down at him with listless expressions, as if they, too, were embarrassed by their garish detail. St. Roch displayed a wounded thigh. St. Germaine released a bevy of roses from her apron. St. Magdalene held an odd-shaped vase. Try as he might, Malone could not become comfortable. He'd been inside many European churches and most exuded a deep sense of time and history. This one seemed only to repel.

"Saunière directed every detail of the decoration," Mark was saying. "Nothing was placed here without his approval."

Mark pointed at one of the statues. "St. Anthony of Padua. We pray to him when searching for something lost."

He caught that irony. "Another message?"

"Clearly. Check out the stations of the cross."

The carvings began at the pulpit, seven along the north wall, then another seven on the south. Each was a colorful bas-relief that depicted a moment in Christ's crucifixion. Their bright patina and cartoonish detail seemed unusual for something so solemn.

"Strange, aren't they?" Mark asked. "When they were installed in 1887, they were common for the area. In Rocamadour, there's a nearly identical set. The Giscard House in Toulouse made those and these. Much has been made of these stations. Conspiratorialists claim they have Masonic origins or are actually some sort of treasure map. None of that's true. But there are messages in them."

Malone noticed some of the curious aspects. The black slave boy who held the wash bowl for Pilate. The veil Pilate wore. A trumpet being sounded as Christ fell with the cross. Three silver discs held aloft. The child confronting Christ, wrapped in a Scottish tartan blanket. A Roman soldier throwing dice for Christ's cloak, the numbers three, four, and five visible on the faces.

"Look at station fourteen," Mark said, gesturing toward the south wall.

Malone stood and walked to the front of the church. Candles flickered before the altar and he quickly noticed the bas-relief beneath. A woman, Mary Magdalene, he assumed, in tears, kneeling in a grotto before a cross formed by two branches. A skull rested at the branch base and he immediately thought of the skull from the lithograph last night in Avignon.

He turned and studied the image of the last station of the cross, number 14, which depicted Christ's body being carried by two men as three women wept. Behind them rose a rocky escarpment above which hung a full moon in the night sky.

"Jesus being carried to the tomb," he whispered to Mark, who'd approached close behind him.

"According to Roman law, a crucified man was never allowed burial. That form of execution was reserved only for those guilty of crimes against the empire, the idea being for the accused to slowly dic on the cross—death taking several days and for all to see, the body left for the carrion birds. Yet supposedly Pilate granted Christ's body to Joesph of Arimathea so that it could be buried. Have you ever wondered why?"

"Not really."

"Others have. Remember, Christ was killed on the eve of the Sabbath. He could not, by law, be buried after the sun set." Mark pointed at station 14. "Yet Saunière hung this representation, which clearly shows the body being carried after dark."

Malone still didn't understand the significance.

"What if instead of being carried *into* the tomb, Christ is being carried *out,* after dark?"

He said nothing.

"Are you familiar with the Gnostic Gospels?" Mark asked.

He was. They were found along the upper Nile in 1945. Seven Bedouin field hands were digging when they came across a human skeleton and a sealed urn. Thinking it contained gold, they smashed the urn open and found thirteen leather-bound codices. Not quite a book, but a close ancestor. The neatly written, ragged-edged texts were all in ancient Coptic, most likely composed by monks who lived at the nearby Pachomian monastery during the fourth century. They contained forty-six ancient Christian manuscripts, their content dating from the second century, the codices themselves fashioned in the fourth century. Some were subsequently lost, used as kindling or discarded, but by 1947 the remainder were acquired by a local museum.

He told Mark what he knew.

"The answer as to why the monks buried the codices came from history," Mark said. "In the fourth century Athanasius, the bishop of Alexandria, wrote a letter that was sent to all the churches in Egypt. He decreed that only the twenty-seven books contained within the recently formulated New Testament could be considered Scripture. All other *heretical* books must be destroyed. None of the forty-six manuscripts in that urn conformed. So the monks at the Pachomian monastery chose to hide the thirteen codices rather than burn them, perhaps waiting for a change in church leadership. Of course, no change ever occurred. Instead, Roman Christianity flourished. But thank heaven the codices survived. These are the Gnostic Gospels we now know. In one, Peter's, it is written, *And as they declared what things they had seen, again they saw three men come forth from the tomb, and two of them supporting one.*"

Malone stared again at station 14. Two men supporting one.

"The Gnostic Gospels were extraordinary texts," Mark said. "Many scholars now say the Gospel of Thomas, which was included in them, may be the closest we have to Christ's actual words. The early Christians were terrified of the Gnostics. The word came from the Greek *gnosis,* which meant 'knowledge.' Gnostics were simply people in the know, but the emerging Catholic version of Christianity eventually eliminated all gnostic thought and teachings."

"And the Templars kept that alive?"

Mark nodded. "The Gnostic Gospels, and several more that theologians today have never seen, are contained in the abbey's library. The Templars were broad-minded when it came to Scripture. There's a lot to be learned from these so-called heretical works."

"How would Saunière know anything of those Gospels? They weren't discovered until decades after his death."

"Perhaps he had access to even better information. Let me show you something else."

He followed Mark back to the church's entrance and they stepped out onto the porch. Above the door was a stone-carved box upon which words were painted.

"Read the writing beneath," Mark said.

Malone strained to make out the letters. Many were faded and hard to decipher, and all were in Latin.

REGNUM MUNID ET OMNEM ORNATUM SAECULI CONTEMPSI,
PROPTER AMOREM DOMININ MEI JESU CHRISTI: QUEM VIDI,
QUEM AMAVI, IN QUEM CREDIDI, QUEM DILEXI

"Translated it means, 'I have had contempt for the kingdom of this world, and all temporal adornments, because of the love of my Lord Jesus Christ, whom I saw, whom I loved, in whom I believed, and whom I worshiped.' On its face an interesting statement, but there are some conspicuous errors." Mark motioned. "The words *scoeculi, anorem, quen,* and *cremini* are all misspelled. Saunière spent one hundred and eighty francs for that carving and for the letters to be painted, which was a sizable sum at the time. We know this because his receipts still exist. He went to a lot of trouble to design this entrance, yet he allowed the misspellings to remain. It would have been easy to repair them, since the letters were only painted."

"Maybe he didn't notice?"

"Saunière? He was a type A personality. Nothing slipped by him."

Mark led him away from the entrance as another wave of visitors entered the church. They stopped in front of the garden with the Visigoth pillar and statue of the Virgin.

"The inscription above the door is not biblical. It's contained within a responsory written by a man named John Tauler early in the fourteenth century. Responsories were prayers or poems used between scriptural readings and Tauler was well known in Saunière's time. So it's possible Saunière simply liked the phrase. But it's pretty unusual."

Malone agreed.

"The misspellings could shed some light on why Saunière

used it. The painted words are *quem cremini,* 'in whom I believed,' but the word should have been *credidi,* yet Saunière allowed the misspelling. Could that mean that he did not believe in Him? And then the most interesting of all. *Quem vidi.* Whom I saw."

Malone instantly saw the significance. "Whatever he found led him to Christ. Whom he saw."

"That's what Dad thought, and I agree. Saunière seemed unable to resist sending messages. He wanted the world to know what he knew, but it was almost as if he realized that no one in his time would understand. And he was right. No one did. Not until forty years after he died did anyone ever notice." Mark looked over at the ancient church. "The whole place is one of reversals. The stations of the cross are hung on the wall backward from every other church in the world. The devil at the door—he's the reverse of good." Then he pointed to the Visigoth pillar a few feet away. "Upside down. Notice the cross and the carvings on the face."

Malone studied the face.

"Saunière inverted the pillar before carving Mission 1891 at the bottom and Penitence, Penitence along the top."

Malone noticed a v with a circle at its center in the bottom right corner. He cocked his head around and envisioned the image inverted. "Alpha and omega?" he asked.

"Some think so. Dad did."

"Another name for Christ."

"That's right."

"Why did Saunière turn the pillar upside down?"

"No one has come up with a good reason."

Mark stepped away from the garden display and allowed others to surge forward for pictures. He then led the way toward the rear of the church, into one corner of the Calvary garden where a small grotto stood.

"This is a replica, too. For the tourists. World War Two took the original. Saunière built it with rocks he would bring back from his forays. He and his mistress would travel off for days at a time and return with a hod full of stones. Odd, wouldn't you say?"

"Depends on what else was in that hod."

Mark smiled. "Easy way to bring back a little gold without arousing suspicion."

"But Saunière seems a strange sort. He could have just been toting rocks."

"Everybody who comes here is a little strange."

"That include your father?"

Mark appraised him with a serious countenance. "No question. He was obsessed. He gave his life to this place, loved every square foot of this village. This was his home, in every way."

"But not yours?"

"I tried to carry on. But I didn't have his passion. Maybe I realized the whole thing was futile."

"Then why hide yourself away in an abbey for five years?"

"I needed the solitude. It was good for me. But the master

had bigger plans. So here I am. A fugitive from the Templars."

"So what were you doing in the mountains when that avalanche came?"

Mark did not answer him.

"You were doing the same thing your mother's doing here now. Trying to atone for something. You just didn't know folks were watching."

"Thank heaven they did."

"Your mother is hurting."

"You and she worked together?"

He noticed the dodge. "For a long time. She's my friend."

"That's a tough nut to crack."

"Tell me about it, but it can be done. She's hurting bad. Lots of guilt and regrets. This could be a second chance for her and you."

"My mother and I parted ways long ago. It was best for both of us."

"Then what are you doing here?"

"I came to my father's house."

"And when you arrived you saw that somebody else's bags were there. Both our passports were left with our stuff. Surely you found them? Yet you stayed."

Mark turned away and Malone thought it an effort to hide a growing confusion. He was more like his mother than he cared to admit.

"I'm thirty-eight years old and still feel like a boy," Mark said. "I've lived the past five years within the sheltered cocoon of an abbey governed by strict Rule. A man I considered a father was kind to me, and I rose to a level of importance I've never known before."

"Yet here you are. Right in the middle of God-knows-what."

Mark smiled.

"You and your mother need to settle things."

The younger man stood somber, preoccupied. "The woman you mentioned last night, Cassiopeia Vitt. I know of her. She and my father sparred for several years. Should she not be found?"

He noticed that Mark liked to avoid answering questions by asking them, much like his mother. "Depends. She a threat?"

"Hard to say. She seemed to always be around, and Dad didn't like her."

"Neither does de Roquefort."

"I'm sure."

"In the archives, last night, she never identified herself and de Roquefort didn't know her name. So if he has Claridon, then he now knows who she is."

"Isn't that her problem?" Mark asked.

"She saved my hide twice. So she needs to be warned. Claridon told me she lives nearby, in Givors. Your mother and I were leaving here today. We thought this quest over. But that's changed. I need to pay Cassiopeia Vitt a visit. I think alone would be best, for now."

"That's fine. We'll wait here. Right now I have a visit of my own to make. It's been five years since I paid respects to my father."

And Mark walked off toward the cemetery's entrance.

FORTY

STEPHANIE POURED HERSELF A CUP·OF HOT COFFEE AND OF-
fered more to Geoffrey, but the younger man refused.

"We're allowed but one cup a day," he made clear.

She sat at the kitchen table. "Is your entire life governed
by Rule?"

"It's our way."

"I thought secrecy was important to the brotherhood, too.
Why do you speak of it so openly?"

"My master, who now resides with the Lord, told me to be
honest with you."

She was perplexed. "How did your master know me?"

"He followed your husband's research closely. That was
long before my time at the abbey, but the master told me of it.
He and your husband spoke on several occasions. The master
was your husband's confessor."

The information shocked her. "Lars made contact with the
Templars?"

"Actually, the Templars contacted him. My master approached your husband, but if your husband knew that he
was of the Templars, he never revealed it. Perhaps he
thought saying it might end the contact. But surely he knew."

"Your master sounds like a curious man."

The younger man's face brightened. "He was a wise man who tried to do good for our Order."

She recalled his defense of Mark hours earlier. "Did my son help with that endeavor?"

"That's why he was chosen seneschal."

"And the fact that he was Lars Nelle's son had nothing to do with that choice?"

"On that, madame, I cannot speak. I only learned who the seneschal was a few hours ago. Here, in this house. So I don't know."

"You know nothing of each other?"

"Very little, and some of us struggle with that. Others revel in the privacy. But we spend our lives together, close as in a prison. Too much familiarity could become a problem. So we're barred by Rule from any intimacy with our fellows. We keep to ourselves, our silence enforced through the service of God."

"Sounds difficult."

"It's the life we choose. This adventure, though." He shook his head. "My master told me I'd discover many new things. He was right."

She sipped more coffee. "Your master was sure that you and I would meet?"

"He sent the journal hoping you'd come. He also sent a letter to Ernst Scoville, which included pages from the journal that related to you. He hoped that would bring you two together. He knew Scoville once didn't care for you—he learned that from your husband. But he realized your resources are great. So he wanted the two of you, together with the seneschal and myself, to find the Great Devise."

She recalled that term and its explanation from earlier. "Does your Order truly believe that there's more to the story of Christ—things the world doesn't know?"

"I have, as yet, not achieved a sufficient level of training to answer your question. Many decades of service are required before I'll be privy to what the Order actually knows. But death, at least to me and from what I have been taught so far, seems a clear finality. Many thousands of brothers died on the battlefields of the Holy Land. Not one of them ever rose and walked away."

"The Catholic Church would call what you just said heresy."

"The Church is an institution created by men and governed by men. Whatever more is made of that institution is also the creation of man."

She decided to tempt fate. "What am I supposed to do, Geoffrey?"

"Help your son."

"How?"

"He must complete what his father started. Raymond de Roquefort cannot be allowed to find the Great Devise. The master was emphatic on this point. That's why he planned ahead. Why I was trained."

"Mark detests me."

"He loves you."

"How would you know that?"

"My master told me."

"He would have no way of knowing that."

"My master knew all." Geoffrey reached into his trouser pocket and withdrew a sealed envelope. "I was told to give this to you when I thought appropriate." He handed her the crinkled packet, then stood from the table. "The seneschal and Mr. Malone have gone to the church. I'll leave you alone."

She appreciated the gesture. No telling what emotions the message might stir, so she waited until Geoffrey had withdrawn to the den, then opened the envelope.

Mrs. Nelle, you and I are strangers, yet I feel I know much about you, all from Lars, who told me what troubled his soul. Your son was different. He kept his torment inside, sharing precious little. On a few occasions I managed to learn some, but his emotions were not as transparent as his father's. Perhaps he inherited that trait from you? And I do not mean to be flippant. What is surely happening at the moment is serious. Raymond de Roquefort is a dangerous man. He is driven by a blindness that has, through the centuries, affected many of our Order. His is a single-mindedness that clouds his vision. Your son fought him for leadership and lost. Unfortunately, Mark does not possess the resolve needed to complete his battles. Starting them seems easy, continuing them even easier, but resolving them has proven difficult. His battles with you. His battles with de Roquefort. His battles with his conscience. All challenge him. I thought that joining the two of you together could prove decisive for you both. Again, I do not know you, but I believe I understand you. Your husband is dead and so much was left unresolved. Perhaps this quest will finally answer all your questions. I offer this advice. Trust your son, forget about the past, think only of the future. That could go a long way to providing peace. My Order is unique among all Christendom. Our beliefs are different, and that is because of what the original brothers learned and passed on. Does that make us less Christian? Or more Christian? Neither, in my opinion. Finding the Great Devise will answer many questions, but I fear that it will raise many more. It will be to you and your son to decide what is best if and when that critical time comes, and hopefully it will, for I have faith in you both. A resurrection has occurred. A second chance has been offered. The dead have risen and now walk again among you. Make good use of that miracle, but a warning: Free your mind from the prejudices in which it has grown comfortable. Open yourself to con-

ceptions more vast, and reason by more certain methods.
For only then will you succeed. May the Lord be with you.

A tear streaked down her cheek. A strange feeling, crying. One she could not remember since childhood. She was highly educated and possessed the experience that decades of working in the top levels of the intelligence business offered. Her career had been spent handling one difficult situation after another. She'd made life-and-death decisions many times. But none of that applied here. She'd somehow left the world of good and bad, right and wrong, black and white, and entered a realm where her innermost thoughts were not only known, but actually understood. This master, a man to whom she'd never spoken a word, seemed to precisely comprehend her pain.

But he was right.

Mark's return was a resurrection. A glorious miracle with endless possibilities.

"Do the words sadden you?"

She looked up. Geoffrey stood in the doorway. She swiped the tears away. "In one way. But in another they bring happiness."

"The master was like that. He knew both joy and pain. Much pain, though, in his final days."

"How did he die?"

"Cancer took him two nights ago."

"You miss him?"

"I was raised alone, without the benefit of family. Monks and nuns taught me about life. They were good to me, but none ever loved me. So hard to grow up without the love of a parent."

The admission struck her heart.

"The master showed me great kindness, perhaps even love, but most of all he placed his trust in me."

"Then don't fail him."

"I won't."

She motioned with the paper. "Is this mine to keep?"

He nodded. "I was only the deliveryman."

She grabbed hold of herself. "Why did Mark and Cotton go to the church?"

"I sensed that the seneschal wanted to talk to Mr. Malone."

She stood from the chair. "Perhaps we, too, should—"

A knock came at the front door. She tensed as her gaze darted to the unlocked latch. Cotton and Mark would have simply walked in. She saw Geoffrey likewise come alert and a gun appeared in his hand. She stepped toward the door and peered through the glass.

A familiar face stared back.

Royce Claridon.

FORTY-ONE

DE ROQUEFORT WAS FURIOUS. FOUR HOURS AGO HE'D BEEN informed that, on the night the master died, the archival security system had recorded a visit at eleven fifty-one PM. The seneschal had stayed inside twelve minutes, then left with two books. The electronic identification tags affixed to every volume identified the two missing tomes as a thirteenth-century codex he knew well and a marshal's report filed in the latter part of the nineteenth century, which he'd also read.

When he'd interrogated Royce Claridon a few hours ago, he'd not made known his familiarity with the cryptogram contained in Lars Nelle's journal. But one was included in the prior marshal's report along with the location where the puzzle had been found—in the abbé Gélis's church located in Coustausa, not far from Rennes-le-Château. He recalled from his reading that the marshal had spoken to Gélis shortly before the priest was murdered and learned that Saunière had also found a cryptogram in his church. When compared, the two were identical. Gélis apparently solved the puzzle and the marshal was told the results, but the solution was not recorded and was never found after Gélis's death. Both the local police and the marshal suspected that the murderer was after something in Gélis's briefcase. Surely, Gélis's decipher. But was the murderer Saunière? Hard to say. The crime was never solved. Still, given what de Roquefort knew, the priest from Rennes would have to be included on any suspect list.

Now the marshal's report was gone. Which might not be all bad since he possessed Lars Nelle's journal, which contained Saunière's cryptogram. Yet was it, as the marshal reported, the same as Gélis's? No way to know without the marshal's report, which was certainly removed from the archives for a reason.

Five minutes ago, while he'd listened through a microphone stuck to a side windowpane as Stephanie Nelle and brother Geoffrey bonded, he'd learned Mark Nelle and Cotton Malone had walked to the church. Stephanie Nelle had even cried after reading what the former master had written. How touching. The master had clearly planned ahead and this whole matter was rapidly spinning out of control. He needed to yank the reins tight and slow the momentum down. So while Royce Claridon dealt with the occupants at Lars Nelle's house, he was going to see about the other two.

The transponder still attached to Malone's rental car had revealed that Malone and Stephanie Nelle returned to Rennes from Avignon in the wee hours. Mark Nelle must have come straight here from the abbey, which was not surprising.

After what happened last night with the woman on the bridge, he'd thought Malone and Stephanie Nelle were no longer important, which was why his men had been instructed only to subdue them. Killing a current and a former American operative would surely bring attention. He'd traveled to Avignon to discover what secrets the palace archives held and to capture Claridon, not to attract the interest of the entire American intelligence community. He'd accomplished all three objectives and managed to obtain Lars Nelle's journal as a bonus. All in all, not a bad night's work. He'd even been willing to let Mark Nelle and Geoffrey go, since away from the abbey they were a far lesser threat. But after learning about the two missing books, that strategy had changed.

"We're in place," a voice said in his ear.

"Stay still until I call for you," he whispered into the lapel mike.

He'd brought six brothers with him and they were now scattered around the village, blending in with the growing Sunday crowd. The day was bright, sunny, and characteristically windy. While the Aude River's valleys were warm and calm, the summits surrounding them were perpetually raked by mountain winds.

He strolled up the main *rue* toward the Church of Mary Magdalene, making no effort to mask his approach.

He wanted Mark Nelle to know he was there.

MARK STOOD AT HIS FATHER'S GRAVE. THE MEMORIAL WAS IN good condition, as were all the graves, since the cemetery now seemed an integral part of the town's growing tourist industry.

For the first six years after his father died, he'd personally tended to the grave, visiting nearly every weekend. He'd also tended to the house. His father had been popular with Rennes' residents since he'd treated the village with kindness and Saunière's memory with respect. That was, perhaps, one reason why his father had included so much fiction about Rennes in his books. The embellished mystery was a money machine for the entire region, and writers who trashed that mystique were not appreciated. Since precious little was known for sure about any aspect of the tale, lots of room for improvisation existed. It also helped that his father was regarded as the man who brought the story to the world's attention, though Mark knew that a relatively unknown French book by Gérard de Sède, *Le Trésor Maudit,* published in the late 1960s, was what first ignited his father's curiosity. He'd always thought the title—*The Accursed Treasure*—apt, especially after his father suddenly died. Mark had been a teenager when he'd first read his father's book, but it had been years later, while he was in graduate school, honing his knowledge of medieval history and religious philosophy, that his father told him what was really at stake.

"The heart of Christianity is the resurrection of physical bodies. It's the fulfillment of the Old Testament promise. If Christians will not one day be resurrected, then their faith is useless. No resurrection means the Gospels are all a lie—the Christian faith is only for this life—there's no more after. It's the resurrection that makes everything performed for Christ worthwhile. Other religions preach about paradise and the afterlife. But only Christianity offers a God who became man, died for His followers, then rose from the dead to rule forever.

"Think about it," his father had said. "Christians can have a lot of different beliefs on a lot of subjects. But they all agree on the resurrection. It's their universal constant. Jesus rose from the dead for them alone. Death was conquered for them alone. Christ is alive and working toward *their* redemption. The kingdom of heaven is waiting for them, as they, too, will be raised from the dead to live forever with the Lord. There's meaning in every tragedy, since the resurrection gives hope for a future."

Then his father asked the question that had floated in his memory ever since.

"What if that never happened? What if Christ simply died, dust to dust?"

Indeed, what if?

"Think of all the millions who were slaughtered in the name of the risen Christ. During the Albigensian Crusade alone fifteen thousand men, women, and children were burned to death for simply denying the teachings of the crucifixion. The Inquisition murdered millions more. The Holy Land Crusades cost hundreds of thousands of lives. All for the so-called risen Christ. Popes for centuries have used Christ's sacrifice as a way to motivate warriors. If the resurrection never happened, so there's no promise of an afterlife, how many of those men do you think would have faced death?"

The answer was simple. Not a single one.

What if the resurrection had never happened?

Mark had just spent five years searching for an answer to that question within an Order the world thought eradicated seven hundred years ago. Yet he'd come away as perplexed as when he was first brought to the abbey.

What had been gained?

More important, what had been lost?

He shook the confusion from his mind and refocused on his father's tombstone. He'd commissioned the slab and watched while it had been laid in place one dreary May afternoon. His father had been found a week earlier, hanging from a bridge half an hour to the south of Rennes. Mark had been at home in Toulouse when the call came from the police.

He remembered his father's face when he identified the body—the ashen skin, a gaping mouth, dead eyes. A grotesque image he feared would never leave him.

His mother had returned to Georgia right after the funeral. They'd spoken little during the three days she was in France. He was twenty-seven years old, just starting at the university in Toulouse as a graduate assistant, ill prepared for life. But he wondered now, eleven years later, if he was any more prepared. Yesterday he would have killed Raymond de Roquefort. What happened to all that he'd been taught? Where was the discipline he thought he'd acquired? De Roquefort's failings were easy to understand—a false sense of duty powered by ego—but his own weaknesses were perplexing. In the span of three days, he'd gone from seneschal to fugitive. From security to chaos. From purpose to wandering.

And for what?

He felt the press of the gun beneath his jacket. The reassurance it offered was troubling—just one more new and strange sensation that brought him comfort.

He stepped from his father's grave and crept across to Ernst Scoville's resting place. He'd known the reclusive Belgian and had liked him. The master had apparently known of him, too, since he'd sent Scoville a letter only last week. What had de Roquefort said yesterday about the two mailings? *I've tended to one of the receivers.* Apparently so. But what else had he said? *And will shortly tend to the other.* His mother was in danger. They all were. But there was little that could be done. Go to the police? No one would believe them. The abbey was well respected, and not a single brother would speak out against the Order. All that would be found was a quiet monastery devoted to God. Plans existed for the secretion of all things related to the brotherhood, and not one of the men inside the abbey would fail.

Of that he was sure.

No, they were on their own.

MALONE WAITED IN THE CALVARY GARDEN FOR MARK TO RE-
turn from the cemetery. He'd not wanted to intrude on something so personal since he fully understood the unsettling
emotions the man was surely experiencing. He was only ten
when his father died, but the sorrow he'd felt at knowing that
he would never see his dad again had never faded. Unlike
with Mark, there was no cemetery for him to visit. His father's grave had been at the bottom of the North Atlantic inside the crushed hulk of a sunken submarine. He'd tried
once to find out the details of what happened, but the entire
incident remained classified.

His father had loved the Navy and the United States—he'd
been a patriot who willingly gave his life for his country.
And that realization always made Malone proud. Mark Nelle
had been lucky. He'd shared many years with his father.
They'd grown to know one another and shared life. But in a
lot of ways he and Mark were similar. Both of their dads had
been committed to their work. Both were gone. Neither
death possessed a good explanation.

He stood by the Calvary and watched as more visitors
streamed in and out of the cemetery. Finally, he spotted Mark
following a Japanese group out through the gate.

"That was tough," Mark said as he approached. "I miss
him."

He decided to pick up where they'd left off. "You and your
mother are going to have to come to terms."

"There's a lot of bad feelings there, and seeing his grave
just brought them into focus again."

"She has a heart. It's encased in iron, I know, but it's still
there."

Mark smiled. "Appears you know her."

"I've had some experience."

"At the moment, we need to concentrate on whatever the master has concocted."

"You two dodge the issue well."

Mark smiled again. "Comes with the genes."

He glanced at his watch. "It's eleven thirty. I need to head out. I want to pay a visit to Cassiopeia Vitt before nightfall."

"I'll draw you a map. It's not a long drive from here."

They left the Calvary garden and turned toward the main *rue*. A hundred feet away Malone spotted a short, rugged-looking man, hands stuffed into the pockets of a leather jacket, marching straight for the church.

He grabbed Mark's shoulder. "We've got company."

Mark followed his gaze and saw de Roquefort, too.

Malone quickly assessed their options as he spotted three more short-hairs. Two stood ahead at the Villa Béthanie. Another blocked the alley that led up to the car park.

"Any suggestions?" Malone said.

Mark stepped toward the church. "Follow me."

STEPHANIE OPENED THE DOOR AND ROYCE CLARIDON ENTERED the house. "Where did you come from?" she asked, motioning for Geoffrey to lower his weapon.

"They took me from the palace last night and drove me here. They kept me in a flat two streets over, but I managed to slip away a few minutes ago."

"How many brothers are in the village?" Geoffrey asked Claridon.

"Who are you?"

"His name is Geoffrey," Stephanie said, hoping her compatriot understood to offer precious little.

"How many brothers are here?" Geoffrey asked again.

"Four."

Stephanie stepped toward the kitchen window and gazed

out at the street. The cobbles were deserted in both directions. But she was concerned about Mark and Malone. "Where are those brothers?"

"I don't know. I heard them say you were in Lars's house, so I came straight here."

She didn't like that response. "We couldn't help you last night. We had no idea where they'd taken you. We were knocked unconscious trying to catch de Roquefort and the woman. By the time we woke up, everyone was gone."

The Frenchman held up his palms. "It is all right, madame, I understand. There was nothing you could do."

"Is de Roquefort here?" Geoffrey asked.

"Who?"

"The master. Is he here?"

"No names were given." Claridon faced her. "But I heard them say that Mark is alive. Is that true?"

She nodded. "He and Cotton walked to the church, but they should be back shortly."

"A miracle. I thought he was gone forever."

"You and me both."

His gaze raked the room. "I've not been inside this house in some time. Lars and I spent a lot of time here."

She offered him a seat at the table. Geoffrey positioned himself near the window, and she noticed an edge to his otherwise cool demeanor.

"What happened to you?" she asked Claridon.

"I was bound until this morning. They untied me so I could relieve myself. In the bathroom, I climbed out the window and came straight here. They will surely be looking for me, but there was nowhere else to go. Getting out of this town is quite difficult, since there is but one way in and out." Claridon fidgeted in the chair. "Might I trouble you for some water?"

She stood and filled a glass from the tap. Claridon downed it in one swallow. She refilled the glass.

"I was terrified of them," Claridon said.

"What do they want?" she asked.

"They seek their Great Devise, as Lars did."

"And what did you tell them?" Geoffrey asked, with a hint of scorn in his tone.

"I told them nothing, but they asked precious little. I was told that my questioning would be later today, after they tended to something else. But they failed to say what that was." Claridon stared at her. "Do you know what they want from you?"

"They have Lars's journal, the book from the auction, and the lithograph of the painting. What more could they want?"

"I think it's Mark."

The words visibly stiffened Geoffrey.

She wanted to know, "What do they want with him?"

"I have no clue, madame. But I wonder if any of this is worth bloodshed."

"Brothers have died for nearly nine hundred years for what they believed," Geoffrey said. "This is no different."

"You talk as though you're of the Order."

"I'm only quoting history."

Claridon drank his water. "Lars Nelle and I studied the Order for many years. I have read that history you speak of."

"What did you read?" Geoffrey asked, amazement in his voice. "Books written by people who know nothing. They write of heresy and idol worship, of kissing each other on the mouth, of sodomy, and of the denial of Jesus Christ. Not a word of which is true. All lies designed to destroy the Order and take its wealth."

"Now you truly speak like a Templar."

"I speak like a man who cherishes justice."

"Is that not a Templar?"

"Should that not be all men?"

Stephanie smiled. Geoffrey was quick.

MALONE FOLLOWED MARK BACK INTO THE CHURCH OF MARY Magdalene. They hustled down the center aisle, past nine rows of pews and gawkers, toward the altar. There Mark veered right and entered a small anteroom through an open doorway. Three camera-toting visitors stood inside.

"Could you excuse us?" Mark said to them in English. "I'm with the museum and we need this room for a few moments."

None questioned his obvious authority and Mark gently closed the door behind them. Malone looked around. The space was naturally illuminated by the light from a stained-glass window. A row of empty cupboards dominated one wall. The other three were all of wood. No furniture was inside.

"This was the sacristy," Mark said.

De Roquefort was no more than a minute from being upon them, so he wanted to know, "I assume you have something in mind?"

Mark stepped toward the cupboard and searched with his fingertips above the top shelf. "Like I told you, when Saunière built the Calvary garden, he constructed the grotto. He and his mistress would go down into the valley and collect stones." Mark continued to search for something. "They'd come back with hods full of rocks. There."

Mark withdrew his hand and grabbed hold of the cupboard, which swung open to reveal a windowless space beyond. "This was Saunière's hiding place. Whatever else he brought back with those rocks was stored here. Few know of this addition. Saunière created it during the church remodeling. Plans for this building, prior to 1891, show it as an open room."

Mark withdrew an automatic pistol from beneath his jacket. "We'll wait in here and see what happens."

"Does de Roquefort know of this room?"

"We'll find out shortly."

FORTY-TWO

DE ROQUEFORT STOPPED OUTSIDE THE CHURCH. ODD THAT HIS targets had fled inside. But no matter. He was going to personally tend to Mark Nelle. His patience was at an end. He'd taken the precaution of consulting with his officers before leaving the abbey. He wasn't going to repeat the former master's mistakes. His tenure would at least carry the appearance of a democracy. Thankfully, yesterday's escape and the two shootings had galvanized the brotherhood onto a singular path. All agreed that the former seneschal and his ally must be returned for punishment.

And he intended to deliver.

He surveyed the street.

The crowd was growing. A warm day had brought out the tours. He turned to the brother standing beside him. "Go inside and assess the situation."

A nod and the man walked off.

He knew the church's geography. Only one way in and out. The stained-glass windows were all fixed, so they would have to shatter one to escape. He saw no policemen, which was normal for Rennes. Little ever happened here except the spending of money. The commercialization sickened him. If it was his decision, all tours of the abbey would be stopped. He realized the bishop would question that move, but he'd already decided to limit access to only a few hours on Saturdays, citing the brothers' need for more solitude. That the bishop would understand. He fully intended on restoring many of the old ways, practices that had long been abandoned, rituals that once separated the Templars from all other religious orders. And for that he would need the abbey's gates locked far more than they were open.

The brother he'd sent inside exited the church and walked his way.

"They're not there," the man said as he drew close.

"What do you mean?"

"I searched the nave, the sacristy, the confessionals. They're not inside."

He did not want to hear that. "There's no other exit."

"Master, they're not there."

His gaze locked on the church. His mind swirled with possibilities.

Then the answer was clear.

"Come," he said. "I know precisely where they are."

STEPHANIE WAS LISTENING TO ROYCE CLARIDON, NOT AS A wife and mother on a mission important to her family, but as the head of a covert government agency that dealt routinely in espionage and counterespionage. Something was out of place. Claridon's sudden appearance was too convenient. She knew little about Raymond de Roquefort, but she knew enough to realize that either Claridon had been allowed to escape or, worse, the prickly little man sitting across from her was in league with the enemy. Either way she had to watch what she said. Geoffrey, too, had apparently sensed something since he was offering precious little to the Frenchman's many questions—too many inquiries for a man who'd just survived a life-and-death experience.

"Was the woman last night in the palace Cassiopeia Vitt,

the *Ingénieur* mentioned in the letter to Ernst Scoville?" she asked.

"I would assume. A she-devil."

"She may have saved us all."

"How? She interfered, as she did with Lars."

"You're alive right now thanks to her interference."

"No, madame. I am alive because they want information."

"What I wonder is why you're even here," Geoffrey said from his position by the window. "Escaping from de Roquefort is not easy."

"You did."

"And how would you know that?"

"They spoke of you and Mark. Apparently there was shooting. Brothers were hurt. They're angry."

"Did they mention attempting to kill us?"

A moment of uneasy silence passed.

"Royce," Stephanie said. "What else might they be after?"

"I only know that two books are missing from their archive. There was a mention of that."

"You just said a moment ago that you possessed no clue as to why they wanted Madame Nelle's son." Suspicion laced Geoffrey's declaration.

"And I don't. But I know they want the two missing books."

Stephanie glanced at Geoffrey and saw not a hint of acquiescence in the younger man's expression. If indeed he and Mark possessed the books de Roquefort sought, no admission came from his eyes.

"Yesterday," Claridon said, "you showed me Lars's journal and the book—"

"Which de Roquefort has."

"No. Cassiopeia Vitt stole both from him last night."

Another new piece of information. Claridon knew an awful lot for a man whom his captors supposedly ignored.

"So de Roquefort needs to find her," she made clear. "As we do."

"It seems, madame, that one of the books Mark took from their archive also contains a cryptogram. De Roquefort wants that book back."

"Is this more of what you overheard?"

Claridon nodded. "*Oui*. They believed me asleep, but I was listening. One of their marshals, from Saunière's time, discovered the cryptogram and recorded it in the book."

"We have no books," Geoffrey said.

"What do you mean?" Astonishment filled the man's face.

"We have no books. We left the abbey in a great rush and took nothing with us."

Claridon came to his feet. "You're a liar."

"Bold words. Can you prove the allegation?"

"You're a man of the Order. A warrior of Christ. A Templar. Your oath should be enough to prevent you from lying."

"And what prevents you?" Geoffrey asked.

"I don't lie. I've been through a difficult ordeal. I hid in an asylum for five years to avoid being a prisoner of the Templars. Do you know what they planned to do to me? Grease my feet and hold them before a hot brazier. Cook my skin from the bone."

"We have no books. De Roquefort is chasing a shadow."

"But that's not so. Two men were shot during your escape, and both said Mark carried a rucksack."

She perked at the information.

"And how would you know that?" Geoffrey asked.

DE ROQUEFORT ENTERED THE CHURCH, FOLLOWED BY THE brother who'd just been inside. He walked down the center aisle and entered the sacristy. He had to give Mark Nelle credit. Few knew about the church's secret room. It was not part of any tour, and only Rennes purists would have any inkling the concealed space existed. He'd often thought it curious that the domain's operators did not exploit Saunière's addition to the church's architecture—secret rooms always added to any mystery—but there were a lot of things about the church, the town, and the story that defied explanation.

"When you came in before, was the entrance to this room open?"

The brother shook his head and whispered, "Closed, Master."

He gently shut the door. "Allow no one to enter."

He approached the cupboard and withdrew his gun. He'd never actually seen the secret chamber that lay beyond, but he'd read enough accounts from previous marshals who'd investigated Rennes to know that a concealed room existed. If he recalled correctly, the release mechanism was in the top right corner of the cupboard.

He reached up and located a metal lever.

He knew that once he yanked down, the two men on the other side would be alerted and he had to assume they were armed. Malone certainly could handle himself and Mark Nelle had proven he was not a man to underestimate.

"Prepare yourself," he said.

The brother withdrew a short-barreled automatic and aimed at the cupboard. He popped the latch and quickly stepped back, gun pointed, waiting for what would happen next.

The cupboard inched open, then stopped.

He stayed at the far right edge and, with his foot, pivoted the door wide open.

The secret room was empty.

MALONE STOOD CLOSE TO MARK INSIDE THE CONFESSIONAL. They'd waited inside the hidden room for a couple minutes, able to observe the sacristy through a tiny Judas hole strategically placed in the cupboard. Mark had watched as one of the brothers entered the sacristy, saw the room empty, and left. They'd waited a few more seconds, then exited, watching from the doorway as the brother left the church. Seeing no other brothers inside, they'd quickly hustled to the confessional and stepped inside just as de Roquefort and the brother returned.

Mark had correctly surmised that de Roquefort would know of the secret room, but that he wouldn't share that knowledge with anyone unless absolutely necessary. When they'd spotted de Roquefort waiting outside, sending another brother inside to investigate, they'd lingered only long enough to buy a couple of minutes to change locations, since once the scout returned and reported they were missing de Roquefort would immediately surmise where they were hiding. After all, there was only one way in and out of the church.

"Know your enemy and know yourself," Mark whispered as de Roquefort and his minion entered the sacristy.

Malone smiled. "Sun Tzu was a wise man."

The door to the sacristy closed.

"We'll give it a few seconds, then we're out of here," Mark said.

"Could be more men outside."

"I'm sure there are. We'll take our chances. I've got nine shots."

"Let's don't start a shootout, unless there's no other choice."

The sacristy door stayed closed.

"We need to go," Malone said.

They exited the confessional, turned right, and headed for the door.

STEPHANIE SLOWLY CAME TO HER FEET, STEPPED CLOSE TO Geoffrey, and calmly took the gun from his grip. She then whirled, cocked the hammer, and rushed forward, pressing the barrel to Claridon's skull. "You slimy little scum. You're with them."

Claridon's eyes went wide. "No, madame. I swear I am not."

"Open his shirt," she said.

Geoffrey ripped away the buttons, exposing a microphone taped to the thin chest.

"Come. Quick. I need help," Claridon screamed.

Geoffrey slammed his fist into Claridon's jaw and sent the impish man to the floor. Stephanie turned, gun in hand, and spotted through the window a short-hair running toward the front door.

A kick and the door swung open.

Geoffrey was ready.

He'd positioned himself to the left of the entrance and, as the man burst inside, Geoffrey spun the attacker around. Stephanie saw a gun in the short-hair's hand, but Geoffrey deftly kept the barrel pointed down, pivoted on his heel, and kicked the man into the wall. Allowing no time to react, he delivered another kick to the abdomen that brought a yelp. When the man keeled forward, the breath gone from him, Geoffrey propelled him to the floor with a blow to the spine.

"They teach you that at the abbey?" she asked, impressed.

"That and more."

"Let's get out of here."

"Hold one second."

Geoffrey darted from the kitchen back toward the bedroom and returned with Mark's knapsack. "Claridon was right. We have books and I can't leave without them."

She noticed an earpiece on the man Geoffrey had subdued. "He was listening to Claridon, and is surely in communication with others."

"De Roquefort is here," Geoffrey said with conviction.

She grabbed her world phone from the kitchen counter. "We need to find Mark and Cotton."

Geoffrey approached the open front door and carefully

peered in both directions. "You'd think more brothers would be here by now."

She stepped up behind him. "Could be they're occupied at the church. We'll head there following the outer wall, through the car park, staying off the main *rue*." She handed the gun back to him. "You watch my back."

He smiled. "With pleasure, madame."

DE ROQUEFORT STARED INTO THE EMPTY SECRET ROOM. Where were they? There was simply no other place to hide within the church.

He slammed the cupboard back into place.

The other brother surely saw the moment of confusion that had passed across his face when they'd discovered the hiding place bare. He washed any doubt from his eyes.

"Where are they, Master?" the brother asked.

Considering the answer, he stepped to the stained-glass window and gazed out through one of the clear segments. The Calvary garden below was still busy with visitors. Then he saw Mark Nelle and Cotton Malone rush into the garden and turn toward the cemetery.

"Outside," he calmly said, stepping toward the sacristy door.

MARK THOUGHT THE TRICK WITH THE SECRET ROOM MIGHT buy them enough time to make an escape. He was hoping de Roquefort had brought only a small contingent. But three more brothers had been waiting outside—one on the main *rue,* another blocking the alley to the car park, and a final one positioned outside the Villa Béthanie, preventing the tree garden from becoming an escape route. De Roquefort had apparently not thought the cemetery a threat since it was walled with a fifteen-hundred-foot drop on the other side.

But that was precisely where Mark was headed.

He now thanked heaven for the many late-night explorations he and his father had once performed. The locals frowned on people visiting the cemetery after dark, but that was the best time, his father would say. So they'd many times scoured around, looking for clues, trying to make sense of Saunière and his seemingly inexplicable behavior. On a few forays they'd been interrupted, so they'd improvised another way out than through the skull-and-crossbones gate.

Time to put that discovery to good use.

"I'm afraid to ask how we're going to get out of here," Malone said.

"It's scary, but at least the sun's shining. Every other time I've done it has been at night."

Mark turned right and scampered down the stone stairs to the lower part of the cemetery. Fifty or so people were scattered around, admiring the memorials. Beyond the wall the cloudless sky was a brilliant blue and the wind moaned like a stricken soul. Clear days were always breezy in Rennes, but the cemetery air was motionless, the church and presbytery blocking the strongest gusts, which came from the south and west.

He hustled straight for a monument that lay adjacent to the east wall, beneath a canopy of elms that draped the earth in long shadows. He noticed that the crowd loomed mainly on the upper level, where the grave of Saunière's mistress sat. He hopped onto a thick tombstone and clambered up onto the wall.

"Follow me," he said as he jumped down on the other side, rolled once, then came to his feet, brushing off grit.

He looked back as Malone leaped the eight feet down to the narrow track.

They were standing at the base of the wall, on a rocky footpath that measured about four feet wide. Anomalous beech

and pines sustained the downward slope beyond, beaten back
by the wind, their branches twisted and interlaced, their roots
stuck between clefts in the rock.

Mark pointed left. "This path ends just ahead, beyond the
château, with nowhere to go." He turned. "So we have to go
this way. It takes us around to the car park. There's an easy
way up there."

"No wind here, but when we round that corner—" Malone
pointed ahead. "—I imagine it'll get breezy."

"Like a hurricane. But we have no choice."

FORTY-THREE

DE ROQUEFORT BROUGHT ONE BROTHER WITH HIM AS HE EN-
tered the cemetery, the remaining three waited outside.
Clever what Mark Nelle had done, using the secret room as
a diversion. They'd most likely stayed inside only long
enough for his scout to leave the church. Then they hid in the
confessional until he'd ensconced himself in the sacristy.

Inside the parish close he stopped and calmly surveyed the
graves, but did not see his quarry. He told the brother standing next to him to search left and he went right, where he
came across Ernst Scoville's grave.

Four months ago, when he'd first learned of the former
master's interest in Scoville, he'd sent a brother to monitor the
Belgian's activities. Through a listening device installed on
Scoville's telephone his spy had learned about Stephanie
Nelle, her plans to visit Denmark then France, and her intent

to obtain the book. But when it became clear that Scoville did not like Lars Nelle's widow and was merely leading her on, intent on thwarting her efforts, a speeding car on the Rennes incline solved the problem of his potential interference. Scoville was not a player in the unfolding game. Stephanie Nelle was and, at the time, nothing could be allowed to impede her movement. De Roquefort had personally handled Scoville's killing, involving no one at the abbey since he could ill afford to explain why outright murder was necessary.

The brother returned from the other side of the cemetery and reported, "Nothing."

Where could they have gone?

His gaze settled on the tawny gray wall that lined the outer edge. He stepped to a spot where the wall rose only breast-high. Rennes sat on the backbone of a summit with slopes as steep as pyramids on three sides. Objects in the valley below were lost in a grayish haze that blanketed the colorful earth, like some far-off Lilliputian world, the basin, highways, and towns as if seen on an atlas. The wind from beyond the wall washed over his face and dried his eyes. He planted both hands on top, leveraged himself up, and hinged his body forward. He glanced right. The rocky ledge was barren. Then he looked left and caught a glimpse of Cotton Malone turning from the wall's north side to its west.

He dropped back down.

"They're on a ledge moving toward the Tour Magdala. Stop them. I'm going to the belvedere."

STEPHANIE LED THE WAY AS SHE AND GEOFFREY FLED THE house. A sunburned lane paralleled the west wall and led northward to the car park and beyond to Saunière's domain. Geoffrey was clearly alight with anticipation, and for a man who appeared only in his late twenties he'd handled himself with a professional ease.

Only scattered houses stood in this corner of town. Firs and pines climbed skyward in patches.

Something whizzed by her right ear and pinged off the limestone of the building just ahead. She whirled to see the short-hair from the house taking aim fifty yards back. She dove behind a parked car that nestled close to the rear of one of the houses. Geoffrey dropped to the ground, rolled, then hinged up and fired two shots from between his outstretched legs. The pop, like a firecracker, was dulled by the howling wind. One of the bullets found its mark and the man cried out in pain, then grabbed at his thigh and fell.

"Good shot," she said.

"I couldn't kill him. I gave my word."

They came to their feet and rushed ahead.

MALONE FOLLOWED MARK. THE ROCKY ESCARPMENT, LINED by spikes of brown grass, had narrowed, and the wind, which before was only a nuisance, had now become a hazard, molesting them with gale force, its monotonous murmur masking all other noise.

They were on the town's west side. The lofty stem of copses from the north slope were gone. Nothing but bare rock plunged downward, gleaming in the fiery afternoon sun, colored by tufts of moss and heather.

The belvedere Malone had crossed two nights ago, chasing after Cassiopeia Vitt, spanned twenty feet above them. The Tour Magdala stood ahead and he could see people atop the tower admiring the distant valley. He wasn't wild about the view. Heights affected his head like wine—one of those weaknesses that he'd hid from the government psychologists who were once required, from time to time, to evaluate him for duty. He risked one glance down. Scant brushwood dotted the steeply inclined plane for several hundred feet. Then a short ledge leveled, and below that an even steeper drop began.

Mark was ten feet ahead of him. He saw him glance back, stop, then turn and level his gun, pointing the barrel his way.

"Was it something I said?" he yelled.

The wind buffeted Mark's arm and shook the weapon. Another hand came up to steady the aim. Malone caught the glare in the man's eye and turned back to see one of the short-hairs coming straight for them.

"Far enough, brother," Mark hollered over the wind.

The man held a Glock 17, similar to the one Mark gripped.

"If that weapon comes up, I'll shoot you," Mark made clear.

The man's arm stopped its rise.

Malone did not like his predicament and pressed himself against the wall to give them room for the duel.

"This is not your battle, brother. I realize you're simply doing what the master ordered. But if I shoot you, even in the leg, you'll go over the edge. Is it worth it?"

"I'm bound to follow the master."

"He's leading you into peril. Have you even considered what you're doing?"

"That's not my responsibility."

"Saving your life is," Mark said.

"Would you shoot me, Seneschal?"

"Without question."

"Is what you seek important enough to harm another Christian?"

Malone watched as Mark pondered the question—and he wondered if the resolve he noted in the eyes was matched with the courage to follow through. He, too, had faced a similar dilemma—several times. Shooting someone never came easy. But sometimes it simply had to be done.

"No, brother, it's not worth a human life." And Mark lowered his gun.

In the corner of his eye, Malone saw movement. He turned to see the other man take advantage of Mark's concession. The Glock started to rise as the man's other hand whipped across to meet the weapon, surely to help steady the shot he was about to take.

But he never fired.

A pop muffled by the wind came from Malone's left and the short-hair was thrown back as a bullet sank into his chest. He couldn't tell if the man was wearing a protective vest or not, but it didn't matter. The close shot scrambled his balance and the man's stocky frame teetered. Malone rushed toward him, trying to prevent a fall, and caught sight of two tranquil eyes. He recalled the look from Red Jacket atop the Round Tower. Two more steps were all he needed to reach him, but the wind swept the brother off the promontory and the body rolled downward like a log.

He heard a scream from above. Some of the visitors on the belvedere had apparently witnessed the man's fate. He watched as the body continued to roll, finally settling on a ledge far below.

He turned to Mark, who still held the gun level.

"You okay?"

Mark lowered the weapon. "Not really. But we need to go."

He agreed.

They turned and scampered down the stony track.

DE ROQUEFORT RUSHED UP THE STAIRS THAT LED TO THE belvedere. He heard a woman scream and saw excitement as people flocked to the wall. He moved close and asked, "What happened?"

"A man fell off the edge. Rolled a long way."

He elbowed his way to the wall. As in the parish close, the stone was nearly a meter wide, making it impossible to see down to the base of the outer wall.

"Where did he fall?" he asked.

"There," a man said, pointing.

He followed the outstretched finger and saw a figure in a dark jacket with light trousers far down the barren slope, lying still. He knew who it was. Damn. He planted his palms on the rough stone and pushed himself up onto the wall. Pivoting on his stomach, he cocked his head left and saw Mark Nelle and Cotton Malone making their way toward a short incline that led up to the car park.

He dropped back down and retreated to the steps.

He pressed the SEND button on the radio clipped to his waist and whispered into the lapel mike, "They're coming your way, at the wall's edge. Contain them."

STEPHANIE HEARD A GUNSHOT. THE POP APPEARED TO HAVE come from the other side of the wall. But that made no sense. Why would anyone be out there? She and Geoffrey were a hundred feet shy of the car park—which, she noticed, was filled with vehicles, including four buses nestled close to the stone water tower.

They slowed their advance. Geoffrey shielded the gun behind his thigh as they calmly walked ahead.

"There," Geoffrey whispered.

She saw the man, too. Standing at the far end, blocking the alley down to the church. She turned back and saw another short-hair strolling up the lane behind them.

Then she spotted Mark and Malone as they ran up from the other side of the wall and hopped over the knee-high stone.

She trotted toward them and asked, "Where have you two been?"

"Out for a stroll," Malone said.

"I heard shooting."

"Not now," Malone said.

"We have company," she made clear, pointing to the two men.

Mark scanned the scene. "De Roquefort is orchestrating this whole thing. Time to leave. But I don't have the keys to our car."

"I have mine," Malone said.

Geoffrey handed over the knapsack.

"Good job," **Mark** said. "Let's go."

DE ROQUEFORT HUSTLED PAST THE VILLA BÉTHANIE AND IG-nored the many visitors making their way toward the Tour Magdala, the tree garden, and the belvedere.

He turned right at the church.

"They're attempting to leave by car," a voice said in his ear.

"Allow them," he said.

MALONE BACKED FROM HIS PARKING SPOT AND THREADED HIS way around the other cars to the alley leading to the main *rue*. He noticed that the short-hairs made no attempt to stop them.

That worried him.

They were being herded.

But to where?

He crept through the alley, past the souvenir kiosks, and turned right onto the main *rue,* allowing the car to coast down the incline toward the town gate.

Past the restaurant, the crowd thinned and the street cleared.

Ahead, he spotted Raymond de Roquefort, standing in the middle of the lane, blocking the gate.

"He means to challenge you," Mark said from the rear seat.

"Good, because I can play chicken with the best of them."

He gently rested his foot atop the accelerator.

A couple of hundred feet and closing.

De Roquefort stayed rooted.

Malone saw no weapon. Apparently the master had concluded his presence alone might stop them. Beyond, Malone saw the road was clear, but a sharp curve lay just outside the gate and he hoped no one decided to come around it in the next few seconds.

He rammed his foot to the floorboard.

Tires grabbed pavement and, with a lurch, the car shot forward.

A hundred feet.

"You plan to kill him," Stephanie said.

"If I have to."

Fifty feet.

Malone kept the wheel steady and stared straight at de Roquefort as the man's form grew larger in the windshield. He braced himself for the body's impact and willed his hands to hold tight.

A hurried form leaped from the right and shoved de Roquefort out of the car's path.

They roared out through the gate.

DE ROQUEFORT REALIZED WHAT HAD HAPPENED AND WAS NOT happy. He'd fully prepared himself to challenge his adversary, ready for whatever would come, and he resented the intrusion.

Then he saw who'd saved him.

Royce Claridon.

"That car would have killed you," Claridon said.

He pushed the man off him and rose to his feet. "That remained to be seen." Then he asked what he really wanted to know. "Was anything learned?"

"They discovered my ruse and I was forced to call for help."

Anger seethed through him. Again, nothing had gone right. One salvation, though, rang through his brain.

The car they'd left in. Malone's rental.

Still equipped with an electronic monitor.

At least he'd know exactly where they went.

FORTY-FOUR

MALONE DROVE AS FAST AS HE DARED DOWN THE TWISTING IN-cline to ground level. There he turned west for the main high-way and half a mile later veered south toward the Pyrénées.

"Where are we going?" Stephanie asked him.

"To see Cassiopeia Vitt. I was going alone, but I think it's time we all get acquainted." He needed something to distract him. "Tell me about her," he said to Mark.

"I don't know much. I heard that her father was a wealthy Spanish contractor, her mother a Muslim from Tanzania. She's brilliant. Degrees in history, art, religion. And she's rich. She inherited lots of the money and has made even more. She and Dad clashed many times."

"Over what?" Malone wanted to know.

"Proving that Christ did not die on the cross is a mission of hers. Twelve years ago religious fanaticism was viewed much differently. People weren't all that concerned with the Taliban or al Qaeda. Then, Israel was the hot spot and

Cassiopeia resented the way Muslims were always depicted as extremists. She hated the arrogance of Christianity and the presumptiveness of Judaism. Her quest was one of truth, Dad would say. She wanted to strip away the myth and see just how much alike Jesus Christ and Muhammad really were. Common ground—common interests. That kind of thing."

"Isn't that exactly what your father wanted to do?"

"Same thing I used to say to him."

Malone smiled. "How far to her château?"

"Less than an hour. We turn west a few miles ahead."

Malone studied his rearview mirrors. Still no one was following them. Good. He slowed the car as they entered a town identified as St. Loup. Being Sunday, everything was closed except for a gasoline station and convenience store just to the south. He turned in and came to a stop.

"Wait here," he said as he climbed out. "I have to tend to something."

Malone turned off the highway and drove the car down a graveled path, deeper into the thick forest. A sign indicated that GIVORS—A MEDIEVAL ADVENTURE IN THE MODERN WORLD—lay half a mile ahead. The drive from Rennes had taken a little less than fifty minutes. They'd headed west most of the time, passing the ruined Cathar fortress of Montségur, then turning south toward the mountains where rising slopes sheltered river valleys and tall trees.

The two-car-wide avenue was well maintained and roofed by leafy beech trees that cast a dreamy stillness in the lengthening shadows. The entrance opened into a clearing matted in short grass. Cars littered the field. Slender columns of pine and fir lined the perimeter. He stopped and they all climbed out. A placard in French and English announced their location.

GIVORS ARCHÁEOLOGICAL SITE

WELCOME TO THE PAST. HERE, AT GIVORS, A SITE FIRST
OCCUPIED BY LOUIS IX, A CASTLE IS BEING CONSTRUCTED
USING MATERIALS AND TECHNIQUES ONLY AVAILABLE TO
13TH-CENTURY CRAFTSMEN. A MASONED TOWER WAS THE VERY
SYMBOL OF A LORD'S POWER AND THE CASTLE AT GIVORS WAS
DESIGNED AS A MILITARY FORTRESS WITH THICK WALLS AND
MANY CORNER TOWERS. THE SURROUNDING ENVIRONS
PROVIDED AN ABUNDANCE OF WATER, STONE, EARTH, SAND,
AND WOOD, WHICH WERE ALL NEEDED FOR ITS CONSTRUCTION.
QUARRIERS, STONE HEWERS, MASONS, CARPENTERS,
BLACKSMITHS, AND POTTERERS ARE NOW LABORING, LIVING
AND DRESSING EXACTLY AS THEY WOULD HAVE SEVEN
CENTURIES AGO. THE PROJECT IS PRIVATELY FUNDED AND THE
CURRENT ESTIMATE IS 30 YEARS WILL BE NEEDED TO
COMPLETE THE CASTLE. ENJOY YOUR TIME IN THE
13TH CENTURY.

"Cassiopeia Vitt funds all this herself?" Malone asked.

"Medieval history is one of her passions," Mark said.
"They knew her well at the university in Toulouse."

Malone had decided that the direct approach would be
best. Surely Vitt anticipated that he'd eventually locate her.

"Where does she live?"

Mark pointed east, where the branches of oaks and elms,
closed like a cloister, shaded another lane. "The château is
that way."

"These cars for visitors?" he asked.

Mark nodded. "They give tours of the construction site to
raise revenue. I took it once, years ago, right after the work
began. It's impressive what she's doing."

He started off toward the lane leading to the château.
"Let's go say hello to our hostess."

They walked in silence. In the distance, on the steep side

of a rising slope, he spied the dreary ruin of a stone tower, its layers yellowed with moss. The dry air was warm and still. Purple heather, broom, and wildflowers carpeted the low earth on both sides of the lane. Malone imagined the clash of arms and shouts of battle that centuries ago would have echoed through the valley as men fought for its dominance. Overhead, a murder of screaming crows flew past.

A hundred or so yards down the lane he saw the château. It filled a sheltered hollow that provided a clear measure of seclusion. Dark red brick and stone were arranged in symmetrical patterns over four stories, flanked by two ivy-crowned towers and topped with slanting slate roofs. Greenery spread out across the façade like rust on metal. Traces of a moat, now filled with grass and leaves, surrounded three sides. Slender trees rose in the rear and hedges of clipped yew guarded its base.

"Some house," Malone said.

"Sixteenth century," Mark noted. "I was told that she bought the château and the surrounding archaeological site. She calls the place Royal Champagne, after one of Louis XV's cavalry regiments."

Two cars were parked out front. A late-model Bentley Continental GT—about $160,000, Malone recalled—and a Porsche Roadster, cheap by comparison. There was also a motorcycle. Malone approached the cycle and examined the left rear tire and muffler. The shiny chrome was scarred.

And he knew precisely how that had happened.

"That's where I shot."

"Quite right, Mr. Malone."

He turned. The cultured voice had come from the portico. Standing outside the open front door was a tall woman, lean as a jackal, with shoulder-length auburn hair. Her features reflected a leonine beauty reminiscent of an Egyptian goddess—thin brows, brooding cheeks, blunt nose. The skin was the color of mahogany, and she was dressed in a tasteful V-neck tank that exposed her toned shoulders and capped a knee-length, safari-print silk skirt. Leather sandals sheathed her feet. The ensemble was casual but elegant, as if she were off to stroll the Champs-Élysées.

She threw him a smile. "I've been expecting you." Her gaze caught his and he registered determination in the deep pools of her dark eyes.

"That's interesting, because I only decided to come see you an hour ago."

"Oh, Mr. Malone, I'm sure I've been high on your priority list since at least two nights ago, when you shot my cycle in Rennes."

He was curious. "Why lock me in the Tour Magdala?"

"I was hoping to use the time to leave quietly. But you extricated yourself much too quickly."

"Why shoot at me in the first place?"

"Nothing would have been learned from talking to the man you assaulted."

He noticed the melodious tone of her voice, surely designed to be disarming. "Or perhaps you didn't want me to talk to him? Anyway, thanks for saving my hide in Copenhagen."

She brushed his gratitude away. "You would have found a way out on your own. I just hastened the process."

He saw her glance over his shoulder. "Mark Nelle. I am pleased to finally meet you. Glad to see you didn't die in that avalanche."

"I see you still like to interfere in other people's business."

"I don't consider it interfering. Merely monitoring the progress of those who interest me. Like your father." Cassiopeia stepped past Malone and extended a hand to Stephanie. "And I'm pleased to meet you. I knew your husband well."

"From what I hear, you and Lars were not the best of friends."

"I can't believe anyone would say that." Cassiopeia looked at Mark with clear mischief. "Did you tell your mother such a thing."

"No. He didn't," Stephanie said. "Royce Claridon told me."

"Now, he's a man to watch. Placing your trust in that one will bring nothing but trouble. I warned Lars about him, but he wouldn't listen."

"On that we agree," Stephanie said.

Malone introduced Geoffrey.

"You're of the brotherhood?" Cassiopeia asked.

Geoffrey said nothing.

"No, I wouldn't expect you to answer. Still, you are the first Templar I've met civilly."

"Not true," Geoffrey said, pointing to Mark. "The seneschal is of the brotherhood and you met him first."

Malone wondered about the volunteered information. So far, the young man had been tight-lipped.

"Seneschal? I'm sure there's quite a story there," Cassiopeia said. "Why don't you come inside. My lunch was being prepared, but when I saw you I told the chamberlain to set more plates. They should be about finished with that."

"Great," Malone said. "I'm starving."

"Then let's eat. We have much to discuss."

They followed her inside and Malone took in the expensive Italian chests, rare armored knights, Spanish torch holders, Beauvais tapestries, and Flemish paintings. Everything seemed a cavalcade for the connoisseur.

They followed her into a spacious dining room lined with gilded leather. Sunlight poured in through casement windows draped with elaborate lambrequin and doused the white-clothed table and marble floor in verdant shades. A twelve-branched electrified candelabrum hung unlit. Attendants were laying out gleaming silverware at each place setting.

The ambience was impressive, but what caught Malone's undivided attention was the man sitting at the far end of the table.

Forbes Europe ranked him the eighth-wealthiest person on the Continent, his power and influence in direct proportion to his billions of euros. Heads of state and royalty knew him well. The queen of Denmark called him a personal friend. Worldwide charities counted on him as a generous benefactor. For the past year Malone had spent at least three days a week visiting with him—talking books, politics, the world, how life sucks. He came and went from the man's estate as if he were part of the family and, in many respects, Malone felt that he was.

But now he seriously questioned all that.

He actually felt like a fool.

But all Henrik Thorvaldsen could do was smile. "About time, Cotton. I've been waiting two days."

PART
FOUR

FORTY-FIVE

DE ROQUEFORT SAT IN THE PASSENGER SEAT AND CONCEN-
trated on the GPS screen. The transponder attached to Malone's rental car was working perfectly, the tracking signal
transmitting strongly. One brother drove while Claridon and
another brother occupied the rear seat. De Roquefort was
still irritated with Claridon's interference back in Rennes.
He had no intention of dying and would have eventually
leaped out of the way, but he'd truly wanted to see if Cotton
Malone possessed the resolve to drive through him.

The brother who'd fallen down the rocky incline had died,
shot in the chest before he fell. A Kevlar vest had prevented
the bullet from doing any damage, but the fall had broken the
man's neck. Thankfully, none of them carried identification,
but the vest was a problem. Equipment like that signaled sophistication, but nothing linked the dead man to the abbey.
All the brothers knew Rule. If any of them were killed outside the abbey, their bodies would go unidentified. Like the
brother who'd leaped from the Round Tower, Renne's casu-
alty would end up in a regional morgue, his remains eventually consigned to a pauper's grave. But before that happened,
procedure called for the master to dispatch a clergyman, who
would claim the remains in the name of the Church, offering
to provide a Christian burial at no cost to the state. Never had

that offer been refused. And while arousing no suspicion, the gesture ensured that a brother received his proper internment.

He'd not rushed leaving Rennes, first searching Lars Nelle's and Ernst Scoville's houses and finding nothing. His men had reported that Geoffrey had carried a rucksack, which was handed over to Mark Nelle in the car park. Surely it contained the two stolen books.

"Any idea where they went?" Claridon asked from the backseat.

He pointed to the screen. "We'll know shortly."

After questioning the injured brother who'd eavesdropped on Claridon's conversation inside Lars Nelle's house, he'd learned that Geoffrey had said precious little, obviously suspicious of Claridon's motivations. Sending Claridon in there had been a mistake. "You assured me you could find those books."

"Why do we need them? We have the journal. We should be concentrating on deciphering what we have."

Maybe, but it bothered him that Mark Nelle had chosen those two volumes from the thousands in the archives. "What if they contain information different from the journal?"

"Do you know how many versions of the same information I've come across? The entire Rennes story is a series of contradictions stacked atop one another. Let me explore your archives. Tell me what you know and let's see what, together, we have."

A good idea, but unfortunately—contrary to what he'd led the Order to believe—he knew precious little. He'd been counting on the master leaving the requisite message for his successor, in which the most coveted information was always passed from leader to leader, as had been done from the time of de Molay. "You'll get that opportunity. But first we must take care of this."

He thought again of the two dead brothers. Their deaths

would be seen by the collective as an omen. For a religious society heaped in discipline, the Order was astoundingly superstitious. And violent death was not common—yet two had occurred in a matter of days. His leadership could now well be questioned. *Too much, too fast* would be the cry. And he'd be forced to listen to all objections since he'd openly challenged the last master's legacy, in part because that man had ignored the brothers' wishes.

He asked the driver for an interpretation of the GPS readout. "How far to their vehicle?"

"Twelve kilometers."

He gazed out beyond the car windows at the French countryside. Once, no stretch of sky had been true to the eye unless a tower rose on the horizon. By the twelfth century Templars had populated this land with well over a third of their total estates. The entire Languedoc should have become a Templar state. He'd read of plans in the Chronicles. How fortresses, outposts, supply depots, farms, and monasteries had all been strategically established, each connected by a series of maintained roads. For two hundred years the brotherhood's strength had been carefully preserved, and when the Order failed to establish a fiefdom in the Holy Land, eventually surrendering Jerusalem back to the Muslims, the aim had been to succeed in the Languedoc. All was well under way when Philip IV struck his death blow. Interestingly, Rennes-le-Château was never mentioned in the Chronicles. The town, in all of its previous incarnations, played no role in Templar history. There'd been Templar fortifications in other parts of the Aude Valley, but nothing at Rhedae, as the occupied summit was then called. Yet now the tiny village seemed an epicenter, and all because of an ambitious priest and an inquisitive American academician.

"We're approaching the car," the driver said.

He'd already instructed caution. The other three brothers he'd brought to Rennes were returning to the abbey, one with a flesh wound to his thigh after Geoffrey shot at him. That made three wounded men, along with two dead. He'd sent word that he wanted a council with his officers when he returned to the abbey, which should quell any discontent, but first he needed to know where his quarry had gone.

"Up ahead," the driver said. "Fifty meters."

He stared out the window and wondered about Malone and company's choice of refuge. Odd that they would come here.

The driver stopped the car, and they climbed out.

Parked cars surrounded them.

"Bring the handheld unit."

They walked and, twenty meters later, the man holding the portable receiver stopped. "Here."

De Roquefort stared at the vehicle. "That's not the car they left Rennes in."

"The signal is strong."

He motioned. The other brother searched beneath and found the magnetic transponder.

He shook his head and stared at the walls of Carcassonne, which stretched skyward ten meters away. The grassy area before him had once formed the town moat. Now it served as a car park for the thousands of visitors who came each day to see one of the last existing walled cities from the Middle Ages. The time-tanned stones had stood when Templars roamed the surrounding land. They'd borne witness to the Albigensian Crusade and the many wars thereafter. And never once were they breached—truly a monument to strength.

But they said something about cleverness, too.

He knew the local myth, from when Muslims controlled the town for a short time in the eighth century. Eventually, Franks came from the north to reclaim the site and, true to their way, laid a long siege. During a sally the Moorish king was killed, which left the task of defending the walls to his daughter. She was the clever one, creating an illusion of greater numbers by sending the few troops she possessed running from tower to tower and stuffing the clothing of the dead with straw. Food and water eventually ran out for both sides. Finally, the daughter ordered the last sow be caught and fed the final bushel of corn. She then hurled the pig out over the walls. The animal smashed into the earth and its belly burst forth with grain. The Franks were shocked. After such a long siege, apparently the infidels still possessed enough food to feed their pigs. So they withdrew.

A myth, he was sure, but an interesting tale of ingenuity.

And Cotton Malone had shown ingenuity, too, transferring the electronic tag to another vehicle.

"What is it?" Claridon asked.

"We've been led astray."

"This is not their car?"

"No, monsieur." He turned and started back for their vehicle. Where had they gone? Then a thought occurred to him. He stopped. "Would Mark Nelle know of Cassiopeia Vitt?"

"*Oui,*" Claridon said. "He and his father discussed her."

Is it possible that was where they'd gone? Vitt had interfered three times of late, and always on Malone's side. Maybe he sensed an ally there.

"Come." And he started for the car again.

"What do we do now?" Claridon wanted to know.

"We pray."

Claridon still had not moved. "For what?"

"That my instincts are accurate."

FORTY-SIX

MALONE WAS FURIOUS. HENRIK THORVALDSEN HAD KNOWN far more about everything and had said absolutely nothing. He pointed at Cassiopeia. "She one of your friends?"

"I've known her a long time."

"When Lars Nelle was alive. You knew her then?"

Thorvaldsen nodded.

"And did Lars know of your relationship?"

"No."

"So you played him for a fool, too." Anger punctuated his voice.

The Dane seemed forced to submerge his defensiveness. After all, he was cornered. "Cotton, I understand your irritation. But one can't always be forthcoming. Multiple angles have to be explored. I'm sure that when you worked for the U.S. government you did the same thing."

He did not rise to the bait.

"Cassiopeia kept watch on Lars. He knew of her, and in his eyes, she was a nuisance. But her real chore was to protect him."

"Why not just tell him?"

"Lars was a stubborn man. It was simpler for Cassiopeia to watch him quietly. Unfortunately, she could not protect him from himself."

Stephanie stepped forward, her face set for combat. "This is what his profile warned about. Questionable motives, shifting allegiances, deceit."

"I resent that." Thorvaldsen glared at her. "Especially since Cassiopeia looked after you two, as well."

On that point Malone could not argue. "You should have told us."

"To what end? As I recall, you both were intent on coming to France—especially you, Stephanie. So what would have been gained? Instead, I made sure Cassiopeia was there, in case you needed her."

Malone wasn't going to accept that hollow explanation. "For one thing, Henrik, you could have provided us with background on Raymond de Roquefort, whom you both obviously know. Instead, we went in blind."

"There's little to tell," Cassiopeia said. "When Lars was alive all the brothers did was watch him, too. I never made actual contact with de Roquefort. That's only happened during the past couple of days. I know as much about him as you do."

"Then how did you anticipate his moves in Copenhagen?"

"I didn't. I simply followed you."

"I never sensed you there."

"I'm good at what I do."

"You weren't so good in Avignon. I spotted you at the café."

"And your trick with the napkin, dropping it so you could see if I was following? I wanted you to know I was there. Once I saw Claridon, I knew de Roquefort would not be far behind. He's watched Royce for years."

"Claridon told us about you," Malone said, "but he didn't recognize you in Avignon."

"He's never seen me. What he knows is only what Lars Nelle told him."

"Claridon never mentioned that fact," Stephanie said.

"There's a lot I'm sure Royce failed to mention. Lars never realized, but Claridon was far more of a problem for him than I ever was."

"My father hated you," Mark said, disdain in his tone.

Cassiopeia appraised him with a cool countenance. "Your father was a brilliant man, but he was not schooled in human nature. His was a simplistic view of the world. The conspiracies he sought, the ones you explored after he died, are far more complicated than either of you could imagine. This is a quest for knowledge that men have died seeking."

"Mark," Thorvaldsen said, "what Cassiopeia says about your father is true, as I'm sure you realize."

"He was a good man who believed in what he did."

"He was, indeed. But he likewise kept many things to himself. You never knew he and I were close friends, and I regret you and I never came to know one another. But your father wanted our contacts confidential, and I respected his desire even after his death."

"You could have told me," Stephanie said.

"No, I couldn't."

"Then why are you talking to us now?"

"When you and Cotton left Copenhagen, I came straight here. I realized you would eventually find Cassiopeia. That's precisely why she was in Rennes two nights ago—to draw you in her direction. Originally, I was to stay in the background and you were not to know of our connection, but I changed my mind. This has gone too far. You need to know the truth, so I'm here to tell it to you."

"So good of you," Stephanie said.

Malone stared at the older man's hooded eyes. Thorvaldsen was right. He'd played both ends against the middle many times. Stephanie had, too. "Henrik, I haven't been a player in this kind of game in more than a year. I got out because I didn't want to play anymore. Lousy rules, bad odds.

But at the moment I'm hungry and, I have to say, curious. So let's eat, and you tell us all about that truth we need to know."

Lunch was a roasted rabbit seasoned with parsley, thyme, and marjoram, along with fresh asparagus, a salad, and a currant dessert topped with vanilla cream. While he ate, Malone tried to assess the situation. Their hostess seemed the most at ease, but he was unimpressed with her cordiality.

"You specifically challenged de Roquefort last night in the palace," he said to her. "Where'd you learn your craft?"

"Self-taught. My father passed to me his boldness, and my mother blessed me with an insight into the male mind."

Malone smiled. "One day you may guess wrong."

"I'm glad you care about my future. Did you ever *guess wrong* as an American agent?"

"Many times, and folks died from it occasionally."

"Henrik's son on that list?"

He resented the jab, particularly considering she knew nothing of what happened. "Like here, people were given bad information. Bad information leads to bad decisions."

"The young man died."

"Cai Thorvaldsen was in the wrong place at the wrong time," Stephanie made clear.

"Cotton is right," Henrik said as he stopped eating. "My son died because he was not alerted to the danger around him. Cotton was there and did what he could."

"I didn't mean to imply that he was to blame," Cassiopeia said. "It was only that he seemed anxious to tell me how to run my business. I simply wondered if he could run his own. After all, he did quit."

Thorvaldsen sighed. "You have to forgive her, Cotton. She's brilliant, artistic, a *cognoscenta* in music, a collector of antiques. But she inherited her father's lack of manners. Her mother, God rest her precious soul, was more refined."

"Henrik fancies himself my surrogate father."

"You're lucky," Malone said, scrutinizing her carefully, "that I didn't shoot you off that motorcycle in Rennes."

"I didn't expect you to escape the Tour Magdala so quickly. I'm sure the domain operators are quite upset about the loss of that casement window. It was an original, I believe."

"I'm waiting to hear that truth you spoke about," Stephanie said to Thorvaldsen. "You asked me in Denmark to keep an open mind about you and what Lars thought important. Now we see that your involvement is far more than any of us realized. Surely, you can understand how we'd be suspicious."

Thorvaldsen laid down his fork. "All right. What's the extent of your knowledge about the New Testament?"

An odd question, Malone thought. But he knew Stephanie was a practicing Catholic.

"Among other things, it contains the four Gospels—Matthew, Mark, Luke, and John—which tell us about Jesus Christ."

Thorvaldsen nodded. "History is clear that the New Testament, as we know it, was formulated during the first four centuries after Christ as a way to universalize the emerging Christian message. After all, that's what *catholic* means—'universal.' Remember, unlike today, in the ancient world politics and religion were one and the same. As paganism declined, and Judaism retreated within itself, people began searching for something new. The followers of Jesus, who were merely Jews embracing a different perspective, formed their own version of the Word, but so did the Carpocratians, the Essenes, the Naassenes, the Gnostics, and a hundred other emerging sects. The main reason the Catholic version survived, while others faltered, was its ability to impose its belief *universally*. They grafted onto the Scriptures so much authority that eventually no one could question their validity without being deemed a heretic. But there are many problems with the New Testament."

The Bible was a favorite of Malone's. He'd read it and much historical analysis and knew all about its inconsistencies. Each Gospel was a murky mixture of fact, rumor, legend, and myth that had been subjected to countless translations, edits, and redactions.

"Remember, the emerging Christian Church existed in the Roman world," Cassiopeia was saying. "In order to attract followers, the Church fathers had to compete not only with a variety of pagan beliefs, but also their own Jewish beliefs. They also needed to set themselves apart. Jesus had to be more than a mere prophet."

Malone was becoming impatient. "What does this have to do with what's happening here?"

"Think what finding the bones of Christ would mean for Christianity," Cassiopeia said. "That religion revolves around Christ dying on the cross, resurrecting, and ascending into heaven."

"That belief is a matter of faith," Geoffrey quietly said.

"He's right," Stephanie said. "Faith, not fact, defines it."

Thorvaldsen shook his head. "Let's remove that element from the equation for a moment, since faith also eliminates logic. Think about this. If a man named Jesus existed, how would the chroniclers of the New Testament know anything about His life? Just consider the language dilemma. The Old Testament was written in Hebrew. The New was penned in Greek, and any source materials, if they even existed, would have been in Aramaic. Then there's the issue of the sources themselves.

"Matthew and Luke tell of Christ's temptation in the wilderness, but Jesus was alone when that occurred. And Jesus's prayer in the Garden of Gethsemane. Luke says He uttered it after leaving Peter, James, and John *a stone's throw away.* When Jesus returned He found the disciples asleep and was immediately arrested, then crucified. There's absolutely no mention of Jesus ever saying a word about the prayer in the garden or the temptation in the wilderness. Yet we know its every detail. How?

"All of the Gospels speak of the disciples fleeing at Jesus's arrest—so none of them was there—yet detailed accounts of the crucifixion are recorded in all four. Where did these details come from? What the Roman soldiers did, what Pilate and Simon did. How would the Gospel writers know any of that? The faithful would say the information came from God's inspiration. But the four Gospels, these so-called Words of God, conflict with each other far more than they agree. Why would God offer only confusion?"

"Maybe that's not for us to question," Stephanie said.

"Come now," Thorvaldsen said. "There are too many examples of contradictions for us to simply dismiss them as intentional. Let's look at it in generalities. John's Gospel mentions much that the other three—the so-called synoptic Gospels—completely ignore. The tone in John is also different, the message more refined. John's is like an entirely different testimony. But some of the more precise inconsistencies start with Matthew and Luke. Those are the only two that say anything of Jesus's birth and ancestry, and even they conflict. Matthew says Jesus was an aristocrat, descended from David, in line to be king. Luke agrees with the David connection, but points to a lesser class. Mark went an entirely different direction and spawned the image of a poor carpenter.

"Jesus's birth is likewise told from differing perspectives. Luke says shepherds visited. Matthew called them *wise men.* Luke said the holy family lived in Nazareth and journeyed to Bethlehem for a birth in a manger. Matthew says the family was well off and lived in Bethlehem, where Jesus was born—not in a manger, but in a house.

"But the crucifixion is where the greatest inconsistencies exist. The Gospels don't even agree on the date. John says the day before Passover, the other three say the day after. Luke described Jesus as meek. *A lamb.* Matthew goes the other way—for him Jesus *brings not peace, but the sword.* Even the Savior's final words varied. Matthew and Mark say it was, *My God, my God, why have you forsaken me?* Luke says, *Father, into your hands I commit my spirit.* John is even simpler. *It is finished.*"

Thorvaldsen paused and sipped his wine.

"And the tale of the resurrection itself is completely riddled with contradictions. Each Gospel has a different version of who went to the tomb, what was found there—even the days of the week are unclear. And as to Jesus's appearances after the resurrection—none of the accounts agree on any point. Would you not think that God would have at least been reasonably consistent with His Word?"

"Gospel variations have been the subject of thousands of books," Malone made clear.

"True," Thorvaldsen said. "And the inconsistencies have been there from the beginning—largely ignored in ancient times, since rarely did the four Gospels appear together. Instead, they were disseminated individually throughout Christendom—one tale working better in some places than in others. Which, in and of itself, goes a long way toward explaining the differences. Remember, the idea behind the Gospels was to demonstrate that Jesus was the Messiah predicted in the Old Testament—not to be an irrefutable biography."

"Weren't the Gospels just a recording of what had been passed down orally?" Stephanie asked. "Wouldn't errors be expected?"

"No question," Cassiopeia said. "The early Christians believed Jesus would return soon and the world would end, so they saw no need to write anything down. But after fifty years, with the Savior still not having returned, it became important to memorialize Jesus's life. That's when the earliest Gospel, Mark's, was written. Matthew and Luke came next, around 80 C.E. John came much later, near the end of the first century, which is why his is so different from the other three."

"If the Gospels were entirely consistent, wouldn't they be even more suspect?" Malone asked.

"These books are more than simply inconsistent," Thorvaldsen said. "They are, quite literally, four different versions of the Word."

"It's a matter of faith," Stephanie repeated.

"There's that word again," Cassiopeia said. "Whenever a problem exists with biblical texts, the solution is easy. *It's faith.* Mr. Malone, you're a lawyer. If the testimony of Matthew, Mark, Luke, and John were offered in a court as proof Jesus existed, would any jury so find?"

"Sure, all of them mention Jesus."

"Now, if that same court was required to state which one of the four books is correct, how would it rule?"

He knew the right answer. "They're all correct."

"So how would you resolve the differences among the testimonies?"

He didn't answer, because he didn't know what to say.

"Ernst Scoville did a study once," Thorvaldsen said. "Lars told me about it. He determined that there was a ten to forty percent variation among the Gospels of Matthew, Mark, and Luke on any passage you cared to compare. *Any passage.* And with John, which is not one of the synoptics, the percentage was much higher. So Cassiopeia's question is fair, Cotton. Would these four testimonies have any probative value, beyond establishing that a man named Jesus may have lived?"

He felt compelled to say, "Could all of the inconsistencies be explained by the writers simply taking liberties with an oral tradition?"

Thorvaldsen nodded. "That explanation makes sense. But what compounds its acceptance is that nasty word *faith*. You see, to millions, the Gospels are not the oral traditions of radical Jews establishing a new religion, trying to secure converts, recounting their tale with additions and subtractions necessary for their particular time. No. The Gospels are the Word of God, and the resurrection is its keystone. For their Lord to have sent His son to die for them, and for Him to be physically resurrected and ascend into heaven—that set them far apart from all other emerging religions."

Malone faced Mark. "Did the Templars believe this?"

"There's an element of Gnosticism to the Templar creed. Knowledge is passed to the brothers in stages, and only the highest in the Order know all. But no one has known that knowledge since the loss of the Great Devise during the 1307 Purge. All of the masters who came after that time were denied the Order's archive."

He wanted to know, "What do they think of Jesus Christ today?"

"The Templars look equally to both the Old and New Testaments. In their eyes, the Jewish prophets in the Old Testament predicted the Messiah, and the writers of the New Testament fulfilled those predictions."

"It is like the Jews," Thorvaldsen said, "of whom I may speak since I am one. Christians for centuries have said that Jews failed to recognize the Messiah when He came, which was why God created a new Israel in the form of the Christian Church—to take the place of the Jewish Israel."

"His blood be upon us and upon our children," Malone muttered, quoting what Matthew had said about the Jews' willingness to accept that blame.

Thorvaldsen nodded. "That phrase has been used for two millennia as a reason for killing Jews. What could a people expect from God when they'd rejected His own son as their

Messiah? Words that some unknown Gospel writer penned, for whatever reason, became the rally cry of murderers."

"So what Christians finally did," Cassiopeia said, "was separate themselves from that past. They named half the Bible the Old Testament, the other the New. One was for Jews, the other for Christians. The twelve tribes of Israel in the Old were replaced by the twelve apostles in the New. Pagan and Jewish beliefs were assimilated and modified. Jesus, through the writings of the New Testament, fulfilled the prophecies of the Old Testament, thereby proving His messianic claim. A perfectly assembled package—the right message, tailored to the right audience—all of which allowed Christianity to utterly dominate the Western world."

Attendants appeared, and Cassiopeia signaled for them to clear away the lunch dishes. Wineglasses were refilled and coffee was passed around. As the last attendant withdrew, Malone asked Mark, "Do the Templars believe in the actual resurrection of Christ?"

"Which ones?"

A strange question. Malone shrugged.

"Those today—of course. With few exceptions, the Order follows traditional Catholic doctrine. Some adjustments are made to conform to Rule, as all monastic societies must. But in 1307? I have no idea what they believed. The Chronicles from that time are cryptic. Like I said, only the highest officers within the Order could have spoken on that subject. Most Templars were illiterate. Even Jacques de Molay could not read or write. So only a few within the Order controlled what the many thought. Of course, the Great Devise existed then, so I assume seeing was believing."

"What is this Great Devise?"

"I wish I knew. That information has been lost. The Chronicles speak little of it. I assume it's evidence of what the Order believed."

"Is that why they search for it?" Stephanie asked.

"Until recently, they haven't really searched. There's been little information relating to its whereabouts. But the master told Geoffrey that he believed Dad was on the right track."

"Why does de Roquefort want it so bad?" Malone asked Mark.

"Finding the Great Devise, depending on what's there, could well fuel the reemergence of the Order onto the world scene. That knowledge could also fundamentally change Christendom. De Roquefort wants retribution for what happened to the Order. He wants the Catholic Church exposed as hypocritical, the Order's name cleared."

Malone was puzzled. "What do you mean?"

"One of the charges leveled against the Templars in 1307 was idol worshiping. Some sort of bearded head the Order supposedly venerated, none of which was ever proven. Yet even now Catholics pray to images routinely, the Shroud of Turin being one of those."

Malone recalled what one of the Gospels said about Christ's death—*after they had taken him down they wrapped him in a sheet*—symbolism so sacred that a later pope decreed that mass should always be said upon a linen tablecloth. The Shroud of Turin, which Mark mentioned, was a cloth of herringbone weave on which was displayed a man—six feet tall, sharp nose, shoulder-length hair parted down the center, full beard, with crucifixion wounds to his hands, feet, and scalp, and scourge marks ravaging his back.

"The image on the shroud," Mark said, "is not of Christ. It's Jacques de Molay. He was arrested in October 1307 and in January 1308 he was nailed to a door in the Paris Temple in a manner similar to that of Christ. They were mocking him for his lack of belief in Jesus as Savior. France's grand inquisitor, Guillaume Imbert, orchestrated that torture. Afterward, de Molay was wrapped in a linen shroud the Order kept in the Paris Temple for use during induction ceremonies. We now know lactic acid and blood from de Molay's traumatized body mixed with the frankincense in the cloth and etched the image. There's even a modern equivalent. In 1981 a cancer patient in England left a similar trace of his limbs on bedsheets."

Malone recalled the late 1980s when the Church finally broke with tradition and allowed microscopic examination and carbon dating on the Shroud of Turin. The results indicated that there were no outlines or brushstrokes. The coloration lay upon the linen. Dating showed that the cloth came not from the first century, but from the late thirteenth to the mid-fourteenth century. But many contested those findings, saying the sample had been tainted, or was from a later repair to the original cloth.

"The image on the shroud fits de Molay physically," Mark said. "There are descriptions of him in the Chronicles. By the time he was tortured his hair had grown long, his beard was unkempt. The cloth that wrapped de Molay's body was removed from the Paris Temple by one of Geoffrey de Charney's relatives. De Charney burned at the stake in 1314 with de Molay. The family kept the cloth as a relic and later noticed that an image had settled upon it. The shroud initially appeared on a religious medallion that dated to 1338 and was first displayed in 1357. When it was shown, people immediately associated the image with Christ, and the de Charney family did nothing to dissuade that belief. That went on until the late sixteenth century when the Church took possession of the shroud, declaring it *acheropita*—not made by human hand—deeming it a holy relic. De Roquefort wants to take the shroud back. It's the Order's, not the Church's."

Thorvaldsen shook his head. "That's foolishness."

"It's how he thinks."

Malone noticed the annoyed look on Stephanie's face. "The Bible lesson was fascinating, Henrik. But I'm still waiting for the truth about what's happening here."

The Dane smiled. "You're such a joy."

"Chalk it up to my bubbly personality." She displayed her phone. "Let me make myself real clear. If I don't get some answers in the next few minutes, I'm calling Atlanta. I've had my fill of Raymond de Roquefort, so we're going public with this little treasure hunt and ending this nonsense."

FORTY-SEVEN

MALONE WINCED AT STEPHANIE'S DECLARATION. HE'D BEEN wondering when her patience would run out.

"You can't do that," Mark said to his mother. "The last thing we need is for the government to be involved."

"Why not?" Stephanie asked. "That abbey should be raided. Whatever they're doing is certainly not religious."

"On the contrary," Geoffrey said in a tremulous voice. "Great piety exists there. The brothers are devoted to the Lord. Their lives are consumed with His worship."

"And in between you learn about explosives, hand-to-hand combat, and how to shoot a weapon like a marksman. A bit of a contradiction, wouldn't you say?"

"Not at all," Thorvaldsen declared. "The original Templars were devoted to God *and* were a formidable fighting force."

Stephanie was clearly not impressed. "This is not the thirteenth century. De Roquefort has both an agenda and the might to press that agenda onto others. Today we call him a terrorist."

"You haven't changed a bit," Mark spat out.

"No, I haven't. I still believe that covert organizations with money, weapons, and chips on their shoulders are problems. My job is to deal with them."

"This doesn't concern you."

"Then why did your master involve me?"

Good question, Malone thought.

"You didn't understand when Dad was alive, and you don't now."

"Then why don't you clear up my confusion?"

"Mr. Malone," Cassiopeia said in a pleasant tone. "How would you like to see the castle restoration project?"

Apparently their hostess wanted to speak with him alone. Which was fine—he had some questions for her, too. "I'd love that."

Cassiopeia pushed back her chair and stood from the table. "Then let me show you. That'll give everyone else here time to talk—which, clearly, needs to happen. Please, make yourselves at home. Mr. Malone and I will return in a short while."

He followed Cassiopeia outside into the bright afternoon. They strolled back down the shaded lane, toward the car park and the construction site.

"When finished," Cassiopeia told him, "a thirteenth-century castle will stand exactly as it did seven hundred years ago."

"Quite an endeavor."

"I thrive on grand endeavors."

They entered the construction site through a broad wooden gate and strolled into what appeared to be a barn with sandstone walls that housed a modern reception center. Beyond loomed the smell of dust, horses, and debris, where a hundred or so people milled about.

"The entire foundation for the perimeter has been laid and

the west curtain wall is coming along," Cassiopeia said, pointing. "We're about to start the corner towers and central buildings. But it takes time. We have to fashion the bricks, stone, wood, and mortar precisely as was done seven hundred years ago, using the same methods and tools, even wearing the same clothes."

"Do they eat the same food?"

She smiled. "We do make some modern accommodation."

She led him through the construction area and up the slope of a steep hill to a modest promontory, where everything could be clearly seen.

"I come here often. One hundred and twenty men and women are employed down there full time."

"Quite a payroll."

"A small price to pay for history to be seen."

"Your nickname, *Ingénieur*. Is that what they call you? Engineer?"

"The staff gave me that name. I'm trained in medieval building techniques. I've designed this entire project."

"You know, on the one hand, you're an arrogant bitch. On the other, you can be rather interesting."

"I realize my comment at lunch, about what happened with Henrik's son, was inappropriate. Why didn't you strike back?"

"For what? You didn't know what the hell you were talking about."

"I'll try not to make any more judgments."

He chuckled. "I doubt that, and I'm not that sensitive. I long ago developed a lizard skin. You have to in order to survive in this business."

"But you're retired."

"You never really quit. You just stay out of the line of fire more often than not."

"So you're helping Stephanie Nelle simply as a friend?"

"Shocking, isn't it?"

"Not at all. In fact, it's entirely consistent with your personality."

Now he was curious. "How do you know about my personality?"

"Once Henrik asked me to be involved, I learned a great deal about you. I have friends in your former profession. They all spoke highly of you."

"Glad to know folks remember."

"Do you know much about me?" she asked.

"Just a thumbnail sketch."

"I have many peculiarities."

"Then you and Henrik should get along well."

She smiled. "I see you know him well."

"How long have you known him?"

"Since childhood. He knew my parents. Many years ago, he told me of Lars Nelle. What Lars was working on fascinated me. So I became Lars's guardian angel, though he thought of me as the devil. Unfortunately, I couldn't help him on the last day of his life."

"Were you there?"

She shook her head. "He'd traveled south to the mountains. I was here when Henrik called and told me the body had been found."

"Did he kill himself?"

"Lars was a sad man, that was plain. He was also frustrated. All those amateurs who'd seized on his work and twisted it beyond recognition. The puzzle he tried to solve has remained a mystery a long time. So, yes, it's possible."

"What were you protecting him from?"

"Many tried to encroach on his research. Most of them were ambitious treasure hunters, some opportunists, but eventually Raymond de Roquefort's men appeared. Luckily, I was always able to conceal my presence from them."

"De Roquefort is now master."

She crinkled her brow. "Which explains his renewed search efforts. He now commands all the Templar resources."

She apparently knew nothing about Mark Nelle and where he'd been living the past five years, so he told her, then said, "Mark lost to de Roquefort in the selection of a new master."

"So this is personal between them?"

"That's certainly part of it." But not all, he thought, as he stared down and watched a horse-drawn cart work its way across the dry earth toward one of the partial walls.

"The work being done today is for the tourists," she said, noticing his interest. "Part of the show. We'll return to serious building tomorrow."

"The sign out front said it'll take thirty years to finish."

"Easily."

She was right. She did possess many peculiarities.

"I intentionally left Lars's notebook for de Roquefort to find in Avignon."

That revelation shocked him. "Why?"

"Henrik wanted to talk to the Nelles privately. It's why we're here. He also said that you're a man of honor. I trust precious few people in this world, but Henrik is one I do. So I'm going to take him at his word and tell you some things no one else knows."

MARK LISTENED AS HENRIK THORVALDSEN EXPLAINED. HIS mother appeared interested, too, but Geoffrey simply stared at the table, hardly blinking, seemingly in a trance.

"It's time you fully understand what Lars believed," Henrik said to Stephanie. "Contrary to what you may have thought, he was not some crackpot chasing after treasure. A serious purpose lay behind his inquiries."

"I'll ignore your insult, since I want to hear what you have to say."

A look of irritation crept into Thorvaldsen's eyes. "Lars's theory was simple, though it really was not his. Ernst Scoville formulated most of it, which involved a novel look at the Gospels of the New Testament, especially with how they dealt with the resurrection. Cassiopeia hinted at some of this earlier.

"Let's start with Mark's. His was the first Gospel, written around AD 70, perhaps the only Gospel the early Christians possessed after Christ died. It contains six hundred sixty-five verses, yet only eight are devoted to the resurrection. This most remarkable of events only rated a brief mention. Why? The answer is simple. When Mark's Gospel was written, the story of the resurrection had yet to develop, and the Gospel ends without mention of the fact that the disciples believed Jesus had been raised from the dead. Instead, it tells us that the disciples fled. Only women appear in Mark's version of what happened, and they ignore a command to tell the disciples to go to Galilee so the risen Christ could meet them there. Rather, the women, too, are confused and flee, telling no one what they saw. There are no angels, only a young man dressed in white who calmly announces that *He has risen*. No guards, no burial clothes, and no risen Lord."

Mark knew everything Thorvaldsen had just said was true. He'd studied that Gospel in great detail.

"Matthew's testimony came a decade later. The Romans had by then sacked Jerusalem and destroyed the Temple. Many Jews had fled into the Greek-speaking world. The Orthodox Jews who stayed in the Holy Land viewed the new Jewish Christians as a problem—as much of one as the Romans were. Hostility existed between the Orthodox Jews and the emerging Jewish Christians. Matthew's Gospel was probably written by one of those unknown Jewish Christian scribes. Mark's Gospel had left many unanswered questions, so Matthew changed the story to suit his troubled time.

"Now the messenger who announces the resurrection

becomes an angel. He descends in an earthquake, with a face like lightning. Guards are struck down. The stone has been removed from the tomb, and an angel perches upon it. The women are still gripped with fear, but it is rapidly replaced with joy. Contrary to the women in Mark's account, the women here rush out to tell the disciples what's happened and actually confront the risen Christ. Here, for the first time, the risen Lord is actually described. And what did the women do?"

"They took hold of His feet and worshiped Him," Mark softly said. "Later, Jesus appeared to His disciples and proclaimed that *'all authority in heaven and on earth has been given to me.'* He tells them he'll always be with them."

"What a change," Thorvaldsen said. "The Jewish Messiah named Jesus has now become Christ to the world. In Matthew, everything is more vivid. Miraculous, too. Then comes Luke, sometime around AD 90. By then the Jewish Christians had moved further away from Judaism, so Luke radically modified the resurrection story to accommodate this change. The women are at the tomb again, but this time they find it empty and go tell the disciples. Peter returns and sees only the discarded burial clothes. Then Luke tells a story that appears nowhere else in the Bible. It involves Jesus traveling in disguise, encountering certain disciples, sharing a meal, then, when recognized, vanishing. There is also a later encounter with all of the disciples where they doubt His flesh, so He eats with them, then vanishes. And only in Luke do we find the story of Jesus's ascension into heaven. What's happened? A sense of rapture has now been grafted onto the risen Christ."

Mark had read similar Scripture analyses in the Templar archives. Learned brothers had for centuries studied the Word, noting errors, evaluating contradictions, and hypothesizing on the many conflicts in names, dates, places, and events.

"Then there's John," Thorvaldsen said. "The Gospel written the furthest away from Jesus's life, around AD 100. There are so many changes in this Gospel, it's almost as if John talks of a totally different Christ. No Bethlehem birth—Nazareth is Jesus's birthplace here. The other three talk of a three-year ministry. John says only one. The Last Supper in John occurred on the day before the Passover—the crucifixion on the day the Passover lamb was slaughtered. This is different from the other Gospels. John also moved the cleansing of the Temple from the day after Palm Sunday to a time early in Christ's ministry.

"In John, Mary Magdalene alone goes to the tomb and finds it empty. She never even considers a resurrection, but instead thinks the body has been stolen. Only when she returns with Peter and *the other disciple* does she see two angels. Then the angels are transformed into Jesus Himself.

"Look how this one detail, about who was in the tomb, changed. Mark's young man dressed in white became Matthew's dazzling angel, which Luke expanded to two angels, which John modified to two angels who become Christ. And was the risen Lord seen in the garden on the first day of the week, as Christians are always told? Mark and Luke said no. Matthew, yes. John said not at first, but Mary Magdalene did see Him later. What happened is clear. Over time, the resurrection was made more and more miraculous to accommodate a changing world."

"I assume," Stephanie said, "you don't adhere to the principle of biblical inerrancy?"

"There's nothing whatsoever literal within the Bible. It's a tale riddled with inconsistencies, and the only way they can be explained is through the use of faith. That may have worked a thousand years ago, or even five hundred years ago, but that explanation is no longer acceptable. The human mind today questions. Your husband questioned."

"So what was it Lars meant to do?"

"The impossible," Mark muttered.

His mother looked at him with strangely understanding eyes. "But that never stopped him." The voice was low and melodious, as if she'd just realized a truth that had long lain hidden. "If nothing else, he was a wonderful dreamer."

"But his dreams had a basis," Mark said. "The Templars once knew what Dad wanted to know. Even today, they read and study Scripture that's not a part of the New Testament. The Gospel of Philip, the Letter of Barnabas, the Acts of Peter, the Epistle of the Apostles, the Secret Book of John, the Gospel of Mary, the Didache. And the Gospel of Thomas, which is to them perhaps the closest we have to what Jesus may have actually said, since it has not been subjected to countless translations. Many of these so-called heretical texts are eye opening. And that was what made the Templars special. The true source of their power. Not wealth or might, but knowledge."

MALONE STOOD UNDER THE SHADE OF TALL POPLARS THAT DOTted the promontory. A cool breeze eased past and dulled the sun's rays, reminding him of a fall afternoon at the beach. He was waiting for Cassiopeia to tell him what nobody else knew. "Why did you allow de Roquefort to have Lars Nelle's notebook?"

"Because it's useless." A crinkle of amusement slipped into her dark eyes.

"I thought it contained Lars's private thoughts. Information he never published. The key to everything."

"Some of that is true, but it's not the key to anything. Lars created it just for the Templars."

"Would Claridon have known that?"

"Probably not. Lars was a secretive man. He told no one everything. He said once that only the paranoid survived in his line of work."

"How do you know this?"

"Henrik was aware. Lars never spoke of the details, but he told Henrik of his encounters with the Templars. On occasion, he actually believed he was speaking to the Order's master. They talked several times, but eventually de Roquefort entered the picture. And he was altogether different. More aggressive, less tolerant. So Lars created the notebook for de Roquefort to focus on—not unlike the misdirection Saunière himself used."

"Would the Templar master have known this? When Mark was taken to the abbey, he had the notebook with him. The master kept it hidden until a month ago, when he sent it to Stephanie."

"Hard to say. But if he sent the notebook to Stephanie, it's possible the master calculated that de Roquefort would again chase after it. He apparently wanted Stephanie involved, so what better way than to bait her with something irresistible?"

Smart, he had to admit. And it worked.

"The master surely felt Stephanie would use the considerable resources at her disposal to aid the quest," she said.

"He didn't know Stephanie. Too stubborn. She'd try it on her own first."

"But you were there to help."

"Lucky me."

"Oh, it's not that bad. We never would have met otherwise."

"Like I said, lucky me."

"I'll take that as a compliment. Otherwise my feelings might be hurt."

"I doubt you bruise so easily."

"You handled yourself well in Copenhagen," she said. "Then again in Roskilde."

"You were in the cathedral?"

"For a while, but I left when the shooting started. It would have been impossible for me to help without revealing my presence, and Henrik wanted that kept secret."

"And what if I had been unable to stop those men inside?"

"Oh, come now. You?" She threw him a smile. "Tell me something. How shocked were you when the brother leaped from the Round Tower?"

"Not something you see every day."

"He fulfilled his oath. Trapped, he chose death rather than risk the Order's exposure."

"I assume you were there because of my mention to Henrik that Stephanie was coming for a visit."

"Partly. When I heard of Ernst Scoville's sudden demise, I learned from some of the older men in Rennes that he'd spoken with Stephanie and that she was coming to France. They're all Rennes enthusiasts, spending their days playing chess and fantasizing about Saunière. Each one of them lives in a conspiratorialist dream. Scoville bragged that he meant to get Lars's notebook. He didn't care for Stephanie, though he'd led her to believe otherwise. Obviously he, too, was unaware that the journal was by and large meaningless. His death aroused *my* suspicions, so I contacted Henrik and learned of Stephanie's impending Danish visit. We decided that I should go to Denmark."

"And Avignon?"

"I had a source at the asylum. No one believed Claridon was crazy. Deceitful, untrustworthy, an opportunist— certainly. But not insane. So I watched until you returned to claim Claridon. Henrik and I knew there was something in the palace archives, just not what. As Henrik said at lunch, Mark never met Henrik. Mark was much tougher to deal with than his father. He only occasionally searched. Something, perhaps, to keep his father's memory alive. Whatever he may have found, he kept totally to himself. He and Claridon connected for a while, but it was a loose association.

Then, when Mark disappeared in the avalanche and Claridon retreated to the asylum, Henrik and I gave up."

"Until now."

"The quest is back on, and this time there may well be somewhere to go."

He waited for her to explain.

"We have the book with the gravestone and we also have *Reading the Rules of the Caridad*. Together, we might actually be able to determine what Saunière found, since we're the first to have so many pieces of the puzzle."

"And what do we do if we find anything?"

"As a Muslim? I'd like to tell the world. As a realist? I don't know. The historical arrogance of Christianity is nauseating. To it, every other religion is an imitation. Amazing, really. All of Western history is shaped by its narrow precepts. Art, architecture, music, writing—even society itself became Christianity's servants. That simple movement ultimately formed the mold from which Western civilization was crafted, and it could all be predicated on a lie. Wouldn't you like to know?"

"I'm not a religious person."

Her thin lips creased into another smile. "But you're a curious man. Henrik speaks of your courage and intellect in reverent terms. A bibliophile, with an eidetic memory. Quite a combination."

"And I can cook, too."

She chuckled. "You don't fool me. Finding the Great Devise would mean something to you."

"Let's just say that it would be a most unusual find."

"Fair enough. We'll leave it at that. But if we're successful, I look forward to seeing your reaction."

"You're that confident there's something to find?"

She swept her arms toward the distant outline of the Pyrénées. "It's out there, no question. Saunière found it. We can, too."

STEPHANIE AGAIN CONSIDERED WHAT THORVALDSEN HAD SAID about the New Testament, and made clear, "The Bible is not a literal document."

Thorvaldsen shook his head. "A great many Christian faiths would take issue with that statement. For them, the Bible is the Word of God."

She looked at Mark. "Did your father believe the Bible was not the Word of God?"

"We debated the point many times. I was, at first, a believer, and I'd argue with him. But I came to think like he did. It's a book of stories. Glorious stories, designed to point people toward a good life. There's even greatness in those stories—if one practices their moral. I don't think it's necessary that it's the Word of God. It's enough that the words are a timeless truth."

"Elevating Christ to deity status was simply a way of elevating the importance of the message," Thorvaldsen said. "After organized religion took over in the third and fourth centuries, so much was added to the tale that it's impossible any longer to know its core. Lars wanted to change all that. He wanted to find what the Templars once possessed. When he first learned of Rennes-le-Château years ago, he immediately believed the Templar's Great Devise was what Saunière had located. So he devoted his life to solving the Rennes puzzle."

Stephanie was still not convinced. "What makes you think the Templars secreted anything away? Weren't they arrested quickly? How was there time to hide anything?"

"They were prepared," Mark said. "The Chronicles make that clear. What Philip IV did wasn't without precedent. A hundred years earlier there was an incident with Frederick II, the king of Germany and Sicily. In 1228 he arrived in the Holy Land as an excommunicate, which meant he could not command a crusade. The Templars and Hospitallers stayed loyal to the pope and refused to follow him. Only his German Teutonic knights stood by his side. Ultimately, he negotiated a peace treaty with the Saracens that created a divided Jerusalem. The Temple Mount, which was where the Templars were headquartered, was given by that treaty to the Muslims. So you can imagine what the Templars thought of him. He was as amoral as Nero and universally hated. He even tried to kidnap the Order's master. Finally he left the Holy Land in 1229, and as he made his way to the port at Acre, the locals threw excrement on him. He hated the Templars for their disloyalty, and when he returned to Sicily, he seized Templar property and made arrests. All of which was recorded in the Chronicles."

"So the Order was ready?" Thorvaldsen asked.

"The Order had already seen, firsthand, what a hostile ruler could do to it. Philip IV was similar. As a young man he'd applied for Templar membership and had been refused, so he harbored a lifelong resentment toward the brotherhood. Early in his reign, the Templars actually saved Philip when he tried to devalue the French currency and the people revolted. He fled to the Paris Temple for refuge. Afterward, he felt beholden to the Templars. And monarchs never want to owe anyone. So, yes, by October 1307 the Order was ready. Unfortunately, nothing is recorded that tells us the details of what was done." Mark's gaze bored into Stephanie. "Dad gave his life to try to solve that mystery."

"He did love looking, didn't he?" Thorvaldsen said.

Though answering the Dane, Mark continued to face her. "It was one of the few things that actually brought him joy. He wanted to please his wife and himself and, unfortunately, he could do neither. So he opted out. Decided to leave us all."

"I never wanted to believe he killed himself," she said to her son.

"But we'll never know, will we?"

"Perhaps you may," Geoffrey said. And for the first time the young man lifted his gaze from the table. "The master said you might learn the truth of his death."

"What do you know?" she asked.

"I know only what the master told me."

"What did he tell you about my father?" Anger gripped Mark's face. Stephanie could never recall seeing him vent that emotion on anyone but her.

"That will have to be learned, by you. I don't know." The voice was strange, hollow, and conciliatory. "The master told me to be tolerant of your emotion. He made clear you're my senior, and I should offer you nothing but respect."

"But you seem to be the only one with answers," Stephanie said.

"No, madame. I know but markers. The answers, the master said, must come from all of you."

FORTY-EIGHT

MALONE FOLLOWED CASSIOPEIA INTO A LOFTY CHAMBER WITH a raftered ceiling and paneled walls hung with tapestries that depicted cuirasses, swords, lances, casques, and shields. A black marble fireplace dominated the long room, which was lit by a glittering chandelier. The others joined them from the dining room and he noticed serious expressions on all of their faces. A mahogany table sat beneath a set of mullioned windows, across which were spread books, papers, and photographs.

"Time we see if there are any conclusions we can reach," Cassiopeia said. "On the table is everything I have on this subject."

Malone told the others about Lars's notebook and how some of the information contained within it was false.

"Does that include what he said about himself?" Stephanie asked. "This young man here—" She pointed at Geoffrey. "—sent me pages from the journal—pages his master cut out. They talked about me."

"Only you know if what he said was true or more misdirection," Cassiopeia said.

"She's right," Thorvaldsen said. "The notebook is, by and large, not genuine. Lars created it as Templar bait."

"Another point you conveniently failed to mention back in Copenhagen." Stephanie's tone signaled she was once again annoyed.

Thorvaldsen was undaunted. "The important thing was that de Roquefort thought the journal genuine."

Stephanie's back straightened. "You son of a bitch, we could have been killed trying to get it back."

"But you weren't. Cassiopeia kept an eye on you both."

"And that makes what you did right?"

"Stephanie, you've never withheld information from one of your agents?" Thorvaldsen asked.

She held her tongue.

"He's right," Malone said.

She whirled and faced him.

"How many times did you tell me only part of the story? And how many times did I complain later that it could have gotten me killed? And what did you say? *Get used to it.* Same here, Stephanie. I don't like it any better than you do, but I got used to it."

"Why don't we stop arguing and see if we can come to some consensus as to what Saunière may have found," Cassiopeia said.

"And where would you suggest we start?" Mark asked.

"I'd say Marie d'Hautpoul de Blanchefort's gravestone would be an excellent spot, since we have Stüblein's book that Henrik purchased at the auction." She motioned to the table. "Opened to the drawing."

They all stepped close and gazed at the sketch.

"Claridon explained about this in Avignon," Malone said, and he told them about the wrong date of death—1681 as opposed to 1781—the Roman numerals—MDCOLXXXI—containing a zero, and the remaining set of Roman numerals—LIXLIXL—etched into the lower right corner.

Mark grabbed a pencil off the table and wrote 1681 and 59, 59, 50 on a pad. "That's the conversion of those numbers. I'm ignoring the zero in the 1681. Claridon's right, no zero in Roman numerals."

Malone pointed at the Greek letters on the left stone. "Claridon said they were Latin words written in the Greek alphabet. He converted the lettering and came up with *Et in arcadia ego*. And in Arcadia I. He thought it might be an anagram, since the phrase makes little sense."

Mark studied the words with intensity, then asked Geoffrey for the rucksack, from which he removed a tightly folded towel. He gently unwrapped the bundle and revealed a small codex. Its leafs were folded, then sewn together and bound—vellum, if Malone wasn't mistaken. He'd never seen one he could actually touch.

"This came from the Templar archives. I found it a few years ago, right after I became seneschal. It was written in 1542 by one of the abbey's scribes. It's an excellent reproduction of a fourteenth-century manuscript and recounts how the Templars re-formed after the Purge. It also deals with the time from December 1306 until May 1307, when Jacques de Molay was in France and little is known of his whereabouts."

Mark gently opened the ancient volume and carefully

paged through until he found what he was looking for. Malone saw the Latin script was a series of loops and fioriture, the letters joined together from the pen not being lifted from the page.

"Listen to this."

Our master, the most reverend and devoted Jacques de Molay, received the pope's envoy on 6 June 1306 with the pomp and courtesy reserved for those of high rank. The message stated that His Holiness Pope Clement V hath summoned Master de Molay to France. Our master intended to comply with that order, making all preparations, but prior to leaving the island of Cyprus, where the Order hath established its headquarters, our master learned that the leader of the Hospitallers had also been summoned, but hath refused the command, citing the need to remain with his Order in time of conflict. This aroused great suspicion in our master and he consulted with his officers. His Holiness had likewise instructed our master to travel unrecognized and with a small retinue. This raised more questions since why would His Holiness care how our master moved through the lands. Then a curious document was brought to our master titled De Recuperatione Terrae Sanctae. Concerning the Recovery of the Holy Land. The manuscript was written by one of Philip IV's lawyers and it outlined a grand new crusade to be headed by a Warrior King designed to retake the Holy Land from the infidels. This proposal was a direct affront to the plans of our Order and caused our master to question his summons to the King's court. Our master made it known that he greatly distrusted the French monarch, though it would be both foolish and inappropriate for him to voice that mistrust beyond the walls of our Temple. In a mood of caution, being not a careless man and remembering the treachery from long ago of Frederick II, our master laid plans that our wealth and knowledge must be safeguarded. He prayed that he might be in error but saw no reason to be unprepared. Brother Gilbert de Blanchefort was summoned and ordered to take away the treasure of the Temple in advance. Our master then told de Blanchefort, "We of the Order's leadership could be at risk. So none of us are to know what you know and you must assure that what you know is passed to others in an appropriate manner." Brother de Blanchefort, being a learned man, set about to accomplish his mission and quietly secreted all that the Order had acquired. Four brothers were his allies and they used four words, one for each of them, as their signal. ET IN ARCADIA EGO. *But the letters are but a jumble for the true message. A rearrangement tells precisely what their task entailed.* I TEGO ARCANA DEI.

"I conceal the secrets of God," Mark said, translating the last line. "Anagrams were common in the fourteenth century, too."

"So de Molay was ready?" Malone asked.

Mark nodded. "He came to France with sixty knights, a hundred fifty thousand gold florins, and twelve pack horses hauling unminted silver. He knew there was going to be trouble. That money was to be used to buy his way out. But there's something contained within this treatise that is little known. The commander of the Templar contingent in the Languedoc was Seigneur de Goth. Pope Clement V, the man who summoned de Molay, was named Bertrand de Goth. The pope's mother was Ida de Blanchefort, who was related to Gilbert de Blanchefort. So de Molay possessed good inside information."

"Always helps," Malone said.

"De Molay also knew something on Clement V. Prior to his election as pope, Clement met with Philip IV. The king had the power to deliver the papacy to whomever he wanted.

Before he gave it to Clement, he imposed six conditions. Most had to do with Philip getting to do whatever he wanted, but the sixth concerned the Templars. Philip wanted the Order dissolved, and Clement agreed."

"Interesting stuff," Stephanie said, "but what seems more important at the moment is what the abbé Bigou knew. He's the man who actually commissioned Marie's gravestone. Would he have known of a connection between the de Blanchefort family secret and the Templars?"

"Without a doubt," Thorvaldsen said. "Bigou was told the family secret by Marie d'Hautpoul de Blanchefort herself. Her husband was a direct descendant of Gilbert de Blanchefort. Once the Order was suppressed, and Templars started burning at the stake, Gilbert de Blanchefort would have told no one the location of the Great Devise. So that family secret has to be Templar-related. What else could it be?"

Mark nodded. "The Chronicles speak of carts topped with hay moving through the French countryside, each headed south toward the Pyrénées, escorted by armed men disguised as peasants. All but three made the journey safely. Unfortunately, there's no mention of their final destination. Only one clue in all the Chronicles. *Where is it best to hide a pebble?*"

"In the middle of a rock pile," Malone said.

"That's what the master said, too," Mark said. "To the fourteenth-century mind, the most obvious location would be the safest."

Malone gazed again at the gravestone drawing. "So Bigou had this gravestone carved that, in code, says that he conceals the secrets of God, and he went to the trouble of publicly placing it. What was the point? What are we missing?"

Mark reached into the rucksack and extracted another volume. "This is a report by the Order's marshal written in 1897. The man was investigating Saunière and came across another priest, the abbé Gélis, in a nearby village, who found a cryptogram in his church."

"As Saunière did," Stephanie said.

"That's right. Gélis deciphered the cryptogram and wanted the bishop to know what he learned. The marshal posed as the bishop's representative and copied the puzzle, but he kept the solution to himself."

Mark showed them the cryptogram and Malone studied the lines of letters and symbols. "Some sort of numeric key unscrambles it?"

Mark nodded. "It's impossible to break without the key. There are billions of possible combinations."

"There was one of these in your father's journal, too," he said.

"I know. Dad found it in Noël Corbu's unpublished manuscript."

"Claridon told us about that."

"Which means de Roquefort has it," Stephanie said. "But is it part of the fiction of Lars's journal?"

"Anything Corbu touched has to be suspect," Thorvaldsen made clear. "He embellished Saunière's story to promote his damn hotel."

"But the manuscript he wrote," Mark said. "Dad always believed it contained truth. Corbu was close with Saunière's mistress up until she died in 1953. Many believed she told him things. That's why Corbu never published the manuscript. It contradicted *his* fictionalized version of the story."

"But surely the cryptogram in the journal is false?" Thorvaldsen said. "That would have been the very thing de Roquefort would have wanted from the journal."

"We can only hope," Malone said, as he noticed an image of *Reading the Rules of the Caridad* on the table. He lifted the letter-sized reproduction and studied the writing beneath the little man, in a monk's robe, perched on a stool with a finger to his lips, signaling quiet.

ACABOCE A°
DE 1681

Something was wrong, and he instantly compared the image with the lithograph.

The dates were different.

"I spent this morning learning about that painting," Cassiopeia said. "I found that image on the Internet. The painting was destroyed by fire in the late 1950s, but prior to that the canvas had been cleaned and readied for display. During the restoration process it was discovered that 1687 was actually 1681. But of course, the lithograph was drawn at a time when the date was obscured."

Stephanie shook her head. "This is a puzzle with no answer. Everything changes by the minute."

"You're doing precisely what the master wanted," Geoffrey said.

They all looked at him.

"He said that once you combined, all would be revealed."

Malone was confused. "But your master specifically warned us to *Beware the engineer*."

Geoffrey motioned to Cassiopeia. "Perhaps you should beware of her."

"What does that mean?" Thorvaldsen asked.

"Her race fought the Templars for two centuries."

"Actually, the Muslims trounced the brothers and sent them packing from the Holy Land," Cassiopeia declared. "And Spanish Muslims kept the Order in check here in the Languedoc when the Templars tried to expand their sphere south, beyond the Pyrénées. So your master was right. Beware the engineer."

"What would you do if you found the Great Devise?" Geoffrey asked her.

"Depends on what there is to find."

"Why does that matter? The Devise is not yours, regardless."

"You're quite forward for a mere brother of the Order."

"Much is at stake here, the least of which is your ambition to prove Christianity a lie."

"I don't recall saying that was my ambition."

"The master knew."

Cassiopeia's face screwed tight—the first time Malone had seen agitation in her expression. "Your master knew nothing of my motives."

"And by keeping them hidden," Geoffrey said, "you do nothing but confirm his suspicion."

Cassiopeia faced Henrik. "This young man could be a problem."

"He was sent by the master," Thorvaldsen said. "We shouldn't question."

"He's trouble," Cassiopeia declared.

"Maybe so," Mark said. "But he's part of this, so get used to him."

She stayed calm and unruffled. "Do you trust him?"

"Doesn't matter," Mark said. "Henrik's right. The master trusted him and that's what matters. Even if the good brother can be irritating."

Cassiopeia did not push the point, but on her brow was written the shadow of mutiny. And Malone did not necessarily disagree with her impulse.

He turned his attention back to the table and stared at the color images taken at the Church of Mary Magdalene. He noticed the garden with the statue of the Virgin and the words MISSION 1891 and PENITENCE, PENITENCE carved into the face of the upside-down Visigoth pillar. He shuffled through close-up shots of the stations of the cross, pausing for a moment on station 10, where a Roman soldier was gambling for Christ's cloak, the numbers three, four, and five visible on the dice faces. Then he paused on station 14, which showed Christ's body being carried under cover of darkness by two men.

He remembered what Mark had said in the church, and he couldn't help wondering. Was their route *into* the tomb or *out*?

He shook his head.

What in the world was happening?

FORTY-NINE

5:30 PM

DE ROQUEFORT FOUND THE GIVORS ARCHAEOLOGICAL SITE, which was clearly denoted on the Michelin map, and approached with a measure of caution. He did not want to announce his presence. Even if Malone and company were not there, Cassiopeia Vitt knew him. So on arriving, he ordered the driver to slowly cruise through a grassy meadow that served as a car park until he found the Peugeot matching the make and color he remembered, with a rental sticker on the windshield.

"They're here," he said. "Park."

The driver did as instructed.

"I'll explore," he told the other two brothers and Claridon. "Wait here, and remain out of sight."

He climbed out into the late afternoon, a blood ball of summer sun already fading over the surrounding walls of limestone. He sucked in a deep breath and savored cool, thin air that reminded him of the abbey. They'd clearly risen in altitude.

A quick visual survey and he spotted a tree-shaded lane cast in long shadows and decided that direction seemed best, but he stayed off the defined path, making his way through the tall trees, a tapestry of flowers and heather carpeting the violet ground. The surrounding land had all once been a Templar domain. One of the largest commanderies in the Pyrénées had crowned a nearby promontory. It had been a factory, one of several locations where brothers labored night and day crafting the Order's weapons. He knew that great skill had gone into compacting wood, leather, and metal into shields that could not be easily split. But the sword had been the brother knight's true friend. Barons often loved their swords more than their wives, and tried to retain the same one all of their lives. Brothers cradled a similar passion, which Rule encouraged. If a man was expected to lay down his life, the least that could be done was allow him the weapon of his choice. Templar swords, however, were not like those of barons. No hilts adorned with gilt or set with pearls. No end knobs capped in crystal containing relics. Brother knights required no such talismans, as their strength came from a devotion to God and obedience to Rule. Their companion had been their horse, always one with quickness and intelligence. Each knight was allocated three animals, which were fed, combed, and tricked out each day. Horses were one of the means whereby the Order flourished, and the coursers, the palfreys, and especially the destriers responded to the brother knights' affection with an unmatched loyalty. He'd read of one brother who returned home from the Crusades and was not embraced by his father, but was instantly recognized by his faithful stallion.

And they were always stallions.

To ride a mare was unthinkable. What had one knight said? *The woman to the woman.*

He kept walking. The musty scent of twigs and boughs stirred his imagination, and he could almost hear the heavy hooves that had once crushed the tender mosses and flowers. He tried to listen for some sound, but the clicking of grasshoppers interfered. He was mindful of electronic surveillance but had, so far, sensed none. He continued to thread a path through the tall pines, moving farther away from the lane, deeper into the woods. His skin heated, and sweat beaded on his brow. High above him, rock crannies groaned from a wind.

Warrior monks, that's what the brothers became.

He liked that term.

St. Bernard of Clairvaux himself justified the Templars' entire existence by glorifying the killing of non-Christians. *Neither dealing out death nor dying, when for Christ's sake, contains anything criminal but rather merits glorious reward. The soldier of Christ kills safely and dies the more safely. Not without cause does he bear the sword. He is the instrument of God for the punishment of evildoers and for the defense of the just. When he kills evildoers it is not homicide, but malicide, and he is considered Christ's legal executioner.*

He knew those words well. They were taught to every inductee. He'd repeated them in his mind as he'd watched Lars Nelle, Ernst Scoville, and Peter Hansen die. All were heretics. Men who'd stood in the Order's way. Malice doers. Now there were a few more names to be added to that list. Those of the men and women who occupied the château that was coming into view, beyond the trees, in a sheltered hollow among a succession of rock ridges.

He'd learned something of the château from the background information he'd ordered earlier, before leaving the abbey. Once a sixteenth-century royal residence, one of Catherine de Médicis' many homes, it had been spared destruction in the Revolution due to its isolation. So it remained a monument to the Renaissance—a picturesque mass of turrets, spires, and perpendicular roofs. Cassiopeia Vitt was clearly a woman of means. Houses such as this required great sums of money to buy and maintain, and he doubted she conducted tours as a way to supplement the income. No, this was the private residence of an aloof soul, one that had three times interfered in his business. One that must be tended to.

But he also needed the two books Mark Nelle possessed.

So rash acts were out of the question.

The day was fast falling, deep shadows already starting to engulf the château. His mind whirled with possibilities.

He had to be sure they were all inside. His current vantage point was too close. But he spied a thick stand of beech trees two hundred meters away that would provide an unobstructed view of the front entrance.

He had to assume that they expected him to come. After what happened in Lars Nelle's house, they surely realized Claridon was working for him. But they might not expect him here this soon. Which was fine. He needed to return to the abbey. His officers were awaiting him. A council had been called that demanded his presence.

He decided to leave the two brothers in the car here to watch. That would be enough for now.

But he'd be back.

FIFTY

8:00 PM

STEPHANIE COULD NOT RECALL THE LAST TIME SHE AND MARK had sat and talked. Perhaps not since he was a teenager. That was how deep the chasm between them ran.

Now they had retreated to a room atop one of the château's towers. Before sitting, Mark had swung open four oriel windows, allowing the keen evening air to wash over them.

"You may or may not believe this, but I think about you and your father every day. I loved your father. But once he came across the Rennes story, he changed his focus. That whole thing took him over. And at the time, I resented that."

"Which I can understand. Really, I can. What I don't understand is why you made him choose between you and what he thought was important."

His sharp tone bristled through her, and she forced herself to remain calm. "The day we buried him, I knew how wrong I'd been. But I couldn't bring him back."

"I hated you that day."

"I know."

"Yet you just flew home and left me in France."

"I thought that was what you wanted."

"It was. But for the past five years I've had a lot of time to reflect. The master championed you, though I'm only now realizing what he meant by a lot of his comments. In the Gospel of Thomas, Jesus says, *Whoever does not hate their father and mother as I do cannot be my disciple.* Then He says, *Whoever does not love their father and mother as I do cannot be my disciple.* I'm beginning to understand those contradictory statements. I hated you, Mother."

"But do you love me, too?"

Silence loomed between them, and it tore at her heart.

Finally, he said, "You're my mother."

"That's not an answer."

"It's all you're going to get."

His face, so much like Lars's, was a study in conflicting emotions. She didn't press. Her chance to demand anything had long passed.

"Are you still head of the Magellan Billet?" he asked.

She appreciated the change in subject. "As far as I know, but I've probably pushed my luck the past few days. Cotton and I haven't been inconspicuous."

"He seems like a good man."

"The best. I didn't want to involve him, but he insisted. He worked for me a long time."

"It's good to have friends like that."

"You have one, too."

"Geoffrey? He's more my oracle than a friend. The master swore him to me. Why? I don't know."

"He would defend you with his life. That much is clear."

"I'm not accustomed to people laying down their lives for me."

She recalled what the master had said in his note to her, about Mark not possessing the resolve to finish his battles. She told him exactly what the master wrote. He listened in silence.

"What would you have done if you'd been elected master?" she asked.

"A part of me was glad I lost."

She was amazed. "Why?"

"I'm a college professor, not a leader."

"You're a man in the middle of an important conflict. One that other men are waiting to see resolved."

"The master is right about me."

She stared at him with undisguised dismay. "Your father would be ashamed to hear you say that." She waited for his anger to come, but Mark merely sat silent, and she listened to the rattle of insects from outside.

"I probably killed a man today," Mark said in a whisper. "How would Dad have felt about that?"

She'd been waiting for a mention. He'd not said a word about what had happened since they'd left Rennes. "Cotton told me. You had no choice. The man was given an option and he chose to challenge you."

"I watched the body roll down. Strange, the feeling that goes through you knowing you'd just taken a life."

She waited for him to explain.

"I was glad the trigger had been pulled, since I survived. But another part of me was mortified, because the other man hadn't."

"Life is one choice after another. He chose wrong."

"You do it all the time, don't you? Make those kinds of decisions?"

"They happen every day."

"My heart is not cold enough for that."

"And mine is?" She resented the implication.

"You tell me."

"I do my job, Mark. That man chose his fate, not you."

"No. De Roquefort chose it. He sent him out on that precipice, knowing there'd be a confrontation. He made the choice."

"And that's the problem with your Order, Mark. Unquestioned loyalty is not a good thing. No country, no army, no leader has ever survived who insisted on such foolishness. My agents make their own choices."

A moment of strained silence passed.

"You're right," he finally muttered. "Dad would be ashamed of me."

She decided to risk it. "Mark, your father's gone. He's been dead a long time. For me, you've been dead five years. But you're here now. Is there no room within you for forgiveness?" Hope laced her plea.

He stood from the chair. "No, Mother. There's not."

And he walked from the room.

MALONE HAD TAKEN REFUGE OUTSIDE THE CHÂTEAU, UNDER A shady pergola overgrown with greenery. Only insects disturbed his tranquility, and he watched as bats fluttered across the dimming sky. A little while ago Stephanie had taken him aside and told him that a call to Atlanta, requesting a complete dossier on their hostess, had revealed that Cassiopeia Vitt's name did not appear in any of the terrorist databases the U.S. government maintained. Her personal history was unremarkable, though she was half Muslim and these days that raised, if nothing else, a red flag. She owned a multicontinent conglomerate, based in Paris, involved in a broad spectrum of business ventures with assets in the billion-euro range. Her father started the company and she inherited control, though she was little involved with its everyday operation. She also was the chairwoman for a Dutch foundation that worked closely with the United Nations on international AIDS relief and world famine, particularly in Africa. No foreign government considered her a threat.

But Malone wasn't sure.

New threats arose every day and from the strangest places.

"So deep in thought."

He looked up to see Cassiopeia standing beyond the pergola. She wore a tight-fitting black riding habit that suited her.

"I was actually thinking about you."

"I'm flattered."

"I wouldn't be." He motioned to her outfit. "I wondered where you disappeared to."

"I try to ride every evening. Helps me think."

She stepped under the enclosure. "I had this built years ago as a tribute to my mother. She loved the outdoors."

Cassiopeia sat on a bench opposite him. He could tell there was a purpose to her visit.

"I saw earlier that you have doubts about all this. Is it because you refuse to challenge your Christian Bible?"

He didn't really want to talk about it, but she seemed eager. "Not at all. It's because *you* choose to challenge the Bible. Seems everyone involved in this quest has an ax to grind. You, de Roquefort, Mark, Saunière, Lars, Stephanie. Even Geoffrey, who's a bit different to say the least, has an agenda."

"Let me tell you a few things and maybe you'll see this is not personal. At least, not with me."

He doubted that, but he wanted to hear what she had to say.

"Did you know that in all of recorded history only one crucified skeleton has ever been found in the Holy Land."

He didn't.

"Crucifixion was alien to the Jews. They stoned, burned, decapitated, or strangled to accomplish capital punishment. Mosaic law only allowed a criminal who'd already been executed to hang on wood as *additional* punishment."

"For he that is hanged is accursed by God," he said, quoting Deuteronomy.

"You know your Old Testament."

"We do have some culture back in Georgia."

She smiled. "But crucifixion was a common form of Roman execution. Varrus in 4 BC crucified more than two thousand. Florus in AD 66 killed nearly four thousand. Titus in AD 70 executed five hundred a day. Yet only one crucified skeleton has ever been found. That was in 1968, just north of Jerusalem. The bones dated from the first century, which excited a lot of people. But the dead man was not Jesus. His name was Yehochanan, about five and a half feet tall, twenty-four to twenty-eight years old. We know because of information inscribed on his ossuary. He'd also been tied to the cross, not nailed, and neither of his legs was broken. Do you understand the significance of that detail?"

He did. "Suffocation was how you died on the cross. The head would eventually droop forward, and oxygen deprivation set in."

"Crucifixion was a public humiliation. Victims weren't supposed to die too soon. So to delay death a piece of wood was attached behind the abdomen that could be sat on, or a piece at the feet that could be stood upon. That way, the accused could support himself and breathe. After a few days, if the victim had not exhausted his strength, soldiers broke the legs. That way he could no longer support himself. Death came quickly after that."

He recalled the Gospels. "A crucified person couldn't defile the Sabbath. The Jews wanted the bodies of Jesus and the two criminals executed with Him down by nightfall. So Pilate ordered the legs of the two criminals broken."

She nodded. "*But when they came to Jesus, and found that he was already dead, they did not break his legs.* That's from John. Ever wonder why Jesus died so quickly? He'd only been hanging a few hours. It usually took days. And why didn't the Roman soldiers break His legs anyway, just to be sure he died? Instead, John says, they pierced His side with a lance and blood and water poured forth. But Matthew, Mark, and Luke never mention this happening."

"What's your point?"

"Of all the tens of thousands who were crucified, only one skeleton has ever been found. And the reason is simple. In Jesus's time, burial was deemed an honor. No greater horror existed than for your body to be left for the animals. Each of Rome's supreme penalties—burned alive, cast to the beasts, or crucifixion—had one thing in common. No body to bury. Crucifixion victims were left hanging until the birds picked their bones clean, then what was left was tossed into a common grave. Yet all four Gospels agree that Jesus died in the ninth hour, three PM, then was taken down and buried."

He began to understand. "The Romans would not have done that."

"This is where the story gets complicated. Jesus was condemned to death with the Sabbath only a few hours away. Yet He's ordered to die by crucifixion, one of the slowest ways to kill a person. How could anyone think He'd be dead before nightfall? Mark's Gospel says even Pilate was puzzled by such a quick death, asking a centurion if everything was in order."

"But wasn't Jesus mistreated before He was nailed to the cross?"

"Jesus was a strong man in the prime of his life. He was accustomed to walking great distances in the heat. Yes, he endured the scourge. According to law, thirty-nine lashes were to be given. But we're not told anywhere in the Gospels if this number was administered. And after his torment, he was apparently strong enough to address His accusers in a forcible way. So little evidence exists of any weakened condition. Yet Jesus dies in a mere three hours—without His legs being broken—His side supposedly pierced by a lance."

"The prophecy from Exodus. John speaks of it in his Gospel. He said all those things happened so Scripture would be fulfilled."

"Exodus speaks of Passover restrictions and that none of the meat may be taken outside the house. It had to be eaten within one house *with no broken bones*. That has nothing to do with Jesus. John's reference to it was a weak attempt at continuity with the Old Testament. Of course, as I said, the other three Gospels never even mention the lance."

"I assume your point, then, is that the Gospels are wrong."

"None of the information contained within them makes sense. They contradict not only themselves, but history, logic, and reason. We're left to believe that a crucified man, without His legs broken, died within three hours, and was then afforded the honor of being buried. Of course, from a religious standpoint it makes perfect sense. Early theologians were attempting to attract followers. They needed to elevate Jesus from a man to the god Christ. The gospel writers all wrote in Greek and would have known their Hellenic history. Osiris, the consort of the Greek god Isis, died at the hands of evil on a Friday, then was resurrected three days later. Why not Christ, too? Of course, for Christ to physically rise from the dead, there would have to be an identifiable body. No bones picked clean by birds and tossed into a common grave would do. Hence, the burial."

"This is what Lars Nelle was trying to prove? That Christ did not rise from the dead?"

She shook her head. "I have no idea. All I know is that the Templars knew things. Important things. Enough to transform a band of nine obscure knights into an international force. Knowledge was what fueled that expansion. Knowledge that Saunière rediscovered. I want that knowledge."

"How could there be any proof of anything, one way or another?"

"There must be. You've seen Saunière's church. He left a lot of hints, and they all point in one direction. There must be something out there—enough to convince him to keep the Templars looking."

"We're dreaming."

"Are we?"

He noticed that evening had finally dissolved into darkness, the surrounding hills and forest a mass of silhouette.

"We have company," she whispered.

He waited for her to explain.

"On the ride, I worked my way up one of the promontories. I spotted two men. One to the north, the other south. Watching. De Roquefort found you quickly."

"I didn't think the trick with the transponder would slow him down long. He'd assume we'd come here. And Claridon would show him the way. They spot you?"

"I doubt it. I was careful."

"This could get dicey."

"De Roquefort is a man in a hurry. He's impatient, particularly if he feels cheated."

"You mean the journal?"

She nodded. "Claridon will know it's riddled with mistakes."

"But de Roquefort found us. We're within his sights."

"He must know precious little. Otherwise, why bother? He'd simply use his resources and search himself. No, he needs us."

Her words made sense, as had everything else she'd said. "You rode out expecting them, didn't you?"

"I thought we were being watched."

"You always so suspicious?"

She faced him. "Only when people mean to hurt me."

"I assume you've considered a course of action?"

"Oh, yes. I have a plan."

FIFTY-ONE

DE ROQUEFORT SAT BEFORE THE ALTAR IN THE MAIN CHAPEL, dressed once more in his formal white cassock. The brothers filled the pews before him, chanting words that dated back to the Beginning. Claridon was in the archives, poring through documents. He'd instructed the archivist to allow the impish fool access to whatever he requested—but also to keep a close watch over him. The report from Givors was that Cassiopeia Vitt's château seemed down for the night. One brother watched the front, another the rear. So while little else could be done, he decided to tend to his duties.

A new soul was about to be welcomed into the Order.

Seven hundred years ago, any initiate would have been of legitimate birth, free of debt, and physically fit to wage war. Most were celibates, but married men had been allowed honorary status. Criminals were not a problem, nor were excommunicates. Both were allowed redemption. Every master's duty had been to ensure that the brotherhood grew. Rule made clear, *If any secular knight, or other man, wishes to leave the mass of perdition and abandon this century, do not deny him entry.* But it was St. Paul's words that had formed the modern standard for induction. *Approve the spirit if it comes from God.* And the candidate kneeling before him represented his first attempt to implement that dictate. It disgusted him that such a glorious ceremony was forced to take place in the dead of night behind locked gates. But such was the way of the Order. His legacy—what he wanted noted in the Chronicles long after his death—would be a return to the light.

The chanting stopped.

He stood from the oak chair that had served since the Beginning as the master's perch.

"Good brother," he said to the candidate, who knelt before him, hands on a Bible. "You ask a great thing. Of our Order, you see only the façade. We live in this resplendent abbey, we eat and drink well. We have clothes, medicine, education, and spiritual fulfillment. But we live under harsh commandments. It is hard to make yourself the serf to another. If you wish to sleep, you may be awakened. If you are wakeful, you may be ordered to lie down. You may not want to go where directed, but you must. You will hardly do anything that you wish. Can you suffer well these hardships?"

The man, probably in his late twenties, his hair already cropped short, his pale face clean-shaven, looked up and said, "I will suffer all that is pleasing to God."

He knew that the candidate was typical. He'd been found at university several years ago, and one of the Order's precepts had monitored the man's progress while learning the family tree and personal history. The fewer attachments, the better, and thankfully the world abounded with drifting souls. Eventually, direct contact was made and, being receptive, the initiate was slowly schooled in Rule and asked the questions candidates had been asked for centuries. Was he married? Engaged? Had he ever made a vow or pledge to another religious society? Any debts he could not pay? Any hidden illnesses? Was he beholden to a man or woman for any reason?

"Good brother," he said to the candidate, "in our company, you must not seek riches, nor honor, nor bodily ease. Instead, you must seek three things. First, renounce and reject the sins of this world. Second, do the service of our Lord. And third, be poor and penitent. Will you promise to God and our Lady that all the days of your life you will obey the master of this Temple? That you will live in chastity, without personal property? That you will uphold the customs of this house? That you will never leave this Order, neither through strength nor weakness, in worse times nor better?"

Those words had been used since the Beginning, and de Roquefort recalled when they'd been uttered to him, thirty years ago. He still felt the flame that had been ignited within him—a fire that now burned with a raging intensity. To be a Templar was important. It meant something. And he was determined to ensure every candidate who donned the robe during his tenure understood that devotion.

He faced the kneeling man.

"What do you say, brother?"

"De par dieu." For God's sake, I will do it.

"Do you understand that your life may be required?" And after what had happened the past few days, this inquiry seemed even more important.

"Without question."

"And why would you offer your life for us?"

"Because my master ordered it."

The correct answer. "And you would do so without challenge?"

"To challenge would be to violate Rule. My task is to obey."

He motioned to the draper, who produced from a wooden chest a long twill cloth.

"Stand," he said to the candidate.

The young man came to his feet, dressed in a black wool robe that covered his thin frame from shoulder to bare feet.

"Remove your garment," he said, and the robe was lifted over his head. Beneath, the candidate was dressed in a white shirt and black trousers.

The draper approached with the cloth and stood off to one side.

"You have removed the shroud of the material world," de Roquefort made clear. "Now we embrace you with the cloth of our membership and we celebrate your rebirth as a brother in our Order."

He motioned and the draper came forward and wrapped the cloth around the candidate. De Roquefort had seen many a grown man cry at this moment. He himself had fought to suppress his own emotions when the same cloth had been wrapped around him. No one knew how old this particular shroud was, but one had reverently remained in the initiation chest since the Beginning. He well knew the tale of one of the early cloths. Used to wrap Jacques de Molay after the master had been nailed to a door in the Paris Temple. De Molay had lain within the linen for two days, unable to move from his wounds, too weak to even rise. While he had, bacteria and chemicals from his body had stained the fibers and generated an image that fifty years later began to be venerated by gullible Christians as the body of Christ.

He'd always thought that fitting.

The master of the Knights Templar—the head of a supposed heretical order—became the mold from which all subsequent artists fashioned Christ's face.

He stared out at the assembly. "You see before you our newest brother. He wears the shroud that symbolizes rebirth. It's a moment we've all experienced, one that joins us to each other. When chosen as your master I promised a new day, a new Order, a new direction. I told you that no longer would the few know more than the many. I told you that I would find our Great Devise."

He stepped forward.

"In our archives, at this moment, is a man who possesses knowledge we need. Unfortunately, while our former master did nothing, others, not of this Order, have been searching. I have personally followed their efforts, watched and studied their movements, waiting for a time when we would join that search." He paused. "That time has come. I have brothers beyond the walls searching at this moment, and more of you will follow."

As he spoke, he allowed his gaze to drift across the church to the chaplain. He was an Italian with a solemn countenance, the chief prelate, the Order's highest-ranking ordained cleric. The chaplain headed the priests, about a third of the brothers, men who chose a life devoted solely to Christ. The chaplain's words carried much weight, particularly given that the man spoke sparingly. Earlier, when the council had convened, the chaplain had voiced his concern about the recent deaths.

"You're moving too fast," the chaplain declared.

"I'm doing what the Order desires."

"You're doing what you desire."

"Is there a difference?"

"You sound like the previous master."

"On that point he was correct. And though I disagreed with him on a great many things, I obeyed him."

He'd resented the younger man's directness, especially in front of the council, but he knew that many respected the chaplain.

"What would you have me do?"

"Preserve the brothers' lives."

"The brothers know that they may be called upon to lay down their lives."

"This is not the Middle Ages. We're not waging a crusade.

These men are devoted to God and pledged their obedience to you, as proof of their devotion. You have no right to take their lives."

"I intend to find our Great Devise."

"To what end? We've endured without it for seven hundred years. It's unimportant."

He'd been shocked.

"How can you say such a thing? It's our heritage."

"What could it possibly mean today?"

"Our salvation."

"We're already saved. The men here all possess good souls."

"This Order does not deserve banishment."

"Our banishment is self-imposed. We're content within it."

"I'm not."

"Then this is your fight, not ours."

His anger had risen.

"I don't intend to be challenged."

"Master, less than a week and you've already forgotten from whence you came."

Staring at the chaplain, he tried to read the features on the stiff face. He'd meant what he said earlier. He was not going to be challenged. The Great Devise must be found. And the answers lay with Royce Claridon and the people inside Cassiopeia Vitt's château.

So he ignored the indifferent look from the chaplain and concentrated on the crowd seated before him.

"My brothers. Let us pray for success."

FIFTY-TWO

Malone was in Rennes, strolling into the Church of Mary Magdalene, and the same garish detail gave him the same uncomfortable feeling. The nave was empty, save for a solitary man standing before the altar, dressed in a priestly black robe. When the man turned, the face was familiar.

Bérenger Saunière.

"Why are you here?" Saunière asked in a shrill voice. "This is my church. My creation. No one's but mine."

"How is it yours?"

"I took the chance. No one but me."

"Chance of what?"

"Those who challenge the world always face risk."

Then he noticed a gaping hole in the floor, just before the altar, and steps leading into blackness.

"What's down there?" he asked.

"The first step along the way to truth. God bless all those who guarded that truth. God bless their generosity."

The church encasing him suddenly dissolved and he was surrounded by a treed plaza that spread out before the American embassy in Mexico City. People rushed by in all directions, and the sounds of horns blaring, tires squealing, and diesel engines grew loud.

Then gunshots.

Coming from a car that had ground to a stop. Men emerged. Firing at a middle-aged woman and a young Danish diplomat who were enjoying their lunch in the shade. Marines guarding the embassy reacted, but they were too far away.

He reached for his gun and fired.

Bodies dropped to the pavement. Cai Thorvaldsen's head exploded as bullets meant for the woman found him. He shot two of the men who'd started the mélange, then felt his shoulder tear as a bullet pierced through him.

The pain jarred his senses.

Blood poured from the wound.

He stammered back, but shot his assailant. The bullet penetrated the dark face, which once again became that of Bérenger Saunière.

"Why did you shoot me?" Saunière calmly asked.

The walls of the church re-formed and the stations of the cross appeared. Malone spotted a violin lying on one of the pews. A metal plate rested on the strings. Saunière floated over and scattered sand on the plate. Then he drew a bow across the strings and, as sharp notes rang out, the sand arranged itself into a distinct pattern.

Saunière smiled. "Where the plate does not vibrate, the sand stands still. Change the vibration and another pattern is created. A different one every time."

The statue of the grimacing Asmodeus came to life, and the devil-like form left the holy water fount at the front door and drifted toward him.

"Terrible is this place," the demon said.

"You are not welcome here," Saunière screamed.

"Then why did you include me?"

Saunière didn't answer. Another figure emerged from the

shadows. The little man in the brown monk's robe from *Reading the Rules of the Caridad*. His finger was still to his lips, signaling quiet, and he carried the stool upon which was written ACABOCE A°1681.

The finger came away and the little man said, "I am alpha and omega, the beginning and end."

Then the little man vanished.

A woman appeared, her face obscured, dressed in dark clothing with no detail. "You know my grave," she said.

Marie d'Hautpoul de Blanchefort.

"Are you afraid of spiders?" she asked. "They'll not hurt you."

Upon her chest Roman numerals appeared, bright like the sun. LIXLIXL. A spider materialized beneath the symbols, the same design from Marie's tombstone. Between the tentacles were seven dots. Yet the two spaces near the head were bare. With her finger, Marie traced a line from her neck, down her chest, across the blazing letters to the image of the spider. An arrow appeared where her finger had been.

The same two-tipped arrow from the tombstone.

He was floating. Away from the church. Through the walls, out into the courtyard, and into the flower garden where the statue of the Virgin stood upon the Visigoth pillar. The stone was no longer a dingy gray, worn by weather and time. Instead, the words PENITENCE, PENITENCE and MISSION 1891 gleamed.

Asmodeus reappeared. The demon said, "By this sign you will conquer him."

Lying before the Visigoth pillar was Cai Thorvaldsen. A patch of oily asphalt lay beneath him, crimson with blood, his limbs stretched at contorted angles, like Red Jacket from the Round Tower. His eyes were frozen open, alight with shock.

He heard a voice. Sharp, crisp, mechanical. And he saw a television with a mustached man reporting the news, talking about the death of a Mexican lawyer and a Danish diplomat, the reason for the murders unknown.

And the aftermath.

"Seven dead—nine injured."

Malone came awake.

He'd dreamed of Cai Thorvaldsen's death before—many times, in fact—but never in relation to Rennes-le-Château. His mind was apparently filled with thoughts he'd found difficult to avoid when he'd tried, two hours ago, to fall asleep. He'd finally managed to drift off, ensconced in one of the many chambers of Cassiopeia Vitt's château. She'd assured him that their minders outside would be watched and they'd be ready if de Roquefort chose to act during the night. But he agreed with her assessment. They were safe, at least until tomorrow.

So he'd slept.

But his mind had continued to play out the puzzle.

Most of the dream faded away, but he recalled the last portion—the television anchor reporting on the attack in Mexico City. He'd learned later that Cai Thorvaldsen had been dating the Mexican lawyer. She was a tough, gutsy lady investigating a mysterious cartel. The local police learned there'd been threats she'd ignored. Police had been in the area, but curiously none of them were around when the gunmen emerged from a roadster. She and the younger Thorvaldsen had been sitting on a bench, eating their lunch. Malone had been nearby, on his way back to the embassy, in town on assignment. He'd used his automatic to take down two attackers before two others realized he was there. He never saw the third and fourth men, one of whom planted a slug in his left shoulder. Before he lapsed into unconsciousness he'd managed to shoot his attacker, and the final man was taken out by one of the marine guards from the embassy.

But not before a lot of bullets found a lot of people.

Seven dead—nine injured.

He sat up from the bed.

He'd just solved the Rennes riddle.

FIFTY-THREE

ABBEY DES FONTAINES
1:30 AM

DE ROQUEFORT SWIPED THE MAGNETIC CARD ACROSS THE SENsor pad and the electronic bolt released. He entered the brightly lit archives and threaded his way through the restricted shelves to where Royce Claridon sat. On the table before Claridon were stacks of writings. The archivist sat to one side, watching patiently as he'd been ordered to do. He motioned for the man to withdraw.

"What have you learned?" he asked Claridon.

"The materials you pointed me to are interesting. I never realized the extent of this Order's existence after the 1307 Purge."

"There's much to our history."

"I found an account of when Jacques de Molay was burned at the stake. Many brothers apparently watched that spectacle in Paris."

"He walked to the stake on March 13, 1314, with his head held high and told the crowd, *It is only right that at so solemn a moment, when my life has so little time to run, I should reveal the deception that has been practiced and speak up for the truth.*"

"You memorized his words?"

"He's a man to know."

"Many historians blame de Molay for the Order's demise. He was said to be weak and complacent."

"And what do the accounts you've read say about him?"

"He seemed strong and determined and planned ahead before he traveled from Cyprus to France in the summer of 1307. He actually anticipated what Philip IV had planned."

"Our wealth and knowledge were safeguarded. De Molay made sure of that."

"That Great Devise." Claridon shook his head.

"The brothers made sure it survived. De Molay made sure."

Claridon's eyes looked weary. Though the hour was late, de Roquefort functioned best at night. "Did you read de Molay's final words?"

Claridon nodded. *"God will avenge our death. Woe will come ere long to those who condemned us."*

"He was referring to Philip IV and Clement V, who conspired against him and our Order. The pope died less than a month later, and Philip succumbed seven months after that. None of Philip's heirs produced a male son, so the Capetian royal line extinguished itself. Four hundred and fifty years later, during the Revolution, the French royal family was imprisoned, just like de Molay, in the Paris Temple. When the guillotine finally severed the head of Louis XVI, a man plunged his hand into the dead king's blood and flicked it into the crowd, shouting, *Jacques de Molay, thou art avenged.*"

"One of yours?"

He nodded. "A brother—caught up in the moment. There to watch the French monarchy be eliminated."

"This means a lot to you, doesn't it?"

He wasn't particularly interested in sharing his feelings with this stranger, but he wanted to make clear, "I'm master."

"No. There's more here. More to this."

"Is analysis part of your specialty, too?"

"You stood in front of a speeding car, challenging Malone to run you down. And you would have roasted the flesh from my feet with no remorse."

"Monsieur Claridon, thousands of my brothers were arrested—all for the greed of a king. Several hundred were burned at the stake. Ironically, only lies would have liberated them. The truth was their death sentence, since the Order was guilty on none of the charges leveled against it. Yes. This is intensely personal."

Claridon reached for Lars Nelle's journal. "I've some bad news. I've read a good part of Lars's notes and something is wrong."

He did not like the sound of that statement.

"There are errors. Dates are wrong. Locations differ. Sources incorrectly noted. Subtle changes, but to a trained eye they're obvious."

Unfortunately, de Roquefort was not knowledgeable enough to know the difference. He was actually hoping the journal would increase his awareness. "Are they merely entry errors?"

"At first I thought so. Then, as I noticed more and more, I came to doubt that. Lars was a careful man. A lot of the information in the journal I helped accumulate. These are intentional."

De Roquefort reached for the journal and paged through until he found the cryptogram. "What of this? Correct?"

"I would have no way of knowing. Lars never told me if he learned the mathematical sequence that unravels it."

He was concerned. "Are you saying the journal is useless?"

"What I'm saying is that there are errors. Even some of the entries from Saunière's personal diary are wrong. I read some of those myself long ago."

De Roquefort was confused. What was happening here? He thought back to the last day of Lars Nelle's life, to what the American had said to him.

"You couldn't find anything, even if it were right before your eyes."

Standing in the trees, he'd resented Nelle's attitude but admired the man's courage—considering a rope was wrapped around the older man's neck. A few minutes earlier he'd watched as the American fastened the rope to a bridge support, then looped the noose. Nelle had then hopped onto the stone wall and stared out into the dark river below.

He'd followed Nelle all day, wondering what he was doing in the high Pyrénées. The village nearby possessed no connection to either Rennes-le-Château or any of Lars Nelle's known research. Now it was nearing midnight and blackness enveloped the world around them. Only the gurgle of water running beneath the bridge disturbed the mountain stillness.

He stepped from the foliage onto the road and approached the bridge.

"I wondered if you were going to show yourself," Nelle said with his back to him. "I assumed an insult would draw you out."

"You knew I was there?"

"I'm accustomed to brothers following me." Nelle finally turned toward him and pointed at the rope around his neck. "If you don't mind, I was just about to kill myself."

"Death apparently doesn't frighten you."

"I died a long time ago."

"You fear not your God? He does not allow suicide."

"What God? Dust to dust, that's our fate."

"What if you're wrong?"

"I'm not."

"And what of your quest?"

"It's brought nothing but misery. And why does my soul concern you?"

"It doesn't. But your quest is another matter."

"You've watched me a long time. Your master has even spoken to me himself. Too bad the Order will have to continue the quest—without me leading the way."

"You're aware we were watching?"

"Of course. Brothers have tried for months to obtain my journal."

"I was told you're a strange man."

"I'm a miserable man who simply doesn't want to live any longer. A part of me regrets this. For my son, whom I love. And for my wife, who loves me in her own way. But I have no desire to live any longer."

"Are there not quicker ways to die?"

Nelle shrugged. *"I detest guns, and something about poison seems offensive. Bleeding to death wasn't appealing, so I opted for hanging."*

He shrugged. *"Seems selfish."*

"Selfish? I'll tell you what's selfish. What people have done to me. They believe that Rennes hides everything from the reincarnated French monarchy to aliens from space. How many searchers have visited with their equipment to desecrate the land? Walls have been torn out, holes dug, tunnels excavated. Even graves opened and corpses exhumed. Writers have postulated every conceivable wild theory—all designed to make money."

He wondered about the strange suicide speech.

"I've watched while mediums held séances and

*clairvoyants carried on conversations with the dead. So
much has been fabricated, the truth is now actually
boring. They forced me to write that gibberish. I had to
embrace their fanaticism in order to sell books. People
wanted to read drivel. It's ridiculous. I even laugh at
myself. Selfish? All those morons are the ones who
should be given that label."*

"And what is the truth about Rennes?" he calmly
asked.

"I'm sure you'd love to know."

He decided to try another approach. "You realize that
you're the one person who may be able to solve
Saunière's puzzle."

"May be able? I did solve it."

He recalled the cryptogram he'd seen in the marshal's
report filed in the abbey's archives, the one abbés Gélis
and Saunière found in their churches, the one Gélis may
have perhaps died solving.

"Can't you tell me?" There was almost a plea to his
question, one he did not like.

"You're like all the rest—in search of easy answers.
Where's the challenge in that? It took me years to
decipher that combination."

"And I assume you wrote little down?"

"That's for you to discover."

"You're an arrogant man."

"No, I'm a screwed-up man. There's a difference. You
see, all those opportunists, who came for themselves and
left with nothing, taught me something."

He waited for an explanation.

"There's absolutely nothing to find."

"You're lying."

Nelle shrugged. "Maybe? Maybe not."

He decided to leave Lars Nelle to his task. "May you
find your peace." He turned and walked away.

"Templar," Nelle called out.

He stopped and turned back.

"I'm going to do you a favor. You don't deserve it, because all you brothers did was cause me aggravation. But your Order didn't deserve what happened to it, either. So I'll give you a clue. Something to help you along. It's not written down anywhere. Not even in the journal. Only you'll have it and, if you're smart, you might even solve the puzzle. You have a paper and pencil?"

He came back close to the wall, fished into his pocket, and produced a small note pad and pen, which he handed to Nelle. The older man scribbled something, then tossed the pen and pad to him.

"Good luck," Nelle said.

Then the American leaped over the side. He heard the rope go taut and a quick pop as the neck snapped. He brought the pad close to his eyes and in the faint moonlight read what Lars Nelle had written.

GOODBYE STEPHANIE

Nelle's wife was named Stephanie. He shook his head. No clue. Just a final salutation from husband to wife.

Now he wasn't so sure.

He'd decided that leaving the note with the body would ensure a determination of suicide. So he'd grabbed hold of the rope, pulled the corpse back up, and stuffed the paper into Nelle's shirt pocket.

But had the words really been a clue?

"On the night Nelle died, he told me that he solved the cryptogram and offered me this." He grabbed a pencil from the table and wrote GOODBYE STEPHANIE on a pad.

"How's that a solution?" Claridon asked.

"I don't know. I never even thought it was, until this moment. If what you're saying is true, that the journal contains intentional errors, then we were meant to find it. I searched for that journal while Lars Nelle was alive, then after with the son. But Mark Nelle kept it locked away. Then when the son turned up here, at the abbey, I learned he was carrying the journal with him in the avalanche. The master took possession of it and kept it under lock until just a few weeks ago." He thought back to Cassiopeia Vitt's apparent misstep in Avignon. Now he knew it was no mistake. "You're right. The journal's worthless. We were meant to have it." He pointed to the pad. "But maybe these two words have meaning."

"Or maybe they're more misdirection?"

Which was possible.

Claridon studied them with clear interest. "What precisely did Lars say when he gave you this?"

He told him exactly, ending with, *"A clue to help you along. If you're smart, you might even solve the puzzle."*

"I recall something Lars mentioned to me once." Claridon searched the tabletop until he found some folded papers. "These are the notes I made in Avignon from Stüblein's book concerning Marie d'Hautpoul's gravestone. Look here." Claridon pointed to a series of Roman numerals. MD-COLXXXI. "This was carved into the stone and is supposedly her date of death. 1681. And that's discounting the *O,* since there is no such Roman numeral. But Marie died in 1781, not 1681. And her age is in error, too. She was sixty-eight, not sixty-seven, as noted, when she died." Claridon gripped the pencil and wrote 1681, 67, and GOODBYE STEPHANIE on the pad. "Notice anything?"

He stared at the writing. Nothing stood out, but he was never good with puzzles.

"You have to think like a man in the eighteenth century. Bigou was the person who created the gravestone. The solution would be simple in one respect, but difficult in another because of endless possibilities. Break up the date 1681 into two numbers—16 and 81. One plus six equals seven. Eight plus one equals nine. Seven, nine. Then look at sixty-seven. You can't invert the seven, but the six becomes a nine when turned over. So, seven, nine again. Count the letters in what Lars wrote to you. Seven for GOODBYE. Nine for STEPHANIE. I think he did leave you a clue."

"Open the journal to the cryptogram and try."

```
Y E N S Z N I M G L C Y • R A T E H O X
O • E O T + T E C T N G A + D E Z B O F
V O U P H R P A + D Y S T L R D A • X T
L P O C X F E I S R A V H G C K L N H N
R D M R M A A N R J ) S • M B D Q A D P
R I E U Z O O T U O J I F S O E A L B N
T N A T ) G R E Y I O E ) T R U X ) W H
K X V E V L A L P E N + L O Z J K J D G
N U E + N G E K O • I X A Z V R + S I Z
S N S I C E T B + X G A C S E D X V U A
Y V L K B • ) N B W V K T P I B • J T Y
O U P E O M S U L Z R V ) J R S B + C E
P A T S X E • F X ) H N M Z H • Y T B C
```

Claridon leafed through the pages and found the drawing.

"There are several possibilities. Seven, nine. Nine, seven. Sixteen. One, six. Six, one. I'll start with the most obvious. Seven, nine."

He watched as Claridon counted across the rows of letters and symbols, stopping at the seventh, then the ninth, jotting down the character displayed. When he finished, there appeared ITEGOARCANADEI.

"It's Latin," he said, seeing the words. *"I tego arcana dei."* He translated. "I conceal the secrets of God."

Damn.

"That journal *is* useless," he yelled. "Nelle planted his own puzzle."

But another thought surged through his brain. The marshal's report. It, too, had contained a cryptogram, one obtained from the abbé Gélis. One supposedly solved by the abbé. One the marshal had noted was identical to the one Saunière found.

He must have it.

"There's another drawing in one of the books Mark Nelle has."

Claridon's eyes were aflame. "I assume you're going to get it."

"When the sun rises."

FIFTY-FOUR

GIVORS, FRANCE
1:30 AM

MALONE STOOD IN THE SALON, THE SPACIOUS ROOM LIT BY lamps, the others crowded around the table. He'd awakened them all a few minutes ago.

"I know the answer," he told them.

"For the cryptogram?" Stephanie asked.

He nodded. "Mark told me about Saunière's personality. Bold and brash. And I agree with what you said the other day, Stephanie. The church in Rennes is not a signpost to a treasure. Saunière would never have telegraphed that information, but he just couldn't resist a little pointing. Trouble is, you need a lot of pieces to assemble this puzzle. Luckily, we have most of them."

He reached for the book *Pierres Gravées du Languedoc,*

still open to Marie d'Hautpoul's gravestones. "Bigou is the fellow who left the real clues. He was fleeing France, never to return, so he hid cryptograms in both churches and left two carved stones over an empty grave. There's the wrong date of death, 1681, the wrong age, sixty-seven, and look at these Roman numerals at the bottom—LIXLIXL—fifty, nine, fifty, nine, fifty. If you add those together you get one hundred sixty-eight. He also made reference to the painting *Reading the Rules of the Caridad* in the parish register. Remember, in Bigou's time the date was not obscured. So he would have seen 1681, not 1687. There's a pattern here."

He pointed to the drawing of the gravestone.

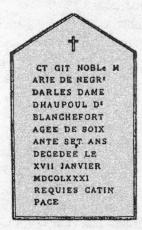

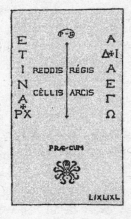

"Look at the spider carved into the bottom. Seven dots were intentionally placed between the legs, with two spaces left blank. Why not just include a dot between them all? Then look what Saunière did in the garden outside the church. He takes the Visigoth pillar, turns it upside down, and carves Mission 1891 and Penitence, Penitence into its face. I know this is going to sound crazy, but I just dreamed the connection among all these."

Everyone smiled, but no one interrupted him.

"Last year, Henrik, when Cai and all the others were killed

in Mexico City—I dream about it from time to time. Tough to get those images out of your brain. There were a lot of dead and wounded that day—"

"Seven dead. Nine wounded," Stephanie muttered.

The same thought seemed to rush unbidden into each of their minds and he saw understanding, especially on Mark's face.

"Cotton, you might just be right." Mark sat down at the table. "1681. Add the first two and last two digits. Seven, nine. The carving on the pillar. Saunière turned it upside down to send a message. He erected it in 1891, but invert that date and you have 1681. The pillar is upside down to lead us in the right direction. Seven, nine again."

"Then count the letters," Malone said. "Seven in *Mission*. Nine in *Penitence*. That's more than a coincidence. And the one hundred sixty-eight from the Roman numerals on the gravestone. That total is there for a reason. Add the one to the six and eight and you get seven and nine. The pattern's everywhere." He reached for a color image of station 10 from inside the Church of Mary Magdalene. "Look here. Where the Roman soldier is throwing the dice for Christ's cloak. On the dice face. A three, four, and five. When Mark and I were in the church I wondered why these particular numbers were chosen. Mark, you said Saunière personally oversaw every detail that went into that church. So he selected these numbers for a reason. I think the sequence is what's important. The three is first, then the four, then five. Three plus four is seven, four plus five is nine."

"So seven, nine solves the cryptogram?" Cassiopeia said.

"One way to find out." Mark motioned and Geoffrey handed him the rucksack. Mark carefully opened the marshal's report and found the drawing.

He then started applying the seven, nine sequence, moving through the thirteen lines of letters and symbols. As he did, he wrote each selected character down.

```
Y E N S Z N T M G L N Y Y R A E F V H E
O · M O T + P E C T H P E R + A + B L Z
V O U P H R E I + D U S T L E G R , D F
L P O R X F O N S R T V H V G + C R K R
R D E U M A E T R + R O A U · S M B A Q
R I O + A O 1 L U J N R Z K M A O X E M
T N A F O G R N E O Y + M P F Q L E , +
K X V O , L T K Y I U D · S G T S X O I
N U E + V G A N P E E S L E + U P S Q M
S N L I N G , L O + P A Q D L X D V G P
Y V E K C · T U B G , H S M S C · L Y ,
O U P T B M + B L V O V + N A X W X S U
P A T S O E S F X · C T I W B · T Y + O
```

TEMPLIERTRESORENFOUIAULAGUSTOUS

"It's French," Cassiopeia said. "Bigou's language."

Mark nodded. "I see them."

He added spaces so the message made sense.

TEMPLIER TRESOR EN FOUI AU LAGUSTOUS

"Templar treasure can be found at lagustous," Malone translated.

"What's lagustous?" Henrik asked.

"I have no idea," Mark said. "And I don't remember any mention of such a place in the Templar archives."

"I've lived in this region all my life," Cassiopeia said, "and know of no such locale."

Mark appeared frustrated. "The Chronicles specifically say that the carts carrying the Devise came south to the Pyrénées."

"Why would the abbé have made things so easy?" Geoffrey calmly asked.

"He's right," Malone said. "Bigou could have built in a safeguard so that just solving the sequence would not be enough."

Stephanie looked puzzled. "I wouldn't say this has been easy."

"Only because the pieces are so scattered, some lost forever," Malone said. "But in Bigou's time, everything existed, and he erected the tombstone for all to see."

"But Bigou hedged his bet," Mark said. "The marshal's report specifically notes that Gélis found a cryptogram identical to Saunière's in his church. During the eighteenth century Bigou served that church, as well as Rennes, so he hid a marker in each."

"Hoping that a person of curiosity would find one of them," Henrik said. "Which is precisely what happened."

"Gélis actually solved the puzzle," Mark said. "We know that. He told the marshal. He also said he was suspicious of Saunière. Then a few days later he was murdered."

"By Saunière?" Stephanie asked.

Mark shrugged. "No one knows. I always thought the marshal might be suspect. He disappeared from the abbey within weeks of Gélis's murder and specifically didn't note in his report the solution to the cryptogram."

Malone pointed to the pad. "Now we have it. But we need to find out what *lagustous* is."

"It's an anagram," Cassiopeia said.

Mark nodded. "Just like on the gravestone where Bigou used *Et in arcadia ego* as an anagram for *I tego arcana dei*. He could have done the same thing here."

Cassiopeia was studying the pad and her gaze beamed with recognition.

"You know, don't you?" Malone asked.

"I think I do."

They all waited.

"In the tenth century a wealthy baron named Hildemar came to know a man named Agulous. Hildemar's relatives resented Agulous's influence over him, and, in direct opposition to his family, Hildemar turned over all his lands to Agulous, who converted his castle into an abbey that Hildemar himself joined. While kneeling in prayer inside the abbey's chapel, Agulous and Hildemar were slain by Saracens. Both were eventually made Catholic saints. There's a town there still. About ninety miles from here. St. Agulous." She reached for the pen and converted *lagustous* into *St. Agulous*.

"There were Templar sites there," Mark said. "A large commandery, but it's gone."

"That castle, which became an abbey, is still there," Cassiopeia made clear.

"We need to go," Henrik said.

"That could be a problem." And Malone cut a glance to Cassiopeia. They'd not told the others about the men outside, so he did now.

"De Roquefort will act," Mark said. "Our hostess, here, allowed him to have Dad's journal. Once he learns the thing is worthless, his attitude will change."

"We need to leave here unnoticed," Malone said.

"There's a lot of us," Henrik said. "Such an exit would be a challenge."

Cassiopeia smiled. "I like challenges."

FIFTY-FIVE

7:30 AM

DE ROQUEFORT THREADED HIS WAY THROUGH THE FOREST OF tall pines, the ground beneath him silvered with white heather. A honey scent hung in the morning air. The rocky clefts of red limestone surrounding him were shrouded by a wispy fog. An eagle soared in and out of the haze, on the prowl for breakfast. He'd eaten his with the brothers, the meal taken in the traditional silence as Scripture was read to them.

He had to give Claridon credit. He'd deciphered the cryptogram with the seven, nine combination and unlocked the secret. Unfortunately, the message was useless. Claridon told him that Lars Nelle had found a cryptogram within an unpublished manuscript by Noël Corbu, the man who'd promulgated much of the fiction about Rennes in the mid-twentieth century. But had Nelle changed the puzzle or had Saunière? Was the frustrating solution what drove Lars Nelle to suicide? All that effort and when he finally deciphered what Saunière left, he was told nothing. Was that what Nelle meant when he'd declared *There's absolutely nothing to find*?

Hard to know.

But he was damn well going to find out.

A horn blared in the distance from the direction of the castle. The workday was probably about to begin. Ahead, he spied one of his sentries. He'd communicated with the man by cell phone on the trip north from the abbey and learned that all was quiet. Through the trees he caught sight of the château, a couple of hundred meters away, bathed in a filtered morning glow.

He approached the brother who reported that an hour ago a group of eleven men and women had arrived on foot from the construction site. All period-dressed. They'd been inside ever since. The second sentinel had reported that the rear of the building remained quiet. No one had entered or left. Plenty of inside movement came two hours ago—lights on in rooms, servant activity. Cassiopeia Vitt herself emerged at one point and walked to the stables, then back.

"There also was activity around one AM," the brother said to him. "Bedroom lights came on, then a downstairs room was lit. About an hour later the lights went off. Seems they all woke up for a while, then went back to sleep."

Perhaps their night had been as revealing as his own. "But no one left the house?"

The man shook his head.

He reached for the radio in his pocket and communicated with the team leader for the ten knights he'd brought with him. They'd parked their vehicles half a mile away and were hiking through the forest toward the château. He'd ordered that they quietly ring the building, then await his instruction. He was now informed that all ten were in place. Counting the two already here and himself, thirteen armed men—more than enough to accomplish the task.

Ironic, he thought. The brothers were once again at war with a Saracen. Seven hundred years ago, Muslims defeated the Christians and retook the Holy Land. Now another Muslim, Cassiopeia Vitt, had involved herself in Order business.

"Master."

His attention was diverted to the château and the front entrance, where people were exiting, all dressed in the colorful peasant garb of the Middle Ages. The men in plain brown cottes with cords tied about their waists, legs sheathed in dark hose, feet covered by thin shoes. A few sported cockers tied about their ankles. The women wore long gray gowns and heuks tied around their hips with apron strings. Straw hats, broad-brimmed caps, headrails, and hoods covered the heads. Yesterday, he'd noticed how all of the workers at the Givors site wore authentic clothing, part of the anachronistic atmosphere the place was surely designed to evoke. A couple of the workers started jostling with one another in good humor as the group turned and slowly headed for the lane leading back to the castle site.

"Perhaps some sort of meeting," the brother standing next to him said. "They came and are returning to the construction site."

He agreed. Cassiopeia Vitt personally oversaw the Givors project, so it was reasonable to assume workers would meet with her.

"How many went in?"

"Eleven."

He counted. The same had exited. Fine. Time to act. He raised the radio to his lips and said, "Move in."

"What are our orders?" the voice on the other end of the radio asked.

He was tired of toying with his opponent.

"Do what is necessary to contain them until I get inside."

He entered the château through the kitchen, an enormous room loaded with stainless steel. Fifteen minutes had passed since he gave the order to take the house and the siege had proceeded without a shot. In fact, the occupants had been eating their breakfast when the brothers made their way through the ground floor. Men stationed at all the exits and outside the dining room windows had destroyed any hope of escape.

He was pleased. He did not want to attract any attention.

As he moved through the many rooms, he admired the walls covered in colorful brocade, the painted ceilings, carved pilasters, glass chandeliers, and furniture sheathed in varying shades of damask. Cassiopeia Vitt possessed taste.

He found the dining room and prepared himself to face Mark Nelle. The others would be killed, their bodies buried in the forest, but Mark Nelle and Geoffrey would be returned to face discipline. He needed to make an example of them. The death of the brother in Rennes must be avenged.

He stepped through a spacious foyer and entered the dining room.

Brothers ringed the room, their weapons drawn. His gaze raked the long table and he registered six faces.

None of which he recognized.

Instead of seeing Cotton Malone, Stephanie Nelle, Mark Nelle, Geoffrey, and Cassiopeia Vitt, the men and women gathered around the table were strangers, all six dressed in jeans and shirts.

Workers from the construction site.

Damn.

They'd escaped right before his eyes.

He contained his rising anger. "Hold them here until I return," he said to one of the knights.

He left the house and calmly strolled down the treed lane toward the car park. Only a few vehicles present this early. But Cotton Malone's rental, which had been parked there when he arrived earlier, was gone.

He shook his head.

Now he was at a loss, with no idea where they'd gone.

One of the brothers he'd left inside the château ran up from behind. He wondered why the man had left his post.

"Master," the man said. "One of the people inside the château told me that Cassiopeia Vitt asked them to come to the château early today, dressed in their work outfits. Six of them switched clothing and were all told by Vitt to enjoy their breakfast."

That much he'd already surmised. What else?

The man handed him a cellular phone. "That same employee said a note was left that indicated you'd be coming. When you did, he was to give you this phone, along with this."

He unfolded and read from a scrap of paper.

The answer has been found. I will call before the sun sets with information.

He needed to know, "Who wrote this?"

"The employee said it was left with his change of clothes along with an instruction that it be given directly to you."

"How did you get it?"

"When he mentioned your name, I simply told him I was you and he handed it to me."

What was happening here? Was there a traitor among his enemy? Apparently so. Since he possessed no idea where they'd gone, little choice remained.

"Withdraw the brothers and return to the abbey."

FIFTY-SIX

10:00 AM

MALONE MARVELED AT THE PYRÉNÉES, WHICH WERE SO MUCH like the Alps in appearance and majesty. Separating France from Spain, the crests seemed to roll to infinity, each jagged peak crowned with bright snow, the lower elevations a mixture of green slopes and purple crags. Between the summits lay sun-scorched valleys, deep and foreboding, the haunts of Charlemagne, the Franks, Visigoths, and Moors.

They'd taken two cars—his rental and Cassiopeia's Land Rover, which she kept parked at the construction site. Their exit from the château had been clever—the ruse apparently working, since there'd been no tails—and, once away, he'd given both cars a thorough searching for any electronic trackers. He had to give Cassiopeia credit. She was imaginative.

An hour ago, before heading up into the mountains, they'd stopped and purchased clothes at a shopping plaza outside Ax-les-Thermes, a thriving spa resort that catered to hikers and skiers. Their colorful tunics and long gowns had won them some strange looks, but they were now dressed in jeans, shirts, boots, and fleece jackets, ready for what lay ahead.

St. Agulous perched on the rim of a precipice, surrounded by terraced hills, at the end of a narrow highway that corkscrewed a path up through a cloud-dimmed pass. The village, not much larger than Rennes-le-Château, was a mass of time-worn limestone buildings that seemed to have merged with the rock beyond.

Malone stopped short of entering the town, easing off into the trees, down a narrow dirt lane. Cassiopeia cruised in behind him. They climbed out into sharp mountain air.

"I don't think it's a good idea for all of us to just ride in there," he said. "This doesn't look like a place that receives a whole lot of tourists."

"He's right," Mark said. "Dad always approached these villages cautiously. Let me and Geoffrey do it. Just a couple of guys out hiking. That's not unusual for summer."

"You don't think I'd make a good impression?" Cassiopeia asked.

"Making an impression is not your problem," Malone said, grinning. "Getting folks to forget that impression is the problem."

"And who put you in charge?" Cassiopeia asked.

"I did," Thorvaldsen declared. "Mark knows these mountains. He speaks the language. Let him and the brother go."

"Then, by all means," she said. "Go."

MARK LED THE WAY AS HE AND GEOFFREY STROLLED THROUGH the main gate and into a tight plaza shaded by trees. Geoffrey still carried the rucksack with the two books, so they appeared as a couple of hikers out for the afternoon. Pigeons circled above the jumble of black slate roofs, dueling with a blast of wind that whistled through the clefts, shoving clouds northward over the mountains. A fountain in the center of the plaza trickled with water, green with age. No one was in sight.

A cobbled street radiating from the plaza was well kept and checkered with scattered sunlight. The tap of horned feet announced the appearance of a shaggy goat, which vanished down another side lane. Mark smiled. Like so many in this region, this was not a clock-driven place.

One vestige of any former glory came from the church, which rose at the end of the plaza. A set of wide narrow steps led up to a Romanesque door. The building itself, though, was more Gothic, its bell tower an odd octagonal shape that immediately arrested Mark's attention. He could not recall seeing another like it in the region. The size and grandeur of the church spoke of a lost prosperity and power.

"Interesting that a small town like this has a church that size," Geoffrey said.

"I've seen others like it. Five hundred years ago, this was a thriving market center. So a church would have been a must."

A young woman appeared. Sun freckles gave her the air of a country girl. She smiled, then entered a small general store. Next door stood what appeared to be a post office. Mark wondered about the strange vagary of fate that had apparently preserved St. Agulous from the Saracens, Spaniards, French, and Albigensian Crusaders.

"Let's start in there," he said, pointing at the church. "The local priest may be helpful."

They entered a compact nave topped by a star-spangled ceiling of vivid blue. No statuary decorated the plain stone walls. A wooden cross hung above the simple altar. Worn boards, each at least two feet wide, probably hewn centuries ago from the surrounding primeval forest, sheathed the floor and creaked with each step. Where the church at Rennes was animated in obscene detail, an unnatural quiet reigned in this nave.

Mark noticed Geoffrey's interest in the ceiling. He knew what he was thinking. The master had worn a robe of blue with gold stars in the last days of his life.

"Coincidence?" Geoffrey asked.

"I doubt it."

From the shadows near the altar emerged an older man. His crooked shoulders were poorly concealed under a loose brown frock. He walked with a jerky, stooped gait that reminded Mark of a puppet on a string.

"Are you the abbé?" he asked the man in French.

"*Oui,* monsieur."

"What's the name of this church?"

"The Chapel of St. Agulous."

Mark watched as Geoffrey strolled forward, past where they stood, to the first pew before the altar. "This is a quiet place."

"Those who live here belong only to themselves. It is indeed a peaceful location."

"How long have you been abbé?"

"Oh, for many years. No one else seems to want to serve here. But I do like it."

Mark recalled what he knew. "This area was once a hiding place for the Spanish brigands, wasn't it? They would slip into Spain, terrorize the locals, rob farmhouses, then slip back over the mountains, safe here in France, out of reach of the Spanish."

The priest nodded. "To plunder Spain, they had to live in France. And never once did they touch a Frenchman. But that was a long time ago."

He continued to study the church's austere interior. Nothing suggested that the building harbored any great secret.

"Abbé," he said. "Have you ever heard the name Bérenger Saunière?"

The older man thought for a moment, then shook his head.

"Is that a name anyone has ever mentioned in this village?"

"I'm not accustomed to monitoring my parishioners' conversations."

"Nor did I mean to say that you were. But is it a name you recall anyone mentioning?"

He shook his head again.

"When was this church built?"

"In 1732. But the first building was erected here in the thirteenth century. Many came after. So unfortunate, but nothing remains from those early structures."

The older man's attention was diverted to Geoffrey, who was still wandering near the altar.

"Does he bother you?" Mark asked.

"What is he looking for?"

Good question, Mark thought. "Perhaps he's in prayer, wanting to be near the altar?"

The abbé faced him. "You don't lie well."

Mark realized the old man standing before him was far smarter than he wanted his listener to believe. "Why don't you tell me what I want to know."

"You look just like him."

He fought to repress his surprise. "You knew my father?"

"He came to this area many times. He and I spoke often."

"Did he tell you anything?"

The priest shook his head. "You know better."

"Do you know what I'm to do?"

"Your father told me that if you ever made it here, you should already know what it is for you to do."

"You know he's dead?"

"Of course. I was told. He took his own life."

"Not necessarily."

"That's fanciful thinking. Your father was an unhappy man. He came here looking but, sadly, found nothing. That frustrated him. When I heard that he took his own life, I was not surprised. There was no peace for him on this earth."

"He spoke to you about those things?"

"Many times."

"Why did you lie to me about never hearing the name Bérenger Saunière?"

"I didn't lie. I've never heard that name before."

"My father never mentioned him?"

"Not once."

Another riddle stood before him, as frustrating and irritating as Geoffrey, who was now walking back toward them. The church surrounding him clearly contained no answers, so he asked, "What about the abbey of Hildemar, the castle he turned over to Agulous in the tenth century? Is any of that still standing?"

"Oh, yes. Those ruins still exist. Up in the mountains. Not far."

"It's no longer an abbey?"

"Goodness no. It hasn't been occupied in three hundred years."

"Did my father ever mention the place?"

"He visited there many times, but found nothing. Which only added to his frustration."

They needed to go. But he wanted to know, "Who owns the abbey ruins?"

"They were bought years ago. By a Dane. Henrik Thorvaldsen."

PART
FIVE

FIFTY-SEVEN

DE ROQUEFORT STARED ACROSS THE TABLE AT THE CHAPLAIN. The priest had been waiting for him when he returned to the abbey from Givors. Which was fine. After their confrontation yesterday, he needed to speak with the Italian, too.

"You will not ever question me," he made clear. He possessed the authority to remove the chaplain if, as Rule stated, *he caused disturbances or was more a hindrance than an asset.*

"It's my job to be your conscience. Chaplains have served masters in this way since the Beginning."

What went unsaid was the fact that any decision to remove the chaplain had to be approved by the brotherhood. Which could prove difficult, since this man was popular. So he retreated a bit. "You'll not challenge me before the brothers."

"I was not challenging you. Merely noting that the deaths of two men weigh heavily on all of our minds."

"And not on mine?"

"You must tread carefully."

They were sitting behind the closed door of his chamber,

the window open, the distant waterfall a gentle roar. "That approach has taken us nowhere."

"Whether you realize it or not, those men dying has shaken your authority. There's talk already, and you've only been master a few days."

"I will not tolerate dissension."

A sad but tranquil smile came to the chaplain's lips. "You sound just like the man you so opposed. What's changed? Has the seneschal so affected you?"

"He's not seneschal any longer."

"Unfortunately, that's the only name I know him by. You apparently know far more."

But he wondered if the cagey Venetian sitting across from him was being truthful. He'd heard talk, too, his spies reporting that the chaplain was quite interested in what the master was doing. Far more than any spiritual adviser needed to be. He wondered if this man, who professed to be his friend, was positioning himself for more. After all, he'd done the same thing years ago himself.

He actually wanted to talk about his dilemma, explain what happened, what he knew, seek some guidance, but sharing that with anyone would be foolhardy. Claridon was bad enough, but at least he was not of the Order. This man was altogether different. He had the potential to become an enemy. So he voiced the obvious. "I'm searching for our Great Devise, and I'm close to locating it."

"But at the price of two dead."

"Many have died for what we believe," he said, voice rising. "In the first two centuries of our existence, twenty thousand brothers gave their lives. Two more dying now is insignificant."

"Human life has a much greater value now than then." He noticed the chaplain's voice had lowered into a whisper.

"No, the value is the same. What's changed is *our* lack of dedication."

"This is not a war. There are no infidels holding the Holy Land. We're talking about finding something that most likely doesn't exist."

"You speak blasphemy."

"I speak the truth. And you know it. You think finding our Great Devise will change everything. It will change nothing. You must still garner the respect of all who serve you."

"Doing what I promised will generate that respect."

"Have you thought this quest through? It's not as simple as you think. The issues here are far greater than they were in the Beginning. The world is no longer illiterate and ignorant. You have much more to contend with than the brothers did then. Unfortunately for you, there exists not one mention of Jesus Christ in any secular Greek, Roman, or Jewish historical account. Not one reference in any piece of surviving literature. Just the New Testament. That's the whole sum of His existence. And why is that? You know the answer. If Jesus lived at all, He preached His message in the obscurity of Judea. No one paid Him any mind. The Romans couldn't have cared less, provided He wasn't inciting rebellion. And the Jews did little more than argue among themselves, which suited the Romans. Jesus came and went. He was inconsequential. Yet He now commands the attention of billions. Christianity is the world's largest religion. And He is, in every sense, *their* Messiah. The risen Lord. And nothing you find will change that."

"What if His bones are there?"

"How would you know they're His bones?"

"How did those nine original knights know? And look at what they accomplished. Kings and queens bowed to their will. How else can that be explained except through what they knew."

"And you think they shared that knowledge? What did they do—show the bones of Christ to each king, each monetary donor, each one of the faithful?"

"I have no idea what they did. But whatever their method it proved effective. Men flocked to the Order, wanting to be a part of it. Secular authorities courted its favor. Why can't that be again?"

"It can. Only not in the manner you think."

"It galls me. For all we did for the Church. Twenty thousand brothers, six masters, all died defending Jesus Christ. The Knights Hospitallers' sacrifice cannot compare. Yet there is not one Templar saint, and there are many canonized Hospitallers. I want to right that injustice."

"How is that possible?" The chaplain did not wait for him to answer. "What *is* will not change."

He thought again of the note. THE ANSWER HAS BEEN FOUND. And the phone resting in his pocket. I WILL CALL BEFORE THE SUN SETS WITH INFORMATION. His fingers lightly caressed the bulge of the cell phone in his trouser pocket. The chaplain was still talking, murmuring more about "the quest for nothing." Royce Claridon was still in the archives, searching.

But only one thought raced through his mind.

Why won't the phone ring?

"HENRIK," MALONE SCREAMED. "I CAN'T TAKE MUCH MORE OF this."

He'd just listened to Mark's explanation that the ruins of the nearby abbey belonged to Thorvaldsen. They stood in the trees, half a mile from St. Agulous, where they'd parked and waited.

"Cotton, I had no idea that I own that property."

"We're supposed to believe that?" Stephanie said.

"I don't give a damn whether you believe me or not. I knew nothing of this till a moment ago."

"How do you explain it then?" Malone asked.

"I can't. I can only say that Lars borrowed a hundred and

forty thousand dollars from me three months before he died. He never said what the money was for and I didn't ask."

"You just gave him that much money with no questions?" Stephanie asked.

"He needed it, so I gave it to him. I trusted him."

"The abbé in town said the buyer bought the property from the regional government. They were divesting themselves of the ruins and had few takers, as it's up in the mountains and in poor condition. It was sold at auction here in St. Augulous." Mark faced Thorvaldsen. "Yours was the high bid. The priest knew Dad and said he wasn't the one who actually bid."

"Then Lars engaged someone to do it on his behalf, because it was not me. He then placed the title in my name to give him cover. Lars was quite paranoid. If I owned that property and knew it, I would have said something last night."

"Not necessarily," Stephanie murmured.

"Look, Stephanie. I'm not afraid of you or any one of you. I don't have to explain myself. But I consider you all my friends, and if I owned the property and knew it, I'd tell you."

"Why don't we assume Henrik is telling the truth," Cassiopeia said. She'd stayed uncharacteristically quiet during the debate. "And get on up there. Darkness comes quick in the mountains. I for one want to see what's there."

Malone agreed. "She's right. Let's go. We can fight about this later."

The drive up into the higher elevations took fifteen minutes and required strong nerves and good brakes. They followed the abbé's directions and eventually caught sight of the crumbling priory, resting on an eagle's aerie, its shattered square tower flanked by a merciless precipice. The road ended about half a mile from the ruins and the hike up, along a trail of emaciated rock flowered with thyme, beneath a canopy of great pines, took another ten minutes.

They entered the site.

Signs of neglect lay everywhere. The thick walls were bare and Malone allowed his fingers to slip along the gray-green granite schist, each stone surely quarried from the mountains and worked with faithful patience by ancient hands. A once grand gallery opened to the sky with columns and capitals that centuries of weather and light had tarnished beyond recognition. Moss, orange lichens, and gray wiry grass littered the ground, the stone floor long ago returned to sand. Grasshoppers sang a loud castanet.

The rooms were hard to delineate, as the roof and most of the walls lay collapsed, but the monk cells were evident, as was a large hall and another spacious room that might have been a library or scriptorium. Malone knew that life here would have been frugal, thrifty, and austere.

"Quite a place you own," he said to Henrik.

"I was just admiring what a hundred and forty thousand dollars could buy twelve years ago."

Cassiopeia seemed enthralled. "You can imagine the monks harvesting a meager crop from the little bit of fertile soil. Summers here were brief, the days short. You can almost hear them chanting."

"This place would have been sufficiently forlorn," Thorvaldsen said. "An oblivion only for themselves."

"Lars titled this property in your name," Stephanie said, "for a reason. He came here for a reason. Something has to be here."

"Perhaps," Cassiopeia noted. "But the abbé in town told Mark that Lars found nothing. This could be more of the perpetual chases he engaged in."

Mark shook his head. "The cryptogram led us here. Dad was here. He didn't find anything, but he thought it important enough to buy. This has to be the place."

Malone sat atop one of the chunks of stone and stared up at the sky. "We have maybe five or six hours of daylight left. I suggest we make the most of it. I'm sure it gets pretty cold up here at night, and these fleece-lined jackets aren't going to be enough."

"I brought some equipment and gear in the Rover," Cassiopeia said. "I assumed we could be underground, so I have light bars, flashlights, and a small generator."

"Well, aren't you Johnny-on-the-spot," Malone said.

"Here," Geoffrey called out.

Malone glanced farther into the decayed priory. He'd not noticed that Geoffrey had wandered off.

They all hustled deeper into the ruin and found Geoffrey standing outside what was once a Romanesque doorway. Little remained of its craftsmanship beyond a faint image of human-headed bulls, winged lions, and a palm-leaf motif.

"The church," Geoffrey said. "They carved it from rock."

Malone could see that indeed the walls beyond were not human-made, but were part of the precipice that towered above the former abbey. "We'll need those flashlights," he said to Cassiopeia.

"No, you won't," Geoffrey said. "There's light inside."

Malone led the way in. Bees hummed in the shadows. Dusty shafts of light poured through slits cut through the rock at varying angles, apparently designed to take advantage of the drifting sun. Something caught his eye. He stepped close to one of the rock walls, hewn smooth but now bare of any decoration except a carving about ten feet above him. The crest consisted of a helmet with a swathe of linen dropping on each side of a male face. The features were gone, the nose worn smooth, the eyes blank and lifeless. On top was a sphinx. Below was a stone shield with three hammers.

"That's Templar," Mark said. "I've seen another like it at our abbey."

"What's it doing here?" Malone asked.

"The Catalans who lived in this region during the fourteenth century had no love for the French king. Templars were treated with kindness here, even after the Purge. That's one reason the area was chosen as a refuge."

The ponderous walls rose high to a rounded ceiling. Frescoes surely once adorned everything, but not a remnant remained. Water leaking in through the porous rock had long ago erased all artistic vestiges.

"It's like a cave," Stephanie said.

"More a fortress," Cassiopeia noted. "This could well have been the abbey's last line of defense."

Malone had been thinking the same thing. "But there's a problem." He motioned to the dim surroundings. "No other way out."

Something else caught his attention. He stepped close and focused on the wall, most of which rose in shadow. He strained hard. "I wish we had one of those flashlights."

The others approached.

Ten feet up he saw the faint remnants of letters roughly hewn on the gray stone.

"*P, R, N, V, I, R,*" he asked.

"No," Cassiopeia said. "There's more. Another *I,* maybe an *E* and another *R.*"

He strained in the dimness to interpret the writing.

PRIER EN VENIR.

Malone's mind came alive. He recalled the words at the center of Marie d'Hautpoul's gravestone. REDDIS RÉGIS CÉLLIS ARCIS. And what Claridon said about them in Avignon.

Reddis *means "to give back, to restore something previously taken." Regis derives from* rex, *which is king. Cella refers to a storeroom. Arcis stems from arx—a stronghold, fortress, citadel.*

The words had seemed meaningless at the time. But perhaps they simply needed rearranging.

Storeroom, fortress, restore something previously taken, king.

By adding a few prepositions, the message might be, *In a storeroom, at a stronghold fortress, restore something previously taken from the king.*

And the arrow that stretched down the center of the gravestone, between the words, starting at the top with the letters P-S and ending at PRÆ-CUM.

Præ-cum. Latin for "pray to come."

He stared again at the letters scratched into the rock.

PRIER EN VENIR

French for "pray to come."

He smiled and told them what he thought. "The abbé Bigou was a clever one, I'll give him that."

"That arrow on the gravestone," Mark said, "had to be significant. It's dead in the center, in a place of prominence."

Malone's senses were now alert, his mind surging through the information, and he started to take notice of the floor. Many of the flagstones were gone, the remaining cracked and misshapen, but he noticed a pattern. A series of squares, framed by a narrow stone line, ran from front to back and left to right.

He counted.

In one of the framed rectangles he tallied seven stones across, nine down. He counted another section. The same. Then another.

"The floor is arranged seven, nine," he told them.

Mark and Henrik moved toward the altar, themselves counting. "And there are nine sections from the rear door to the altar," Mark said.

"And seven go across," Stephanie said, as she finished finding a final floor section near an outer wall.

"Okay, we seem to be in the right place," Malone said. He thought again about the headstone. *Pray to come.* He gazed up at the French words scratched into the stone, then down at the floor. Bees continued to buzz near the altar. "Let's get those light bars and that generator in here. We need to see what we're doing."

"I think we also need to stay tonight," Cassiopeia said. "The nearest inn is in Elne, thirty miles away. We should camp here."

"We have supplies?" Malone asked.

"We can get them," she said. "Elne is a fairly good-sized town. We can buy what we need there without drawing any attention. But I don't want to leave."

He could see that none of the others wanted to go, either. An excitement was stirring. He could feel it, too. The riddle was no longer some abstract concept, impossible to understand. Instead, the answer lay somewhere around them. And contrary to what he'd told Cassiopeia yesterday, he wanted to find it.

"I'll go," Geoffrey said. "Each of you needs to stay and decide what we do next. It's for you, not me."

"We appreciate that," Thorvaldsen said.

Cassiopeia reached into her pocket and produced a wad of euros. "You'll need money."

Geoffrey took the funds and smiled. "Just give me a list and I'll be back by nightfall."

FIFTY-EIGHT

MALONE RAKED THE FLASHLIGHT'S BEAM ACROSS THE INSIDE of the church, searching the rock walls for more clues. They'd off-loaded all of the equipment Cassiopeia had brought and hauled it into the abbey. Stephanie and Cassiopeia were outside, fashioning a camp. Henrik had volunteered to locate firewood. He and Mark had come back inside to see if there was anything they'd missed.

"This church has been empty a long time," Mark said. "Three hundred years, the priest in town said."

"Must have been remarkable in its day."

"This type of construction isn't unusual. There are subterranean churches all over the Languedoc. At Vals, up near Carcassonne, is one of the most famous. It's in good shape. Still has frescoes. All the churches in this region were painted. That was the style. Unfortunately, little of that art has survived anywhere thanks to the Revolution."

"Must have been a tough life up here."

"Monastics were a rare breed. They had no newspapers, radio, television, music, theater. Only a few books and the frescoes in church as intoxicants."

Malone continued to survey the almost theatrical darkness that surrounded him, broken only by a chalky fading light that colored the few details as though snow lay heavy inside.

"We have to assume the cryptogram in the marshal's report is authentic," Mark said. "There's no reason to think it's not."

"Except the marshal disappeared shortly after he filed the report."

"I always believed that particular marshal was driven like de Roquefort. I think he went after the treasure. He must have known the story of the de Blanchefort family secret. That information, and the fact that Abbé Bigou may have known the secret, has been a part of our Chronicles for centuries. He could have assumed that Bigou left both cryptograms and that they led to the Great Devise. Being an ambitious man, he went to get it himself."

"Then why record the cryptogram?"

"What did it matter? He had the solution, which the Abbé Gélis gave him. No one else even had a clue as to what it meant. So why not file the report and show your master that you've been working?"

"Using that line of thinking, the marshal could have killed Gélis and simply gone back and recorded what happened afterward as a way to cover his tracks."

"That's entirely possible."

Malone stepped close to the letters—PRIER EN VENIR— scratched in the wall. "Nothing else survived in here," he muttered.

"That's true. Which is a shame. There are lots of niches, and those would have all contained statues. Combined with the frescoes, this would have once been a decorated place."

"So how did those three words manage to survive?"

"They barely have."

"Just enough," he said, thinking maybe Bigou had made sure.

He thought again of Marie de Blanchefort's gravestone. The double-sided arrow and PRÆ-CUM. Pray to come. He stared at the floor and the seven–nine arrangement. "Pews would have once been in here, right?"

"Sure. Wooden. Long gone."

"If Saunière learned the solution to the cryptogram from Gélis or solved it himself—"

"The marshal said in his report that Gélis didn't trust Saunière."

Malone shook his head. "Could be more misdirection by the marshal. Saunière clearly deduced something, unbeknownst to the marshal. So let's assume he found the Great Devise. From everything we know, Saunière returned to it many times. You were telling me back in Rennes about how he and his mistress would leave town, then return with rocks for the grotto he was building. He could have come here to make a withdrawal from his private bank."

"In Saunière's day, that trip would have been easy by rail."

"So he would have needed to be able to access the cache, while at the same time keeping the location secret."

He stared up again at the carving. PRIER EN VENIR. Pray to come.

Then he knelt.

"Makes sense, but what do you see from there that I don't from here?" Mark asked.

His gaze searched the church. Nothing was left inside save the altar, twenty feet away. The stone top was about three inches thick, supported by a rectangular support fashioned from granite blocks. He counted the blocks in one horizontal row. Nine. Then he counted the number vertically. Seven. He shone the flashlight beam onto the lichen-infested stones. Thick wavy lines of mortar were still there. He traced several of the paths with the light, then brought the beam up toward the underside of the granite top.

And saw it.

Now he knew.

He smiled.

Pray to come.

Clever.

DE ROQUEFORT WAS NOT LISTENING TO THE TREASURER'S prattle. Something about the abbey's budget and overages. The abbey was funded with an endowment that totaled in the millions of euros, funds long ago acquired and religiously maintained so as to ensure that the Order would never suffer financially. The abbey was nearly self-supporting. Its fields, farms, and bakery produced the majority of its needs. Its winery and dairy generated much of their drink. And water was in such abundance that it was piped down to the valley, where it was bottled and sold all across France. Of course, a lot of what was needed to supplement meals and mainte-nance had to be purchased. But income from wine and water sales, along with visitors' fees, more than provided the nec-essary sources. So what was all this about overages?

"Are we in need of money?" he interrupted and asked.

"Not at all, Master."

"Then why are you bothering me?"

"The master must be informed of all monetary decisions."

The idiot was right. But he didn't want to be bothered. Still, the treasurer might be helpful. "Have you studied our financial history?"

The question seemed to catch the man off guard. "Of course, Master. It's required of all who become treasurer. I'm presently teaching those below me."

"At the time of the Purge, what was our wealth?"

"Incalculable. The Order held over nine thousand land es-tates, and it's impossible to value that acreage."

"Our liquid wealth?"

"Again, hard to say. There would have been gold dinars, Byzantine coins, gold florins, drachmas, marks, along with unminted silver and gold. De Molay came to France in 1306 with twelve pack horses loaded with unminted silver, which was never accounted for. Then there is the matter of the items we held for safekeeping."

He knew what the man was referring to. The Order had pioneered the concept of safe depositories, holding wills and precious documents for men of means, along with jewels and other personal items. Its reputation for trustworthiness had been impeccable, which allowed the service to flourish throughout Christendom—all, of course, at a fee.

"The items being held," the treasurer said, "were lost at the Purge. The inventories were with our archives, which disappeared, too. So there's no way to even estimate what was being held. But it's safe to say that the total wealth would be in the billions of euros today."

He knew about hay carts hauled south by four chosen brothers and their leader, Gilbert de Blanchefort, who'd been instructed first to tell no one of his hiding place, and second to assure that what he knew was *passed to others in an appropriate manner*. De Blanchefort performed his job well. Seven hundred years had passed, and still the location was a secret.

What was so precious that Jacques de Molay ordered its secretion with such elaborate precautions?

He'd wondered about the answer to that inquiry for thirty years.

The phone in his cassock vibrated, which startled him.

Finally.

"What is it, Master?" the treasurer asked.

He caught hold of himself. "Leave me, now."

The man stood from the table, bowed, then withdrew. De Roquefort flipped open the phone and said, "I hope this is not a waste of my time."

"How can the truth ever be a waste of time?"

He instantly recognized the voice.

Geoffrey.

"And why would I believe a word you say?" he asked.

"Because you're my master."

"Your loyalty was to my predecessor."

"While he breathed, that's true. But after his death, my oath to the brotherhood commands that I be loyal to whoever wears the white cassock—"

"Even if you don't care for that man."

"I believe you did the same for many years."

"And assaulting your master is part of your loyalty?" He'd not forgotten the slap to the temple from a gun butt before Geoffrey and Mark Nelle escaped the abbey.

"A necessary demonstration for the seneschal's benefit."

"Where did you obtain this phone?"

"The former master gave it to me. It was to be of use during our excursion beyond the walls. But I decided on a different use."

"You and the master planned well."

"It was important to him that we succeed. That's why he sent the journal to Stephanie Nelle. To involve her."

"That journal is worthless."

"So I am told. But that was new information to me. I only learned yesterday."

He asked what he wanted to know. "Have they solved the cryptogram? The one in the marshal's report?"

"Indeed, they have."

"So tell me, brother. Where are you?"

"St. Agulous. At the ruined abbey just to the north of the village. Not far from you."

"And our Great Devise is there?"

"This is where all clues lead. They are, at this moment, working to locate the hiding place. I was sent to Elne for supplies."

He was beginning to believe the man on the other end of the phone. But he wondered if that was from desperation or good judgment. "Brother, I'll kill you if this is a lie."

"I don't doubt that declaration. You've killed before."

He knew he shouldn't, but he had to ask, "And who have I killed?"

"Surely you were responsible for Ernst Scoville's death. Lars Nelle? That's more difficult to determine, at least from what the former master told me."

He wanted to probe further but knew that any interest he showed would be nothing but a tacit admission, so he simply said, "You are a dreamer, brother."

"I've been called worse."

"What's your motive?"

"I want to be a knight. You're the one who makes that determination. In the chapel, a few nights ago, when you arrested the seneschal, you made clear that that wasn't going to happen. I determined then that I'd be taking a different course—one the former master would not like. So I went along. Learned what I could. And waited until I could offer what you really want. In return, I seek only forgiveness."

"If what you say is true, you shall have it."

"I'll be returning to the ruin shortly. They plan to camp there through the night. You've already seen how resourceful they are, both individually and collectively. Though I'd never presume to substitute my judgment for yours, I'd recommend decisive action."

"I assure you, brother, my response will be most decisive."

FIFTY-NINE

MALONE STOOD AND MARCHED TOWARD THE ALTAR. IN THE beam of his flashlight he'd noticed that there was no mortar joint beneath the top slab. The seven–nine arrangement of the support stones had drawn his attention, and kneeling had allowed him to see the crack.

At the altar he bent down and shone the light closer. "This top is not attached."

"I wouldn't expect it to be," Mark said. "Gravity held them in place. Look at it. The thing's what? Three inches thick and six feet long?"

"Bigou hid his cryptogram in the altar column in Rennes. I wondered why he chose that particular hiding place. Unique, wouldn't you say? To get to it, he had to lift the slab enough to free the locking pin, then slide the glass vial into the niche. Shift the top back and you have a great hiding place. But there's more to it. Bigou was sending a message by that selection." He set the flashlight down. "We need to move this."

Mark walked to one end and Malone positioned himself at the other. Grasping each side with his hands, he tested to see if the stone would move.

It did, ever so slightly.

"You're right," he said. "It's just sitting there. I don't see any reason for niceties. Shove it off."

Together, they waddled the stone left and right, then worked it enough so that gravity allowed it to crash to the floor.

Malone stared into the rectangular opening they'd exposed and saw loosely packed stones.

"The thing is full of rocks," Mark said.

Malone smiled. "Sure is. Let's get 'em out."

"For what?"

"If you were Saunière and didn't want anyone to follow your tracks, that stone top is a good deterrent. But these rocks would be even better. Like you told me yesterday. We need to think like folks thought a hundred years ago. Look around. Nobody would have come here looking for treasure. This was nothing but a ruin. And who would have disassembled this altar? The thing has been standing here for centuries unmolested. But if someone did do all that, why not another layer of defense."

The rectangular support stood about three feet off the floor, and they quickly tossed the stones aside. Ten minutes later the support was empty. Dirt filled the bottom.

Malone hopped inside and thought he detected a gentle vibration. He bent down and probed with his fingers. The parched soil possessed the consistency of desert sand. Mark shone the light while he scooped the earth away with a cupped hand. Six inches deep he hit something. With both hands he cleared away a foot-wide crater and saw wooden planks.

He looked up and grinned. "Ain't it nice to be right."

DE ROQUEFORT STORMED INTO THE ROOM AND FACED HIS council. He'd hastily ordered an assemblage of the Order's officers after finishing his telephone conversation with Geoffrey.

"The Great Devise has been found," he said.

Astonishment crossed the assembled faces.

"The former seneschal and his allies have located the hiding place. I have a brother embedded with them as a spy. He's reported their success. It's time to reclaim our heritage."

"What do you propose?" one of them asked.

"We shall take a contingent of knights and seize them."

"More bloodshed?" the chaplain asked.

"Not if the action is handled with care."

The chaplain seemed unimpressed. "The former seneschal and Geoffrey, who apparently is your ally since we know of no other brother in league with them, have already shot two brothers. There's no reason to suggest that they would not shoot more."

He'd heard enough. "Chaplain, this is not a matter of faith. Your guidance is not needed."

"The safety of the members of this Order is all our responsibility."

"And you dare to say that I don't have the safety of this Order in mind?" He allowed his voice to rise. "Do you question my authority? Are you challenging my decision? Tell me, Chaplain, I want to know."

If the Venetian was intimidated, nothing in his countenance betrayed fear. Instead, the man simply said, "You're my master. I owe you allegiance . . . no matter what."

He did not like the insolent tone.

"But, Master," the chaplain continued, "was it not you who said that we should all be a part of decisions of this magnitude?" A few of the other officers nodded. "Did you not tell the brotherhood in conclave that you would chart a new course?"

"Chaplain, we are about to embark on the greatest mission this Order has undertaken in centuries. I have not the time to debate with you."

"I thought giving praise to our Lord and God was our

greatest mission. And that is a matter of faith, to which I am qualified to speak."

He'd had enough. "You are dismissed."

The chaplain did not move. None of the others said a word.

"If you do not leave immediately, I'll have you seized and brought before me later for punishment." He paused a moment. "Which will not be pleasant."

The chaplain stood and tipped his head. "I will go. As you command."

"And we shall talk later, I assure you."

He waited until the chaplain left then said to the others, "We have searched for our Great Devise a long time. It's now within our grasp. What that repository contains does not belong to anyone but us. Our heritage is there. I, for one, intend to claim what is ours. Twelve knights will assist me. I will leave it to you to select those men. Have your choices fully armed and assembled in the gymnasium in one hour."

MALONE CALLED OUT FOR STEPHANIE AND CASSIOPEIA AND told them to bring the shovel they'd off-loaded from Cassiopeia's Rover. They appeared with Henrik, and as they entered the church, Malone explained what he and Mark had found.

"Pretty smart," Cassiopeia said to him.

"I have my moments."

"We need to get the rest of that dirt out of there," Stephanie said.

"Hand me the shovel."

He bailed out the loose soil. A few minutes later three blackened wooden planks were revealed. Half were bound together with metal straps. The other half formed a hinged door that opened upward.

He bent down and lightly caressed the metal. "The iron's

corroded. These hinges are gone. A hundred years of exposure has worked on them." He stood and used the shovel to chip away their remnants.

"What do you mean, *a hundred years*?" Stephanie asked.

"Saunière built that door," Cassiopeia said. "The wood is in fairly good shape, certainly not centuries old. And it appears to have been planed to a smooth finish, which is not something you would see in medieval lumber. Saunière had to have an easy way in and out. So when he found this entrance, he rebuilt the door."

"I agree," Malone said. "Which explains how he handled that heavy stone top. He just slid it halfway off, took out the rocks over the door, climbed down, then put everything back when he was through. From everything I've heard about him, he was in good shape. Damn clever, too."

He wedged the shovel into the gap at the door's edge and fulcrumed the door upward. Mark reached in and grabbed hold. Malone tossed the shovel aside and together they freed the hatch from its frame, exposing a gaping orifice.

Thorvaldsen stared into the void. "Amazing. This might actually be the place."

Stephanie shone a flashlight into the opening. A ladder stood against one of the stone walls. "What do you think? Will it hold?"

"One way to find out."

Malone extended a leg and gently applied weight to the first rung. The ladder was fashioned out of thick lumber, which he hoped was still bound with nails. He could see a few rusted heads. He pressed harder, holding on to the top of the altar support just in case something gave way. But the rung held. He placed his other foot on the ladder and tested more.

"I think it'll hold."

"I'm lighter," Cassiopeia said. "I'd be glad to go first."

He smiled. "If you don't mind, I'd like the honor."

"You see, I was right," she said. "You do want this."

Yes, he did. What lay below was beckoning him, like the search for rare books through obscure shelves. You never knew what might be found.

Still gripping the edge of the altar support, he lowered himself to the second rung. They were about eighteen inches apart. He quickly transferred his hands to the top of the ladder and descended one more rung.

"Feels okay," he said.

He kept heading down, careful to test each rung. Above him, Stephanie and Cassiopeia were searching the darkness with their lights. In the halo of their combined beams he saw that he'd come to the bottom of the ladder. The ground was the next step. Everything was covered with a fine gravel and stones the size of fists and skulls.

"Toss me a flashlight," he said.

Thorvaldsen dropped one of the torches to him. He caught it and focused the beam around him. The ladder rose about fifteen feet from floor to ceiling. He saw that the exit stood in the center of a natural corridor, one that millions of years of rain and melting snow had forged through the limestone. He knew the Pyrénées were riddled with caves and tunnels.

"Why don't you jump off?" Cassiopeia asked.

"It's too easy." He was alert to a chill that had settled in the hollow of his back, one that did not come solely from the cold air. "I'm going to swing around to the back side of the ladder. Drop one of those stones straight down." He positioned himself out of the way.

"You clear?" Stephanie asked.

"Fire away."

The rock plunged through the opening. He followed its path and watched as it struck the ground, then kept going.

Light beams probed the impact site.

"You were right," Cassiopeia said. "That hole was just under the surface, ready for someone to leap off the ladder."

"Drop some more rocks around it and find solid ground."

Four more rained down and thudded onto hard earth. He knew where to leap, so he dropped off the ladder and used the flashlight to examine the booby trap. The cavity was about three feet square and at least three feet deep. He reached inside and retrieved some of the wood that had been laid loosely across the top. The edges were tongue-and-grooved, the boards thin enough to shatter away at the weight of a man, but thick enough to shoulder a layer of silt and gravel. At the bottom of the hole were metal pyramids, sharpened to a point, wide at the base, waiting to snare an unsuspecting intruder. Time had dulled their patina, but not their effectiveness.

"Saunière was serious about this," he said.

"Those could have been Templar traps," Mark noted. "Is that brass?"

"Bronze."

"The Order was expert in metallurgy. Brass, bronze, copper—all were used. The Church forbade scientific experimentation, so they learned things like that from the Arabs."

"The wood on top could not be seven hundred years old," Cassiopeia said. "Saunière must have repaired the Templar's defenses."

Not what he wanted to hear. "Which means this is probably just the first of many traps."

SIXTY

MALONE WATCHED AS STEPHANIE, MARK, AND CASSIOPEIA climbed down the ladder. Thorvaldsen stayed on the surface, waiting for Geoffrey to return, ready to hand down tools, if needed.

"I meant what I said," Mark made clear. "The Templars were pioneers in booby traps. I've read accounts in the Chronicles of techniques they developed."

"Just keep your eyes open," Malone said. "If we want to find whatever there is to find, we have to look."

"It's after three," Cassiopeia said. "The sun will be gone in two hours. It's cold enough down here as it is. Nightfall will be brisk."

His jacket kept his chest warm, but gloves and thermal socks would be welcomed, which were some of the supplies Geoffrey was obtaining. Only the light spilling in from the ceiling illuminated the passageway that stretched in both directions. Without flashlights, Malone doubted if they'd be able to see a finger touch their nose. "Daylight's not going to matter. It's all artificial light down here. We just need Geoffrey to get back with food and warmer clothes. Henrik," he called out. "Let us know when the good brother returns."

"Safe hunting, Cotton."

His mind swelled with possibilities. "What do you make of this?" he asked the others.

"This could be part of a *horreum*," Cassiopeia said. "When the Romans ruled this area they established underground storerooms for holding perishable goods. An early version of a refrigerated warehouse. Several have survived. This could have been one."

"And the Templars knew of it?" Stephanie asked.

"They had them, too," Mark said. "They learned from the Romans. What she says makes sense. When de Molay told Gilbert de Blanchefort to *take away the treasure of the temple in advance,* he could have easily chosen a place like this. Beneath a nondescript church, at a minor abbey, with no connection to the Order."

Malone pointed his flashlight ahead, then turned around and shone the beam in the other direction. "Which way?"

"Good question," Stephanie said.

"You and Mark go that way," he said. "Cassiopeia and I will go the other." He could see that neither Mark nor Stephanie liked that decision. "We don't have time for you two to fight. Put it aside. Do your jobs. That's what you'd tell me, Stephanie."

She didn't argue with him. "He's right. Let's go," she said to Mark.

Malone watched as they dissolved into the blackness.

"Clever, Malone," Cassiopeia whispered. "But do you think it wise to send those two out together? Lots of issues between them."

"Nothing like a little tension to make them appreciate one another."

"That true for me and you, too?"

He aimed his flashlight into her face. "Lead the way and let's find out."

✠

DE ROQUEFORT AND TWELVE BROTHERS APPROACHED THE AN-
cient ruined abbey from the south. They'd avoided the village of St. Agulous and parked their vehicles a kilometer
back in the thick woods. They'd then hiked through a land-
scape of scrub and red rock, steadily rising in altitude. He
knew the entire area was a magnet for outdoor enthusiasts.
Green slopes and purple crags closed around them, but the
path was well marked, perhaps used by the local shepherds
to herd sheep, and the route brought them to within a kilometer of the torn walls and piles of debris that had once been a
place of devotion.

He stopped the entourage and checked his watch. Nearly
four PM. Brother Geoffrey had said that he would return to
the site at four. He looked around. The ruins perched on a
rocky promontory a hundred meters above. Malone's rental
car was parked farther down the slope.

"Into the trees for cover," he ordered. "And everyone stay
down."

A few moments later a Land Rover churned its way up the
sloping graveled path and stopped by the rental. He saw Geoffrey exit the driver's side and noticed the younger man appraise his surroundings, but de Roquefort did not reveal
himself, still not sure if this was a trap.

Geoffrey hesitated at the Land Rover, then opened the rear
hatch and removed two boxes. Grasping both, Geoffrey
started up the path toward the abbey. De Roquefort waited
until he'd passed, then boldly stepped out onto the trail and
said, "I've been waiting, brother."

Geoffrey stopped and turned.

A cold pallor engulfed the younger man's pale face. The
brother said nothing and simply laid the boxes down, reached
beneath his jacket, and brought out a nine-millimeter automatic. De Roquefort recognized the gun. The Austrian-made
weapon was one of several brands the abbey's arsenal
stocked.

Geoffrey chambered a round. "Then bring your men and let's get this over with."

AN INSUFFERABLE TENSION FLUSHED EVERY THOUGHT FROM Malone's mind. He was following Cassiopeia as they inched their way through the underground passage. The path was about six feet wide and eight feet tall, the walls dry and jagged. Fifteen feet of hard earth lay between him and the surface. Tight confines were not his favorite places. Cassiopeia, though, appeared fortified with nerve. He'd seen her kind of courage before in agents who worked best under extreme pressure.

He was alert for more traps, paying careful attention to the gravel ahead of them. He'd always found it amusing in adventure movies when moving parts made of stone and metal, supposedly hundreds or thousands of years old, still functioned as if they'd been greased yesterday. Iron and stone were vulnerable to air and water, their effectiveness limited. But bronze was a different matter. That metal was enduring, which was precisely why it had been created. So more pointed stakes at the bottom of deep holes could be a problem.

Cassiopeia stopped, her light focused ten feet ahead.

"What is it?" he asked.

"Take a look."

He added his beam to hers and saw it.

STEPHANIE HATED ENCLOSED SPACES, BUT SHE WAS NOT ABOUT to voice that concern, especially to her son, who thought little enough of her. So to take her mind off her uncomfortableness she asked, "How would the knights have stored their treasure down here?"

"Carried in a piece at a time. Nothing would have stopped them, short of capture or death."

"That would have taken some effort."

"All they had was time."

They were both intent on the ground ahead of them as Mark gently tested the surface before each step.

"Their precautions would not have been sophisticated," Mark said. "But they would have been effective. The Order possessed vaults all over Europe. Most they guarded, along with rigging traps. Here, secretion itself and a few traps had to do the job without guards. The last thing they would have wanted was to draw attention to this place by having knights around."

"Your father would have loved this." She had to say it.

"I know."

Her light caught something ahead on the passage wall. She grabbed hold of Mark's shoulder and stopped him. "Look."

Carved into the rock were letters.

NON NOBIS DOMINE
NON NOBIS SED NOMINE TUO DA GLORIUM
PAUPERS COMMILITONES CHRISTI TEMPLIQUE SALAMONIS

"What does it say?" she asked.

" 'Not to us, O Lord, not to us, but to Thy name give the glory. Poor Fellow-Soldiers of Christ and the Temple of Solomon.' It's the Templar motto."

"So it's true. This is it."

Mark said nothing.

"May God forgive me," she whispered.

"God has little to do with this. Man created this mess and it's up to man to clean it up." He motioned farther down the passage with his light. "Look there."

She stared into the halo and saw a metal grille—a gate— that opened into another passage.

"Is that where everything is stored?" she asked.

Not waiting for an answer, she moved around him and

had taken only a few steps when she heard Mark cry out, "No."

Then the ground slipped away.

MALONE STARED AT THE SIGHT ILLUMINATED BY THEIR COM-bined lights. A skeleton. Lying prostrate on the cavern floor, the shoulders, neck, and skull propped up against the wall.

"Let's get closer," he said.

They inched ahead and he noticed a slight depression in the floor. He grasped Cassiopeia's shoulder.

"I see it," she said, stopping. "It's a long one. Stretches a couple of yards."

"Those damn pits would have been invisible in their time, but the wood beneath has weakened enough to show them." They moved around the depression, staying on solid ground, and approached the skeleton.

"There's nothing left but bones," she said.

"Look at the chest. The ribs. And the face. Shattered in places. He fell into that trap. Those gashes are from spikes."

"Who is he?"

Something caught his eye.

He bent down and found a blackened silver chain among the bones. He lifted it out. A medallion dangled from the loop. He focused the light. "The Templar seal. Two men on a single horse. It represented individual poverty. I saw a drawing of this in a book a few nights ago. My bet is this is the marshal who wrote the report we've been using. He dis-appeared from the abbey once he learned the solution to the cryptogram from the priest Gélis. He came, figured out the so-lution, but wasn't careful. Saunière probably found the body and just left him here."

"But how would Saunière have figured anything out? How did he solve the cryptogram? Mark let me read that report. According to Gélis, Saunière had not solved the puzzle he found in his church and Gélis was suspicious of him, so he told Saunière nothing."

"That's assuming what the marshal wrote was true. Either Saunière or the marshal killed Gélis to keep the priest from telling anyone what he'd deciphered. If it was the marshal, which seems likely, then he filed the report simply as a way to cover his tracks. A way for no one to think he left the abbey to come here and find the Order's Great Devise for himself. What did it matter that he recorded the cryptogram? There's no way to solve the thing without the mathematical sequence."

He turned his attention away from the dead man and shone his light farther down the passage. "Look at that."

Cassiopeia stood and together they saw a cross with four equal arms, wide at the ends, carved into the rock.

"The cross patee," she said. "Allowed to be worn only by the Templars thanks to a papal decree."

He recalled more of what he'd read in the Templar book. "The crosses were red on a white mantle and symbolized a willingness to suffer martyrdom in fighting infidels." With his flashlight, he traced the lettering above the cross.

PAR CE SIGNE TU LE VAINCRAS

"By this sign ye shall conquer him," he said, translating. "Those same words are in the church at Rennes, above the holy water fount at the door. Saunière put them there."

"Constantine's declaration when he first fought Maxentius. Before the battle, he supposedly saw a cross on the sun with those words emblazoned beneath."

"With one difference. Mark said there was no *him* in the original phrase. Only *By this sign ye shall conquer.*"

"He's right."

"Saunière inserted *le* after *tu*. At the thirteenth and fourteenth position in the phrase. 1314."

"The year Jacques de Molay was executed."

"Seems Saunière enjoyed a touch of irony in his symbolism, and he got the idea right here."

He searched more of the darkness and saw that the passage ended twenty feet ahead. But before that, a metal grille locked by a chain and hasp blocked a path that led off into another direction.

Cassiopeia saw it, too. "Seems we found it."

A rumble came from behind them and someone shouted, "No."

They both turned.

SIXTY-ONE

DE ROQUEFORT STOPPED AT THE ENTRANCE TO THE RUINS AND motioned his men to flank out to either side. The site was uncomfortably quiet. No movement. No voices. Nothing. Brother Geoffrey stood beside him. He remained worried that he was being set up. Which was why he'd come with firepower. He was pleased with his council's selection of knights—these men were some of the best in his ranks, experienced fighters of unquestioned courage and fortitude— which he might well need.

He peered around a pile of lichen-encrusted rubble, deeper into the decayed structure, past billows of standing grass. The bright dome of sky overhead was fading as the sun beat a retreat behind the mountains. Darkness would arrive shortly. And he worried about the weather. Squalls and rain came without warning in the Pyrenean summer.

He motioned and his men advanced forward, clambering over boulders and collapsed wall sections. He spied a campsite among three partial walls. Wood had been arranged for a fire that had yet to be lit.

"I'll go in," Geoffrey whispered. "They're expecting me."

He saw the wisdom of that move and nodded.

Geoffrey calmly walked into the open and approached the camp. Still no one was around. Then the younger man disappeared deeper into the ruins. A moment later he emerged and signaled for them to come.

De Roquefort told his men to wait and only he stepped into the open. He'd already directed his lieutenant to attack if necessary.

"Only Thorvaldsen is in the church," Geoffrey said.

"What church?"

"The monks cut a church into the rock. They've discovered a portal beneath the altar that leads to caves. The others are beneath us exploring. I told Thorvaldsen that I was going to retrieve the supplies."

He liked what he was hearing.

"I'd want to meet Henrik Thorvaldsen."

With gun in hand, he followed Geoffrey into the dungeon-like cavity carved from the rock. Thorvaldsen stood with his back to them, gazing down into what was once a support for the altar.

The old man turned as they came close.

De Roquefort raised his gun. "Not a word. Or it will be your last."

THE EARTH BENEATH STEPHANIE'S FEET HAD GIVEN WAY AND her legs were collapsing into one of the traps they'd tried so hard to avoid. What had she been thinking? Seeing the words etched into the rock and then the metal gate waiting to be opened, she'd realized that her husband had been right. So she'd abandoned caution and raced forward. Mark had tried to stop her. She heard him scream, but it had been too late.

She was already heading down.

Her hands went skyward in an attempt to balance and she readied herself for the bronze stakes. But then she felt an arm encase her chest in a tight embrace. Then she was falling backward, to the ground, which she struck, another body cushioning her impact.

A second later, quiet.

Mark lay beneath her.

"You okay?" she asked, rolling off him.

Her son raised himself off the gravel. "Those rocks felt lovely on my back."

Heavy footsteps sounded in the darkness behind them, accompanied by two orbs of waggling light. Malone and Cassiopeia appeared.

"What happened?" Malone asked.

"I was careless," she said, standing, brushing herself off.

Malone shone a light down into the rectangular hole. "That would have been a bloody fall. It's full of stakes, all in good shape."

She came close, stared down into the opening, then turned and said to Mark, "Thanks, son."

Mark was rubbing the back of his neck, working the pain from his muscles. "No problem."

"Malone," Cassiopeia said. "Take a look."

Stephanie watched as Malone and Cassiopeia studied the Templar motto she and Mark had found. "I was headed to that gate when the hole got in the way."

"Two of them," Malone muttered. "At opposite ends of this corridor."

"There's another grille?" Mark asked.

"With another inscription."

She listened as Malone told them what they'd found.

"I agree with you," Mark said. "That skeleton has to be our long-lost marshal." He fished a chain from beneath his shirt. "We all wear the medallion. They're given at induction."

"Apparently," Malone said, "the Templars hedged their bets and separated the cache." He motioned to the floor trap. "And they made it a challenge to find. The marshal should have been more careful." Malone faced Stephanie. "As we all should."

"I understand," she said. "But, as you so often remind me, I'm not a field agent."

He smiled at her sarcasm. "So let's see what's behind that grille."

✠

DE ROQUEFORT AIMED THE SHORT BARREL OF HIS WEAPON DIrectly at Henrik Thorvaldsen's furrowed brow. "I'm told you're one of the wealthiest men in Europe."

"And I'm told you're one of the most ambitious prelates in recent memory."

"You shouldn't listen to Mark Nelle."

"I didn't. His father told me."

"His father didn't know me."

"I wouldn't say that. You followed him around enough."

"Which turned out to be a waste of time."

"Did that make it easier for you to kill him?"

"Is that what you think? That I killed Lars Nelle?"

"Him and Ernst Scoville."

"You know nothing, old man."

"I know you're a problem." Thorvaldsen motioned to Geoffrey. "I know he's a traitor to his friend. And his Order."

De Roquefort watched as Geoffrey absorbed the insult, disdain sweeping into the younger man's pale gray eyes, then just as quickly dissipating.

"I'm loyal to my master. That's the oath I took."

"So you betrayed us for your oath?"

"I don't expect you to understand."

"I don't, and never will."

De Roquefort lowered his gun, then gestured for his men. They swarmed into the church and he motioned for silence. A few hand signals and they instantly understood that six were to position themselves outside and the remaining six to encircle the interior.

MALONE STEPPED AROUND THE TRAP STEPHANIE HAD EXPOSED and approached the metal grille. The others followed. He noticed a heart-shaped padlock suspended from a chain. "Brass." He caressed the gate. "But the gate is bronze."

"The padlock and chain have to be from Saunière's time," Mark said. "Brass was a rare Middle Age commodity. Zinc was needed to make it and that was hard to come by."

"The lock is a *cœur-de-brass*," Cassiopeia said. "They were once prevalent all over this region to fasten slave chains."

None of them moved to open the gate and Malone knew why. Another trap could lie in wait.

With his boot, he gently brushed the soil and gravel beneath his feet and tested the earth. Solid. He used his light and examined the gate's exterior. Two bronze hinges supported the right edge. He shone the light through the grille. The corridor beyond right-angled sharply a few feet inside and nothing could be seen past the bend. Great. He tested the chain and lock. "This brass is still strong. We're not going to be able to pound it away."

"How about cutting it?" Cassiopeia asked.

"That would work. But with what?"

"The bolt cutters I brought. They're in the tool bag topside, by the generator."

"I'll go get them," Mark said.

"ANYBODY UP THERE?"

The words echoed from inside the hollow altar support and startled de Roquefort. Then he quickly realized that the voice was Mark Nelle's. Thorvaldsen moved to answer, but de Roquefort grabbed the crooked old man and clamped a hand across the mouth before he could utter a sound. He then signaled for one of the brothers, who rushed forward and grabbed the kicking Dane, a new hand sheathing Thorvaldsen's mouth. He pointed and the prisoner was dragged to a far corner of the church.

"Answer him," he mouthed to Geoffrey.

This would be an interesting test of his newfound ally's loyalty.

Geoffrey stuffed his gun between his belt and stepped to the altar. "I'm here."

"You're back. Good. Any problems?"

"None. Bought everything on the list. What's happening down there?"

"We found something, but we need bolt cutters. They're in the tool bag by the generator."

He watched as Geoffrey moved toward the generator and removed a pair of heavy-duty bolt cutters.

What had they found?

Geoffrey tossed the tool down.

"Thanks," Mark Nelle said. "You coming?"

"I'll stay here with Thorvaldsen and keep an eye on things. We don't need any uninvited guests."

"Good idea. Where's Henrik?"

"Unpacking what I bought and getting the camp ready for the night. The sun's nearly gone. I'll go help him."

"You might want to get the generator ready and the power cords unraveled for the light bars. We may need those shortly."

"I'll take care of it."

Geoffrey lingered a moment more then stepped away from the altar and whispered, "He's gone."

De Roquefort knew what had to be done. "Time to take command of this expedition."

MALONE GRIPPED THE BOLT CUTTERS AND WORKED THE TEETH around the brass chain. He then compressed the handles and allowed the spring-action to bite clean through the metal. A snap signaled success and the chain, with hasp, slipped to the ground.

Cassiopeia bent down and retrieved them. "There are museums around the world that would love to have this. I'm sure not many have survived in this condition."

"And we just cut it," Stephanie said.

"There wasn't a whole lot of choice," Malone said. "We're kind of in a hurry." He pointed a flashlight through the grille. "Everybody to the side. I'm going to open this thing slowly. It looks clear, but you never know."

He wedged the bolt cutters into the grille, then stepped to one side, using the rock wall for protection. The hinges were stiff and he had to work the grille back and forth. Finally, the portal opened.

He was just about to lead the way inside when a voice called down from above.

"Mr. Malone. I have Henrik Thorvaldsen. I need for you and your companions to come up. Now. I'll give you one minute, then I'm going to shoot this old man dead."

SIXTY-TWO

MALONE WAS THE LAST TO CLIMB UP. WHEN HE STEPPED FROM the ladder he saw that the church was occupied by six armed men along with de Roquefort. Outside, the sun was gone. Inside was now illuminated from the glow of two small fires, the smoke rushing out into the night through the open window slits.

"Mr. Malone, we finally meet in person," Raymond de Roquefort said. "You handled yourself well in the Roskilde cathedral."

"Glad to know you're a fan."

"How did you find us?" Mark asked.

"Certainly no thanks to that phony journal of your father's, clever though he was. He spoke to the obvious and changed the details just enough to make them worthless. When monsieur Claridon deciphered the cryptogram within it, the message, of course, was of no help. He told us that he concealed the secrets of God. Tell me, since you've been down there, does he conceal those secrets?"

"Never got a chance to find out," Malone said.

"Then we should remedy that. But to answer your question—"

"Geoffrey betrayed us," Thorvaldsen said.

Astonishment clouded Mark's face. "What?"

Malone had already noticed the gun in Geoffrey's hand. "That true?"

"I'm a brother in the Temple, loyal to my master. I did my duty."

"Your duty?" Mark screamed. "You lying son of a bitch." Mark lurched toward Geoffrey, but two brothers blocked the way. Geoffrey stayed rooted. "You led me on this whole thing just so de Roquefort could win? Is that what our master meant to you? He trusted you. I trusted you."

"I knew you were a problem," Cassiopeia declared. "Everything about you signaled trouble."

"And you should know," de Roquefort said, "as that's what you have been to me. Leaving Lars Nelle's journal for me to find in Avignon. You thought that would occupy me for a while. But you see, mademoiselle, the loyalty of our brotherhood takes precedence. So your efforts have all been for naught." De Roquefort faced Malone. "I have six men here, six outside—and they know how to handle themselves. You have no weapons, or so brother Geoffrey has informed me. But to be safe." De Roquefort motioned and one of the men frisked Malone, then moved to the others.

"What did you do, call the abbey when you left here to get supplies?" Mark asked Geoffrey. "I wondered why you volunteered. You haven't let me out of your sight in two days."

Geoffrey continued to stand, his face stiff with conviction.

"You're a disgusting excuse for a man," Mark spat out.

"I agree," de Roquefort said, and Malone watched as de Roquefort's gun came level and he fired three shots into Geoffrey's chest. The bullets staggered the younger man back, and de Roquefort finished his assassination with a bullet to the head.

Geoffrey's body collapsed to the floor. Blood poured from the wounds. Malone bit his lip. There was nothing he could do.

Mark lunged at de Roquefort.

The gun was aimed at Mark's chest.

He stopped.

"He assaulted me at the abbey," de Roquefort said. "Attacking the master is punishable by death."

"Not in five hundred years," Mark yelled.

"He was a traitor. To you and to me. Neither of us has any use for him. That's the occupational hazard of being a spy. He surely knew the risk he was taking."

"Do you know the risks you're taking?"

"A strange question coming from a man who killed a brother of this Order. That act is punishable by death, too."

Malone realized this show was for the others present. De Roquefort needed his enemy, at least for the moment.

"I did what I had to," Mark spit out.

De Roquefort clicked the hammer of the automatic into place. "So will I."

Stephanie stepped between the two men, her body blocking Mark's. "And will you kill me, too?"

"If need be."

"But I'm a Christian and I haven't harmed any brothers."

"Words, dear lady. Only words."

She reached up and fished out a chain with a medal from around her neck. "The Virgin. She goes with me wherever I go."

Malone knew de Roquefort could not shoot her. She'd sensed the theater, too, and called his bluff before his men. De Roquefort could not afford to be a hypocrite. He was impressed. It took balls to face down a loaded gun. Not bad for a desk jockey.

De Roquefort lowered the weapon.

Malone rushed toward Geoffrey's bleeding body. One of the men raised a hand to stop him. "I'd drop that arm if I were you," he made clear.

"Let him pass," de Roquefort said.

He came close to the body. Henrik stood staring down at

the corpse. A pained look filled the Dane's face and he saw something he'd not seen in the year he'd known him.

Tears.

"You and I will go back down," de Roquefort said to Mark, "and you'll show me what you found. The others will stay here."

"Screw yourself."

De Roquefort **shrugged** and aimed his gun at Thorvaldsen. "He's a Jew. **Different** rules."

"Don't push it," Malone said to Mark. "Do as he says." He hoped Mark understood that there was a time to hold and a time to fold.

"All right. We'll go down," Mark said.

"I'd like to come," Malone said.

"No," de Roquefort said. "This is a matter for the brother-hood. Though I never considered Nelle one of us, he took the oath, and that counts for something. Besides, his expert-ise might be needed. You, on the other hand, could become a problem."

"How do you know Mark will behave?"

"He will. Otherwise, Christians or no, all of you will die before he could ever climb out that hole."

MARK DESCENDED THE LADDER, FOLLOWED BY DE ROQUEFORT. He pointed left and told de Roquefort about the chamber they'd found.

De Roquefort slid his gun back into a shoulder holster and aimed his flashlight ahead. "You lead the way. And you know what happens if there are any problems."

Mark started walking, his flashlight added to de Roque-fort's beam. They eased their way around the staked hole that had almost claimed Stephanie.

"Ingenious," de Roquefort said as he examined the pit.

They found the open grille.

Mark recalled Malone's warning about more traps and took only baby steps forward. The passage beyond narrowed to about a yard wide, then angled sharply right. After only a few feet, another angle back to the left. One step at a time, he inched ahead.

He made the final turn and stopped.

He shone his light and saw before him a chamber, perhaps ten yards square with a high rounded ceiling. Cassiopeia's assessment that the subterranean vaults might be of Roman origin seemed correct. The gallery formed a perfect repository, and as his light dissolved the darkness, a multitude of wonders came into view.

He first saw statuary. Small colorful pieces. Several enthroned Virgins and Child. Gilded pietàs. Angels. Busts. All in straight rows, like soldiers, across the rear wall. Then the glint of gold from rectangular chests. Some overlaid with ivory panels, others sheathed in a mosaic of onyx and gilt, a few gilded in copper and decorated with coats of arms and religious scenes. Each was too precious for simple storage. They were reliquary caskets, made for the remains of holy saints, probably commandeered in the rush, anything to hold what they needed to transport.

He heard de Roquefort slip off the backpack he was wearing, and suddenly the room was engulfed in a bright orange glow from a battery-powered light bar. De Roquefort handed him one. "These will work better."

He didn't like cooperating with the monster, but knew he was right. He grabbed the light, and they fanned out to see what the room contained.

"COVER HIM UP," MALONE SAID TO ONE OF THE BROTHERS, motioning at Geoffrey.

"With what?" came the question.

"The power cords for the light bars are wrapped in a

blanket. I can use that." He motioned across the church, past one of the burning fires.

The man seemed to consider the inquiry a moment, then said, "*Oui*. Do it."

Malone stomped across the uneven floor and found the blanket, all the while assessing their situation. He returned and draped Geoffrey's body. Three guards had withdrawn to the other fire. The remaining three were stationed near the exit.

"He wasn't a traitor," Henrik whispered.

They all stared at him. "He came in alone and told me that de Roquefort was here. He called him. He had to. The former master made him pledge that, once the Devise was found, de Roquefort would be told. He had no choice. He didn't want to do it, but he trusted the old man. He told me to play along, begged my forgiveness, and said he'd look after me. Unfortunately, I couldn't return the favor."

"That was foolish of him," Cassiopeia said.

"Maybe," Thorvaldsen said. "But his word meant something to him."

"Did he say why he had to tell him?" Stephanie muttered.

"Only that the master foretold a confrontation between Mark and de Roquefort. Geoffrey's task was to ensure one."

"Mark's no match for that man," Malone said. "He's going to need help."

"I agree," Cassiopeia added, talking through her teeth, her mouth not moving.

"The odds aren't good," Malone said. "Twelve men armed, and we're not."

"I wouldn't say that," Cassiopeia whispered.

And he liked the twinkle in her eye.

MARK STUDIED THE TREASURE THAT SURROUNDED HIM. HE'D never seen so much wealth. The reliquary caskets contained a variety of silver and gold, either in coinage or as unminted raw metal. There were gold dinars, silver drachmas, and Byzantine coins, all stacked in neat rows. And jewels. Three chests brimmed with rough stones. Too many to even imagine. Chalices and reliquary vessels caught his gaze, most of ebony, glass, silver, and parcel-gilt. Some were coated with relief figures and dotted in precious stones. He wondered whose remnants they supposedly contained. One he knew for sure. He read the engraving and whispered, "De Molay," as he stared into the reliquary's rock crystal tube.

De Roquefort came close.

Inside the reliquary were bits of blackened bone. Mark knew the tale. Jacques de Molay was roasted alive on an island in the Seine, in the shadow of Notre Dame, shrieking his innocence and cursing Philip IV, who'd dispassionately watched the execution. During the night brothers swam the river and scrounged through the hot ashes. They swam back with the acrid bones of de Molay in their mouths. Now he was staring at one of those mementos.

De Roquefort crossed himself and mumbled a prayer. "Look what they did."

But Mark realized an even greater significance. "This means someone visited this place after March 1314. They must have kept coming back until they all died. Five of them knew about this place. The Black Death surely took them in the mid-1300s. But they never told a soul, and this vault was lost forever." A sadness swept over him at the thought.

He turned and his light revealed crucifixes and statuary of ebonized wood dotting one wall, about forty, the styles varying from Romanesque, to German, to Byzantine, to high Gothic, the intricately carved physical undulations so perfect they seemed to almost breathe.

"It's spectacular," de Roquefort said.

The tally was incalculable, the stone niches that spanned two walls were packed full. Mark had studied in detail the history and purpose of medieval carving from the pieces that survived in museums, but here before him was a broad, spectacular display of Middle Age craftsmanship.

To his right, on a stone pedestal, he spotted an oversized book. The cover still gleamed—gold foil, he surmised—and was dotted with pearls. Someone had apparently opened the volume before, as crumbled parchment lay beneath, scattered like leaves. He bent down, brought the light close to the scraps, and saw Latin. He could read some of the script and quickly determined that it had once been an inventory ledger.

De Roquefort noticed his interest. "What is it?"

"An accounting. Saunière probably tried to examine it when he found this place. But you have to be careful with parchment."

"Thief. That's what he was. Nothing but a common thief. He had no right to take any of this."

"And we do?"

"It's ours. Left for us by de Molay himself. He was crucified on a door, yet told them nothing. His bones are here. This is *ours*."

Mark's attention was diverted to a partially open chest. He shone his light and saw more parchment. He slowly hinged open the lid, which only slightly resisted. He dared not touch the sheets stacked together. So he strained to decipher what was on the top page. Old French, he quickly concluded. He could read enough to know that it was a will.

"Papers the Order was safekeeping. This chest is probably full of thirteenth- and fourteenth-century wills and deeds." He shook his head. "To the end, the brothers made sure their duty was done." He considered the possibilities that lay before him. "What we could learn from these documents."

"This is not all of it," de Roquefort suddenly declared. "No books. Not one. Where's the knowledge?"

"What you see is it."

"You're lying. There's more. Where?"

He faced de Roquefort. "This is it."

"Don't be coy with me. Our brothers secreted away their knowledge. You know that. Philip never found it. So it has to be here. I can see it in your eyes. There's more." De Roquefort reached for his gun and raised the barrel to Mark's brow. "Tell me."

"I'd rather die."

"But would you rather have your mother die? Or your friends up there? Because that's who I'll kill first, while you watch, until I learn what I want to know."

Mark considered the possibility. It wasn't that he was afraid of de Roquefort—strangely, no fear coursed through him—it was simply that he wanted to know, too. His father had searched for years and found nothing. What had the master told his mother about him? *He doesn't possess the resolve needed to complete his battles.* Bullshit. The solution to his father's quest was a short walk away.

"All right. Come with me."

"IT'S AWFUL GLOOMY IN HERE," MALONE SAID TO THE BROTHER who appeared in charge. "Mind if we get the generator going and fire up those lights?"

"We wait for the master to return."

"They're going to need those lights down there, and it takes a few minutes to set things up. Your master may not be inclined to wait when he calls for them." He was hoping the prediction might affect the man's judgment. "What's it going to hurt? We're just rigging up some lights."

"Okay. Go ahead."

Malone withdrew back to where the others stood. "He bought it. Let's set 'em up."

Stephanie and Malone moved toward one set, while Henrik and Cassiopeia grabbed another. The bars consisted of two halogen flood lamps atop an orange tripod. The generator was a small gasoline-powered unit. They positioned the tripods at opposite ends of the church and angled the bulbs upward. Power cords were connected and run back to where the generator sat, near the altar.

A tool bag lay beside the generator. Cassiopeia was reaching inside when one of the guards stopped her.

"I need to hot-wire the power cords. Can't use plugs for this kind of ampage. I'm only going to get a screwdriver."

The man hesitated then stepped back, gun at his side, seemingly ready. Cassiopeia reached into the bag and carefully removed the screwdriver. By the light of the fires, she attached the cords to leads on the generator.

"Let's check out the connections to the lights," she said to Malone.

They casually walked to the first tripod. "My dart gun is in the tool bag," she whispered.

"I assume those are the same little darlings used in Copenhagen?" He kept his lips still as a ventriloquist's.

"They work fast. I just need a few seconds to fire the shots."

She was fiddling with the tripod, not doing anything.

"And how many shots do you have?"

She seemingly finished what she was doing. "Four."

They headed for the other tripod. "We have six guests."

"The other two are your problem."

They stopped at the second tripod. He breathed out, "We'll need a moment of distraction to confuse everybody. I have an idea."

She tinkered with the back of the lights. "About time."

SIXTY-THREE

MARK LED THE WAY BACK DOWN THE SUBTERRANEAN PAS-
sage, past the ladder, toward where Malone and Cassiopeia
had first explored. No light seeped down from the church
above. As they were leaving the treasure chamber he'd retrieved the bolt cutters, as he assumed the other gate would
likewise be chained.

They came to words etched into the wall.

"By this sign ye shall conquer him," de Roquefort said as
he read, then his beam found the second gate. "That it?"

Mark nodded and motioned at the skeleton propped
against the wall. "He came to see for himself." He explained
about the marshal from Saunière's time and the medallion
Malone found, which confirmed the identity.

"Serves him right," de Roquefort said.

"And what you're doing is better?"

"I come for the brothers."

In the halo of his light bar, Mark noticed a slight depression in the earth ahead. Without saying a word, he stepped
around the liar, toward the wall, avoiding the trap that de
Roquefort seemed not to notice, as his focus was on the
skeleton. At the gate, with the bolt cutters, Mark severed another brass chain. He recalled Malone's caution and stepped
to one side as he worked the grille open.

Beyond the entrance were the same two sharp turns. He inched his way forward. Within the golden glow of his lamp he saw nothing but rock.

He turned the first corner, then the second. De Roquefort stood behind him and their combined lights revealed another gallery, this one larger than the first treasure chamber.

The room was dotted with stone plinths of varying shapes and sizes. Atop them were books, all neatly stacked. Hundreds of volumes.

A sick feeling came to Mark's stomach as he realized that the manuscripts would most likely be ruined. Though the chamber was cool and dry, time would have taken a toll on both the leaves and the ink. Much better if they'd been sealed inside another container. But the brothers who had secreted these certainly never imagined that it would be seven hundred years before they'd be retrieved.

He stepped to one of the stacks and examined the top cover. What was once surely gilded silver atop wood boards had turned black. He studied the engravings of Christ and what appeared to be Peter and Paul, which he knew were formed from clay and wax beneath the gilt. Italian craftsmanship. German ingenuity. He gently lifted the cover and brought the light close. His suspicion was confirmed. He could not make out many of the words.

"Can you read it?" de Roquefort asked.

He shook his head. "It needs to be in a laboratory. It will take professional restoration. We shouldn't disturb them."

"Looks like somebody already did that."

And he stared into the spill of de Roquefort's light and saw a pile of books scattered on the floor. Bits and pieces of pages lay about like charred paper from a flame.

"Saunière again," he said. "It'll take years to garner anything useful from these. And that's assuming there's anything to find. Beyond some historical value, they're probably useless."

"This is *ours*."

So what, he thought, for all the good it would do.

But his mind raced with possibilities. Saunière had come to this place. No question. The treasure chamber had provided his wealth—it would have been an easy matter to return from time to time and cart off unminted gold and silver. Actual coins would have raised questions. Bank officials or assay clerks might want to know their source. But the raw metal would have been the perfect currency in the early part of the twentieth century when many economies were either gold- or silver-based.

Yet the abbé had gone a step farther.

He'd used the wealth to fashion a church loaded with hints that pointed to something Saunière clearly believed. Something he was so sure about that he flaunted the knowledge. *By this sign ye shall conquer him.* Words carved not only here underground, but in the Rennes church as well. He visualized the inscription painted above the entrance. *I have had contempt for the kingdom of this world, and all temporal adornments, because of the love of my Lord Jesus Christ, whom I saw, whom I loved, in whom I believed, and whom I worshiped.* Obscure words from an ancient responsory? Maybe. Yet Saunière intentionally chose them.

Whom I saw.

He fanned the light bar around the room and studied the plinths.

Then he saw it.

Where to hide a pebble?

Where, indeed.

MALONE WALKED BACK TO THE GENERATOR, WHERE STEPHANIE and Henrik stood. Cassiopeia was still "working" on the tripod. He bent down and made sure there was gasoline in the engine.

"This thing going to make a lot of noise?" he asked in a low voice.

"We can only hope. But unfortunately they make these units fairly quiet nowadays."

He did not touch the tool bag, not wanting to draw any attention to it. So far none of the guards had bothered to check inside. Apparently the defensive training at the abbey left a lot to be desired. But how effective could it be? Sure, you could learn hand-to-hand combat, how to shoot, how to handle a blade. But the choice of recruits had to be limited, and only so many silk purses could be crafted from a sow's ear.

"All ready," Cassiopeia said loud enough for all to hear.

"I need to get to Mark," Stephanie whispered.

"I understand," Malone said. "But we have to take this a step at a time."

"Do you think for one moment de Roquefort is going to allow him to climb back out of there? He shot Geoffrey with no hesitation."

He saw her agitation. "We're all aware of the situation," he muttered. "Just stay cool."

He, too, wanted de Roquefort. For Geoffrey.

"I need a second with the tool bag," Cassiopeia breathed as she crouched down and stuffed the screwdriver she'd been using back inside. Four of the guards stood across the church, beyond one of the fires. Two more loitered to their left, near the other fire. None seemed to be paying them much attention, confident that the cage was secure.

Cassiopeia stayed crouched by the tool bag, her hand still inside, and gave him a slight nod. Ready. He stood and called out, "We're going to crank the generator."

The man in charge signaled to go ahead.

He turned back and whispered to Stephanie, "After I crank it, we're going over to the two men standing together. I'll take one, you the other."

"With pleasure."

She was anxious and he knew it. "Easy, tiger. It's not as simple as you think."

"Watch me."

MARK APPROACHED ONE OF THE STONE PLINTHS SITTING among the remaining dozen or so. He'd noticed something. While the tops to the others were supported by a variety of pillars, some singular, most in pairs, this one was held aloft by a rectangular-shaped support, similar to the altar above. And what drew his attention was the stone arrangement. Nine compact square blocks across, seven high.

He bent down and shone his light at the underside. No mortar joint appeared above the top row of block. Just like the altar.

"These books have to come off," he said.

"You said not to disturb them."

"It's what's inside this thing that's important."

He laid the light bar down and grabbed a handful of the olden manuscripts. Disturbing them churned up a dust storm. He gently laid them on the gravelly ground. De Roquefort did the same. Three loads each and the top was empty.

"It should slide," he said.

Together they grasped an end and the top moved, much more easily than the altar above since the plinth was half its size. They pushed it free and the chunk of limestone pounded to the ground and split into pieces. Nestled within the plinth Mark saw another container, smaller, about twenty-four inches long, half that wide, and eighteen or so inches tall. Made of gray-beige rock—limestone, if he wasn't mistaken—and in remarkably good condition.

He grabbed the light bar and thrust it into the support. Just as he suspected, writing appeared on one side.

"It's an ossuary," de Roquefort said. "Is it identified?"

He studied the script and was pleased that it was Aramaic.

To be authentic, it would have to be. The custom of laying the dead in underground crypts until all that remained was dry bone, then collecting the bones and depositing them into a stone box was popular with Jews during the first century. He knew that some thousand ossuaries had survived. But only about a quarter of them bore inscriptions that identified their contents—most likely explained by the fact that the vast majority of people from that time were illiterate. Many fakes had appeared through the centuries—one in particular a few years ago had claimed to hold the bones of James, Jesus's half brother. Another test of authenticity would be the type of material used—chalk limestone from quarries near Jerusalem—along with the style of carvings, microscopic examination of the patina, and carbon testing.

He'd learned Aramaic in graduate school. A difficult language made more complicated by its varying styles, its slang, and the many errors of ancient scribes. How the letters were carved was a problem, too. Most times they were shallow, scratched with a nail. Other times they were scrawled across the face haphazardly, like graffiti. Sometimes, like here, they were engraved with a stylus, the letters clear. Which was why these words were not difficult to translate. He'd actually seen them before. He read from right to left as required, then reversed them in his mind.

YESHUA BAR YEHOSEF

"Jesus, son of Joseph," he said, translating.

"His bones?"

"That remains to be seen." He spied the top. "Lift it off."

De Roquefort reached in and grasped the flat lid. He worked it from side to side until the stone released. Then he lifted off the cover and rested it vertically against the ossuary.

Mark sucked a breath.

Inside the repository lay bones.

Some had turned to dust. Many were still intact. A femur. A tibia. Some ribs, a pelvis. What looked like fingers, toes, parts of a spine.

And a skull.

Was this what Sauinère found?

Beneath the skull lay a small book in remarkably good condition. Which was understandable, given it had been sealed within the ossuary, itself sealed within another container. The cover was exquisite, gilded in gold leaf and studded with cut stones arranged in the shape of a cross. Christ lay upon the cross, fashioned also of gold. Surrounding the cross were more stones in shades of crimson, jade, and lemon.

He lifted out the book and blew away the dust and debris from its cover, then balanced it on the corner of the support. De Roquefort came close with his lamp. He opened the cover and read the *incipit,* penned in Latin and written in a running Gothic script without punctuation, the ink a mixture of blue and crimson.

HERE BEGINNETH AN ACCOUNT LOCATED BY THE FOUNDING BROTHERS DURING THEIR EXPLORATION OF THE TEMPLE MOUNT CONDUCTED THROUGH THE WINTER OF 1121 THE ORIGINAL BEING IN SUCH A STATE OF DECAY HAS BEEN COPIED EXACTLY AS IT APPEARED IN A LANGUAGE THAT ONLY ONE OF OUR NUMBER COULD UNDERSTAND BY ORDER OF THE MASTER WILLIAM DE CHARTRES DATED 4 JUNE 1217 THE TEXT HAS BEEN TRANSLATED INTO THE WORDS OF THE BROTHERS AND PRESERVED FOR ALL TO KNOW.

De Roquefort was reading over his shoulder and said, "That book was placed within the ossuary for a reason."

Mark agreed.

"See what follows?"

"I thought you were here for the brothers? Should this not be returned to the abbey and read to all?"

"I'll make that decision after I read it."

He wondered if the brothers would ever know. But he wanted to know, so he studied the script on the next page and recognized the jumble of scribbles and scratches. "It's in Aramaic. I can only read a few words. That language has been gone for two thousand years."

"The *incipit* spoke of a translation."

He carefully lifted the pages and saw that the Aramaic spanned four leaves. Then he saw words he could understand. THE WORDS OF THE BROTHERS. Latin. The vellum had survived in excellent condition, its surface the color of aged parchment. The colored ink, too, was still clear. A title headed the text.

THE TESTIMONY OF SIMON

He started reading.

SIXTY-FOUR

MALONE APPROACHED ONE OF THE BROTHERS, A MAN DRESSED like the other five in jeans and a woolen coat, a cap atop his short hair. At least six more were outside—that's what de Roquefort had said—but he'd worry about them once the six inside the church were subdued.

At least then he'd be armed.

He watched Stephanie as she grabbed a shovel and started

to tend one of the fires, shuffling the timbers and reigniting the flames. Cassiopeia was still at the generator with Henrik, waiting for him and Stephanie to position themselves.

He turned toward Cassiopeia and nodded.

She yanked the starter cord.

The generator sputtered, then died. Two more pulls and the piston caught, the engine emitting a low rumble. The lights on the two tripods came to life, their glow intensifying with the growing voltage. The halogen bulbs heated fast and condensation started to rise from the glass in wisps of mist that just as quickly vanished.

Malone saw that the event caught the guards' attention. A mistake. On their part. But they'd need a bit more to give Cassiopeia time to fire four air darts. He wondered about her shooting ability, then remembered her marksmanship at Rennes.

The generator continued to growl.

Cassiopeia remained crouched, the tool bag at her feet, seemingly adjusting the dials on the engine.

The lights seemed at full intensity and the guards appeared to have lost interest.

One set of bulbs exploded.

Then the other.

A lightning-white flash mushroomed upward and, in an instant, was gone. Malone used that second to land a punch on the jaw of the brother standing beside him.

The man teetered, then collapsed to the floor.

Malone reached down and disarmed him.

STEPHANIE SCOOPED A BURNING EMBER FROM THE FIRE AND turned to the guard a few feet away, whose attention was on the exploding lights.

"Hey," she said.

The man turned. She lobbed the ember. The chunk of

white-hot timber floated through the air and the guard reached out to deflect the projectile, but the ember struck him in the chest.

The man screamed and Stephanie slammed the flat side of the shovel into the brother's face.

MALONE SAW STEPHANIE TOSS AN EMBER TOWARD THE GUARD, then pound him with the shovel. His gaze then shot toward Cassiopeia as she calmly fired the air gun. She'd already ticked off one shot, as he saw only three men standing. One of the remaining guards reached for his thigh. Another jerked and groped at the back of his jacket.

Both collapsed to the ground.

The last of the short-hairs at the altar saw what was happening to his compatriots and whirled to face Cassiopeia, who was crouched thirty feet away, the air gun aimed directly at him.

The man leaped behind the altar support.

Her shot missed.

Malone knew she was out of darts. It would only be an instant before the brother fired.

He felt the gun in his hand. He hated to use it. The blast would certainly alert not only de Roquefort, but also the brothers outside. So he raced across the church, planted the palms of his hands on the altar support, and, as the brother came up, gun ready, he lunged and used his momentum to kick the brother into the floor.

"Not bad," Cassiopeia said.

"I thought you said you didn't miss."

"He jumped."

Cassiopeia and Stephanie were disarming the downed brothers. Henrik came close and asked, "You okay?"

"My reflexes haven't had to do that in a while."

"Good to know they still work."

"How'd you do that with the lights?" Henrik asked.

Malone smiled. "Just upped the voltage. Works every time." He scanned the church. Something was wrong. Why hadn't any of the brothers outside reacted to the exploding lights? "We should be having company."

Cassiopeia and Stephanie came close, guns in hand.

"Maybe they're out in the ruins, toward the front," Stephanie said.

He stared at the exit. "Or maybe they don't exist."

"I assure you, they existed," a male voice said from outside the church.

A man slowly crept into view, his face shrouded in the shadows.

Malone raised his gun. "And you are?"

The man stopped near one of the fires. His gaze, from deep-set serious eyes, locked on Geoffrey's sheathed corpse. "The master shot him?"

"With no remorse."

The man's face clinched tight and the lips mumbled something. A prayer? Then he said, "I'm chaplain of the Order. Brother Geoffrey called me, too, after he called the master. I came to prevent violence. But we were delayed in arriving."

Malone lowered his gun. "You were part of whatever it was Geoffrey was doing?"

He nodded. "He didn't want to contact de Roquefort, but he gave his word to the former master." The tone was tender. "Now it seems he gave his life, too."

Malone wanted to know, "What's happening here?"

"I understand your frustration."

"No, you don't," Henrik said. "That poor young man is dead."

"And I grieve for him. He served this Order with great honor."

"Calling de Roquefort was stupid," Cassiopeia said. "He invited trouble."

"In the final months of his life, our former master set into motion a complex chain of events. He spoke to me about what he planned. He told me who our seneschal was and why he'd taken him into the Order. He told me of the seneschal's father and what lay ahead. So I pledged my obedience, as did brother Geoffrey. We knew what was happening. But the seneschal did not, nor did the seneschal know of our involvement. I was told not to become involved until brother Geoffrey requested my help."

"Your master is below us with my son," Stephanie said. "Cotton, we need to get down there."

He heard the impatience in her voice.

"The seneschal and de Roquefort cannot coexist," the chaplain said. "They're opposite ends of a long spectrum. For the good of the brotherhood, only one of these men can survive. But my former master wondered if the seneschal could do it alone." The chaplain stared at Stephanie. "Which is why you are here. He believed you'd bring the seneschal strength."

Stephanie appeared not in the mood for mysticism. "My son could die thanks to this foolishness."

"For centuries this Order survived through battle and conflict. That was our way. The former master simply forced a confrontation. He knew de Roquefort and the seneschal would war. But he wanted that war to count for something— to end with something. So he pointed them both toward the Great Devise. He knew it was out there, somewhere, but I doubt if he really believed either one of them would find it. He knew, though, that a conflict would erupt, and a winner would emerge. He also knew that if de Roquefort was the winner, he'd quickly alienate his allies, and he has. The deaths of two brothers weigh heavily on us. All agree there will be more deaths—"

"Cotton," Stephanie said. "I'm going."

The chaplain did not move. "The men outside have been

subdued. Do what you must. There will be no more bloodshed up here."

And Malone heard the words that the somber man had not spoken.

Below us, though, is altogether different.

SIXTY-FIVE

THE TESTIMONY OF SIMON

I have stayed silent, thinking it better for others to preserve a record. Yet none has come forward. So this has been written so that you will know what happened.

The man Jesus spent many years spreading his message throughout the lands of Judea and Galilee. I was the first of his followers, but our number grew since many believed his words possessed great meaning. We traveled with him, watching as he eased suffering, brought hope, and stirred salvation. He was always himself, no matter the day or event. If the masses lauded him, he faced them. When hostility surrounded him, he showed no rage or fear. What others thought of him, said, or did never affected him. He said once, "All of us bear God's image, all are worthy to be loved, all can grow in the spirit of God." I watched as he embraced lepers and the immoral. Women and children were precious to him. He showed me that all were worthy of love. He would say, "God is our father. He cares, loves, and forgives all. No sheep will ever be lost from that shepherd.

Feel free to tell God all, for only in such openness can the heart gain peace."

The man Jesus taught me to pray. He talked of God, the final judgment, and the end of time. I came to think that he could even control the wind and waves since he stood so afar above us. The religious elders taught that pain, sickness, and tragedy were God's judgment and we should accept that wrath with the sorrow of a penitent. The man Jesus said that was wrong and offered the sick the courage to become well, the weak the ability to grow a strong spirit, and nonbelievers the chance to believe. The world seemed to part at his approach. The man Jesus possessed a purpose, he lived his life to fulfill that purpose, and that purpose was clear to those of us who followed him.

But in his travels the man Jesus made enemies. The elders found him a threat in that he offered different values, new rules, and threatened their authority. They worried that if the man Jesus was allowed to roam free and preach change, Rome could well tighten its grip and all would suffer, especially the high priest who served at Rome's pleasure. So it happened that Jesus was arrested for blasphemy and Pilate decreed he should ascend the cross. I was there that day and Pilate drew no joy from the decision, but the elders demanded justice and Pilate could not deny them.

In Jerusalem the man Jesus and six others were taken to a place on the hill and bound by thongs to the cross. Later in the day, the legs of three of the men were broken and they succumbed by nightfall. Two more died the next day. The man Jesus was allowed to linger until the third, when his legs were finally broken. I did not go to him while he suffered. I, and the others who followed him, hid away, afraid that we might be next. After he died, the man Jesus was left on his cross for six more days while birds picked his flesh. He was finally taken from the cross and dropped into a hole dug from the ground. I watched that happen, then fled Jerusalem by way of the desert, stopping in Bethany at the home of Mary called Magdalene and her sister, Martha. They had known the man Jesus and were saddened by his death. They were angry at me for not defending him, for not acknowledging him, for fleeing when he was suffering. I asked them what they would have had me do and their answer was clear. "Join him." But that thought never occurred to me. Instead, to all who asked, I denied the man Jesus and all that he stood for. I left their home, returning days later to Galilee and the comfort of that which I knew.

Two who had traveled with the man Jesus, James and John, also returned to Galilee. Together we shared our grief over the loss of the man Jesus and resumed our life as fishermen. The darkness we all felt consumed us and time did not ease our pain. As we fished on the Sea of Galilee we talked of the man Jesus and all that he did and all that we witnessed. It was on the lake, years ago, that we first met him as he taught from our boat. His memory seemed everywhere upon the waters, which made our grief even harder to escape. One night, as a storm swirled across the lake and we sat on shore eating bread and fish, I thought I saw the man Jesus upon the mist. But when I waded out I knew that the vision was only in my mind. Every morning we broke bread and ate fish. Remembering what the man Jesus once did, one of us would bless the bread and offer it up in praise of God. This act made us all feel better. One day John commented that the broken bread was so like the broken body of the man Jesus. After that, we all started to associate the bread with the body.

Four months passed and one day James reminded us that the Torah proclaimed that one hung upon a tree is accursed. I told him that could not be true of the man Jesus. That was the first time any of us ever questioned the ancient words. They simply could not apply to one so good as the man Jesus. How would a scribe from long ago know that all who were hung upon a tree were accursed. He could not. In a battle between the man Jesus and the ancient words, the man Jesus was the victor.

Our grief continued to torment us. The man Jesus was gone. His voice was silent. The elders survived and their message lived. Not because they were right, but simply because they were alive and speaking. The elders had triumphed over the man Jesus. But how could something so good be wrong? Why would God allow such good to disappear?

Summer ended and the feast of the Tabernacle came, which was a time to celebrate the joy of the harvest. We thought it safe to travel to Jerusalem and take part. Once there, during the procession to the altar, it was read from the Psalms that the Messiah shall not die, but shall live and recount the deeds of the Lord. One of the elders proclaimed that though the Lord has chastened the Messiah sorely, He has not given him over unto death. But rather, the stone that the builders rejected has become the head of the corner. In the Temple we listened to readings from Zechariah, which told that one day the Lord would come and living waters would flow from Jerusalem and the Lord would become king over all the earth. Then one evening I came upon another reading from Zechariah. He spoke of a pouring out from the House of David and of a spirit of compassion and supplication. It was said that when we look on him whom they have pierced, we shall mourn for him as one weeps over a firstborn.

Listening, I thought of the man Jesus and what happened to him. The reader seemed to speak directly to me when he spoke of God's plan to strike the shepherd so that the sheep may scatter. At that moment a love took hold of me that would not let go. That night I journeyed outside Jerusalem to the spot where the Romans had buried the man Jesus. I knelt above his mortal remains and wondered how a simple fisherman could be the source of all truth. The high priest and scribes had judged the man Jesus a fraud. But I knew they were wrong. God did not require obedience to ancient laws in order to achieve salvation. God's love was boundless. The man Jesus had many times said that, and in accepting his death with great courage and dignity, the man Jesus had given one final lesson to us all. In ending life we find life. Loving is to be loved.

All doubt left me. Grief vanished. Confusion became clarity. The man Jesus was not dead. He was alive. Resurrected within me was the risen Lord. I felt his presence as clearly as when he once stood beside me. I recalled what he said to me many times. "Simon, if you love me you will find my sheep." I finally knew that loving as he loved will allow anyone to know the Lord. Doing as he did will allow us all to know the Lord. Living as he lived is the way to salvation. God had come from heaven to dwell within the man Jesus and through his deeds and words the Lord became known. The message was clear. Care for the needy, comfort the distressed, befriend the rejected. Do those things and the Lord will be pleased. God took the man Jesus's life so that we could see. I was merely the first to accept that truth. The task became clear. The message must live through me and others who likewise believe.

When I told John and James of my vision they saw, too. Before we left Jerusalem, we returned to the place of my vision and dug from the earth the remains of the man Jesus. We took him with us and laid him in a cave. We returned the next year and gathered his bones. Then I wrote this account which I placed with the man Jesus, for together they are the Word.

SIXTY-SIX

MARK WAS BOTH CONFUSED AND AMAZED. HE KNEW SIMON.

He was called first Cephas in Aramaic, then Petros, rock, in Greek. Eventually he became Peter and the Gospels proclaimed that Christ said, *Upon this rock I shall build my church.*

The testimony was the first ancient account he'd ever read that made sense. No supernatural events or miraculous apparitions. No actions contrary to history or logic. No inconsistent details that cast doubt on credibility. Just the testimony by a simple fisherman of how he'd borne witness to a great man, one whose good works and kind words lived on after his death, enough to inspire him to continue the cause.

Simon certainly did not possess the intellect or ability to fashion the type of elaborate religious ideas that would come much later. His understanding was confined to the man Jesus, whom he knew, and whom God had reclaimed through a violent death. In order to know God, to be a part of Him, it was clear to Simon that he must emulate the man Jesus. The message could only live if he, and others after him, breathed life into it. In that simple way, death could not contain the man Jesus. A resurrection would occur. Not literal, but spiritual. And within the mind of Simon, the man Jesus had arisen—he lived again—and from that singular beginning, during an autumn night six months after the man Jesus was executed, the Christian Church was born.

"Those arrogant assholes," de Roquefort muttered. "With their grand churches and theologies. Every bit of it is wrong."

"No, it's not."

"How can you say that? There's no elaborate crucifixion, no empty tomb, no angels announcing the risen Christ. That's fiction, created by men for their own benefit. This testimony here has meaning. It all started with one man realizing something in *his* mind. Our Order was wiped from the face of the earth, our brothers tortured and murdered, in the name of the so-called resurrected Christ."

"The effect is the same. The Church was born."

"Do you think for one minute the Church would have flourished if its entire theology was based on the personal revelation of one simple man? How many converts do you think it would have obtained?"

"But that's exactly what happened. Jesus was an ordinary man."

"Who was elevated to the status of a god by later men. And if anyone challenged that determination, they were deemed a heretic and burned at the stake. The Cathars were wiped from the face of the earth right here in the Pyrénées for not believing."

"Those early Church fathers did what they did. They had to embellish in order to survive."

"You condone what they did?"

"It's done."

"And we can undo it."

A thought occurred to him. "Saunière surely read this."

"And told no one."

"That's right. Even he saw the futility of it."

"He told no one because he would have lost his private treasure trove. He had no honor. He was a thief."

"Perhaps. But the information obviously affected him. He left so many clues in his church. He was a learned man and could read Latin. If he found this, which I'm sure he did, he understood it. Yet he placed it back in its hiding place and locked the gate when he left." He stared down into the ossuary. Was he looking at the bones of the man Jesus? A wave a sadness swept through him as he realized all that remained of his father were bones, too.

He locked his gaze on de Roquefort and asked what he truly wanted to know. "Did you kill my father?"

MALONE WATCHED AS STEPHANIE HUSTLED TOWARD THE LADder, a gun from one of the guards in her hand. "Going somewhere?"

"He may hate my guts, but he's still my son."

He understood she had to go, but she wasn't going alone. "I'm coming, too."

"I prefer to do this alone."

"I don't give a damn what you prefer. I'm coming."

"I am, too," Cassiopeia said.

Henrik grabbed her arm. "No. Let them do it. They need to resolve this."

"Resolve what?" Cassiopeia demanded.

The chaplain stepped forward. "The seneschal and the master must challenge each other. His mother was involved for a reason. Let her be. Her destiny is below with them."

Stephanie disappeared down the ladder and Malone watched from above as she hopped to one side, avoiding the pit. He then followed her down, lamp in one hand, gun in the other.

"Which way?" Stephanie whispered.

He signaled for quiet. Then he heard voices. From his left, toward the chamber he and Cassiopeia had found.

"That way," he mouthed.

He knew the path was free of traps until almost to the chamber entrance. Still, they inched ahead slowly. When he spied the skeleton and the words etched into the wall, he knew just ahead they'd have to be cautious.

The voices were clearer now.

"I ASKED IF YOU KILLED MY FATHER," MARK SAID IN A LOUD tone.

"Your father was a weak soul."

"That's not an answer."

"I was there the night he ended his life. I followed him to the bridge. We talked."

Mark was listening.

"He was frustrated. Angry. He'd solved the cryptogram, the one in his journal, and it told him nothing. Your father simply lacked the strength to carry on."

"You know nothing of my father."

"On the contrary. I watched him for years. He moved from issue to issue, never resolving a single one. It brought him problems professionally and personally."

"He apparently found enough to lead us here."

"No. Others found that."

"You made no attempt to stop him from hanging himself?"

De Roquefort shrugged. "Why? He was intent on dying, and I saw no advantage in stopping him."

"So you just walked away and let him die?"

"I didn't interfere in something that did not concern me."

"You son of a bitch." He took a step forward. De Roquefort leveled his gun. He still held the book from the ossuary. "Go ahead. Shoot me."

De Roquefort seemed unfazed. "You killed a brother. You know the penalty."

"He died because of you. You sent him."

"There you go again. One set of rules for yourself, another for the rest of us. You pulled the trigger."

"In self-defense."

"Lay the book down."

"And what will you do with it?"

"What the masters in the Beginning did. I'll use it against Rome. I always wondered how the Order rose so quickly. When popes tried to merge us with the Knights Hospitallers, over and over we stopped them. And all because of that book and those bones. The Roman Church could not take the chance of either being made public.

"Imagine what those medieval popes thought when they learned that the physical resurrection of Christ was a myth. Of course, they couldn't be sure. That testimony could be as fictitious as the Gospels. Still, the words are compelling and the bones hard to ignore. There were thousands of relics floating around then. Pieces of saints adorned every church. Everyone believed so easily. No reason to think these bones would have been ignored. And these were the greatest relics of them all. So masters used what they knew, and the threat worked."

"And today?"

"Just the opposite. Too many people who believe nothing. Lots of questions exist in the modern mind and few answers in the Gospels. That testimony, though, is another matter. It would make sense to a great many people."

"So you're going to be a modern-day Philip IV."

De Roquefort spit on the ground. "That's what I think of him. He wanted this knowledge so he could control the Church—so that his heirs could control it, too. But he paid for his greed. Him and his entire family."

"Do you think for one minute you could control anything?"

"I have no desire to control. But I would like to see the faces of all those pompous prelates as they explain away the testimony of Simon Peter. After all, his bones rest at the heart of the Vatican. They built a cathedral around his grave and named the basilica for him. He's their first saint, their first pope. How will they explain away his words? Wouldn't you like to listen as they try?"

"Who's to say they're his?"

"Who's to say Matthew, Mark, Luke, and John's words are theirs?"

"Changing everything might not be so good."

"You're as weak as your father. No stomach for a fight. You'd bury this away? Tell no one? Allow the Order to languish in obscurity, tainted by the slander of a greedy king? Weak men like you are why we find ourselves in this situation. You and your master were well suited to one another. He was a weak man, too."

He'd heard enough and, without warning, raised his left hand, which held the lamp, angling the bright bar so that its strongest glow momentarily flashed in de Roquefort's eyes. The instant of discomfort caused de Roquefort to squint, and his hand with the gun dropped as he raised his other arm to shield his eyes.

Mark kicked the gun from de Roquefort's grip, then rushed from the chamber. He emerged from the open gate, turned back toward the ladder, but took only a few steps.

Ten feet ahead he saw another light and spotted Malone and his mother.

Behind him, de Roquefort emerged.

"Halt" came the command, and he stopped.

De Roquefort stepped close.

He saw his mother raise a gun.

"Get down, Mark," she yelled.

But he stayed standing.

De Roquefort was now directly behind him. He felt the barrel of the gun at the back of his head.

"Lower your weapon," de Roquefort said to her.

Malone displayed a gun. "You can't shoot us both."

"No. But I can shoot this one."

MALONE CONSIDERED HIS OPTIONS. HE COULDN'T GET A SHOT at de Roquefort without hitting Mark. But why had Mark stopped, allowing de Roquefort the opportunity to corral him?

"Lower the gun," Malone said quietly to Stephanie.

"No."

"I would do as he says," de Roquefort made clear.

Stephanie did not move. "He's going to shoot him anyway."

"Maybe," Malone said. "But let's not provoke it."

He knew she'd lost her son once through mistakes. She was not about to have him taken from her again. He studied Mark's face. Not a speck of fear. He motioned with his light at the book in Mark's grasp.

"That what this was all about?"

Mark nodded. "The Great Devise, along with a lot of treasure and documents."

"Was it worth it?"

"That's not for me to say."

"It was," de Roquefort declared.

"So what now?" Malone asked. "Nowhere for you to go. Your men are down."

"Your doing?"

"Some. But your chaplain is here with a contingent of knights. Seems there's been a revolt."

"That remains to be seen," de Roquefort said. "I'll only say it one more time, Ms. Nelle, lower your gun. As Mr. Malone correctly notes, what do I have to lose by shooting your son?"

Malone was still assessing the situation, his mind checking off options. Then, in the ambient glow from Mark's lamp, he spotted it. A slight depression in the floor. Hardly noticeable, except if you knew what to look for. Another floor trap spanning the width of the passage and extending from where he stood all the way to Mark. He cut his gaze back and saw in the younger man's eyes the fact that he knew it existed. A slight nod of the head and he realized why Mark had stopped. He'd wanted de Roquefort to come after him. He needed him to come.

Apparently it was time to end this.

Here and now.

He reached out and wrenched the gun from Stephanie's grasp.

"What are you doing?" she asked.

Back to de Roquefort, he mouthed, "The floor," and he saw that she registered what he'd said.

Then he faced their dilemma.

"Wise move," de Roquefort said to him.

Stephanie went silent, apparently understanding. But he doubted that she really did. He turned his attention back across the passage. His words, meant for Mark, were said to de Roquefort.

"Okay. Your move."

MARK KNEW THIS WAS IT. THE MASTER HAD WRITTEN TO HIS mother that he did not possess the resolve needed to complete his battles. Starting them seemed easy, continuing them even easier, but resolving them had always proven difficult. Not anymore. His master had formed the stage and the players had acted out the script. Time for the finale. Raymond de Roquefort was a menace. Two brothers were dead because of him, and there was no telling where it all would stop. No way could he and de Roquefort exist within the Order together. His master had apparently known that. Which was why one of them had to go.

He knew that just a step ahead was a deep gouge in the floor, the bottom of which he hoped was lined with bronze stakes. In his rage to hurl forward, unconcerned with everything around him, de Roquefort possessed no idea of that danger. Which was precisely how his enemy would administer the Order. The sacrifices that thousands of brothers had made for seven hundred years would be wasted on arrogance.

When he'd read Simon's testimony he'd finally been provided a historical affirmation of his own religious skepticism. He'd always been troubled by biblical contradictions and their weak explanations. Religion, he feared, was a tool used by men to manipulate other men. The human mind's need to have answers, even to questions that possessed no answer, had allowed the unbelievable to become gospel. Somehow a comfort came in believing that death was not an end. There was more. Jesus supposedly proved that by physically resurrecting Himself, and offering that same salvation to all who believed.

But there was no life after death.

Not literally.

Instead, what others made of your life was how you lived on. In remembering what the man Jesus said and did, Simon Peter realized that his dead friend's beliefs were actually resurrected within him. And preaching that message, doing what Jesus had done, became the measure of Simon's salvation. None of us should judge anyone, only ourselves. Life is not infinite. A set time defines us all—then, just as the bones in the ossuary showed, to dust we return.

He could only hope that his life had meant something and that others would remember him by that meaning.

He sucked a breath.

And tossed the book at Malone, who caught it.

"Why did you do that?" de Roquefort asked.

Mark saw that Malone knew what he was about to do.

And suddenly so did his mother.

He spotted it in her eyes as they shimmered with tears. He wanted to tell her that he was sorry, that he was wrong, that he shouldn't have judged her. She seemed to read his thoughts and took a step forward, which Malone blocked with his arm.

"Get out of the way, Cotton," she said.

Mark used that moment to inch forward, the ground still hard.

"Go," de Roquefort said to him. "Get the book back."

"Certainly."

Another step.

Still hard.

But instead of walking toward Malone as de Roquefort ordered, he ducked to avoid the gun barrel at his head and whirled, ramming his elbow into de Roquefort's ribs. The man's muscular abdomen was hard and he knew he was no match for the older warrior. But he owned an advantage. Where de Roquefort was readying himself for a fight, he simply wrapped his arms around the other man's chest and revolved them both forward, propelling his feet off the ground and sending them down to the floor that he knew would not hold.

He heard his mother scream *no,* then de Roquefort's gun exploded.

He'd shoved the hand holding the weapon outward, but there was no telling where the bullet had gone. They crashed into the false floor, their combined weight enough to obliterate the covering. De Roquefort had surely expected to hit hard earth, ready to spring into action. But as they slammed into the hole, Mark released his grip from around de Roquefort's body and freed his arms, which allowed the full force of the stakes to grind into his enemy's spine.

A groan seeped from de Roquefort's lips as he opened his mouth to speak. Only blood gurgled out.

"I told you the day you challenged the master that you'd

regret what you did," Mark whispered. "Your tenure is over."

De Roquefort tried to speak, but the breath left him as blood spilled from his lips.

Then the body went limp.

"You okay?" Malone asked from above.

He raised up. His shifting weight caused de Roquefort to settle farther onto the stakes. Grit and gravel covered him. He leveraged himself out of the cavity, then swiped away the grime. "I just killed another man."

"He would have killed you," Stephanie said.

"Not a good reason, but it's all I've got."

Tears streamed down his mother's face. "I thought you were gone again."

"I was hoping to avoid those stakes, but I didn't know if de Roquefort would cooperate."

"You had to kill him," Malone said. "He never would have stopped."

"What about the gunshot?" Mark asked.

"Whizzed by close," Malone said. He motioned with the book. "This what you're after?"

Mark nodded. "And there's more."

"I asked before. Was it worth it?"

He pointed back down the passage. "Let's go have a look and you tell me."

SIXTY-SEVEN

MARK STARED OUT ACROSS THE CIRCULAR HALL. THE BROTHERS were once again adorned in their formal dress, convened in conclave, about to select a master. De Roquefort was dead, laid in the Hall of Fathers last night. At the funeral the chaplain had challenged de Roquefort's memory, and the vote had been unanimous that he be denied. As he'd listened to the chaplain's speech, Mark had realized that what happened over the past few days was all necessary. Unfortunately, he'd killed two men, one with regret, the other without relish. He'd begged the Lord's forgiveness for the first death, but felt only relief that de Roquefort was gone.

Now the chaplain was speaking again, to the conclave.

"I tell you brothers. Destiny has been at work, but not in the manner in which our most recent master contemplated. His was the wrong way. Our Great Devise is back because of the seneschal. He was the former master's chosen successor. He was the one sent on the quest. He faced down his enemy, placed our well-being above his own, and fulfilled what masters have attempted for centuries."

Mark saw hundreds of heads bobbing in agreement. Never had he moved men in such a way before. His had been a solitary existence in academia, his weekend forays with his father, then alone, the only adventure he'd ever known until the past few days.

The Great Devise had been quietly taken from the earth yesterday morning and returned to the abbey. He and Malone had personally removed the ossuary, along with its testimony. He'd shown the chaplain what they'd found and it was agreed that the new master would decide what to do next.

Now that decision was at hand.

This time Mark did not stand with the Order's officers. He was merely a brother, so he'd taken his place among the somber mass of men. He'd not been selected as one for the conclave, so he watched with all the others as the twelve went about their task.

"There is no question what must be done," one of the conclave members said. "The former seneschal should be our master. Let it be."

Silence gripped the room.

Mark wanted to speak in protest. But Rule forbid it, and he'd broken enough for a lifetime.

"I agree," another conclave member said.

The remaining ten all nodded.

"Then it shall be," the nominator said. "He that was our seneschal shall now be our master."

Applause erupted as more than four hundred brothers signaled their approval.

Chanting started.

Beauseant.

He was no longer Mark Nelle.

He was master.

All eyes focused on him. He emerged from the brothers and entered the circle formed by the conclave. He stared at men he admired. He'd joined the Order simply as a means to fulfill what his father had dreamed and to escape his mother. He'd stayed because he'd come to love both the Order and its master.

Words from John came to mind.

In the beginning was the Word, and the Word was with God, and the Word was God. Through him all things were made. In him was life, and that life was the light of men. The light shines in the darkness, but the darkness has not understood it. He was in the world, and though the world was made through him, the world did not recognize him. He came to that which was his own, but his own did not receive him. Yet to all who received him, to those who believed in his name, he gave the right to become children of God.

Simon Peter recognized and received Him, as had all who came after Simon, and their darkness became light. Perhaps thanks to Simon's singular realization, they were all now children of God.

The shouts subsided.

He waited until the hall went silent.

"I had thought perhaps that it was time for me to leave this place," he softly said. "The past few days have brought many difficult decisions. Because of the choices I made, I believed my life as a brother over. I killed one of our number and for that I am sorry. But I was given no choice. I killed the master, but for that I feel nothing." His voice rose. "He challenged all that we believe. His greed and recklessness would have been our downfall. He was concerned with *his* needs, *his* wants, not *ours*." A strength surged through him as he again heard the words of his mentor. *Remember all that I taught you.* "As your leader, I'll chart a new course. We'll come from the shadows, but not for revenge or justice, but to claim a place in this world as the Poor Fellow-Soldiers of Christ and the

Temple of Solomon. That's who we are. That's what we shall be. There are great things for us to do. The poor and down-trodden need a champion. We can be their savior."

Something Simon wrote came to mind. *All of us bear God's image, all are worthy to be loved, all can grow in the spirit of God.* He was the first master in seven hundred years to be guided by those words.

And he intended to follow them.

"Now, good brothers, it's time that we say goodbye to brother Geoffrey, whose sacrifice made this day possible."

MALONE WAS IMPRESSED WITH THE ABBEY. HE, STEPHANIE, Henrik, and Cassiopeia had been welcomed earlier and given a complete tour, the first non-Templars ever afforded that honor. Their guide, the chaplain, had showed them every recess and patiently explained its history. Then he'd left, saying that the conclave was about to begin. He'd returned a few minutes ago and escorted them into the chapel. They'd come to attend Geoffrey's funeral, allowed there thanks to the integral role they'd played in finding the Great Devise.

They sat in the first row of pews, directly before the altar. The chapel itself was magnificent, a cathedral in its own right, a place that had harbored the Knights Templar for centuries. And Malone could feel their presence.

Stephanie sat beside him, Henrik and Cassiopeia beside her. He heard the breath leave her as the chanting stopped and Mark entered from behind the altar. While the other brothers wore russet cassocks with their heads sheathed, he was dressed in the white mantle of the master. Malone reached over and grasped her trembling hand. She threw him a smile and gripped hard.

Mark stepped to Geoffrey's simple coffin.

"This brother gave his life for us. He kept his oath. For that he will have the honor of being buried in the Hall of Fathers.

Before this, only masters were there. Now they will be joined by this hero."

No one said a word.

"Also, the challenge made to our former master by brother de Roquefort is hereby rescinded. His place of honor is restored in the Chronicles. Let us now say good-bye to brother Geoffrey. Through him we have been re-born."

The service lasted an hour and Malone and the others fol-lowed the brothers underground into the Hall of Fathers. There the coffin was placed in the *locolus* beside the former master's.

Then they headed outside to their cars.

Malone noticed a calm in Mark and a thaw in his relation-ship with his mother.

"And what now for you, Malone?" Cassiopeia asked.

"Back to bookselling. And my son is coming to spend a month with me."

"A son? How old?"

"Fourteen, going on thirty. He's a handful."

Cassiopeia grinned. "A lot like his father, then."

"More like his mother."

He'd been thinking about Gary a lot the past few days. Seeing Stephanie and Mark struggle with each other brought back some of his own failings as a father. But you'd never know it from Gary. Where Mark became resentful, Gary was brilliant in school, athletic, and had never once objected to Malone moving to Copenhagen. Instead, he'd encouraged him to go, realizing that his father needed to be happy, too. Malone felt a lot of guilt about that decision. But he looked forward to his time with his son. Last year had been their first summer in Europe. This year they planned on traveling to Sweden, Norway, and England. Gary loved to travel—another thing they had in common.

"Going to be a good time," he said.

Malone, Stephanie, and Henrik would drive to Toulouse and catch a flight to Paris. From there, Stephanie would fly home to Atlanta. Malone and Henrik would travel back to Copenhagen. Cassiopeia was headed to the château in her Land Rover.

She was standing by her car when Malone walked over.

Mountains ringed them on all sides. In a couple of months winter would blanket everything with snow. Part of a cycle. As clear in nature as in life. Good, then bad, then good, then more bad, then more good. He remembered telling Stephanie when he retired that he was fed up with the nonsense. She'd smiled at his naïveté and said that so long as the earth was inhabited, there'd be no calm place. The game was the same everywhere. Only the players changed.

That was okay. The experience of the past week had taught him that he was a player and always would be. But if anyone asked, he'd tell them he was a bookseller.

"Take care of yourself, Malone," she said. "I won't be watching your back anymore."

"I have a feeling you and I'll see each other again."

She threw him a smile. "You never know. It's possible."

He walked back to his car.

"What about Claridon?" Malone asked Mark.

"He begged forgiveness."

"And you graciously granted it."

Mark smiled. "He said de Roquefort was going to roast the skin off his feet and a couple of brothers confirmed that. He wants to join us."

Malone chuckled. "Are you guys ready for that?"

"Our ranks were once filled with far worse men. We'll survive. I look at him as my personal penance."

Stephanie and Mark spoke a moment in a quiet tone. They'd already said their goodbyes in private. She appeared calm and relaxed. Apparently their salutation had been amenable. Malone was glad. Peace needed to be made there.

"What will happen with the ossuary and testimony?" Malone asked Mark. No brothers were nearby, so he felt safe discussing the point.

"That will stay sealed away. The world is content with what it believes. I'm not going to mess with that."

Malone agreed. "Good idea."

"But this Order will reemerge."

"That's right," Cassiopeia said. "I've already talked to Mark about becoming involved in the charitable organization I head. The worldwide AIDS effort and famine prevention could use an influx of capital, and this Order now has a lot to spend."

"Henrik has lobbied hard, too, for us to get involved with his favorite causes," Mark said. "And I've agreed to help there. So the Knights Templar will be busy. Our skills can be put to great use."

He extended his hand, which Mark shook. "I believe the Templars are in good hands. The best of luck to you."

"You, too, Cotton. And I still want to know about that name."

"You call me one day and I'll tell you all about it."

They climbed into the rental with Malone driving. As they settled in and buckled their seat belts, Stephanie said, "I owe you one."

He stared over at her. "That's a first."

"Don't get accustomed to it."

He smiled.

"Use it wisely."

"Yes, ma'am."

And he cranked the car.

WRITER'S NOTE

While sitting at a café in Højbro Plads, I decided that my protagonist had to live in Copenhagen. It is truly one of the world's great cities. So Cotton Malone, bookseller, became a new addition to that busy square. I also spent time in southern France discovering much of the history and many of the locales that ended up in this story. Most of the plot came to me while traveling, which is understandable, given the inspiring qualities of Denmark, Rennes-le-Château, and the Languedoc. But it's time to know where the line was drawn between fact and fiction.

The crucifixion of Jacques de Molay, as depicted in the prologue, and the possibility of his image being that on the Shroud of Turin (chapter 46) are the conclusions of Christopher Knight and Robert Lomas. I was intrigued when I discovered the idea in their work, *The Second Messiah,* so I wove their innovative concept into the story. Much of what Knight and Lomas say—as related by Mark Nelle in chapter 46—makes sense and is likewise consistent with all of the scientific dating evidence amassed from the shroud over the past twenty years.

The Abbey des Fontaines is fictional, but is largely based on bits and pieces from many Pyrenean retreats. The locales in Denmark all exist. The cathedral at Roskilde and Christian

IV's crypt (chapter 5), are truly magnificent, and the view from the Round Tower in Copenhagen (chapter 1) does in fact harken back to another century.

Lars Nelle is a composite of many men and women who have devoted their lives to writing about Rennes-le-Château. I read many sources, some bordered on the bizarre, others on the ridiculous. But in their own way each offered a unique insight into this truly mysterious place. Along that line, several points to be made:

The book *Pierres Gravées du Languedoc* by Eugène Stüblein (first mentioned in chapter 4) is part of the Rennes folklore, though no one has ever seen a copy. As related in chapter 14, the book is catalogued in the *Bibliothèque Nationale* in Paris, but the volume is missing.

The original gravestone of Marie d'Hautpoul de Blanchefort is gone, most likely destroyed by Saunière himself. But a sketch was supposedly made of it on June 25, 1905, by a visiting scientific society, the drawing eventually published in 1906. But at least two versions of that supposed sketch exist, so it's hard to know for sure about the original.

All of the facts relevant to the d'Hautpoul family and their connection to the Knights Templar are real. As detailed in chapter 20, the abbé Bigou was Marie's confessor and did in fact commission her gravestone ten years after her death. He likewise fled Rennes in 1793 and never returned. Whether he actually left behind secret messages is conjecture (all part of the Rennes lure), but the possibility does make for an intriguing story.

The murder of the abbé Antoine Gélis happened, and in the manner as depicted in chapter 26. Gélis was indeed connnected to Saunière, and some have speculated that Saunière may have been involved in his death. But no evidence exists for such a link and the crime remains, to this day, unsolved.

Whether there is a crypt beneath the church at Rennes will

never be known. As stated in chapters 32 and 39, local officials will not allow any exploration. But the lords of Rennes have to be buried somewhere and, to date, their crypt has not been located. The references to the crypt supposedly found in the parish journal, as mentioned in chapter 32, are real.

The Visigoth pillar noted in chapter 39 exists and is on display in Rennes. Saunière indeed inverted the pillar and carved words upon it. The connection between 1891 (1681, when inverted) to Marie d'Hautpoul de Blanchefort's gravestone (and the 1681 references there) does indeed stretch the bounds of coincidence, but all that exists. So perhaps there is a message there somewhere.

All of the buildings and all that Saunière fashioned relative to the church at Rennes are real. Tens of thousands of visitors each year experience Saunière's domain. The 7/9 connection is my invention, based on observations I made while studying the Visigoth pillar, the stations of the cross, and various other items in and around the Rennes church. To my knowledge, no one has written of this 7/9 connection, so perhaps this will be my personal addition to the Rennes saga.

Noël Corbu lived in Rennes and his part in forging much of the fiction about the place is true (chapter 29). An excellent book, *The Treasure of Rennes-le-Château: A Mystery Solved,* by Bill Putnam and John Edwin Wood, deals with Corbu's fabrications. Corbu did purchase Saunière's domain from the priest's elderly mistress. Most agree that if Saunière knew anything, he may well have told his mistress. One part of the legend (probably another Corbu fabrication) is that the mistress told Corbu the truth before dying in 1953. But we'll never know. What we do know is that Corbu profited from the fiction of Rennes, and he was the source, in 1956, for the first newspaper stories about the supposed treasure. As stated in chapter 29, Corbu did pen a manuscript about Rennes, but the pages disappeared after his death in 1968.

Eventually, the Rennes legend was memorialized in a 1967 book, *The Accursed Treasure of Rennes-le-Château,* by Gérard de Sède, which is recognized as the first book on the subject. A lot of fiction is contained there, most of which is a regurgitation of Corbu's original 1956 story. Eventually Henry Lincoln, a British filmmaker, came upon the tale and is credited with the popularization of Rennes.

The painting *Reading the Rules of the Caridad,* by Juan de Valdes Leal, presently hangs in the Spanish chapter church of Santa Caridad. I relocated it to France since its symbolism was irresistible. Consequently, its inclusion into the Rennes story is my invention (chapter 34). The papal palace at Avignon is accurately portrayed, except for the archives, which I concocted.

Cryptograms are indeed part of the Rennes story. The ones contained herein, however, came from my imagination.

The castle reconstruction site at Givors is based on an actual project that is presently ongoing in Guédelon, France, where craftsmen are building a thirteenth-century castle using the tools and raw materials of that time. The endeavor will indeed take decades and the site is open to the public.

The Templars, of course, existed and their history is accurately reflected. Their Rule is likewise quoted with accuracy. The poem in chapter 10 is real, author is unknown. All that the Order accomplished, as detailed throughout the book, is true and stands as a testament to an organization that was clearly ahead of its time. As to the Templar lost wealth and knowledge, neither has been found since the October 1307 purge, though Philip IV of France did indeed search in vain. The account of carts headed for the Pyrenees (chapter 48) is based on ancient historical references, though nothing can be known for sure.

Unfortunately there are no chronicles of the Order. But perhaps those documents await some adventurer who will one day find the lost Templar cache. The induction ceremony in chapter 51 is reproduced accurately using the words required by Rule. But the burial ceremony, as detailed in chapter 19 is fictional, though first-century Jews did indeed bury their dead in a similar fashion.

The Gospel of Simon is my creation. But the alternate concept of how Christ may have been "resurrected" came from an excellent book, *Resurrection, Myth or Reality* by John Shelby Spong.

The conflicts between the four books of the New Testament relative to the resurrection (chapter 46), have challenged scholars for centuries. The fact that only one crucified skeleton has ever been found (chapter 50) does raise questions, as do many comments and statements made throughout history. One in particular, attributed to Pope Leo X (1513–1521) caught my attention. Leo was a Medici, a powerful man backed by powerful allies, heading a Church that, at the time, ruled supreme. His statement is short, simple, and strange for the head of the Roman Catholic Church.

Indeed, it was the spark that generated this novel.

It has served us well, this myth of Christ.

An Interview with the Author

Question: The subject of your new novel deals with the Knights Templar. Who exactly were they?

Steve Berry: The Knights Templar were a monastic military order formed in Jerusalem at the beginning of the twelfth century with the mandate of protecting Christian pilgrims on route to the Holy Land. Their full name was The Poor Fellow-Soldiers of Christ and the Temple of Solomon at Jerusalem, but they came to be known as the Knights Templar. Never before had a group of secular knights banded together and taken monastic vows. They lived by a strict set of rules and went on to become the first standing army since Roman times, fighting alongside the Crusaders for the Holy Land. From humble beginnings (the original nine knights relied on alms from traveling pilgrims) the Templars rose to earn the backing of the Holy See and many European monarchs. Within two centuries of being formed, they became the owners of some 9,000 tax-free estates, subject only to papal authority, powerful enough to defy all secular authority.

Q: Weren't they a bit before their time?

SB: No question. In fact, putting to use their vast wealth, the Templars essentially invented banking as we know it. The Church, of course, forbade the lending of money for interest. The Templars, being clever, changed the manner in which loans were paid, giving themselves room to charge impressive fees for their lending. In time, the Order routinely financed kings and nations. It also invented the check. Pilgrims headed to the Holy Land, instead of carrying their money for thieves to seize, deposited funds with the local Temple; obtained a receipt; then presented that receipt when they arrived, whereupon their funds were returned by that Temple. Quite an accomplishment for the twelfth century. The Templars also operated safe-deposit boxes and helped perfect the concept of a security interest in personal property and land.

Q: So what happened to the Knights Templar?

SB: The Order simply became too powerful. Pope Innocent II exempted the Templars from all secular authority. This privilege bred an arrogance which was hard for the Templars to conceal. A few of the masters even openly challenged the authority of kings. The Order's private nature, reflected in secret meetings and rituals, also aided in its downfall. The King of France, Philip IV, used all this when he set out to destroy them. The Templars maintained a strong presence in France, and Philip felt threatened by their presence. He also desperately needed funds to support his war against England. So, on October 13, 1307 Philip ordered all the Templars arrested on the grounds of heresy, since this was the only charge that would allow him to seize their money and assets. Many were tortured and, as a result, ridiculous confessions were given. These included trampling and spitting on the cross, committing acts of sodomy, and worshiping an idol.

Seven years of trial and tribulations followed the 1307 purge and, in 1311, Pope Clement V formally disbanded the Order. Several hundred Templars were eventually executed. Finally, on March 19, 1314 the last master, Jacques de Molay, was burned at the stake. De Molay is said to have cursed Philip and Pope Clement as he burned, asking both men to join him in death within a year. Whether he actually uttered the curse or if it's simply an apocryphal tale, we may never know. What's for certain is this: Clement died one month later and Philip seven months after that.

Q: Jacques de Molay figures prominently in *The Templar Legacy*. Was he interesting to write about?

SB: On the one hand he was a tough, defiant leader. On the other, he was politically inept and embarrassingly arrogant.

His underestimation of Philip IV cost the Order dearly, but he's now generally regarded as a martyr. For seven years after being arrested de Molay suffered torture and inhumane conditions, but he never disclosed the location of the Order's wealth or knowledge. By all accounts, he died proudly.

Q: What about that Templar treasure and wealth? Was any of it ever found?
SB: Philip looked in vain, but to this day no remnant of either has been discovered. There have been countless theories as to what the treasure and the knowledge entailed and where they might have ended up, everything from the European continent, to Scotland, to even America, where the Templars supposedly sailed in the thirteenth century. But nothing has ever been proven. What better fodder for a novelist?

Q: How did you become interested in the Templars?
SB: I've always been fascinated with them, and writing this book gave me the chance to study the Order in detail. It was important that they be presented as they were, not as some Hollywood stereotype, though a few liberties had to be taken to make sure the story remained a thriller. Their 686 rules, though, are a fascinating read. Obedience was paramount. Contrary to Sir Walter Scott and *Ivanhoe,* they were forbidden from participating in tournaments; they spoke sparingly without laughter; they did not bathe; they slept with the lights on and dressed; and they were not allowed to gamble or hunt, play games, or grow their hair, though their beards could be unkempt. By papal order the knights were allowed to wear a white mantle with a red cross, while the remainder of the Order wore different colored mantles. Within *The Templar Legacy* there's an initiation ceremony which I tried to re-create accurately. That was quite an elaborate event. The hierarchy was simple: The master was in absolute charge, aided by seneschals, who

commanded the knights (all of noble heritage) and the sergeants (warriors of non-noble background). Chaplains were the clerics and the rest of the Order were comprised of artisans, farmers, craftsmen, and administrators. Tens of thousands joined. Tens of thousands died fighting. Quite an organization. And the term "warrior-monks"—what a marvelous contradiction.

Q: The French town of Rennes-le-Château is crucial to the story. What makes this place so mysterious?
SB: Rennes is located in the Languedoc, an unspoiled region of southern France. There are many mysteries surrounding this village that link it with everything from the Holy Grail to Noah's Ark, from the Ark of the Covenant to the treasures of the Temple of Solomon. In the 1950s the owner of a local hotel used the story of the priest Bérenger Saunière as an attraction to draw visitors. He suggested that, after finding parchments in an ancient pillar in the local church, Saunière, sometime around 1891, found a great treasure. This story, published in the local newspaper, caught national attention. A French book by Gérard de Sède published in 1967 brought further attention. People started flocking to the area and serious treasure hunting got under way—so serious that, when people's houses began to collapse due to the tunneling, the town halted all unauthorized excavation.

Q: Has anything ever been found?
SB: Not a thing, but the myths and legends live on. Saunière's renovated church is still there today. It is indeed a place of contradiction and perhaps sublime messages. More garish than beautiful, after a visit it's easy to see why conspiratorialists find fuel there for the imagination.

Q: What about Bérenger Saunière, what kind of man was he?

SB: A unique one. Saunière was born in 1852, the eldest of seven children. He entered the seminary in 1874, was ordained as a priest in 1879, then was appointed abbé at Rennes-le-Château in June 1885. He was outspoken, was an antirepublican, possessed a glass eye, and often played the lottery. He also maintained an amorous relationship with Marie Denarnaud, who lived with him as his housekeeper. During his life, he openly spent huge amounts of money building and entertaining. Then he defied the Church and refused to account for his expenditures. Ultimately, he was relieved of his position as a priest. His appeal went all the way to the Vatican but remained unresolved at the time of his death in 1917. Even in death, though, strange things happened. His body was laid out for viewing, covered by a cloth edged with red pom-poms. As the locals walked by to pay their respects, inexplicably they each plucked the pom-poms off one at a time. In another contradiction, he died absolutely penniless, as all of his assets had been transferred to Marie beforehand. It wasn't until forty years after he died that his tale took on mythical proportions. I had a lot of fun bringing him back to life and reliving his exploits.

Q: Did you actually visit Rennes-le-Château?
SB: I did, and it's quite a place. There's a charged air about the village. And, though the area's commercialism has spread, a pall of intrigue remains, particularly at dusk when the shadows fall. While researching *The Templar Legacy*, I visited Rennes, Avignon, the Pyrenees, and other locales throughout the Languedoc. Quite a spectacular part of the world.

Q: Puzzles play a part in the quest for the Templar treasure. Are the cryptograms that appear throughout the story real or something from your imagination?
SB: No, they were a common form of encryption in the eighteenth and nineteenth centuries. They would have been

nearly impossible to decipher without knowing the mathematical key. It was a simple, but effective, means of keeping a secret. These played a part in the Rennes mystery, as one was found among Saunière's writings, the message of which has never been learned. I thought they'd be fun to use here.

Q: Some gravestones also play a pivotal role in the quest. Were they real or more fiction?

SB: The two gravestones of Marie d'Hautpoul de Blanchefort are a matter of great controversy. No one has ever seen the actual stones, but there are drawings of what they may have looked like. Problem is, the drawings differ from one another. These gravestones figure prominently in the Rennes legend so they had to be included. Lots of symbolism and subliminal messages here, so many that great liberties could be taken in their use. All is explained in the Writer's Note at the end of the book.

Q: *The Templar Legacy* introduces a new protagonist, Cotton Malone. Where did he come from?

SB: He was born in Copenhagen. I was sitting at a café in Højbro Plads, a popular Danish square, when I conceived him. I love that city and that square, so I decided Cotton would own a bookshop right there. I wanted a character with government ties and a background that made him a formidable opponent, but I also wanted him to be a person possessed of freedom. Since I personally love rare books, it was natural that Cotton would too, so he became a Justice Department operative turned bookseller who manages, from time to time, to find himself immersed in trouble. I also gave him an eidetic memory, since, well, who wouldn't like one of those? At the same time, Cotton is clearly a man in conflict. His marriage has failed, he maintains a difficult relationship with his teenage son, and he's tired of the risks that seem to follow him even in retirement. Yet that past keeps haunting him, calling him back, forcing him to make tough choices.

Q: Will Cotton Malone be back?
SB: Definitely. This is the first of many adventures for him and his supporting cast of characters.

Read on for an excerpt of
Steve Berry's thriller

The Venetian Betrayal

Published by Ballantine Books

COPENHAGEN, DENMARK
SATURDAY, APRIL 18 , THE PRESENT
11:55 P.M.

THE SMELL ROUSED COTTON MALONE TO CONSCIOUSNESS. Sharp, acrid, with a hint of sulfur. And something else. Sweet and sickening. Like death.

He opened his eyes.

He lay prone on the floor, arms extended, palms to the hardwood, which he immediately noticed was sticky.

What happened?

He'd attended the April gathering of the Danish Antiquarian Booksellers Society a few blocks west of his bookshop, near the gaiety of Tivoli. He liked the monthly meetings and this one had been no exception. A few drinks, some friends, and lots of book chatter. Tomorrow morning he'd agreed to meet Cassiopeia Vitt. Her call yesterday to arrange the meeting had surprised him. He'd not heard from her since Christmas, when she'd spent a few days in Copenhagen. He'd been cruising back home on his bicycle, enjoying the comfortable spring night, when he'd decided to check out the unusual meeting location she'd chosen, the Museum of Greco-Roman Culture—a preparatory habit from his former profession. Cassiopeia rarely did anything on impulse, so a little advance preparation wasn't a bad idea.

* * *

He'd found the address, which faced the Frederiksholms canal, and noticed a half-open door to the pitch-dark building—a door that should normally be closed and alarmed. He'd parked his bike. The least he could do was close the door and phone the police when he returned home.

But the last thing he remembered was grasping the doorknob.

He was now inside the museum.

In the ambient light that filtered in through two plate-glass windows, he saw a space decorated in typical Danish style—a sleek mixture of steel, wood, glass, and aluminum. The right side of his head throbbed and he caressed a tender knot.

He shook the fog from his brain and stood.

He'd visited this museum once and had been unimpressed with its collection of Greek and Roman artifacts. Just one of a hundred or more private collections throughout Copenhagen, their subject matter as varied as the city's population.

He steadied himself against a glass display case. His fingertips again came away sticky and smelly, with the same nauseating odor.

He noticed that his shirt and trousers were damp, as was his hair, face, and arms. Whatever covered the museum's interior coated him, too.

He stumbled toward the front entrance and tried the door. Locked. Double dead bolt. A key would be needed to open it from the inside.

He stared back into the interior. The ceiling soared thirty feet. A wood-and-chrome staircase led up to a second floor that dissolved into more darkness, the ground floor extending out beneath.

He found a light switch. Nothing. He lumbered over to a desk phone. No dial tone.

A noise disturbed the silence. Clicks and whines, like gears working. Coming from the second floor.

His training as a Justice Department agent cautioned him to keep quiet, but also urged him to investigate.

So he silently climbed the stairs.

The chrome banister was damp, as were each of the laminated risers. Fifteen steps up, more glass-and-chrome display cases dotted the hardwood floor. Marble reliefs and partial bronzes on pedestals loomed like ghosts. Movement caught his eye twenty feet away. An object rolling across the floor. Maybe two feet wide with rounded sides, pale in color, tight to the ground, like one of those robotic lawn mowers he'd once seen advertised. When a display case or statue was encountered, the thing stopped, retreated, then darted in a different direction. A nozzle extended from its top and every few seconds a burst of aerosol spewed out.

He stepped close.

All movement stopped. As if it sensed his presence. The nozzle swung to face him. A cloud of mist soaked his pants.

What was this?

The machine seemed to lose interest and scooted deeper into the darkness, more odorous mist expelling along the way. He stared down over the railing to the ground floor and spotted another of the contraptions parked beside a display case.

Nothing about this seemed good.

He needed to leave. The stench was beginning to turn his stomach.

The machine ceased its roaming and he heard a new sound.

Two years ago, before his divorce, his retirement from the government, and his abrupt move to Copenhagen, when he'd lived in Atlanta, he'd spent a few hundred dollars on a stainless-steel grill. The unit came with a red button that, when pumped, sparked a gas flame. He recalled the sound the igniter made with each pump of the button.

The same clicking he heard right now.

Sparks flashed.

The floor burst to life, first sun yellow, then burnt orange, finally settling on pale blue as flames radiated outward, consuming the hardwood. Flames simultaneously roared up the walls. The temperature rose swiftly and he raised an arm to shield his face. The ceiling joined the conflagration, and in less than fifteen seconds the second floor was totally ablaze.

Overhead sprinklers sprang to life.

He partially retreated down the staircase and waited for the fire to be doused.

But he noticed something.

The water simply aggravated the flames.

The machine that started the disaster suddenly disintegrated in a muted flash, flames rolling out in all directions, like waves searching for shore.

A fireball drifted to the ceiling and seemed to be welcomed by the spraying water. Steam thickened the air, not with smoke but with a chemical that made his head spin.

He leaped down the stairs two at a time. Another swoosh racked the second floor. Followed by two more. Glass shattered. Something crashed.

He darted to the front of the building.

The other gizmo that had sat dormant sprang to life and started skirting the ground-floor display cases.

More aerosol spewed into the scorching air.

He needed to get out. But the locked front door opened to the inside. Metal frame, thick wood. No way to kick it open. He watched as fire eased down the staircase, consuming each riser, like the devil descending to greet him. Even the chrome was being devoured with a vengeance.

His breaths became labored, thanks to the chemical fog and the rapidly vanishing oxygen. Surely someone would call the fire department, but they'd be no help to him. If a spark touched his soaked clothes . . .

The blaze found the bottom of the staircase.

Ten feet away.